ADAM J. SCHOLTE

THE
BEGINNING
OF THE
END

THE RAMULAS CHRONICLES

ISBN: 978-1-922757-58-6 (Paperback)
          978-1-922757-59-3 (eBook)

 A catalogue record for this book is available from the National Library of Australia

Editor: Jason Martin
Proofread by: Sarah Kate Hill
Cover Design: Ocean Reeve Publishing and Firda Graphic
Design and Typeset: Ocean Reeve Publishing
Printed in Australia by Ocean Reeve Publishing and Clark & Mackay Printers

Published by Adam J. Scholte and Ocean Reeve Publishing
www.oceanreevepublishing.com

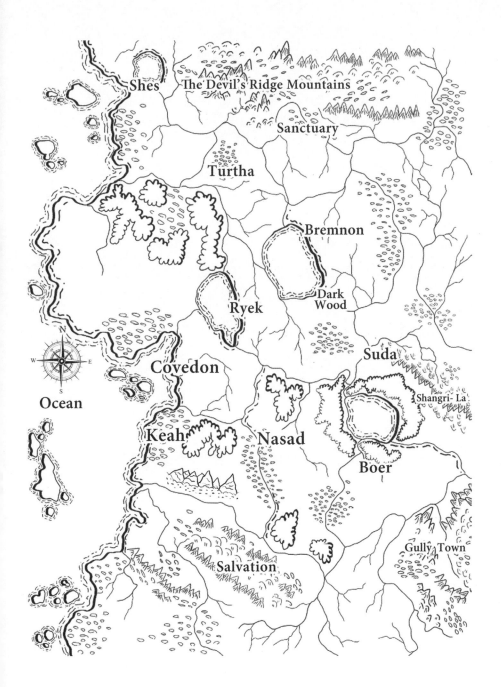

Prologue

The air was forced from Ramulas' body as he hit the ground. He frantically picked himself up and dusted the dirt from his clothes. The light from the moon allowed him to see his house across the field of growing wheat.

He worried about Oriel; did she escape from the warlords, or had they captured her?

The sound of footsteps caused Ramulas to turn, and what he saw shocked him to the core. Two legion soldiers stood near a grove of trees one hundred yards away in his field. 'By the gods,' he whispered.

What were they doing here? *This can't be real,* he thought to himself.

The soldiers unsheathed their swords and ran toward Ramulas. A burst of cold rushed through him as his mouth dried. They were coming quickly, and he didn't know what to do.

Then he turned and ran for his house as fast as he could. Ramulas wanted to call for help, but he knew there would be none. The only people nearby were his wife and daughters.

The thought of his family caused him to change direction toward the barn. At least there he would find something to fight them with.

Then Ramulas knew he would not reach it in time. He heard them coming closer and he dared not look back. Before he knew what had happened, something hit him from behind, and Ramulas was sent sprawling to the ground.

Shock flooded through Ramulas as he realised one of the legion soldiers was on top of him. With a burst of energy, he twisted and kicked the soldier from him before scuttling away as he saw a knife embedded in the back of the legionnaire. He couldn't understand how it got there.

It took a moment to comprehend that the lifeless body would no longer be a threat. Noise from across the field caused Ramulas to turn and see a person dressed in a cloak fighting the remaining soldier.

Feelings of uncertainty and fear almost overwhelmed him. Who would win this fight, and what would they do to his family?

He knew with all certainty that he would be the only one that could help his family. All his negative emotions were washed away in a sea of rage. He ran to a nearby wagon, picked up a hoe, and raced toward the fight.

'What are you doing on my farm?' he shouted, swinging the weapon over his head.

Ramulas gasped in shock as both combatants faced him. The person in the cloak was a young woman. She stabbed the soldier in the throat before jumping away as he fell to his knees, holding his wound. When he fell face-first to the ground, she casually walked over to retrieve her knife.

'What are you doing here?' Ramulas asked her in disbelief.

'You are welcome.'

'What?'

'I said, "you are welcome",' she replied, wiping her knife on the soldier's uniform, 'I saved the lives of you and your family. You should say "thank you".'

Ramulas turned away from her in disbelief.

***

Ramulas walked into his house, shaking his head. The nightmares were getting worse. He knew that he needed to fix his troubles, but how? As soon as Ramulas lay in bed, dreams of the fog came again.

When the whiteness dissipated, Ramulas was in Oriel's cavern, and she greeted him with a worried expression.

'What did you do?' she asked. 'The warlords knew where we were when you screamed. Then they came to attack us. I felt their magic follow you. Tell me what happened.'

Ramulas shook his head. 'None of this is real. I want you to leave me alone.'

'Ramulas, this is real, and if you don't accept it, everyone in your world will die.'

This statement jolted him, and Ramulas looked at Oriel. 'Two legion soldiers came to my house and attempted to kill me.'

'Then how did you survive? Soldiers from the legion are ruthless killers. Did you use your magic?'

'No, someone helped me.'

'Who?'

'I don't know. She left after killing them.'

Oriel waved her hands in front of Ramulas and murmured for a second, and then her eyes widened. 'The warlords were able to send the crystal through. Once it anchors, the crystal will form an exit doorway into your world. You must find it and take it far from your home.' Ramulas shook his head, not understanding what was happening. His heart beat inside his chest like a drum. 'If the crystal is not moved, then more soldiers will come through and they will keep coming until they kill you and your family.'

Frustration built up within Ramulas. 'What do you expect me to do? I am a farmer and nothing more. Now leave me alone.'

Oriel smiled sadly. 'That is where you are wrong. I can feel that your daughters have inherited some of your magic.'

'What magic?'

Oriel waved her hands and a battle-axe and war hammer—both wooden—appeared before him. 'In your old life, you were a battle mage. These weapons were made by you.'

'But they are made from wood—'

'Hold them and you will know the truth. You must find the crystal and take it to the Symiak mountains.'

'I can't go to the Symiak mountains. What about my family?' he asked.

'Your journey may be dangerous. You must leave them behind.'

Ramulas tentatively reached for the weapons in a way that someone would reach for a poisonous spider. He gasped in shock as he touched the weapons and they transformed into silver.

A kaleidoscope of images rushed through Ramulas' mind: fragmented visions of him using the weapons proficiently as well as practising magic.

It all became too much, and he dropped the weapons at his feet. 'I don't want any of this. I want you out of my dreams.'

Oriel smiled sadly, knowing that Ramulas was the only one with the power to save her—he just needed to believe in himself. She thought back to the day that she escaped.

1

'Who are these people to spread rumours of rebellion against the warlords and the legions?'

The speaker's name was Remus; he was the leader of the warlords who ruled this world with magic. As a warlord, his word was law. To question or defy his word was to challenge him.

Remus looked to his left and saw Redemption, one of the three captains who oversaw the first legion. Redemption's face betrayed no emotion as Remus spoke; every other sign of rebellion had been crushed.

Redemption knew this would be no different. One of the spies had found a note in a nearby town. It spoke of a prophecy and hope of overthrowing the warlords. Before the people of that town were slaughtered, they said the note came from this town.

'The prophecy of the Avenger has surfaced once more,' Remus said as he felt the note in his hand. 'We need to show the common people he is nothing but a myth. Prepare the legion.' Redemption gave a slight bow before walking away.

Remus despised the common people. They showed weakness by caring for their families. All Remus needed to do was hold a man's wife or child, and they would do anything. Caring for others was the ultimate weakness.

Remus watched the captain walk away with his black cloak flowing behind him. He thought of how he needed to rule the people with an iron fist. It was natural for small pockets of the people to oppose his rule.

Remus expected—even looked forward to—this. Examples would be made of these rebels; others would learn to be compliant.

Why could the common people not see that being ruled by the warlords was what they needed?

***

The sun had just begun to climb over the horizon. Waiting behind a line of cypress trees, Remus could feel the slight change in temperature as the sunlight shone on his robes. The mudbrick huts were a dull brown, each with open doorways and windows. Straw thatch covered the huts, and Remus thought they would burn easily.

He sat on his mountillo, a horse-like creature with overlapping layers of hardened skin, which acted as armour. They had been magically bred for war and were very hard to kill.

'They know we are here.'

Remus turned his head in agonising slowness to look at Redemption. The captain fought back the urge to flinch at Remus' gaze. One hundred soldiers of the first legion waited in two columns in their red leather and black armour. They showed no reaction to their captain speaking out of turn.

Remus inhaled slowly while opening his robe to show a red breast plate covered in magical symbols. Turning back towards the town, he sighed as an evil smile played across his face.

'That's good. I want them to know that rebellion of any form must be crushed. Let them see us.'

Redemption held up his hand and made several chopping motions. The soldiers fanned out into a semicircle and began to move through the trees toward the town.

Remus looked down to his left. 'Oriel, I want every man, woman, and child found. An example must be made.'

At first, she did not respond. Oriel gave a slight toss of her head, sending a lock of her black hair tumbling down her green robe. She thought of all the families that Remus had killed before and how helpless she had felt.

A family was the one thing that Oriel had never been granted and always yearned for. Today would be the day that she would make a difference.

'Now, Oriel,' Remus whispered through clenched teeth.

She sent a fleeting, defiant look at Remus before running toward the tree line as her robe turned to smoke. Her skin tingled with the casting of the spell.

Oriel's bones, ligaments, and muscles stretched and reformed; within moments, she had transformed into a giant black hunting cat. Her new form stood four feet at the shoulder and was covered in rippling muscles.

She raced past the first row of huts as soldiers began kicking in doors. Oriel could smell the fear of every single person within the town. She used that fear to locate and flush them from the places they were hiding.

The sounds of fighting and women screaming shattered the peaceful morning. She knew where she needed to go and what needed to be done. This small town only had four children, and she would save them. Taking a quick look behind her, Oriel saw that the soldiers were busy.

She needed to hurry.

Sprinting as fast as she could, Oriel reached the last hut and burst through the door, finding it to be only a small room.

Inside she was confronted by a man, two women, and four children.

The man held a wooden staff in his hands so tight that his knuckles had turned white. He had positioned himself in front of the two screaming women who had thrown themselves over the children.

'Git! Go on, git,' the man said fearfully as he jabbed the staff at Oriel.

Time was running short, and she had to move fast. Flattening her ears, Oriel gave a soft growl and lowered her body to the floor. The man stood back with a sharp intake of breath. Oriel pounced and landed on top of him, which brought more screaming from the women. Oriel let out a roar and leapt toward the women. Landing in front of them, Oriel swiped at the woman with her claws. The women received minor scratches and torn clothing.

However, they stubbornly refused to leave the children. Oriel was forced to separate the women. She clamped her jaws on the arm of one of the women, who screamed in terror. With a toss of her head, Oriel sent the woman flying into the man.

They fell into a jumbled heap and Oriel bit the other woman on the rump. With a scream, she ran towards the other adults.

The two women called out to the children as they huddled on either side of the man. Oriel shot forward, raking at their clothing with her claws as she roared. The three adults were attacked from all sides, and when they found themselves at the door, they turned and ran screaming outside.

Turning toward the children, Oriel saw their eyes wide with fear as they held on to one another. With a thought, she transformed back into her human form and made her way to the children. She looked down at the three girls and a boy, all under eight. Oriel smiled at the children. As their expressions changed from fear to amazement, she knelt down in front of them.

'There are some very bad people outside and I don't want them to find you. Come with me and I will take you to a safe place.' Oriel held out both hands as she gave a comforting smile to the children.

A girl of six summers with blonde locks slowly reached out and took Oriel's hand.

'Good girl. Now, we must all move quickly.'

Oriel moved to the front door. Leading the children out into the forest, Oriel sat them on the ground fifty yards from the edge of the town. Oriel waved her hands through the air, and a ten-foot bubble formed around the children.

'No matter what you see or hear, do not make a sound and do not move. I will come for you soon.'

The children gave slight nods and Oriel raced back toward Remus.

The smell of blood and smoke filled the air within the town.

A crying woman was silenced with a loud slap. Keeping her human form, Oriel made her way to where the residents were on their knees in front of Remus and the soldiers of the first legion. There were sixty people. She slowly walked by the prisoners who softly begged for mercy and took her place next to Remus.

Unfolding a sheet of paper, Remus held it out before him and spoke softly as he read from it: *'The time of the Avenger is almost upon us. Soon our days of living under the warlords' tyranny will come to an end. The Avenger is coming, brothers and sisters. He will bring our freedom.'*

He looked up from the piece of paper and cocked his head to the side as if deep in thought. Someone from this town had been passing this message to others.

'Oriel, are they all accounted for?' he asked softly.

'Yes.'

'The Avenger!' Remus exploded as he stepped forward, crushing the paper in his fist. 'The Avenger is a myth spread by rebels to give hope of an uprising against the warlords. An example must be made.' Lowering his voice, Remus said, 'All of them.'

With a slight hand gesture, Redemption sent the soldiers into the crowd. Men and women screamed as they were forced to stand in front of the huts.

Oriel turned her head, knowing what was to come. She had witnessed Remus' fury countless times before. But this time it would be different; there would be no mass crucifixion. This time, Remus would send a more ominous message.

'No, my child—you must watch,' Remus said as he gently held her chin and turned her back toward the people.

Lengths of chain were laid in front of the townspeople. Each person had a collar placed around their neck, and it was attached to the chain in front of them. When the soldiers were finished, the chains were wrapped around the huts. Five huts had people chained together facing outward. It had become deathly quiet, except for the shallow breathing of the prisoners and the soft rattle of the chains.

'Burn it; burn it all,' Remus ordered.

As the soldiers pulled torches from their packs and began lighting them with flints, the prisoners realised their fate and began to pull on the chains while screaming for mercy.

The torches were lit and soldiers moved forward and set fire to the huts as they moved through the town. The screams cut through Oriel like a knife, and she prayed it would end soon. To turn away would mean dealing with Remus' fury. Looking at the huts, Oriel saw something that made her heart stop.

The four children she had saved ran through the smoke and burning huts with tears streaming downs their faces and eyes wide with fear.

Remus stiffened when he saw them and gazed questioningly at Oriel. She looked away. In that split second, he knew that Oriel had hidden them. The soldiers caught the children, and Remus gave the signal for them to be thrown into the fires with the screaming prisoners.

Looking down at Oriel, Remus said, 'You dare?'

Oriel vanished with the sound of a pop.

'Where did she go?' Redemption asked.

'The only place she knows. Ready the soldiers. I need to teach Oriel obedience.'

2

Ramulas sat at the kitchen table finishing the morning meal with his two daughters. Across from him, with a mischievous grin on her cherubic face, was Grace, who had just finished her meal and fought to stay still at the table. She did quite well for an energetic eight-year-old.

To his right was Kate, who, at twelve, tried so much to look and act like an older lady. She had the same deep blue eyes as her mother, whereas Grace had dark brown eyes like her father.

Ramulas glanced at the window, where he saw his reflection staring back at him. He had short dark wavy hair, intense brown eyes, and a square jaw. Wide shoulders and a broad chest told a story of a man who made a living through working with his hands.

'Da, can we go soon?' Grace asked. 'You said after we finish eating.'

'Hold on, little one. I will be finished soon. Why don't you check on the horse and cart?'

Grace noisily pushed her chair back from the table and raced out the back door. Kate rolled her eyes at her younger sister and flicked her blonde hair from her face.

'Kate, would you like to come with us to prepare the fields?' Ramulas asked, already knowing the answer.

'I would rather stay at home and help mother,' she replied.

'Oh, you mean talk to your mother about boys?' he said with a smile.

Her mouth fell open, and she struggled to find a reply.

'Now, you leave her be.'

Ramulas looked up to see his wife Jacqueline walk into the kitchen. In his opinion, she was the most beautiful woman in the world. After fifteen years together, he was still mystified at the way her freckles danced across her nose when she smiled, and how her hair reminded him of a living flame as it danced across her shoulders when she moved.

'Hello, my love,' Ramulas said as he walked over to give his wife a kiss. As he held her in his arms, Jacqueline looked up at him and asked, 'How long will you be gone?'

'This should not take too long; me and the little one will be home for the midday meal.'

There was the sound of running coming toward the house, followed by Grace sliding through the door.

'Kate and Lucas sitting in a tree, K-I-S-S—'she began to sing before Kate jumped out of her chair and began to chase her younger sister around the kitchen. Grace squealed with a mixture of delight and mock terror while Kate growled with a look of pure determination, trying to grab hold of her sister. After the third time around the kitchen table, Grace began to lose her breath, and she hid behind Ramulas, who stepped away from Jacqueline.

'Da, she's trying to get me,' Grace cried out, pointing to Kate.

Her angry older sister pulled up in front of Ramulas. 'She's always teasing me about boys,' she said, with her hands in front of her, waiting for a chance to grab at her younger sister.

'Now, you two girls should get along,' he said in a calm voice as he felt Grace clutching his leg.

'Well, Grace needs to be spoken to,' Kate said to Jacqueline, pointing a finger at her hiding sister.

'Yes, I know; your father will talk to her. Won't you dear?' she replied.

'But boys are yuck,' Grace added before squealing and pulling her head behind her father's leg once again.

Ramulas looked up and sighed, thinking, *Why am I always caught in the middle?*

He bent down, scooped Grace into his arms, and walked towards the back door, where he saw drawings by both of his daughters on the nearby wall; this brought back memories of him allowing one drawing each for the girls when they were younger. They had grown so much since then. 'We will be back by midday, and I will have a talk with this little one.'

Once away from the house, he placed Grace on her feet. He squatted in front of her, clenched his square jaw, and slowly shook his finger at Grace.

'You know better than to always annoy Kate.'

Grace attempted to imitate her father by pursing her lips together and shaking her finger back at him. If anything, it only made her look more mischievous.

'Not this time, little one,' Ramulas said as he gently pushed her finger away, 'you need to think about other people's feelings.'

'She's mean to me!' Grace exclaimed.

'I will talk to Kate after, but I need you to think about what you have done.' Ramulas smiled as he stood up. 'Let's check the horse.'

Grace squealed and raced to the barn. Ramulas waited before giving chase. He caught up to Grace just before she reached the stables next to the barn. Ramulas pretended to run out of breath and allow Grace to reach the stables before him. She let out a laugh as her hand slapped against the door.

'Ha! I knew I could beat you, Da.'

'Oh, you sure are fast then, my little brown-eyed girl,' Ramulas said as he ruffled her hair.

As they approached the horse in the stable, Grace held her breath in anticipation. She knew what was about to happen. In soft soothing tones, Ramulas walked up to the stall where the horse moved around restlessly. He opened the door while clicking his tongue. The horse followed Ramulas outside.

Ramulas felt his body tingle as the magic flowed through his body. He silently communicated with the horse to run.

The horse's ears flicked forward and it gave a slight nod before it raced out into the field.

'Are you going to call him back, Da?'

Ramulas shook his head. 'No. We will be working in the fields, and the horse can run while we work.'

'I didn't hear you tell the horse to go.'

Ramulas tapped the side of his head with his finger. 'I talk to animals with my mind.'

Ramulas and Grace loaded tools into the barrow, and Grace looked at Ramulas. 'Does anyone know that you talk to animals?'

'No, you are the only one. Not even your mother knows.'

'I will tell her when we go home,' Grace said proudly.

Ramulas laughed. 'I don't think she will believe you.'

***

Ramulas squinted up at the sky, taking a break from his work. The end of summer had come and gone, and he knew that winter would arrive in a few months. A couple of clouds floated in the sky and the warm sun shone down.

There was much to do, but his mind began to wander. He had had many dreams about being a leader of the people. Daydreams and at night. But these seemed more than just dreams to Ramulas.

He felt that he was more than just a farmer. Ramulas had the feeling of great importance. The person who the people could look to for honour and respect. It would provide his family with a better life than the one they had now.

However, every time these thoughts came to Ramulas, self-doubt washed over him like a great wave. Thoughts of rejection and people laughing at him running for mayor eroded the thoughts and dreams of being a leader.

Before Ramulas knew it, the sun was directly above him, and he knew it was time to head across the fields.

The horse walked into its stall. Ramulas followed and shut the door.

'Little one, come outside; I saw something that I want to show you,' he said to Grace.

Once outside, he led her to a group of bushes behind the stables where they saw a wren hopping around. Ramulas motioned for Grace to follow him quietly as he approached the small bird.

He knelt down on one knee while softly whispering to the wren. Slowly, Ramulas reached out and stroked its back before coaxing it onto the palm of his hand.

Standing up slowly with the wren, Ramulas saw that Grace was barely able to contain her excitement. Her hands were outstretched toward the bird, her face full of anticipation.

Ramulas smiled. 'Take some deep breaths and calm yourself. The bird will only stay on your hand if you are calm and relaxed.'

Grace took a few quick breaths, then whispered, 'I'm calm now, Da— let me hold him.'

He brought his hand over Grace's and looked into her eyes. 'Nice and calm,' he said with a smile.

The wren hopped onto Grace's hand, and she suppressed a squeal of glee. After a few seconds, she brought up her other hand to stroke the bird in a clumsy jerking movement. It flew off into nearby trees.

'Oh, Da—he flew away,' Grace said, full of disappointment.

'That's alright, little one.' Ramulas laughed as he walked over and ruffled her hair. 'This will take some practice.'

***

Ramulas brought the axe down and split the log, sending the two halves spinning to the ground. He picked them up and placed them on top of the stack at the rear of his house. The stack of wood was chest height and ran along the wall of his house.

Nodding to himself, Ramulas knew this would be enough for a few months.

Kate came around the corner looking worried. 'The sheriff is coming with some men.'

Looking toward the house, Ramulas said, 'Quickly, fetch your mother and Grace inside, and wait until I come for you.'

Kate nodded before running off. Ramulas walked around the front of his house just in time to see the sheriff and two regal looking men dressed in puffy silken shirts. As they rode into his farm down the dirt track, Ramulas could see the sheriff's red eagle crest on his brown vest.

Jacqueline stood protectively by the side of the house in front of her prized garden. It was her place of harmony.

Ramulas waved in greeting and forced a smile. 'I was not expecting a visit so early.'

The sheriff swung down from his horse and tilted his head to the two dandies behind him. 'This is Dickson, collector of taxes, and his assistant. You will answer any questions they ask and show them through your farm,' he said in a no-nonsense tone.

'Of course,' Ramulas said as he lowered his eyes to the ground.

Dickson walked up to Ramulas, followed by his assistant, who held a scroll of paper and a stick of charcoal. Dickson smiled, and Ramulas felt an involuntary shiver run through him.

Dickson pointed to himself. 'You do realise that lying or trying to hide things from me is to lie to King Zachary? You wouldn't lie to King Zachary, would you?' he asked with a smug smile.

'Of course not,' Ramulas replied in a soft voice.

'Good. Then let us begin.'

Ramulas knew how to play this game. Dickson made an inventory of everything of value on the farm and the earnings of the wheat crop. When Dickson and his assistant were finished calculating the figures, Ramulas was told that one of every five bushels of wheat were to be put aside for the kingdom.

Ramulas made a show of arguing that this was too much; how was he supposed to feed his family through winter? However, deep down, Ramulas was happy. His family were left with enough to enjoy a comfortable winter.

After the sheriff and the men had left, Ramulas stood at the front of the house. He watched where the men had disappeared as more dreams of being a leader surfaced. *If I were a man of importance, a leader of the people, I would be treated differently. My family would not need to worry about rationing food for the winter.*

Just as the thoughts of being someone else rose to their peak, Ramulas was hit with another wave of negative feelings. He was left wondering where these thoughts came from and what they meant.

3

Oriel found herself in a large stone-walled room with bookshelves lining the walls. Two tables were covered with scrolls, books, and potions.

A portly, balding man walked in, reading from a leather-bound book. He looked up, puzzled to see Oriel in his chambers.

'My child, why are you here? I was not expecting you until tomorrow.'

'I went against Remus' orders, and he is furious with me,' Oriel said as her eyes dropped to the floor.

'What did you do?' he asked as he placed the book on a nearby table and walked over to her.

He wore black leggings and a red vest, which marked him as a red wizard. He was Antok, a senior red wizard and Oriel's teacher.

'When Remus wanted to kill everyone, I hid some children from him, and he found out what I had done.'

Antok recoiled as if slapped. 'Have you done this before?'

Oriel shook her head.

'Then why did you do something so foolish?'

'All I have ever wanted was to have a family. Remus was killing them; I had to do something to help the children.'

Antok fought to regain his breath and slow his heart. 'Child, you must tell me everything.'

Oriel quickly told Antok the details of what had transpired and how she came to be in his chambers. 'Oh, my child, what have you done?'

Antok scolded as he gently held her shoulders, 'What have I been teaching you all these years?'

'To hide how much ability I have and not to draw attention to myself,' she answered softly.

Letting go of her shoulders, Antok took a step back. 'Tell me what you are.'

'I am a child of the light.'

'And what is your purpose?'

'To study magic from the time I was created until I reach maturity. That is when the warlords will consume my soul to replenish their magical powers.'

'You have shown far more ability than those who have come before you—you have absorbed my teachings at a far greater speed, and I have not seen another grow as rapidly as you have.

'I did have something planned for you, but it is too early. I need to think of a way to delay Remus. He will want to consume you when he returns,' Antok said softly.

A soft humming filled the room, seeming to come from everywhere at once. Antok looked left and right. 'What? No, wait—it's too early.'

Remus appeared in front of Antok and turned to Oriel. He clenched his square jaw and slowly shook his finger at her. Oriel took a step back, her eyes widening.

'You have disappointed me, Oriel, and you will be dealt with when I return.' Remus turned to Antok. 'I will arrive in five hours. I want Oriel in her cage.' Without another word, he vanished.

Antok let out a sigh of relief and placed his face in his hands. 'By the legions; he only projected his image here. For a moment, I thought ...' Antok looked up at Oriel as his hands fell from his face. 'For a moment, I thought he was actually here. If he was—'

'What do I do now?' Oriel asked apprehensively.

'Not what do you do—what do *we* do? The blame will be cast on me as well.'

'I'm sorry; I didn't mean for you to get into trouble.'

Antok paced the small room talking softly to himself. Oriel watched her teacher. Of all people, Antok would be able to save her from Remus. She did not want to die. She wanted to live forever.

Antok stopped suddenly and spun to face Oriel with a stern expression. 'You have become more advanced in magic than those who came before you. But everything you do is …' He paused for a moment trying to find the words.

Then his finger shot up in triumph as a smile spread across his face. '*Wrong* is the word. You have so much potential, but you fail to grasp the fundamentals of what I try to teach you.'

'But I become bored and want to have fun.'

'I know you do, but you can learn so much more by following what I teach. I know there is more inside that you have not shown. Now, before you are locked away, come read with me.'

Oriel walked over to Antok and took a book he handed her.

Coming to her teacher was the only place of happiness and safety for her. Oriel wanted to stay here until Remus had calmed down.

***

After hours of reading, Oriel saw that Antok was fully immersed in his studying. She felt the prickling sensation under her skin as she whispered a spell, which tossed Antok's book into the air.

She waited for the usual laughter from her teacher. Something was wrong. He was not smiling.

'Antok, what's wrong?' Oriel asked.

Her teacher's eyes widened in shock; 'Remus has returned early. He searches for you.'

Oriel's heartbeat quickened. 'I'm not going back to my cage. Please, you have to help me.'

Antok walked up to Oriel and gently held onto her shoulders. 'My child,' he said softly. 'You must go back. If Remus finds you here, he will surely kill you. However, if you are in your cage, I will try to calm him and delay your death.'

Oriel looked into Antok's eyes with tears running down her cheeks. 'If you think it best.'

Antok felt a cold sensation squeeze his chest, followed by a sense of helplessness. He wanted to hold Oriel, tell her the truth of who he really was to her, and tell her how much he truly loved her and how proud he was of her achievements. He pushed those thoughts away. 'You should go now.'

Oriel nodded once then vanished.

Antok allowed the tears to roll down his cheeks. He wanted so much to tell Oriel that he was her father. All he could do now was try to persuade Remus from killing her.

***

Remus walked into Antok's chambers accompanied by the other four warlords; Alpha, Beta, Omega, and Gamma, each kept their face covered and were only identified by symbols on their robes. 'Where is she?' he asked, looking around the chambers.

'I have sent Oriel back to her cage.'

'Oriel has defied my orders, and for that, she must be punished.'

Antok's mouth had gone dry. He nervously licked his lips before saying, 'Her magic is still unstable. She will not be mature enough for consumption.'

Remus smiled and held his arms out. 'How lucky I am for you to be concerned for my wellbeing,' Remus said as he came over to the red wizard. He placed his arm around Antok's shoulders as if they were long lost friends.

Antok dared not move a muscle.

He knew what was coming.

Remus sent a bolt of energy through the red wizard's shoulders. Antok felt as though his joints were being stretched through a lake of fire. The pain continued for what seemed an eternity.

Then suddenly it stopped, and he fell to the floor.

Leaning over Antok—who was curled into the fetal position—Remus said, 'You will prepare Oriel for consumption. I want her ready now.' Remus and the other warlords walked out of his chambers laughing as if a joke had been told. But Antok knew they looked forward to acquiring Oriel's powers.

***

Oriel was not ready to die.

She was afraid, frustrated, and wanted more than anything to have a sense of freedom. However, Oriel knew it was her purpose to die. Her soul had been separated from her body when she was born. This made Oriel a being of pure magic, because the soul could absorb endless amounts of energy. She was to learn different aspects of magic until she had reached maturity. This usually took up to five years. Then the warlords would consume her to replenish their magical powers.

The warlords had been in power for over sixty years. Every few years, they had taken the soul of a child and filled it with magical energy until it matured. These magical beings were known as Children of the Light.

This was how the warlords had ruled for this time, keeping themselves young and powerful. Without this process, they would lose their magical powers. This would bring them down to the level of the common man, who they despised. The red wizards would then be more powerful, and that was something they would not tolerate.

A wizard floated up to Oriel's cage. 'You have been summoned.'

He held a silver sphere the size of an apple. He tossed it at Oriel, and her world turned white.

***

She found herself in Antok's chambers, and he did not greet her with his usual smile. Antok stood before her, devoid of emotion. Oriel knew that he was unable to help her with Remus.

19

She opened her mouth to talk, but Antok raised his hand to silence her. 'You have the spirit of the Dragon within you, child. That is your only chance.'

A soft humming filled the room.

'Quickly, my child; you must try to escape. Find the Dragon— that is your means of safety. Look for the Dragon at all costs, and then you will find the one person with the power to help you.' The humming grew louder as the room filled with static energy. A doorway of light appeared in front of them, and the five warlords walked through. Remus came through first with hunger in his eyes. Alpha and Beta stood to Remus' right, while Omega and Gamma fanned out to the left.

Antok forced a smile as he walked over to Remus. 'Oriel is not mature enough, my warlord.'

'Lies!' Remus roared as he sent a stream of energy into Antok, who gasped and fell to the ground in spasms. He had lost all control of his muscles.

'No!' Oriel cried as she ran to Antok, only for Remus to step forward and grab her by the throat with his right hand. He lifted Oriel a foot off the ground and held her at arm's length. She began to flail at his arm and weakly kick as she struggled for air.

Fear almost overwhelmed Oriel at seeing what had happened to Antok. She knew that Remus sought to consume her soul, and she wanted more than anything to live.

Remus smiled as he felt the raw energy flowing from Oriel.

'It seems that this one has matured early.' Remus said, 'She is ready. We will consume her now.'

The four warlords began to chant in soft tones. He held out his free hand and brought it up to Oriel's face. His hand began to glow red, and Oriel could feel the energy coming from Remus.

Antok lay on the floor helpless, his muscles refusing to obey his commands. He closed his eyes and prayed that Oriel would not suffer too much.

Oriel could feel Remus pulling at her life force. She realised that she was about to die. Oriel did the only thing she could think of, and that was to panic.

Antok did not want to witness what was about to happen and closed his eyes, but a shift in the magical energies made him open them at the right moment.

Oriel's eyes began to glow a fierce bright blue, then an explosion filled the small space between her and Remus. They were thrown to opposite sides of the chamber. Oriel hit the wall with a sickening thud and slid to the floor unconscious. Remus was caught in the air by Alpha and Omega's magic and brought gently to the floor.

Remus fumed at what had happened. He pointed to Oriel's still form and said, 'I want Oriel back in her cage until we can find a way to feed off her.'

The warlords stepped forward, picked her up, and vanished.

Remus turned to Antok and said, 'You will not say one word of this to anyone, do you understand?'

Antok slowly nodded, realising that he had regained control of his muscles once again. Remus walked through the doorway of light before it vanished.

Tears filled Antok's eyes, thinking how close he was to telling Oriel that he was her father. A look of pure determination came over him as he said, 'No-one is going to hurt my daughter.'

He rushed into another room where he would find the proper spells and potions that would help with his upcoming fight with the warlords.

***

Oriel woke inside her cage to find a red wizard floating outside. The cage was made of negative strands of energy that would shock Oriel if she touched them.

The red wizard waved his hands through the air, and a fireball appeared in front of him. 'Oriel, you have much to learn; make yourself ready,' he said, tossing the fireball at her.

The fireball hung in front of Oriel. She smiled at the red wizard as she waved her hand. The fireball began to spin in patterns. Anger and defiance flowed through her. Oriel did not want to be compliant anymore.

'This is not what you have been taught. Now you must practise properly,' he said, tossing two more fireballs into the cage.

With a thought, Oriel made all three fireballs spin and dance around her. She smiled and winked at the red wizard.

The mouth of the red wizard fell open as Oriel threw all three fireballs at him. At such close range, he did not have time to bring up his defences. The fireballs engulfed the red wizard, and he fell to his death twenty feet below.

Oriel looked down to see five red wizards watching her. Three of them stood, raised their hands, and increased their chanting. She could see the energy strands of her cage becoming stronger. The other two had opened up a magical doorway below her. The five warlords stepped through the doorway, looked at the dead red wizard then up at her.

Remus floated up from the floor, leading the other warlords to Oriel's cage. 'She's mine.'

A bolt of energy flew from his hand into her cage. Oriel caught it and sent it back twice as fast, hitting Remus in the chest and sending him falling to the floor below.

The other warlords attacked Oriel from all sides. She was able to defend herself from the first two attacks, then a third. Remus floated up again and joined the assault with fury in his eyes.

Oriel was hit from all sides, and she saw an array of lights.

This must be what death is like, Oriel thought when she heard her name being called from a faraway place. The voice was getting louder, and when she turned, Oriel saw Antok fighting the warlords.

Antok wore a magical suit of golden armour, and he held a golden shield. He sent streams of energy at the warlords with each wave of his hand. The warlord's attacks were knocked aside with his shield in showers of multi-coloured sparks.

A warm sensation of hope exploded within Oriel. There was a way out of this. Antok was gaining the upper hand, but she knew it would not last.

'Oriel, you must search for the Dragon—that is your only hope,' he shouted.

Unseen by Antok, Remus rose up silently behind him. 'Father, look out behind you!' Oriel shouted.

His golden suit of armour faltered for a split second as he lowered his shield. Oriel had known that he was her father. He began to say something to his daughter when Remus struck a vicious blow from behind. As Antok fell to his death, two things occurred: first, Antok smiled peacefully; secondly, Oriel went in search of the Dragon.

Oriel screamed as she began to grow. She felt wings form on her back that spread out to touch the sides of the cage. At first, the pain of touching the energy strands caused Oriel to retract her wings. But she ignored the pain and pushed her wings through the walls of the cage, letting a stream of fire flow from her mouth.

Remus and the warlords backed away as power flowed through Oriel. She looked at the warlords with the utmost hatred as she saw their uncertainty. She had the power to destroy them and avenge Antok.

Then pain beyond imagination exploded behind her eyes. Oriel knew at once that she was unprepared for this amount of power.

Remus could not believe what was happening to Oriel. As she continued to grow, the cage that held Oriel dropped to the floor below, and she disappeared in a flash of light. Remus and the other warlords floated down to where the broken cage was, only to find it empty.

'Where is she?' Remus asked in frustration.

The warlords formed a circle around the cage and saw a small black shimmering void floating in the middle.

After waving intricate patterns through the air, one of the warlords replied, 'Oriel has teleported to another world and left a magical black hole to prevent us from following her.'

Remus shook with rage as he screamed, 'I want Oriel found! Without her, we are nothing.'

4

Ramulas' muscles strained as he pulled on the axle of the cart. He felt warm, even though the early morning dew was still visible on the grass. They needed a new cart, but Ramulas knew that he could only afford minor repairs when they went into town later that day.

Grace screamed in terror and ran outside. Ramulas quickly left the barn in time to scoop her up and saw that tears were running down her cheeks and her bottom lip was protruding.

'Little one, what is wrong?'

'They're coming to get me,' she replied fearfully, looking over her shoulder and hugging Ramulas with all her strength.

'Who is coming to get you?' he asked while searching for hidden enemies.

'The druids. Kate said they're coming to take me away.'

Ramulas sighed as he gently patted her on the back. 'No, they're not, little one.'

Ramulas walked into the house and found Kate inside wearing an innocent expression.

'Now, Kate—look how upset you've made Grace. I think you've gone too far,' he said in a stern voice.

'I didn't—' Kate began before seeing the look on her father's face. 'It's not fair! Grace always teases me, and no-one is scared of druids.'

'You went too far Kate. What would you do if someone scared you with stories of druids coming to get you?'

'I'm too old to be frightened by druid stories.'

Ramulas slowly shook his head. 'Now, you two need to get along.'

Grace glared at Kate as she was carried from the room.

***

Sitting at the kitchen table, Ramulas was surprised to see that Grace had finished the morning meal faster than usual.

'Da, may I be excused?'

He nodded, and Grace ran off.

A moment later, Grace crept into the kitchen with a sheet over her head and held both her arms out in front of her. Ramulas was about to say something when Jacqueline placed a hand over his and gave a slight shake of her head.

Grace moved across the floor without making a sound until she had come up behind Kate. Grace let out a low moan and grabbed Kate by the shoulders. Kate turned and jumped out of her chair.

Ramulas and Jacqueline stifled their laughter as Grace pulled off the sheet.

'Da, Kate thought I was a druid,' Grace exclaimed happily.

'I wasn't scared at all,' Kate retorted.

Ramulas gave Kate a knowing look. 'It's not very nice, is it?' He could tell that Kate wanted to protest, so he held up his hand and she remained silent. 'Now, there will be no more of this nonsense about the druids from either of you. I think you need to know the truth about the druids. If you wait until we are on the way to town, I will tell their story.'

Both girls quickly helped their mother pack the cart. As they left the farm, Ramulas began to tell the tale of the druids.

'Many years ago, before your grandparents were born, stories began to spread throughout the land. All manner of monsters and creatures were seen near farms on the outskirts of towns. Soon they were attacking livestock, then the farmers and their families. By the time help had arrived from the town, the monsters had vanished.

'They began to ambush small groups of travellers along the backroads. The king sent his soldiers out from the city of Keah to patrol the backroads and highways. But the creatures were cunning; they learned to avoid the patrols and continued to attack the people. The only place unaffected was the town of Suda. The druids of Suda kept the monsters at bay with their magic.

'The king sent for the druids. When they arrived in Keah, the king asked if the druids could help rid the kingdom of the creatures and monsters. The druids said they would be able to do this. However, because of their beliefs, they would not kill any of the creatures or monsters.

'They would build a network of underground mazes; the druids would then gather the creatures and place them within the mazes. But this would come at a great cost to them. It would take time and change the physical appearance of the druids. The place would be called the Druids' Labyrinth.

'The king replied he would do anything to repay the druids for this deed. The druids walked from the city of Keah and spent the next two years building the network of mazes in the Darkwood and capturing every creature and monster before placing them in the Druids' Labyrinth. Spells and wards were cast over the only entrance to prevent any from leaving.

'After the task was completed, the group of druids made their way to Keah to inform the king. When they were brought into the king's chambers, the druids removed their hoods to reveal that their faces and heads were covered in green scales, and they had no hair; their hands were the same, and their nails were long black talons.

'The king recoiled in shock and ordered the druids to be removed from the city of Keah. The druids attempted to protest, saying they had told the king of the change they would go through.

'But this fell on deaf ears; they were hounded from Keah by the very people they had helped. In the streets of Keah, rotten food and refuse were thrown at the druids as they were chased from the city.

'The druids travelled from town to town seeking shelter, including their hometown of Suda. They were met with the same response; people's fear of the unknown caused them to despise the druids. Each rejection allowed hatred and spite to creep into the once-peaceful druids.

'After several weeks of tireless travel across the lands, the druids found themselves in the Darkwood, where they had designed the Druids' Labyrinth. They could feel the magic call to them from below. The magic promised retribution if the druids entered the labyrinth.

'The head druid spoke. "We offered to help the people of the kingdom, and we were rewarded by them treating us like the monsters we banished. It would be an easy task for us to open the doorway and allow the monsters and creatures to roam free once more. But I wish to give the people an unnamed fear. Let them whisper about us in the fear of not knowing when we will come to take them into the Druids' Labyrinth."

'From time to time, people disappear for no apparent reason, and sightings of druids will spread. People have been placed in the Druids' Labyrinth to fight their way out. No-one has ever escaped.'

'Did that really happen, Da?' Grace asked.

He looked down at her, smiling. 'I saw a druid a long time ago.'

Both girl's eyes lit up at this revelation, and Kate spoke. 'Can you tell us what happened?'

Ramulas drifted off to his very first memory.

***

He stood in a field, as naked as the day he was born. Ramulas felt the distressed horse before he heard it. He ran in the direction of the animal while sending it calming thoughts. Ramulas ran across a road to see the horse had pulled a cart into a ditch along the banks of a river.

The cart had tipped, pinning the driver in the water with only his head above the surface. He ran into the water to push the cart off the man while communicating with the horse.

As he pushed on the side of the cart, the horse moved back a few feet before pulling itself up the bank toward the road. With a groan of wood, the cart was upright, and Ramulas helped the man out of the water. He was a short, stocky man of middle age whose clothes clung to him with moisture.

'I don't know what shocked me more. To see you save me from drowning or that you are naked. Where are your clothes?'

'I don't know,' Ramulas said, perplexed.

'I have not seen you around here. Where are you from?'

Ramulas shrugged and shook his head. 'I don't know.'

It felt extremely strange for Ramulas not to know where he was from, where his clothes were, or anything about who he was.

'I can tell you're not from around here with that funny accent you have. Well, I just can't leave you here after what you have done. Help me reload the cart and I'll take you home and see what we can do.' The man stepped forward and held out his hand. 'The name's Peter.'

'Ramulas,' he answered, surprising himself. His name was the only thing he knew about himself.

Ramulas helped Peter reload items back onto the cart that had fallen off. Peter handed him an old blanket to wrap around himself.

They arrived at Peter's farm a short while later. On the journey, Peter made Ramulas feel at ease by talking about his farm, his wife, and the people who lived nearby. But Ramulas still struggled to remember anything else besides his name.

After placing the cart in the barn and horse in the stable, Peter led Ramulas, still wrapped in the blanket, into his house.

Once inside, he was introduced to Peter's wife, Fran. Ramulas felt extremely awkward meeting this waif of a lady, who greeted him in an apron with her blonde hair tied in a bun.

When Peter told the story of how Ramulas had saved him from certain death, and that his rescuer had lost his memory, Fran guided Ramulas to a bedroom.

'This used to be Jamie's room—our only son. He was a soldier in the king's army,' Fran said with pride. 'He was killed breaking up a barfight.' She looked up at Ramulas with sadness in her eyes.

'I am sorry for your loss.'

'He passed away almost a year ago. Now, he was about your age and build, and you will find some clothes that should fit you.' She gestured to the chest at the end of the bed.

'I could not accept these clothes,' Ramulas said, feeling uncomfortable.

Fran slapped Ramulas on his shoulder, causing him to jump. She looked up at Ramulas with tears in her eyes. 'If you do not accept, then you will be hurting my feelings. After you are dressed, I will make you something to eat.'

She walked out of the room and closed the door behind her. Ramulas stood for a moment, holding the blanket tightly around him, unsure what he should do.

He walked into the kitchen wearing brown leggings and a woollen shirt. Fran gasped as her hands covered her mouth, and she took a tentative step toward Ramulas.

Peter smiled and rose from his chair. 'Now, there's a sight to see. We didn't think we would see anyone wearing those clothes again.' He saw Ramulas' hesitation. 'Come, sit at the table, boy. Food is just about ready.'

The three sat at the table and made small talk while they ate. Both Peter and Fran asked questions and tried to work out the mystery of where Ramulas had come from and who he was.

Peter told Ramulas of how he built the house with his own hands before asking Fran to marry him. He smiled as the couple told of their son helping to maintain the house, but it didn't help Ramulas remember anything.

Ramulas was asked to stay and help on the farm until his memory returned to him. Peter had estimated Ramulas to be about eighteen years old. An extra strong pair of hands would do well on the farm. He was quick to learn all aspects of farming life within the first four months. Peter and Fran were happy to have Ramulas on the farm; he filled the void left by the death of their son.

***

After eighteen months on the farm, Ramulas still could not remember anything of his previous life. Peter was treasurer of the farmers' guild and took Ramulas along to the meetings. He soon found that Ramulas picked things up quickly, and before too long, Peter started to mentor Ramulas in becoming the next leader of the farmers' guild.

At first, Ramulas was hesitant, and other members did not take too kindly to an outsider running for leader in the upcoming election. But with Peter's support, the protests grew silent.

With Peter and Fran's support, Ramulas gained confidence and looked forward to the elections, which were a few weeks away. Peter had convinced the influential people to vote for Ramulas.

One night, Ramulas was woken by the sound of Peter yelling. He jumped out of bed, put on his leggings, and raced outside toward Peter's voice. The moon was full on this cloudless night, showing the ground easily. Just behind the barn, he saw Peter standing in front of Fran, who was crying on the ground.

'If you want to take someone, then let it be me,' he shouted to the trees while standing protectively in front of his wife.

'What's happening?' Ramulas asked as he walked closer.

'No, boy, stay back,' Peter ordered.

A figure dressed in a black hooded robe glided out of the trees and pointed a taloned, scaly hand at Ramulas, who felt an icy fist grab hold of his heart. He whimpered, dropping to his knees. The last thing he saw before blacking out was Peter charging the hooded figure.

***

Ramulas woke with a crying Fran leaning over him. She explained that the druids had come for her, but Peter had taken her place.

Seeing the confusion on Ramulas' face, Fran told him the story of the druids.

The sheriff from Bremnon was told, and he led a party of soldiers and locals to search for Peter. After two days, the search was called off. The next day, Fran sat at the kitchen table with Ramulas.

'You have made us so happy.' She smiled while reaching over and patting his hand. 'I have something to show you. We were going to wait another year, but I think now is the right time.' Fran pushed a piece of paper in front of Ramulas, who picked it up and read it. Ramulas' eyes widened as he realised that he was holding the deed to the farm. His name was alongside Peter and Fran's.

'I cannot accept this,' he protested as he pushed the piece of paper back to Fran.

'Peter told me you would say that. You never asked us for anything; that is why we made this decision.'

Fran stood, placing her hands on the table as she sighed. In the days since the druids took Peter, Fran had aged and seemed weaker every day. She walked toward her room.

'Fran, where are you going?'

'I'm just a little tired. I'm going to bed early. I'll see you on the morrow.'

Ramulas looked outside and saw that there were a few hours of sunlight left in the day. As much as he wanted to comfort Fran, Ramulas knew she needed time alone.

The next morning, Ramulas woke to find Fran had died in her sleep, and the farm now belonged to him. The two people Ramulas saw as parents had died, along with his dreams of becoming the next leader of the farmers' guild.

5

Oriel woke screaming with her hands stretched out wide. Every part of her body burned in agony. However, the pain quickly subsided, and Oriel stopped screaming. She opened her eyes and found that she was in a world of total darkness. She could feel the cold stone floor beneath her.

Oriel was extremely weak from opening the portal that she used to escape and travel to this place. She had also left a magical void so Remus would have difficulty following her.

She was overwhelmed at transforming into a dragon. At the same time, Antok's teachings came to her. He had always said that the greater the magical power you wield, the more it takes from you. *So much power,* Oriel thought—enough to destroy the warlords and avenge her father. But with that power came so much pain.

Oriel could feel that most of her magical ability had left her, and it would take some time to recover.

Oriel's body protested as she stood. She waved her hand and a soft ball of light appeared before her, which illuminated the small cavern she found herself in. Looking down, Oriel saw that she had reverted back to her human form.

A mixture of emotions flooded through Oriel. She was surprised and happy beyond words to have escaped. But where was she? A pang of sadness came over her as she thought about Antok giving his life so that she may live and be free.

But freedom came at a cost.

Oriel walked around the cavern, which was the size of a small castle. Oriel could feel that she was very close to a place of ancient magic. She could feel the magic faintly coming through the walls. There were a few tunnels within the cavern, none of which led to a way out.

Then Oriel felt a magical being to the south. He was the one who had the power to help her. She was unable to walk through the walls of the cavern and reach this person, so she gathered what little magic that remained to send an astral image of herself to find him.

**

'Da, we're at Bremnon,' Grace shouted.

He came out of his daydream just in time. Jacqueline gave him a reassuring smile and patted him on the leg. She and the girls were used to the sporadic times when Ramulas would drift off into his own little world.

Bringing the cart into Bremnon, Ramulas gave a curt nod or a wave to the people he knew. He could feel the anticipation and excitement growing in Jacqueline and his girls, who spoke in hushed tones.

They passed buildings made of wooden frames and brick before coming into the outdoor market. Vendors stood by their stalls calling out to customers. Horses and carts could be heard as they travelled across the cobblestone roads.

A small group of ladies waved at Jacqueline, and she returned the wave.

Turning to Ramulas, Jacqueline said, 'Kate and I will be fine to stop here.'

He pulled the cart to the side of the road, kissing Kate and Jacqueline as they climbed off the cart.

'I will meet you in the market square at midday,' he said as they waved and walked to the group of ladies.

'Da! Apples for the horse,' Grace exclaimed as she jumped down from the cart.

Ramulas watched with a smile as his youngest daughter ran to the fruit vendor near Jacqueline. A few feet from the vendor, Grace turned to wave at her father. His smile disappeared as she tripped and knocked the vendor's table.

The apples had been arranged in a neat pyramid on the table.

That pyramid collapsed in slow motion before Ramulas' eyes. His first thought was that he would have to pay for all the damaged fruit.

In a fluid movement, Kate danced forward, her hands a blur as she caught the falling fruit. She moved from side to side with ease, and within a few seconds, every apple had been rearranged into a pyramid once more.

Kate turned to see a small group of people watching her, their mouths hanging open in shock. Kate became self-conscious and lowered her eyes to the ground.

'How … How did you do that?' Ramulas stammered.

'I don't know,' Kate replied as she went to Jacqueline. 'Mother, can we leave?'

Ramulas looked at his wife expectantly. Jacqueline gave him a stern look before shaking her head. She put a protective arm around Kate and walked away with the group of ladies.

The Feyan vendor smiled at Ramulas and handed Grace two apples. Feyans were mystical people who lived in the forests north of the devil's ridge mountains. They were tall and thin with slightly pointed ears and were said to live at least two hundred years. It was rare to see a full-blooded Feyan in the towns or the city, and only a few came into Bremnon.

Ramulas could only shrug as he walked away with his youngest daughter. He swore to himself that he would talk to Kate about what happened later in the day.

***

Once Jacqueline and Kate had left, Grace had climbed into the front and sat next to her father, she waved happily to anyone who looked their way. Ramulas glanced down at her beaming face. He enjoyed the special bond he had with Grace. Kate was closer to her mother and wanted so much to be a young lady.

Ramulas steered the cart through Bremnon until he arrived at a workshop next to the stables.

'Da, can I help you fix things today?' Grace asked.

'Of course, little one, that's why you are here.'

Ramulas climbed down from the cart, lifted Grace to the ground, and walked into the workshop. He communicated with the horse that it would be fed soon.

Walking into the workshop, they were met by a wiry dark-skinned man whose face was virtually hidden under his long black hair and bushy beard. His eyes lit up when he saw them come in. He wiped his hands on his overalls as he walked to them.

Ramulas led Grace across the open space as she looked to wagons and carts along the wall in various stages of repair.

Ramulas knew this man had Khilli heritage. A small faction of the Khilli tribes people left their hunting grounds generations ago. The ones who lived in towns were known as 'outcasts'.

'Ramulas and little Grace! To what do I owe the honour?'

'I have come for you to fix my cart. When can you start, Thomas?'

'I won't be starting for another hour, and I know you'll be helping me to save some coin.' Thomas laughed as he walked over and slapped Ramulas on the shoulder. 'You should see your face. Bring your cart in, and I'll have your horse seen to.'

Ramulas smiled at his friend. 'Grace and I will be back in an hour. Don't start without me.'

***

Commotion and a gathered crowd had caught Ramulas' attention in the market square. He was curious and led Grace into the crowd. Ramulas pushed his way through the people with Grace behind, and he found out why the crowd had gathered.

36

'Good people of Bremnon,' the sheriff shouted as he stood on a high platform. Next to him, two men were shackled together.

Ramulas thought they might be father and son. The one thing that stood out was that they had been beaten and looked defeated. 'These two have been caught stealing,' the sheriff continued as he looked to the faces in the crowd below him. 'But what's worse, they were caught stealing from the collector of taxes by hiding valuables and avoiding payment.' The sheriff waved to the two miserable-looking men who knelt with their heads bowed.

'They have stolen from King Zachary himself!' The sheriff proclaimed, 'There is only one punishment to fit this foul crime, and that is five years of labour in Gully town!' The sheriff, wearing a sinister smile, held his arms out wide.

The crowd gasped as one. The two prisoners looked at the sheriff in shock.

'Man, that is hard,' Someone nearby said, 'I would rather take my chances with the druids.'

Grace looked up at Ramulas, and before she could speak, he led her away from the crowd.

'I want you to forget everything you saw back there; they're bad people.'

'The men in chains?' she asked.

'Everyone on the platform. Now, let's find other things to amuse ourselves.'

***

They arrived at Thomas' workshop to find tools lying on the floor in an orderly fashion alongside the cart. Thomas leant against the cart with his hands in his pockets, smiling.

'Now that you both have returned, we can start fixing your cart.'

The two men began work on the cart while Grace ran back and forth, retrieving tools.

After a while, Ramulas noticed that Grace was not around, and he had not seen her in some time.

'Thomas, can you finish the cart; I think I'll look for Grace.'

Thomas answered with a grunt from underneath the cart.

Ramulas walked around the workshop, calling out Grace's name, but she was nowhere to be found. Ramulas walked outside the workshop and found her standing outside. She was staring at something down the street.

'What have you found, little one?' Ramulas asked as he squatted beside her.

'Da, isn't she beautiful?' Grace said in awe.

'Who?' he asked, looking at his daughter.

Grace grabbed her father's chin and turned his head to where she was looking.

'Hello, Ramulas. I need your help.'

Ramulas rose to a standing position so quickly that he became slightly dizzy. In front of him was a beautiful young lady of about twenty years of age. She wore flowing green robes and had black hair that seemed to shine in the sunlight. But the most amazing thing, to Ramulas, was her deep blue eyes.

Then he thought of the way she spoke. She had a strange accent that was somehow familiar to Ramulas.

For a moment, it was as if everything around Ramulas had vanished except for the lady before him. There was something special about her; something that he should know, but Ramulas could not grasp what it was.

He was speechless and did not know how to react. She stepped closer to him and held out her hands. Without being aware of his actions, Ramulas felt his hands holding onto hers. A sense of awkwardness came over Ramulas, he did not want to hurt the small woman in front of him.

'I am Oriel,' she said with a reassuring smile as she gave his hands a gentle squeeze.

'Ramulas,' he answered, feeling stupid as he spoke because she had already said his name.

But how did she know him? Ramulas would have remembered a woman like this.

'I am in trouble, and you are the only one with the power to help me.'

'Power?' Ramulas said in shock. 'What power? I am a simple farmer and nothing more.'

'You are far more than just a simple farmer,' Oriel said with a knowing smile.

'Ah, there you are Ramulas, I have just finished your cart,' Thomas said from the doorway.

Ramulas released Oriel's hands and turned to see Thomas walk toward him. As he turned, Grace witnessed Oriel turn to mist and enter her father's body.

'What have you been doing out here with Grace?' Thomas asked.

'We saw a beautiful lady, and Da held her hand,' Grace blurted out.

'Ho ho! Ramulas, my old friend. I always knew there was something about you,' Thomas said as he searched for the lady in question.

Ramulas felt warmth spread throughout his body as he tried to explain Oriel to Thomas, which only caused his friend to laugh.

'I've never seen her before,' Ramulas protested.

'I think I'll walk to the market with you so young Grace and I can discuss your new friend.' Thomas winked before returning to his workshop.

Ramulas turned and saw that Oriel was nowhere to be seen. 'Where did that young lady go, Grace?'

Grace walked up to Ramulas and placed her hand on his chest. 'She's in here, Da.'

As Grace's hand touched his chest, Ramulas could feel something move inside him. It reminded him of a fish swimming in a small pond.

'By the gods,' Ramulas whispered.

At that moment, Thomas walked out of his workshop, and the three of them walked toward the market.

Ramulas walked, deep in thought about Oriel. Every time he placed a hand on his chest, he could feel something move inside him.

What could it be, and where did the lady go? Ramulas did not want to believe that she was somehow inside him.

'You look lost without your lady friend,' Thomas called out.

Ramulas looked across to see both Thomas and Grace whispering and giggling to each other. He knew that asking them to stop would only prolong their game, so Ramulas remained silent and continued walking.

Every now and then, he would touch his chest and wonder what had happened.

***

Oriel had used the last of her magic and sent her astral image in search of the only one with the power to help her. She flew across the land until she came to the town where she felt he was. Remaining invisible, Oriel searched the streets until she saw a small dark-haired girl walk onto the street.

The girl was connected to the one she was seeking. Oriel showed herself to the girl and stroked her hair while smiling. All the girl's thoughts and memories were shared with Oriel. Grace looked up and smiled at her, and then Ramulas walked into the street.

Oriel was shocked when she saw his face; familiar as it was, but before she could dwell on it, Oriel could feel the untapped magical reservoir within him. She looked into his soul and saw that this was a kind-hearted man who cared deeply for his family.

Once Oriel had entered Ramulas' body, she could tell there would be a lot of work before she could have Ramulas ready to face Remus and the Legion.

***

The trio walked through the market, inspecting the stalls until Ramulas saw Jacqueline and Kate talking to the group of women. Thomas saw them as well and bid his farewells before returning to his workshop.

'Your mother and sister are across the market,' Ramulas said, pointing them out to Grace.

She held Ramulas' hand as they walked over to the group of very animated women. He could hear parts of the conversation.

'It will make beautiful dresses.'

'You two will be the talk of Bremnon.'

'What will you tell your husband?'

'Yes, what will you tell me?' Ramulas asked with a smile on his face.

The women and Kate froze for a second, then the three ladies said their goodbyes and disappeared into the crowd.

Ramulas saw that both Jacqueline and Kate were holding bags behind their backs.

'What have you two been up to?' Jacqueline asked, trying to deflect Ramulas' attention away from the bags.

'We met a beautiful lady,' Grace said, 'And Da held her hand.'

'Who is this lady?' Jacqueline asked, curious as to who she might be. In that moment of curiosity, she allowed her bag to swing to the side, which caused Kate to gasp in shock.

'It was someone that I have never seen before,' Ramulas said with his arms out wide, 'she came to me asking for help. I turned away and then she was gone.'

'She had pretty green robes,' Grace added with a smile.

Ramulas looked to the heavens as if asking for assistance, then he looked at the bag that Jacqueline was holding. 'What do you have there?'

Jacqueline smiled while lowering her eyes. 'I love you, Rami.'

Rami was the pet name Jacqueline called him when she wanted something.

'What did you buy?' Ramulas asked, dreading the answer.

Jacqueline smiled while she pulled out the rolls of fabric of various earthen colours. 'I will make clothes for the girls and myself. These were only five silver coins.'

Ramulas almost fell over. 'If I had a spare five silver coins, I would not have to keep fixing the cart. I could have bought a new cart.' Ramulas looked at Jacqueline with pain in his eyes. 'Why did you buy these things when you know we cannot afford it? That was to help us through winter.'

He looked into his wife's eyes and knew she was sorry. 'I just wanted new clothes for the girls.'

'We can't afford these. This was the money for food during the winter. What are we going to do for food?'

Jacqueline sighed. 'I'll go to the store and return some.' Ramulas nodded as he followed Jacqueline.

She led the way back to the store. Ramulas walked in, and the owner walked up to greet him. He carried himself as if he were royalty and everyone was beneath him. Ramulas took an instant disliking to the man.

'Good day to you madam; you have returned, how may I help?'

Jacqueline placed the bags on the counter and smiled at the man. She took out the rolls of fabric, placing them on the counter. 'I have purchased too much, and I wish to return a few of these.'

The owner tutted and quickly shook his head. 'No, I do not want them. Once something is sold, I do not take it back.' Jacqueline gasped in shock before she replied, 'We were just in this store, and you said nothing of the sort. All I want to do is return a few items.'

The owner gave a false smile and shook his head. Jacqueline felt cold with anger. She was at a loss for words and looked to Ramulas for support.

'My wife purchased some items, and we have come to return them,' Ramulas said as he walked over to the counter.

'I am terribly sorry, but these items have left the store and therefore cannot be returned, nor will you get your three silver coins back.'

Ramulas heard Jacqueline and Kate gasp as they heard the lie. Grace watched everyone; she knew something was about to happen, but she wasn't sure what it was.

The store owner stood with a smug smile on his face as he waited for Ramulas and his family to leave.

Taking a step forward, Ramulas said in a low voice, 'Take back your material and return my five silver coins now.'

The owner stepped behind the counter saying, 'If you do not leave at once, I will be forced to call for the sheriff.'

Ramulas followed the owner behind the counter and grabbed him by the front of his shirt and pulled the man close enough so their noses were almost touching. 'I want my money now.'

Out of the corner of his eye, Ramulas saw something coming toward his head. As Ramulas turned, he was struck by a wooden club held by the store owner. A warm sensation flowed through Ramulas as he lifted the store owner off the ground. Looking back, Ramulas saw the scared expressions of Jacqueline and his girls.

He dropped the store owner, who grabbed some of the cloth before running into the street screaming for help.

Walking out of the store, Ramulas could see the owner had found the sheriff. Next to the sheriff stood a tall dark-skinned warrior. His black hair was tied in braids, he was dressed in only a loincloth, and his lean physic spoke of someone whose life was dedicated to fighting.

Ramulas knew it was a Khilli tribesman. They were famous as the most efficient fighters throughout the kingdom, who knew no fear. They were guards for the sheriffs and the royal family.

The reason why only some of the Khilli left their home was unknown. But their legendary skills were known to all.

Ramulas left Jacqueline and the girls at the store. He walked over to the sheriff and felt his heart sink when he realised who it was. It was the sheriff that had recently come to his farm.

'Hello again,' the sheriff said, crossing his burly arms, 'I was at your farm yesterday with the collector of taxes, and now I find you in a dispute over silver coins that were used to pay for fabric.'

This was all Ramulas needed. A day after crying poor to the tax collector, his wife was buying material. This incident would be reported, and he could expect another visit, and this next visit would hurt.

'Yes, my wife spent money she was not supposed to. This money was for food during winter,' Ramulas said apologetically.

The sheriff raised an eyebrow. 'Well, let me deal one thing at a time.'

As the sheriff spoke, the store owner took a small blade from his sleeve and cut the items he was holding. Ramulas saw this and quickly told the sheriff what had happened.

With a slight flick of his hand, the blade disappeared, and he wore a shocked expression. 'I do not know what he is talking about, these were returned damaged,' the store owner said innocently.

Ramulas was about to reply when he saw Oriel standing next to the Khilli tribesman. She frantically pointed behind Ramulas with fear written across her face. Ramulas turned and his heart leapt into his mouth. Across the road outside an inn were two groups of men in the middle of an argument.

One of the groups consisted of enforcers who worked for the inn; the other group had been kicked out and had come back looking for trouble. They were a smaller group than the enforcers, but they held weapons and had a hell hound. The hell hound was three feet at the shoulder and covered in two-inch black spikes, which protruded from its fur.

In the middle of the two groups sat Grace, too terrified to move as the hell hound pulled on its chain attempting to reach her.

Ramulas began running to his daughter, but his legs felt as if they were made of stone.

Ramulas reached out to the mind of the hell hound, sending it calming thoughts. But he was met with a wall of rage. This hell hound had been mistreated since it was a puppy, and all it wanted to do was maim and kill.

Grace was its next intended victim.

***

Grace followed Ramulas out of the store and watched him walk over to the sheriff. She saw a colourful butterfly dance by and jumped up to grab it. It moved away from her, and Grace followed the butterfly until it landed on the ground.

Grace pounced and landed in the middle of the two groups of men. She saw the big black scary dog close to her. Its jaws opened and it pulled on its chain. A low growl grew in the hell hound's throat. The butterfly was forgotten.

'Nice doggy,' she whimpered softly.

The hell hound's mouth opened to show long curved teeth coming toward her. Grace squealed and pulled back just as the massive jaws snapped shut an inch from her face. Grace overbalanced and fell on her behind.

She was too scared to move. All she needed to do was move back. The big dog pulled on its chain and inched its way toward her.

'Hey stop! My daughter is there,' Ramulas called as he ran across the street where Grace was. At that moment, the owner of the hell hound released the chain, and it lunged at Grace.

Ramulas dove forward with his hands outstretched. Everything around him slowed as he seemed to drift toward the hell hound.

The movement of everything had slowed to a virtual standstill.

Then Ramulas' fingertips touched the chain. Stretching and twisting, he grabbed the chain in his left hand. Then everything returned to normal speed.

Ramulas fell stomach-first onto the porch, still holding the chain. Two things happened simultaneously: the hell hound turned to attack Ramulas, and the two groups of men began to fight with Grace in the middle.

Still holding the chain, Ramulas flipped onto his back then spun around holding his feet out towards the hell hound.

Ramulas jerked on the chain and kicked his feet out to catch the hell hound in its chest. It was momentarily stunned by this. But when it recovered, the hound saw Ramulas lying on his back a few feet away. It had forgotten all about Grace and focused on its new target.

The hell hound attempted to bite Ramulas' legs, snapping its head left and right. But the way Ramulas pulled on the chain and had his boots against the animal's chest, it was unable to reach him. After a few seconds, it used its front paws to rake at Ramulas' legs.

Pain shot through Ramulas' legs like hot coals had been dropped down his trousers. He knew that he would not be able to hold on much longer. Ramulas saw Grace watching him with tears streaming down her cheeks, silently pleading for him to do something. 'Run, Grace!' he cried before his legs gave way, and the hell hound leapt for him.

Time slowed once again as Ramulas watched the open jaws come toward him. A glint of silver caught his eye as it flew in from the side and hit the hell hound in the side of its head.

Then time returned to normal.

Ramulas had the breath knocked out of his lungs as the hell hound collapsed on his chest. Grace screamed as the two groups of men fought around her. Looking at the hell hound, Ramulas saw a silver disk the size of a hand.

It was a Khilli throwing disk.

Ramulas pushed down with his right foot and rolled to his right, pushing the dead hell hound off him. He needed to protect Grace.

A blood-curdling scream cut through the air, and a dark blur ploughed into the mass of fighting men.

It was the Khilli warrior.

The Khilli leapt into the air and delivered a flying knee to one of the enforcer's heads, knocking him back. Coming down, the Khilli spun, hitting another opponent, opening his nose and sending an arc of blood into the air. He reached out, grabbing an arm and twisting it, causing a man to scream as it broke. The Khilli danced to the left, sending a kick into a man's chest before spinning and hitting another with the palm of his hand.

The realisation of what the Khilli was doing suddenly hit Ramulas. The Khilli was protecting Grace, attacking anyone who came close to her. After a few seconds, the combatants that were still standing realised the Khilli had joined the fight.

All except for one backed away, not wanting anything to do with the warrior.

A man as tall as the Khilli, but twice as wide with heavily muscled arms, stood his ground. He held a large club that he slapped onto his open palm.

He looked down at the dead hell hound. 'You killed my dog,' the man said as he shook the long dark hair from his eyes.

'Walk away now,' the Khilli said in a soft voice that sent an involuntary shiver through Ramulas.

The man smiled before running at the Khilli with his club raised. The Khilli danced forward and kicked at the man's knee, breaking it with an audible snap. As the man bent forward, the Khilli sent an elbow into the man's face. The man was lifted from the ground to land unconscious on his back.

The Khilli smiled down at Grace before walking over to Ramulas and offering his hand. Ramulas, accepted the hand and allowed the Khilli to pull him to his feet. Ramulas, almost collapsed from the pain in his legs.

Grace ran up to Ramulas, and he picked her up and held her close. Jacqueline and Kate had recovered from the shock and came running over.

The Khilli smiled at Grace. He did not seem out of breath from the fight. 'It is the way of my people to look upon our children as treasures and not allow any harm to come to them.'

Jacqueline and Kate were now holding onto Ramulas while surveying the surrounding carnage.

'Who gave you leave of my side?' shouted the sheriff as he stormed over. 'That will cost you one weeks' reduced rations.' The Khilli visibly stiffened at this.

Ramulas stepped forward with Grace in his arms. 'You cannot take food from him—he saved me and my daughter.'

'Who said he was going to miss out on food?' replied the sheriff with an evil smile.

The sheriff walked up to the hell hound and pulled out the throwing disk before giving it to the Khilli. Ramulas looked across to see the store owner shutting his store.

'What about the return of my coins?' Ramulas asked.

Waving his hand dismissively at Ramulas, the sheriff said, 'Do not do any further business with that store.'

Watching the sheriff and Khilli walk away, Ramulas knew he would not be seeing his money again. He gathered his family and walked to Thomas' workshop. All he wanted to do was go home and put this day behind him.

6

Pip looked across the market at the man who had caught her attention. He had just walked out of a clothing store and began talking to the sheriff. He was clearly not happy with something the store owner had done.

What caught Pip's attention was that the man was covered in a faint purple nimbus of energy. It rose from him like steam from a boiling pot.

Pip smiled to herself as she pulled her hood down lower to cover her hair. It was the same shade of purple as the nimbus covering the stranger. Judging by the lack of reaction from people in the market square, Pip knew she was the only one who could see the energy rising from him.

Her eyes widened when she saw the man's younger daughter approach two groups of men.

The young girl made a beeline toward the hell hound.

Pip's hand slipped into her cloak to touch one of the many throwing knives she carried on her body. She silently berated herself and shook her head quickly.

Taking her hand out of her cloak, Pip thought to herself, *You do not know them. Do not become involved and draw attention to yourself.*

She pushed away the feeling of sadness as the hell hound tried to attack the girl. When her father ran in to grab the chain, the nimbus flared twice as bright while he fought the hell hound.

The Khilli jumped into the two groups of fighting men to protect the little girl.

Pip found herself ducking and weaving in her mind as the Khilli attacked the men. She imagined herself fighting the warrior. After the fourth man went down, Pip knew she would not last long against the warrior. Pip was an excellent fighter and could defeat a man twice her size.

But the Khilli was far better than her.

After the fight had finished, Pip followed the man and his family from a distance. She needed to know more about him. A short way up the street, the family entered a workshop only to exit on a cart a few minutes later.

As the cart turned up the street away from her, Pip saw something about the man that was even stranger. Pip ran as fast as she could through the rear alleyways until she had overtaken the cart.

Pip came out onto the main street and casually leaned against a wall. The cart passed by a minute later, following a procession of horses and wagons.

Then she saw it.

The man's legs, where the hell hound had raked him, had somehow healed. The material of his pants was torn, and bloodstains covered his legs.

But the wounds had healed.

An overwhelming urge to follow this man came over Pip. She glanced around before jumping into the rear of the cart and quickly hid under the tarp.

Pip knew there was something special about this man involving magic, and she wanted to know what it was. However, if he was anything like the magician who burnt her house down, Pip would kill him in the blink of an eye.

***

The ride home was a quiet one as each person was lost in their own thoughts. Grace sat in between Ramulas and Jacqueline, holding her father fiercely and refusing to let go. Every time Grace closed her eyes, she would see the massive jaws coming toward her.

Jacqueline had a myriad of thoughts swirling through her mind. She was shaken by the hell hound's attack on Grace and Ramulas, and she felt very guilty about the purchase of the material that had vanished with the store owner. Was there more to Oriel than what Ramulas had told her?

Kate thought about the hell hound that attacked her father and almost hurt Grace. Then she thought of what had happened with the apples. How did she move in that way? It had never happened to her before.

Ramulas was angry and confused.

No matter how many times he attempted to calm himself about the loss of the money and how it was lost, the anger kept rising within him. They needed that money to buy food for the winter.

Thoughts of the Khilli came to him. He had heard many tales and even seen them a few times in town. But he had never seen one fight before. He was grateful the Khilli helped Grace.

After talking with the sheriff, Ramulas knew he could expect another visit from the collector of taxes. Jacqueline attempted to talk to him a few times, but he kept his eyes on the road.

Thoughts of Oriel came to Ramulas. Who was she and why would she need help from him? He was a simple farmer, but Oriel had said he had power. Did Oriel know about his ability to talk to animals? And if so, how could that help her? And more importantly, what moved inside of him every time he touched his chest.

Jacqueline grabbed him by the hand tightly. Ramulas looked at his wife to see her eyes wide in fear. Following her line of sight, he saw that there was a wall of fog surrounding their farm. The farms on either side were untouched by it; his farm was the only one affected.

Ramulas communicated with his horse and the cart stopped. He stood on his seat. Ramulas could see the top of his roof sticking through the fog. He concentrated before sending a mental net through the fog. After a few moments, he felt weak and needed to sit down.

That's strange, he thought. Not one animal or insect was in the fog.

'Your leg,' Jacqueline cried as he sat down.

Looking down, Ramulas saw the torn material of his trousers and the bloodstains. He gave his wife a questioning look. She then reached over and opened the tear. Ramulas saw that his leg had healed.

He opened the tear with both hands, and Ramulas saw a light scar running down the inside of his thigh. Ramulas quickly checked his other leg to find the same thing had happened. He looked at Jacqueline in shock.

'How … ?' Ramulas said, struggling to find the words.

'I don't know,' she replied with tears in her eyes.

Too many strange things have happened today. Jacqueline knew she could not cry in front of the girls—Grace especially needed her to be strong.

'Rami,' Jacqueline said in fear, 'We cannot go into that fog. I have a bad feeling about it.'

Ramulas looked at the fog and inwardly sighed. After today's events, all he wanted to do was rest. But he knew that he needed to placate Jacqueline and the girls.

'Stay on the cart, and I'll take a look,' he said as he jumped off the cart.

Ramulas quickly disappeared into the fog and walked in tight circles. He could barely see his hands out before him, but he used Jacqueline's voice of concern as a reference to where the cart was.

He stepped out of the white wall. Jacqueline and his girls breathed a sigh of relief. 'There is nothing to worry about with the fog,' he said, climbing onto the cart.

Ramulas communicated with the horse and the cart moved toward the front gate of the farm. The fog opened for them as they reached the gate.

'Rami, I don't like this,' Jacqueline said, squeezing his hand in fear.

Ramulas could see both girls were as scared as their mother. 'Don't worry, it's just a bit of fog.'

Ramulas communicated for the horse to take them into the fog. He noticed that the fog continued to open up for them as the cart moved toward the farmhouse. When Ramulas could see the outlines of his house, he found it extremely hard to breathe.

As the cart entered the fog, Pip rolled out onto the road and watched the family disappear into the white wall. *This is indeed a strange man,* Pip thought. She would return soon.

***

Shigar's eyes popped open, and he fell three feet to the stone-cold floor of his chambers. He jumped straight to his feet and began to move his hands in slow, lazy circles. His fingers opened slightly so he could feel the magical energies flow between them. Only one thing could have disrupted his levitation spell.

The universe had moved.

Something extremely powerful had entered this world; something strong enough to break his concentration. He could feel the residual magical energy, and what he discovered surprised him.

The magical energy was roughly one hundred leagues from the city, Shigar felt as he sat in his chambers within the castle. However, he was unsure which direction the energy was coming from. Shigar had never before felt this kind of magic, and the prospect excited him.

He needed to inform King Zachary of this amazing discovery. But first, he had to replay what had happened. Zachary would be thankful to have a magician working for him.

Shigar walked over to his desk and recited a few phrases from his book. His black robe began to float, making his round belly seem larger. He nervously ran his hands through his short dark hair and beard as he lifted his legs from the floor.

Feeling lighter, Shigar crossed his legs while repeating the phrases from the book. He had been working on this spell for eighteen months, and nothing short of an explosion within his chambers would break his concentration.

Then he felt a ripple in the universe.

A foreign magical energy had entered this world. He felt its presence for about a minute, and then it vanished. Shigar needed to inform King

Zachary, but he knew that he needed to study the books in his vast library. And that could take days.

He was left with a difficult choice of either going to King Zachary immediately without much information or studying for a few days before approaching the king. Then Shigar knew he would be berated for not informing Zachary sooner.

The decision was made.

With a deep sigh, Shigar walked out of his chambers and made his way to Zachary. A minute later, he came across one of the royal pages. He was around twelve years, had short-cropped blond hair, and wore the royal crest of a red eagle on his vest.

'Boy, come here.'

The page ran up to him. 'Yes, magician?'

'I need you to run to the king and inform him that I have something of the utmost importance to tell him. And it is for his ears alone.'

The page nodded and ran off down the hall.

Two royal guards wearing red silken vests with a black eagle over their hearts stood at attention holding pikes by the doorway into Zachary's chambers. They opened the door when they saw Shigar, allowing him to enter.

He entered a lavish chamber of white marble and gold. Tapestries and paintings lined the walls of this large rectangular room.

Plush chairs used by the king's council were scattered about, telling Shigar that a meeting had hastily come to an end.

At the far end, Zachary sat on his throne silently. Shigar sighed inwardly when he saw Princess Aleesha sitting next to her father.

As Shigar walked fifty yards to his king, Zachary's gaze made him feel like a fieldmouse in the presence of a hungry cat.

'This had better be good,' Zachary said as Shigar approached.

Shigar had quickly explained how he had felt the energy of the universe change. He spoke in simplistic terms so Zachary would understand. The last thing he needed was for Zachary and Aleesha to think he was making fools of them. He finished by saying that this magical power could have unforeseen consequences and that he needed several days of study before he would know what course of action to take.

'This could be a conspiracy against my throne. I need my secret agents,' Zachary said as he turned to the right. 'James!' he shouted.

A hulking brute of a man appeared from a doorway hidden behind one of the tapestries. He looked out of place in his silk trousers and red vest that threatened to explode at any moment, with short cropped blond hair and dark eyes devoid of emotion.

'Yes, my lord,' he answered softly.

'Gather my secret agents and bring them to Shigar, he will talk to them about a magical power. I want them to question people to see if anyone is acting strangely. I want this found at any cost. Anyone found in possession of this power will be brought back here for questioning. The agents will not return until it is found.'

James bowed before walking out of the room.

Zachary looked at Shigar expectantly. 'Well, haven't you some study to do?'

Shigar bowed and quickly left the chambers. One thing was certain: if the secret agents found anyone with this power—and they would—Shigar pitied that person and anyone close to them.

***

Shigar walked through the halls of the castle deep in thought.

He felt so alienated in a place he used to call home. Zachary and Shigar had been almost inseparable, but that was before Zachary's wife died. Now, Shigar wanted to find somewhere he could call home.

The magician almost ran into someone. He looked up with an apologetic smile, which quickly faded when he saw who that person was: Princess Aleesha, the only child to King Zachary. She stood before him wearing a light blue flowing robe, her long blonde hair cascading over her shoulders. But he focused on her cold blue eyes and cruel smile.

'Good morning, Aleesha,' Shigar said.

Her face contorted in anger. 'You will call me "Princess"!'

Shigar sighed. He had played this game with Aleesha countless times before, and he knew not to back down.

'Your name is Aleesha, and that is what I will call you,' he replied calmly.

She looked to her left at a Khilli warrior who was her escort. This was a warning for Shigar. 'Father will hear of this, and you will be punished,' she said with a smug smile.

Shigar smiled, shaking his head. 'Your father has told you not to bother members of the royal court, and you also need to learn some manners.'

Aleesha's face was a mask of fury. She knew that she had no power over the magician. Aleesha decided to take her frustrations out on a softer target. A middle-aged servant walked by holding a pile of folded blankets. Aleesha ran up to the man and slapped him hard across the face. The servant gasped and fell to the ground, the blankets landing by his side.

Aleesha wore a shocked expression while holding the left side of her face.

'That man struck me!' she said to the Khilli escort while pointing at the servant. 'He must be punished.'

The Khilli warrior looked to Shigar with a pained expression. The magician knew he wanted no part in this cruel game.

'Should your family be punished instead?' Aleesha asked with a sinister smile.

The Khilli raced in and kicked the servant multiple times; the servant moaned with each blow. Aleesha gave Shigar a triumphant expression before he stormed away.

The magician shook his head as he walked to his chambers.

Aleesha was only fifteen years old. She had become a petulant tyrant since her mother died six years ago. This was made worse by King Zachary, who gave her whatever she wanted.

Shigar smiled to himself as he walked away. From where he was standing, he could see that the Khilli had kicked the blankets and not the servant.

Zachary had created a monster. What happened to the Zachary Shigar once was proud to call his dear friend? The magician was in a castle surrounded by people, but he felt so alone. He wanted to find a place where he belonged.

7

Jacqueline turned to see that the fog was closing in on the cart from behind. Just before they reached the house, the fog rushed in toward the cart.

It seemed to focus on Ramulas.

Every time Ramulas took a breath, the fog surrounding his face would thicken, flowing into his nose and mouth. Jacqueline could see that Ramulas had difficulty breathing and it was getting worse with each breath. Ramulas began coughing uncontrollably as they reached the house. She helped him down from the cart and through the rear door.

'Kate, I want you and Grace to prepare supper,' Jacqueline called out.

'I'll put the horse away,' Grace cried.

Jacqueline looked back to see Grace unhitching the horse. In no time, she was clicking her tongue and leading the horse to the barn.

'Kate, go with your sister and bring her back from the barn.'

Kate ran off into the fog as Jacqueline sat Ramulas on a chair in the kitchen. She noticed the fog did not enter the house. It seemed to sway as if the wind moved through it. However, there was no wind.

Ramulas stood and held onto the table for balance. Jacqueline saw that his eyes were red, and he appeared as if he had not slept in days.

'Are you feeling well, Rami?' she asked with concern.

'Tired; need sleep,' was his reply.

Ramulas shuffled past her in agonising slowness, refusing any help. She followed him into the bedroom and pulled the covers over him when he lay down.

Jacqueline went outside to check on the girls.

***

Eight red wizards sat in a circle around the black hole that Oriel had left behind. Their legs were crossed, eyes glazed, and hands reached out toward the black hole. Thin wisps of energy flowed from their hands to probe the void of the black hole.

Behind each pair of wizards stood a warlord. The warlord held a hand above each wizard in front of him and allowed his magic to flow into them. The warlords used the red wizards as conduits for their magical energies.

The warlords practised higher and more advanced magic, whereas the red wizard dealt with lower levels. The red wizards were closely watched by the warlords and only allowed to attain a certain level of magical knowledge.

The wizards gained their spells through studying and reading. The warlords' magic was part of their being and they never needed to study. However, their power had its limits, and they need respite in between casting.

One of the benefits of lower-level magic was the ability to fall into a trance-like state. This was known as dream-weaving.

As conduits, they were able to manipulate magical energies flowing through them without suffering any physical effects.

Even though the warlords had the same ability to weave and manipulate magic, they felt it was beneath them because it was a lower-level spell.

On rare occasions, there would be a powerful backlash of magical energy, which would kill a red wizard. There were countless red wizards, and they were easily replaced. However, there were only five warlords.

Remus was prepared to destroy hundreds of red wizards to retrieve Oriel. They had been weaving and manipulating their magic for hours without rest, trying to find any sign of where she went.

Walking behind the circle of warlords and red wizards as they worked, Remus noticed a slight shimmering within the black hole. Then he saw the faint outline of a faint blue thread hanging in the air. The blue thread slowly began to spin. Remus reached out as if to grasp the thread, and he heard one of the red wizards gasp.

'My warlord, do not touch it. If it is touched, we will lose our way to Oriel.'

Remus looked at the red wizard that spoke and closed his hand around the blue thread without actually touching it. 'Fool! I know exactly what I am doing.'

Remus held his hand around the thread for a few seconds before taking it away. He opened his hand to see it covered in a light blue aura for a second before fading. 'My dear Oriel, you have left us a way to find you.'

Looking down at the red wizard, he asked, 'How long until we are able to cross into Oriel's new world?'

'One moment, my warlord.'

The red wizard fell back into the dream-weaver state, his fingers dancing intricate patterns in front of him. This changed the wisps of energy flowing into the black hole. They became solid and joined together as a beam of solid white light.

The beam hit the black hole, covering it in a living, moving ball of light for a second. Then the white light was sucked into the black hole.

The red wizard gasped in pain and shook as he fought against being pulled into the black hole. It was feeding off his magic. He could feel its insatiable appetite. He turned to Remus and looked to the warlord for help.

'If you break contact, I will ensure that you suffer for all eternity,' Remus promised.

The red wizard's arms began to shake as sweat formed on his brow. The black hole began to constrict and expand slowly. After a few seconds, the movements increased, and the red wizard gasped in pain.

Then a backlash of energy flux exploded from the black hole towards the red wizard. He closed his eyes and waited for death.

After a moment, he opened his eyes to see Remus had the energy flux in a containment spell and was in the process of pushing it back into the black hole. The red wizard collapsed from mental strain.

'Oh, thank you for saving me, my warlord,' the red wizard gasped.

'I only saved your worthless hide to find out how long it will take us to reach Oriel.'

The red wizard took a few breaths to steady his thoughts before standing up. 'This will be a multi-step process,' he said as he nervously licked his lips. Remus nodded for him to continue. 'The first step will be to slowly stretch the energy strand. This will damage the molecules within the strand; they will then repair themselves allowing the strand to grow slightly.

'This will be a slow process. If we stretch it too far or too many times, it will unravel and vanish. When it is large enough, the strand will change into a doorway, allowing us to go through to Oriel. To have a doorway large enough will take some time.'

'Some time!' Remus roared, his eyes wide in disbelief, 'I cannot wait to find Oriel. I want this done now.' He noticed the red wizard's reaction. 'What is the problem?'

The red wizard held his hands out in a helpless gesture trying to formulate the right words. 'As I said, this is a multi-step process. The second step is to fortify the walls of the tunnel that will take us to Oriel. There are numerous other pathways that branch off the path we need to travel. If they are not closed, we will end up in a totally different world,' he said with a shrug. Letting out a deep sigh, the red wizard continued, 'The third and most difficult step, will be to drop something off in Oriel's new world to act as an anchor. That anchor will open and act as our exit. Someone needs to travel to Oriel's world and drop it off. There is no way to tell if they will be able to return.'

'I don't care what needs to be done, I want everything ready within the week,' Remus whispered menacingly.

'There's just one last little detail,' the red wizard said, meekly holding his thumb and forefinger an inch apart.

'What?' Remus growled.

'By travelling through the doorways, the portal will weaken and collapse within an hour.' Pointing to the spinning blue thread he continued, 'With only a week, it would be difficult to judge how long we will be able to keep it open.'

Remus stood watching the strand of energy slowly rotate in the air. 'I want all magic used to open the passageway to Oriel, and only for this.'

Remus walked away, leaving the warlords and red wizards to continue their work on the black hole.

He needed Oriel's magic. Remus knew that without feeding on her, the warlords' magic would wane and die. Then even the lowly red wizards would be more powerful than the warlords and him. He could not wait for another child of the light to reach maturity.

By that time, the red wizards would have overthrown the warlords.

That was one of the major differences between the warlords and red wizards. Warlords relied on a child of the light every five years for their power, whereas the red wizards gained their lower-level powers through the study of scrolls and books.

He needed Oriel back.

Remus would move heaven, earth, and everything in between to get to her.

***

Ramulas dreamed of the fog.

It was all around him as far as he could see. He did not feel threatened and was not afraid. He felt very much at home in the fog, and he was at peace within himself. Slowly, the fog drifted away from him on all sides simultaneously.

Ramulas found himself standing in his field in the middle of the night. Looking back toward his house, Ramulas saw Oriel.

'Hello, Ramulas,' Oriel said with a smile as she walked toward him, 'I have things I need to show and tell you.'

'Where did you go in Bremnon, and how did you find my farm?'

Oriel sighed. 'This will be difficult for you to understand, but I have come to you from a place far from here. I have come from another world because you are the only one with the power to help me.'

Ramulas held his hands out. 'As I told you before, I am a simple farmer.'

Oriel smiled once more while brushing her hand along Ramulas' arm. 'You are far more than you think, Ramulas, and your life is going to change in ways you could not understand. The journey you must take will be a painful one, but your world will be destroyed if you do not follow the true path.'

Ramulas stood looking at Oriel, who said she had come from another world and he was the only one to help her. He thought he had gone mad.

'What do you know about power?' he asked. 'Why do I need to take a painful journey to save my world?'

'Look at your legs where the hell hound attacked you today.' Ramulas' hands dropped to feel his thighs had healed. He resisted the urge to break eye contact with Oriel.

She smiled. 'After you met me, some of my magic merged with yours, helping to heal you.'

'But where did you go earlier today after we first met?'

'Grace told you,' Oriel said, 'A part of me went inside of your body; now I am a part of you.'

Ramulas felt a wave of cold wash over him as he stepped away from Oriel in shock. He held his hands in front of him. 'None of this can be real. It must be a dream.'

Oriel laughed. 'Ramulas, you have so much to learn in such a short time.'

Oriel saw the confused expression on Ramulas' face and said, 'You are in a dream-like state; this is the only way for me to reach you. I lost most of my magic coming here. As my power grows, I will be able to reach you in other ways.'

'What if I do not want to help you?' he said, crossing his arms. 'What if I do not want to learn?'

Oriel sighed and slowly shook her head. 'Then your world will be ravaged by those pursuing me. They are truly evil, and when the legion finds me, they will enslave everyone in this world. All the warlords of my world have ever known is war and conquest. This world will be an opportunity that they cannot ignore.'

'Then use your magic to stop them from coming to this world.'

'The people of my world are very similar to locusts. My world is dying a slow death through generations of wars. This world is untouched, and when the legions arrive, they will consume and destroy everything. After they have ravaged the kingdom, all that will remain is ashes and bones. The lucky ones will die first. I do not have the power to stop them, but you do.'

'But why would they come to this world?'

'Because they need to kill me in order to replenish their magic,' Oriel said sadly.

'But why did you come to me? I was happy with my life as a farmer,' Ramulas protested.

Oriel walked over to Ramulas, and she could see fear and uncertainty in his eyes.

'You may have thought you were happy with your life. But deep inside, you have always been a leader. And more importantly, you need to know of your life before you were a farmer.'

'What do you know of my life?' Ramulas asked.

'I will tell you soon enough. Now that I have found you, they will come for me; there will be no doubt in that. Allow me to show you the future if you do not stop them.'

Oriel waved her hands around the two of them. The field in which they were standing faded away, and they stood in a town where all of the buildings had been torched. Smoke rose from collapsed structures while embers still glowed in the early morning light. Scores of dead littered the streets, many with limbs and heads cut from their bodies.

Ramulas looked at Oriel in shock. 'Where are we? What happened here?'

'Please, you must not talk,' Oriel whispered. 'We are invisible to them. But if you speak, they will know we are here.'

Ramulas was about to ask who they were when he heard the sound of sandals stomping the ground in unison. People were marching toward them. Ramulas looked to his left and saw a dozen soldiers coming their way.

They were dressed in red leather and segmented black armour, each wore a helmet with metal plates protecting their cheeks, and they walked in rows three. They wore a sword in its scabbard on their hip and a round shield on their back.

As they walked past Ramulas and Oriel, he saw the soldier's faces were cold and emotionless. Following close behind were the survivors of the raid. They were linked together by chains and walked in pairs.

As the captives walked past, Ramulas could hear Oriel inside his mind: *Once they pass, we will follow them. No matter what you see or hear, do not make a sound.*

He absently nodded. Ramulas could now see the captives as they shuffled past. Almost all of them were covered in cuts and abrasions. Their shoulders were slumped in defeat and their eyes devoid of all hope. In its place was total despair.

Then Ramulas' heart skipped a beat.

He saw his friend Thomas shuffle past, his hair and beard matted in blood. It was then that Ramulas realised he was in Bremnon. Then it hit him like a runaway horse. The other familiar faces of the captives were farmers who lived near him.

Thomas fell to his knees in front of Ramulas, pulling the chains of the other captives around him. His breathing was laboured as he vacantly looked around. The other captives had stopped walking as Ramulas stepped forward to help his friend.

Oriel touched Ramulas on the forearm. When he looked at her, she sadly shook her head.

We are here only to witness, Oriel said in his mind, *If we interfere in any way, that will allow Remus to find me a lot sooner. He will only be able to stay a short while, but in that time, he will be able to cause a lot of damage.*

Reluctantly, Ramulas stood his ground while battling the urge to help those he knew.

One of the soldiers walked up to Thomas and kicked him in the side.

'Bastard,' Thomas gasped.

'Get up and walk, or I promise you suffering beyond your imagination,' the soldier said.

Thomas slowly stood with the help of the surrounding captives, and they began to walk forward once more. At the rear of the captives was another group of soldiers. Once they walked past, Ramulas and Oriel followed.

Ramulas and Oriel could hear people screaming in the distance.

They soon came to a makeshift camp outside of Bremnon that held thousands of captives. The stench was almost overwhelming, and the noise of people screaming hit Ramulas like a wall.

'These are the slave camps,' Oriel said, 'These soldiers come from the first legion. They will only need the strongest; the rest … Well, you will soon see.'

Walking into the camp, they saw legion soldiers lined in rows. Chains were removed from the captives and they were separated into groups of men, women, and children.

The groups were placed into separate pens that were next to one another. They were one hundred feet square, had rows of barbed wire wrapped around wooden frames. The pens were overflowing with people pressed against the wire. Cries of children calling out to their mothers and the return calls to their children were filled with despair and anguish.

The children pushed their small arms through the wire reaching for their mother's outstretched hands. The mothers called out reassurances while straining against the wire in their own pen, only to touch the tips of the children's fingers.

Ramulas felt helpless watching the scene before him. He wanted to do something, anything, but there were too many legion soldiers. Even if there was only one soldier, what could he do?

Occasionally a soldier would run through between the pens slapping the hands with the flat of his sword. The hands from both sides would withdraw, only to cautiously venture out a moment later.

A whistle sounded three times, and the captives went deathly quiet. The legion soldiers formed a semicircle in front of the pens, leaving a fifty-yard space.

Ten soldiers walked over to the men's pen. They opened the gate and began to pull men out. The screaming from the women and children began again with renewed intensity.

Five men were pulled from the pen and thrown to the ground. The women and children called out to the men and called to the soldiers for mercy. As the men stood, Ramulas gasped. One of them was Thomas.

A gap opened in the semicircle, and a cart laden with weapons and armour was brought to the five men. Three of the men, resigned to their fate, slowly began to dress in chainmail vests before picking up swords and shields. They walked over to Thomas and the other man and quietly spoke to them. After a few seconds, both men were in shock. Thomas walked away from the group towards the wall of soldiers.

'I will not fight. Do you hear me?' Thomas screamed as he shook his fist at the legion.

Two soldiers removed the cart as the fifth man took a sword and shield. As the cart pulled away, the soldiers cried out as one. 'Retribution!'

The four men panicked and began running around looking for an escape. Desperation and fear consumed Thomas as he realised his fate.

Retribution is one of the three captains of the first legion, Oriel said in Ramulas' mind, *he is one of their best warriors.*

Thomas screamed, realising he had no weapon or shield. He ran around with desperation in his eyes, looking for an escape. One of the other captives tossed him their sword. He caught it in mid-air. Thomas looked at the wall of soldiers before running at them with the sword held high.

Thomas jolted to a stop at the wall of soldiers, and his sword fell from limp fingers. Twin curved red sword exploded through his body. The soldiers cheered as a man walked through their ranks holding Thomas, who was impaled on his twin swords.

He wore loose black leggings and a hooded vest that was opened to show rippling muscles. One thing that stood out was a thin white strip across his eyes. Two narrow slits in the strip allowed him to see.

The piece over Retribution's eyes is made from human bone, Oriel explained.

Retribution walked casually, holding Thomas' weight as if he were not there. Thomas' feet dragged along the dirt when Retribution smiled and nodded to the soldiers, which brought another cheer.

With a casual flick of his wrists, he sent Thomas into the air.

Retribution took three quick steps before leaping into the air. As he passed Thomas' falling body, he swung a sword out in a tight arc, removing Thomas' head. Thomas' body hit the ground with blood spurting from his neck while his feet kicked at the ground for a few seconds.

The way the remaining captives held their swords, Ramulas knew they were scared. Red swords spun lazily in front of Retribution as he swaggered toward the men. The four stood together, unsure what to do. Retribution stopped ten feet from them, shaking his head.

'You have not fought before, that much is obvious,' he offered. 'You will need to separate and attack me from all sides.'

With his twin swords, he motioned to where the four men should stand.

They followed his instructions with apprehension and uncertainty. He even motioned for one of the men to retrieve Thomas' dropped sword.

'Now, when you are ready, attack,' Retribution said as he lowered his head.

He held out both hands and let out a slow breath. The captive behind rushed in with his sword swinging down. Retribution spun to the left at the last moment, raising a sword to deflect the attack. At the same time, he thrust his other sword through the captive's chest.

This broke the spell. The other three rushed Retribution.

He swung both of his swords out in an upward arc, blocking a strike from the captives on either side of him. Retribution delivered a crushing kick into the chest of the captive in front of him. A resounding crack echoed through the crowd as the man's ribs broke under the impact. The captive collapsed to his knees, a gurgling sound coming from him. His broken ribs had punctured his lungs, and he was drowning in his own blood.

With slight flicks of his wrists, Retribution tapped the swords and shields of the remaining two, who did their best not to drop them.

It was clear that Retribution was toying with the captives.

A smile formed on his face as he increased the tempo of his tapping. Occasionally one of his swords would slip through and score a minor cut. Each of these cuts slowly weakened the captives. After a minute, both men struggled to lift their swords and shields. Becoming bored, Retribution skipped to the right and thrust a sword through one of the men's torsos then, with a flick, opened him from stomach to sternum. The man fell as his entrails spilled into the dirt.

The last captive dropped his sword and shield, turned, and ran. Retribution spun and threw his sword like a spear. The weapon impaled the man, who died on his knees. He was held upright by the sword.

Ramulas' world turned white before he found himself in the field once more with Oriel.

'What was that?' he asked in shock.

'I have shown you what will happen if you do not help me.'

Frustration built up inside of Ramulas. 'Why did you come to me? I want none of this, I am a farmer and nothing more. Find someone else to help you.'

Oriel shook her head slowly. 'There is no-one else, and my magic is all but gone.' She then smiled. 'But your true magic has awakened.'

'What does that mean?'

Oriel waved as the fog swept in to claim her.

8

Ramulas woke to the sounds of Jacqueline and his girls in the kitchen. As he walked out to have the morning meal, he recalled the encounter with Oriel in Bremnon and the strange dream he had with her in the fog.

That's all it was, just a dream.

'Do you feel well, my love?' Jacqueline asked.

'I feel a little tired. Why do you ask?'

'After the fog and what it did to you last night, I have never seen you so sick before.'

'I'm fine,' Ramulas replied with a weak smile.

A cold jolt ran through his body. The fog had happened, but what else had actually occurred and what was imagined? What if Oriel showing him the legion was all a dream? Ramulas had never experienced such a vivid dream before.

It must have been because of the stress he had felt the previous day. He was attacked by the hell hound and Jacqueline had lost five silver coins. Ramulas felt ill.

Jacqueline walked over to Ramulas and wrapped her arms around him. She leaned back and looked into his eyes. 'Are you sure there is nothing with this Oriel you met yesterday?'

'No. That was the first time I had seen her. And we need to do something about money. We won't have enough food for winter. I'll try to work something out.'

He remembered the fight with the hell hound. Ramulas looked down and saw that he was still wearing the trousers from yesterday. They were torn, stained with blood, and his legs were fully healed.

He stepped away from his wife. 'A hell hound tore through my pants yesterday, cutting my legs, and now they are healed.'

The conversation with Oriel about his magical ability came back to him. Everything that he remembered yesterday actually happened. But what about Oriel coming to him in his dreams—what did that mean?

A feeling of anxiety washed over him. He felt trapped. He was not ready for this. All Ramulas wanted to do was work out a way to help them survive through winter.

'Da, can I help you outside today?' Grace asked.

'Of course,' he answered, distracted.

Grace picked the food from her plate and raced out of the house. Ramulas walked to the door and Jacqueline stepped in front of him with her arms crossed.

'I do not want you outside until I know you are fine,' she said.

Ramulas smiled as he stepped forward and held her in his arms. 'I'll be fine. There is nothing to worry about,' he lied.

She tried to reply, but he was past her and out the door.

He caught up with Grace at the stables, messing her hair as he looked at some tools. Looking at the sky, Ramulas could see that it would be a clear sunny day, good for working outside. This always brought a smile to his face.

Then despair washed over him as he looked inside the barn. All of his tools were needed to sow next season's crop. Ramulas was caught in a dilemma: sell some tools to feed his family and go a season without wheat, or use the tools to sow his crop and watch his family go hungry.

Frustration and anger built up in Ramulas. Why did Jacqueline have to buy the material with money they did not have?

Thoughts of being a leader returned. Ramulas knew that if he were a person of authority or the mayor, none of this would have happened. Then waves of self-doubt washed over him, and he felt utterly helpless. What was he supposed to do?

'Da, look at this.'

Ramulas turned and his eyes widened in shock. Grace stood ten feet from him with a stick floating in front of her. Her face was screwed in concentration as she waved her hands and focused on the stick.

'By the gods! What is that?'

Grace's expression turned to disappointment when the stick fell to the floor. Then she looked at Ramulas with a triumphant smile.

'What?' He stammered. 'What was that?'

'I made the stick fly.'

'How?'

Grace shrugged. 'I just knew I could do it.'

Ramulas' mind tried to comprehend what he had just seen. Grace could not have made the stick float in the air, but he needed to be sure.

'Show me again,' he asked.

Grace twisted her face in concentration and held her hands above the stick. At first, nothing happened. Then it began to shake before rising a few inches from the ground. Her brown eyes widened as she looked at Ramulas.

His heart skipped a beat as he watched Grace move the stick. 'How can you do this?'

Grace smiled as the stick fell once more. 'I had a dream, and when I woke up, I could do this.'

'Does your mother know?'

She shook her head and Ramulas took her outside to where Jacqueline and Kate were near the house.

'My love, I want you to see what Grace can do.'

Jacqueline smiled at her youngest while Grace concentrated and began to wave her hands toward a four-foot staff leaning against the house.

Jacqueline gasped in shock and covered her mouth as the staff moved. It floated near Kate, who danced forward to grab it.

Then both parents were shocked by what happened next.

In a dazzling display, Kate spun the staff around her body, kicking up clouds of dust from the ground. Then she struck out at several imagined opponents.

Grace squealed in delight and waved her hands. A few small rocks floated up. She waved her hands, and they flew toward Kate. Each rock was knocked aside by the staff.

Grace laughed softly before falling to the ground in a seated position. Jacqueline found it hard to breathe watching her girls, and Ramulas remembered how Kate had moved in Bremnon catching the falling apples.

Kate held the staff the way a seasoned fighter would—her body perfectly balanced with each move, her eyes alert for any threat. 'Kate, where did you learn to do that?' Ramulas asked.

'I woke this morning and just knew I could do it.'

'My girls,' Jacqueline whispered. 'What is happening?'

Grace yawned. 'I'm tired.'

Jacqueline ran over to hug Grace and pick her up from the ground while she waved for Kate to come to her. Once Kate dropped the staff, Ramulas noticed a change in the way Kate moved.

No longer did she hold herself like a seasoned fighter; she returned to a normal girl.

Ramulas' mind was a myriad of swirling thoughts: losing the money, seeing Oriel, and fighting the hell hound. Dreaming about Oriel—and now seeing what his girls could do—was almost too much for him to comprehend. He just wanted to close his eyes and hope for it all to go away.

Then Jacqueline looked to him for support. Even though his wife was a strong person, this had shocked her. He needed to be there for his wife.

Ramulas walked over to his family, not quite knowing what to say. He said the first thing that came to mind. 'What you girls did today cannot be seen by anyone else. We have enough to worry about.'

Both girls nodded, and Ramulas hoped that they would not do this again in front of other people. The last thing he needed was for the girls to show their abilities when the sheriff returned.

That thought brought a lump to Ramulas' throat. He knew that visit would hurt after previously crying poor to the tax collector. He inwardly sighed, not knowing what he would do.

***

Shigar sighed and looked up from his book. The agents had left yesterday and would not stop for anything until they found someone with magical powers.

Zachary had allowed his paranoia to control his emotions, and Shigar regretted telling him about the magic he had felt coming into the kingdom.

The magician felt as empty as his cold and dimly lit chambers. He longed for the days when Zachary's wife was alive. The king had been so warm and welcoming to Shigar. But now, only memories of the past brought a sad smile to his face.

Shigar wanted a way out of this castle, where he felt virtually invisible. He wanted to escape and find a place he could call home, and where the people around him were as family.

The magician thought of the agents who were sent to the north-east. Zachary had changed his mind. The person was to be brought back to Keah and questioned by James. Shigar shuddered at the thought. He had seen the remains of the people questioned by the brute.

Shigar hoped that the person they caught did not have a family.

If they did, the family would be tortured to make the person talk.

***

The red wizard felt strange as he walked down the hallway to inform Remus about Oriel. He was used to telepathically communicating or walking through a magical doorway. But all use of magic was forbidden except that used in the search for Oriel. Arriving at Remus' chambers, he knocked on the door.

Remus opened the door and looked expectantly at the wizard. 'My warlord, Oriel has used her magic, and it has affected the black hole.'

Remus quickly followed the red wizard to the black hole. He saw that the blue energy strand was fluctuating.

'There was a slight ripple of foreign energy,' one of the warlords told Remus. 'We have been holding it until you arrived.' The blue strand of energy had grown; it was a foot long and two inches thick. Remus squatted and cupped his hands around the blue energy. He closed his eyes and stayed in that position for two minutes.

When Remus finally stood and opened his eyes, he was smiling. Oriel had, indeed, used her magic. That, along with the warlords and red wizards working on the black hole, would increase the speed of reaching her.

'She has used her magic. Oriel will become careless, and when she does, we will be ready.'

He motioned for a group of ten wizards over to him. 'You will use magic to construct a crystal that will act as an anchor. I want this ready within a day. It will help us when Oriel uses magic again.'

***

Remus stood with the other warlords and red wizards around the spinning blue energy stand. It had changed once more and was beginning to take shape.

Remus smiled to himself.

His plan had worked out far better than he hoped. The red wizards had constructed the emerald crystal in under eight hours, and he carried it with him at all times. The next time Oriel used her magic and caused a flux within the black hole, they would attempt to throw the crystal into it. The crystal would pulsate when Oriel used her magic, and then it would travel to where she was before transforming into a doorway.

Eight red wizards had died from exhaustion building the energy strand. That did not matter to Remus—he would sacrifice many more to get Oriel.

***

'Hey, girly,' a voice whispered from the shadows of the alley.

Pip spun into a crouch with a throwing knife appearing in each hand. She peered into the alley.

'Ha, you sure are quick,' an old man said, stepping from the shadows.

Pip recognised him and relaxed instantly. He was tall and slim with thinning grey hair. He wore an old jacket over a tattered shirt and leather breeches. But he carried himself with a sense of royalty.

'Hello, Old John. What are you doing in the town of Nasad? I thought you would be in Keah. You know better than to call me from the darkness,' Pip said as she returned her knives.

'Don't you go worrying about me—it's your sister you should be worried about.'

Pip's whole body tensed at the mention of Jenna. She stepped into the alley. 'Tell me.'

'Last I heard, you moved your sister to Bremnon.' Pip nodded. 'Well, I've been hearing some whispers about some powerful magic that is located somewhere in the north, which appeared yesterday. It holds a lot of power, and the king is afraid of it. The king has sent his secret agents out to look for it. Bremnon is one of the places he sent them to. You know how the king's agents are: they look for anything out of place until they find what they're looking for.'

Pip nodded her thanks and walked out of the alley deep in thought. Yesterday was when she saw the man surrounded by a purple aura. She needed to return to Bremnon. She had work to do in the city of Keah, but that would have to wait.

Pip had allowed her parents to be taken to Gullytown and for Jenna to be hurt. She would not let anything else happen to her family.

Pip looked at Old John. 'Tell the master of shadows I will return to Keah soon.'

Old John nodded as Pip prepared to return to Bremnon. She would also use this as an opportunity to spy on the farmer with the purple aura.

***

Ramulas dreamed of the fog and soon found himself in a field behind his farmhouse. He looked up at the moon and stars in the clear night, wondering how he came to be here. Ramulas turned to see a wall of fog rushing towards him, and his world went white.

Ramulas blinked a few times before seeing that he was once again in a cavern with Oriel.

She smiled in greeting. 'Welcome, Ramulas. I have brought you here to ask again for your help.'

He shook his head. 'I told you already—I am a farmer and have no power to help you.'

'That is where you are wrong,' Oriel said. 'Your magic has awakened, and you have also seen this in your daughters.'

A cold sensation exploded within Ramulas as he remembered what Kate and Grace had shown Jacqueline and him. He shook his head. 'I don't want any part of this. Leave me alone and find someone else to help you.'

Oriel smiled sadly. 'You are the only one with the power to help me. The warlords are aware that I have used my magic. They will use this to come here faster. When they arrive, it will be too late.'

Ramulas saw that she was terrified of these warlords, but frustration built within him. 'Why did you come to me when I cannot help you?'

'Because you are also from my world.'

Ramulas staggered and fought against vertigo to stay upright as the cavern spun around him.

'No; that is not possible. I was born here.'

'How old are you?' Oriel asked.

The comment threw Ramulas for a second before he answered. 'Forty summers.'

Oriel shook her head. 'People on the world of Lodec, where we are from, live to two hundred years. You are closer to seventy years of age. Have you ever wondered why the people around you seem to age while you do not?'

The spinning cavern was too much for Ramulas, and he dropped into a sitting position. His mouth was dry and his palms sweaty. The first person he thought of was Jacqueline. His wife had always been beautiful, but he had seen the slight changes of aging around the corners of her eyes.

There had been a few questions about how Ramulas was always looking so young. He had always put it down to good clean living and hard work. *Come to think of it, everyone in my life has aged in some way,* Ramulas thought, *but I have remained youthful.*

This concept truly terrified Ramulas, and he did not want to think about it anymore. He looked up at Oriel.

'Go away, and leave me alone. I do not want to see you again.'

'You must understand what you were before coming to this world. It will help you and your daughters with their abilities, and you will remember your magic.'

Fear and rage flooded through Ramulas as he looked for a way to escape from the situation. He just wanted to find a way to return to the previous morning. Then he would not have gone to town. There would be no money worries and he would not have met Oriel. But he knew no-one could change time.

Ramulas quickly stood to face Oriel. 'Get out of my life!' he screamed.

9

Remus studied the blue energy strand. It had grown and changed shape once again. It resembled the root of a large plant: a larger central root with several thinner roots branching from it.

The four warlords were still pouring their magical energies through the eight red wizards, who sat around the black hole. Four more red wizards had died, but the losses were acceptable for Remus. Looking at the nearest red wizard, Remus could see him manipulate the magical energies. These energies promoted the strand to grow stronger.

'Tell me of Oriel,' Remus said.

One of the red wizards came out of his dream-weaver state and looked at Remus. 'Oriel has been using her magic more frequently. We capture every energy flux created by her and feed it into the strand of energy, helping it to grow.'

'How ironic that Oriel's own magic will lead us right to her. Do you know what she is using this magic for?'

The red wizard shook his head. 'No, we only receive echoes of her magic.'

'Return to work,' Remus said before walking away.

Travelling through the cold stone hallways, Remus made his way to the first legion's barracks. And before he knew it, the three captains of the first legion stood before him.

The three stood silently before him in hooded red vests with hoods pulled back to reveal short-cropped dark hair. Their vests were open to show rippling muscles on their torsos. Their black silk leggings made a soft swishing sound as they walked toward Remus. He knew they could walk silently with a thought.

Each wore a strip of bone across their eyes with a slit in the middle, allowing them to see. They were almost identical and a few inches taller than Remus, broad across the shoulders with muscular arms. He had not heard them talk to each other for over ten years.

He knew they were telepathic.

The only differences between them were the weapons they carried. Retribution had twin swords on his hips, Redemption had twin two-foot spiked metal batons, and Reckoning wore curved metal claws that were strapped to his hands.

'We are opening a doorway in the central chamber; this will allow us to follow Oriel into her new world. I want the first legion ready to travel at a moment's notice,' Remus said. 'I will require two of your best soldiers ready to leave when the portal first opens.'

The three captains smiled before looking at each other in silence for a few moments. Remus knew they were communicating telepathically.

Then as one, they turned to Remus.

We will have supplies stored close to this doorway, Redemption's voice spoke in his mind, *but for the whole of the legion to travel from here to your doorway, even with the help of slaves, will take time.*

Remus frowned and held back a retort. To ask the first legion to speed things up would not be possible. Ten thousand would need to travel through hallways to the central chamber. He did not want to rush things.

'Begin storing supplies immediately. This is a new world we will enter; I do not know how strong their armies will be. But let them be crushed by the first legion,' Remus said as he closed his fist so tight in front of him that his knuckles popped. 'When we retrieve Oriel, she will give us enough power to keep the passageway open. Then we will take what we want and burn the rest.'

As one, the three captains smiled again.

'Increase the legion's training and prepare them for war. I will inform you when the passageway is almost complete,' Remus said before leaving.

Walking back through the labyrinth of hallways to the black hole, Remus was deep in thought. Although he wanted the passageway opened as soon as possible, he knew there were many factors to be considered. To push one of these factors would affect the others; then his dreams would collapse around him.

Patience is a virtue, Remus thought.

He was content to wait. Oriel was not going anywhere, and he was coming to retrieve her with ten thousand legion soldiers, four warlords, and scores of red wizards.

Who did Oriel have to help her?

***

'Stop that this instant!' Jacqueline called out.

Ramulas woke to the urgency in his wife's voice and quickly came out into the kitchen. The sight before Ramulas froze him in his tracks.

Grace waved her hands through the air, magically lifting plates and sending them at Kate, who caught them and stacked them on the table.

'Girls!' Ramulas said.

Grace dropped her hands by her sides and lowered her eyes to the floor. Two plates fell, but Kate danced forward and caught them. 'What did I tell you about doing this?'

'Da, you said not to be seen by anyone else,' Grace answered.

Ramulas was about to answer when he remembered his dream of Oriel—how she had said that he was from her world and that he was seventy and would live to two hundred years.

Ramulas glanced at Jacqueline and the wrinkles at the corner of her eyes seemed more prominent. He felt sick at the thought of what Oriel had said. It could not be true; he did not want it to be.

'Are you feeling well?' Jacqueline asked.

Ramulas nodded. 'I'll be fine,' he lied. 'I'm still thinking about the coins we lost and what's happening with the girls.'

A guilty expression crossed Jacqueline's face, and Ramulas did not know what he would do. It was certain that the sheriff would come soon, and he needed to keep him away from the girls. And the dreams about Oriel were starting to worry him.

***

Pip stood in the shadow of an oak tree one hundred yards from Ramulas' farmhouse. She watched the interaction within the family, and it tore a hole in her heart.

It felt like only yesterday that Jenna and herself were happy with their parents. But at the same time, it seemed like a lifetime ago. So much had changed, and Pip knew that even if her parents came back, things could never be the same.

Then Pip saw something in the girls that surprised her. They both had had very faint purple auras surrounding them, and the father's aura had grown stronger.

She had arrived in town just after the agent and had spoken to Jenna, saying she would return soon, but Pip wanted to see what was special with the girls.

***

For the third consecutive night, Ramulas dreamt of the fog. It swept toward Ramulas like an angry tide. His world turned white.

When his vision returned, he found himself in Oriel's cavern. She stood a few feet away from him.

'Why do you keep coming to me?' Ramulas asked.

'I want to show you what you will be facing. After you have seen the legion, you will have a better understanding of why you need to help me.'

Walking over to the wall of the cavern, Oriel waved her hand, and the wall transformed into a window that looked over a great city.

Oriel reached out and took Ramulas' hand, and they walked through the window. He saw that they floated one hundred feet above the ground, and they could see an enormous army marching down the main street.

Ramulas recognised them as the 'first legion' from his vision of the future. The columns of the army could be seen for miles.

Their sandaled feet hit the polished marble road in unison, sounding like a continuous wave of small explosions. They marched past the front of a large building with marble columns of intricate designs of jade and gold.

In-between each section, soldiers rode strange-looking armoured horses to form cavalry units. Behind these came elephants dressed in armour and ridden by soldiers, accompanied by slaves pulling carts and wagons.

Ramulas thought the structures were things of wonder, but they paled in comparison to the buildings above them: towering domes made of gold and onyx that were fifty feet high and shone in the sunlight.

Each building in the street had open balconies on the first three floors. People in bright coloured silk robes and bright white togas filled each balcony, watching the passing soldiers.

The street was lined with people wearing darker shades of clothing. Oriel explained that these were the lower class.

None of the people, upper or lower class, showed any emotion as the columns marched by.

They just watched silently.

This is ten legions. There are many more, Oriel's voice said in his mind, *and on the balcony are the warlords.*

As the legion's first rank passed the balcony of the large building, they looked toward it and saluted. Ramulas looked at the five men sitting under the balcony. They were dressed in hooded red robes. All of them had their faces covered.

The man in the centre caught Ramulas' attention. He wore a red breastplate covered in magical symbols under his robes. He also held a glowing emerald crystal. It was pulsating like a heartbeat.

The columns of soldiers reminded Ramulas of fire ants: lines of red and black marching with a singular mind. Each soldier carried a shield on their back and a short sword at their hip.

A small boy ran into the columns as they walked past the building. His mother came after him and attempted to catch her son. They were both held by legion soldiers and brought to the balcony.

Ramulas looked at Oriel. She held a finger to her lips, her eyes begging him to be quiet.

The lady fell to her knees at the feet of the robed men. 'Please do not take my son, he is my only child,' she wailed. The man who held the emerald crystal stepped toward her and held out his hand.

Ramulas saw Oriel turn away from the scene.

The lady took the man's hand and instantly began to scream. She began to age as her life force was taken by the man. Her son attempted to break away from the soldiers who held him.

'Nooooo!' Ramulas screamed.

Everyone below had heard him and looked up, searching for where the voice had come from. No-one seemed to notice Oriel and Ramulas, except for the five robed men who stood and floated toward them.

'Why did you do that?' Oriel asked with fear in her voice. 'I don't have enough power to fight one warlord, let alone all five of them.'

With those words, she grabbed Ramulas by the hand, the air around them grew dark and cold.

Then Oriel's hand was pulled out of his.

Ramulas fought panic as his world grew darker. He felt as if he was falling through nothingness. Ramulas heard Oriel calling to him from a far-off place. Turning toward her voice, Ramulas began to spin.

Before Ramulas knew what was happening, his arms flailed through the air, and he did not know which way was up. His hand brushed against something and he twisted toward it.

Ramulas' body collided with something hard, and an explosion of white lights filled his vision.

When Ramulas regained his vision, he found himself lying in his field in the middle of the night. He looked up at the stars, wondering what had happened to Oriel.

***

Remus was pleased with the progress of the energy strand and the crystal. A few red wizards had died, but they were closer to finding Oriel. Two legion soldiers had been magically placed within the crystal.

The soldiers were instructed that they would emerge from the crystal when it was on Oriel's new world. Once there, they were to kill anyone close by and protect the crystal until it anchored.

Once it was anchored, there would be no stopping the legion from coming through.

To celebrate, Remus had ordered a show of force of the first ten legions marching through the city. This was to remind the people who was in control and to prepare the legions for the upcoming invasion.

Then Remus felt Oriel's magical energies. She was somewhere so close he could feel it, and he did well to hide his excitement.

Then the sound of a man screaming gave away her position. The warlords saw the shimmer of energies in the sky and knew where the sound came from. He joined the other warlords floating towards it.

On impulse, he threw the crystal into its centre and it vanished with a *pop*.

Once it was gone, the warlords hurried to the black hole, quickly forgetting the parade of legion soldiers.

The blue energy strand had shattered, and fragmented pieces floated in mid-air. The warlords used magic to probe the black hole. Almost instantly, they found the crystal had landed in Oriel's world.

The way to Oriel's world would need to be rebuilt, and that would take more time. But Remus was pleased. The two soldiers would kill anyone nearby to protect the crystal.

10

Ramulas slammed into the ground, expelling all the air in his lungs with a whoosh. He dusted the dirt from his body as he stood. The light from the moon allowed him to see his house across the field.

He worried about Oriel; did she escape from the warlords, or had they captured her?

Ramulas turned as he heard footsteps behind him, and his eyes widened at the sight of two legion soldiers coming toward him from the trees. 'By the gods,' he whispered.

What were they doing here? *This can't be real,* he thought to himself.

Then the soldiers unsheathed their swords and ran toward Ramulas. A burst of cold rushed through him as his mouth dried. They were coming quickly, and he didn't know what to do.

Then he turned and ran for his house as fast as he could. Ramulas wanted to call for help, but he knew there would be none. The only people nearby were his wife and daughters.

The thought of his family caused him to change direction toward the barn. At least there he would find something to fight them with.

Then Ramulas knew he would not reach it in time. He heard them coming closer and he dare not look back. Before he knew what had happened, something hit him from behind, and Ramulas was sent sprawling to the ground.

***

Pip had decided to stay after seeing the aura surrounding the girls, and she was not disappointed. The eldest used a staff as a seasoned fighter would, and the youngest could move small objects with magic. She congratulated herself on following this man. Once again, her instincts had been right.

As the sun set and the family went inside, Pip's intuition prompted her to stay a while longer. She had learnt never to question her inner voice. Pip watched the purple aura that surrounded the house from the tree line.

When Pip was making ready to leave, the purple aura flared brightly from within the house. She focused and waited. A few minutes later, Pip jumped in surprise when the father appeared out of thin air and fell to the ground.

After dusting himself off, he walked toward the house. He did not see the glowing emerald crystal that dropped one hundred yards behind him, nor the two soldiers in strange armour who emerged from the crystal.

What could this mean? Were the soldiers with the father? Were they good or evil?

Pip knew their true intentions once they drew their swords and ran towards him. Without thinking, Pip gave chase. She knew that the man with the purple aura had a good heart and was a good father. For that reason alone, Pip would support him.

Running across the field, Pip knew she would not reach the soldiers in time. They would catch the father before she arrived.

Without missing a stride, she pulled out two of her throwing knives and sent them spinning ahead.

Both soldiers were hit. The one closest to the father grunted and fell on top of him, the other fell to one knee and reached behind to pull one of her knives from his lower back.

He turned to Pip with a look of open hatred and walked toward her, holding up his shield and short sword. Pip quickly stopped and watched the soldier's movements. She could tell he was hurt, but he was still dangerous. She would need to take care.

As he came closer, Pip saw the father push the other soldier off him. The way the body moved told Pip the soldier was dead. Her eyes flicked back to her opponent as two throwing knives appeared in her hands.

The soldier smiled and shook his head, saying something in a language Pip did not understand.

That thought almost cost Pip her life as he rushed forward with a thrust and slash combination. She ducked and weaved while looking for an opening. Pip frowned, seeing no gaps in the soldier's defence.

Pip was outclassed and out-skilled. All she could do was try to stay out of the way and hope blood loss would slow him down. But she doubted the soldier would allow that to happen.

'What are you doing on my farm?' The father said as he rushed at the soldier with a hoe.

Pip's mouth fell open at the man's stupidity. He was running to his own death. The soldier turned and was distracted for a fraction of a second, and that was all Pip needed.

She threw one of the knives at the soldier's unprotected ankles. He gasped and lowered his shield. Pip jumped and thrust the other knife into the side of the soldier's neck before cartwheeling away.

The soldier dropped to his knees, trying to stem the fountain of blood pumping from the wound. After a few seconds, he collapsed face-first to the dirt.

'What are you doing here?' the father asked in a shaky voice. 'What is going on?'

Pip walked over to the soldier and pulled out one of her knives. 'You are welcome.'

'What?' he replied in a disordered tone.

'I said, "you are welcome",' Pip said as she cleaned the knife on the soldier's uniform. 'I saved your life, and the lives of your family. You should say "thank you".'

The man shook his head as if confused. 'But none of this can be real. Not them, not you. None of this is happening.'

He muttered to himself as he walked back to the house.

Pip almost laughed at him; she had seen people like him act that way before when they saw terrible things. As he walked away, Pip retrieved her knives.

Then she smiled and ran back to where she saw the crystal drop in the field. Pip found the crystal soon enough, even though it had stopped glowing.

She held it in her hand and knew this would mean freedom for Jenna and herself. Pip could leave the thieves guild, and they could lead a normal life and maybe even buy their parents' freedom from Gullytown.

***

Ramulas walked into his house shaking his head. The nightmares were getting worse. He knew that he needed to fix his money troubles, but how? As soon as Ramulas lay in bed, dreams of the fog came again.

When the whiteness dissipated, Ramulas was in Oriel's cavern, and she greeted him with a worried expression.

'What did you do?' she asked. 'The warlords knew where we were when you screamed. Then they came to attack us. I felt their magic follow you. Tell me what happened.'

Ramulas shook his head. 'None of this is real. I want you to leave me alone.'

'Ramulas this is real, and if don't accept it everyone in your world will die.'

This statement jolted him, and Ramulas looked at Oriel. 'Two legion soldiers came to my house and attempted to kill me.'

'Then how did you survive? Soldiers from the legion are ruthless killers. Did you use your magic?'

'No, someone helped me.'

'Who?'

'I don't know. She left after killing them.'

Oriel waved her hands in front of Ramulas and murmured for a second, and then her eyes widened. 'Remus was able to send the crystal through. Once it anchors, the crystal will form an exit doorway into your world. You must find it and take it far from your home.'

Ramulas shook his head, not understanding what was happening.

His heart beat inside his chest like a deer-skin drum.

'If the crystal is not moved then more soldiers will come through and they will keep coming until they kill you and your family.'

Frustration built up within Ramulas. 'What do you expect me to do? I am a farmer and nothing more. Now leave me alone.'

Oriel smiled sadly. 'That is where you are wrong. I can feel that your daughters have inherited some of your magic.'

'What magic?'

Oriel waved her hands and a battleaxe and war hammer made from wood appeared before him. 'In your old life, you were a battle mage. These weapons were made by you.'

'But—'

'Hold them and you will know the truth. You must find the crystal and take it to the Symiak mountains.'

'I can't go to the Symiak mountains. What about my family?' he asked.

'Your journey may be dangerous. You must leave them behind.'

Ramulas tentatively reached for the weapons in a way that someone would reach for a poisonous spider. He gasped in shock as he touched the weapons and they transformed into silver.

A kaleidoscope of images rushed through Ramulas' mind: fragmented visions of him using the weapons proficiently as well as practising magic.

It all became too much, and he dropped the weapons at his feet.

***

Ramulas sat upright in bed. Relief flooded through him as he found himself in his home. He shook his head to clear his thoughts. Again, he had woken late; Jacqueline and his girls were in the kitchen.

He needed to do something about these nightmares with Oriel. They were affecting his life. As Ramulas climbed out of bed, he looked down and was shocked to see dried dirt on his shirt.

A sensation of cold exploded inside of Ramulas and slowly spread throughout his body. He had gone to bed with a clean shirt. How did this happen?

Ramulas charged out into the kitchen and startled Jacqueline and his girls. A plate that Grace had been holding in the air with magic dropped to the floor and smashed. He ignored his wife's questions and went to the barn.

His heartbeat quickened as he entered the building. Ramulas needed to think of a logical explanation for what was happening. He knew that he had to sell something to recoup their money. Then these nightmares would stop.

Looking around the barn, Ramulas saw something that froze him to the spot. Leaning against the wall was the war hammer and battleaxe. Indecision held Ramulas in that place for what seemed an eternity.

Then he walked to the weapons with agonising slowness, hoping they would disappear as he approached. He reached out for the weapons, praying nothing would happen.

Ramulas jumped away as soon as he touched them. Both weapons had turned to silver. Again, visions of him wielding the weapons and using magic came to him.

Ramulas seemed to collapse and fought to stay upright. 'No, no, no. This isn't real. None of this is real.'

He ran out to the rear of the barn and leant against the wall for support. Ramulas thought if he stayed outside for a moment, just for a few breaths, then he would return to the barn and the weapons would not be there.

Ramulas looked down as he sighed and saw two large mounds of dirt by his feet. He didn't know what they were. There had been nothing there the day before. Ramulas dropped to his knees, digging at the closest mound with his hands.

Shock exploded within him as he uncovered the face of one of the legion soldiers. Ramulas' world spun as he jumped away from the two mounds. His heart felt like a horse running through his chest, and panic threatened to overwhelm him.

It was not a dream. Thoughts of Oriel and the legion that would come for her was real.

Then the thought struck him.

The crystal. Ramulas needed to find the crystal and take it to the Symiak mountains. That was over two days' travel from his farm, but if he did not do it, then more soldiers would come and harm his family.

Ramulas raced into the fields, looking for the crystal.

***

Time was lost to Ramulas as he searched.

Several times Grace came to talk to him, but she was sent away. He needed to find this crystal. Ramulas had searched everywhere in the area where the soldiers had come from.

Then it hit him. Ramulas was saved by the young woman who came out of nowhere. Maybe she took the crystal. If she did, how was he going to retrieve it?

'Father?'

Ramulas turned to see Kate. He was about to wave her away when he heard fear and panic in Kate's voice. Something worried her.

'What's wrong?'

Kate turned and pointed toward the house. A wave of cold washed over Ramulas when he saw the sheriff, the collector of taxes Dickson, his assistant, and a mean-looking large black dog. Ramulas protectively placed his arm around Kate. He saw Grace playing nearby.

'Grace, I need you to come here now,' he said in a voice that would not be questioned.

Once Grace came out and saw the large dog, she began to shake with fear. Ramulas put his other arm around her and walked both girls to the house. Jacqueline saw him coming to the house and sighed in relief. The three men waited patiently for Ramulas to come to the house.

'What is the meaning of coming to my house with that mean-looking dog?' Ramulas said.

'This dog has been trained to find any coins you may have hidden on your farm,' Dickson said smugly as he shook the dog's chain.

Ramulas gently pushed his girls into Jacqueline's arms before standing in front of his family. 'What makes you think I have any hidden coins on my farm?'

'The sheriff tells me you spent five silver coins on material. And according to what you told me last time I was here, a person of your circumstance would not have five silver coins for clothing.'

'As I told him,' Ramulas said, pointing to the sheriff, 'my wife spent money that was meant for food.'

'That may be so.' Dickson sighed dramatically. 'But we are here now, and the search will not take long.'

Ramulas stepped forward. 'My daughter was attacked by a hell hound. Your dog is scaring my family. I do not want it on my farm.'

'Well, I am very sorry,' Dickson said with an evil smile, 'but I am only doing my job.'

Dickson reached down to take the chain off the dog. Ramulas heard his girl's whimper. He took a deep breath and attempted to communicate with the dog. Ramulas was quickly inside its thoughts and saw what a sad and brutal life it had experienced. It was kept in a small cage at night, constantly beaten and tortured to keep it mean.

Ramulas sent calming thoughts to the dog. At first, the dog rejected Ramulas' attempts at communication, but after a moment, it accepted him. Ramulas offered the dog a solution to its brutal life.

Dickson smiled at Ramulas as he let the chain fall to the ground. The dog stayed where it was and watched Ramulas.

'Search,' Dickson said as he hit the dog on its back.

In a flash, the dog spun around and took hold of Dickson's hand in its mouth. The dog began to shake its head from side to side viciously. Dickson fell to the ground screaming while blood from his hand covered the ground. Jacqueline and his girls screamed before running into the house and slamming the door shut.

The sheriff and Dickson's assistant watched the scene in horror, unable to process what was happening. Snapping out of his trance, the sheriff ran over and kicked at the dog. It released Dickson's hand and snapped out at the sheriff's leg.

The dog bit the sheriff once on the foot, piercing the boot and drawing blood. As the sheriff collapsed howling and holding his foot, the dog ran toward the main road.

Ramulas felt the dog's elation as it ran for freedom. He bit down on his tongue to prevent himself from laughing. Dickson was cradling his bloody mess of a hand and cried like a baby. Several fingers were broken, and Ramulas was able to see the white of the bone through the back of his hand.

The sheriff sat on the ground holding his bloody foot. He looked down the road after the dog with murder in his eyes.

Dickson's assistant stood shaking uncontrollably. His eyes were wide in shock, and he had a growing wet patch in his groin area.

Ramulas quickly turned and walked into his house. Jacqueline and his girls were huddled in the far corner of the kitchen. They looked at him to see if the danger had passed.

'Everything is fine,' he said with a reassuring smile.

Just behind the door, he found a small pile of rags. Ramulas grabbed a handful and returned outside. Ramulas walked over and handed half the rags to Dickson, and the other half to the sheriff.

'That dog. It attacked me,' Dickson wailed. 'Why would it turn on me of all people?'

Maybe because of all the abuse you have given it, Ramulas thought to himself.

Dickson's assistant was by his side, carefully wrapping the bloodied hand in rags. The sheriff had removed his boot and was tying a rag around his foot.

'Is there anything I can do to help?' Ramulas asked as he fought to keep a straight face.

'Help him onto his horse,' the sheriff said, nodding at Dickson.

Ramulas looked at the horses with respect—they had not shied away during the dog attack. Stepping toward the three horses, Ramulas entered their minds. They had been taught through punishment.

Ramulas closed his eyes and sent calming thoughts into the horses. He then told them what he wanted them to do. 'What are you standing there for?' the sheriff yelled.

'Please forgive me,' Ramulas said, 'but I am still in shock from the attack.'

'Get on with it then,' the sheriff said as he pulled on his boot.

With the assistant's help, Ramulas pulled Dickson from the ground and put him on his horse. Ramulas wanted nothing more than to send all three horses galloping down the road and watch the riders fall to the ground. But he knew the horses would be punished.

Instead, he instructed the horses to walk slow and steady into Bremnon. Ramulas watched the sheriff and assistant mount up before the trio left the farm.

When they had gone, Ramulas tried to comprehend why any man would be cruel to an animal. The thought angered him. Ramulas prayed he did not catch anyone hurting animals.

Then he saw a note dropped by the sheriff. Ramulas picked it up and was shocked at its contents. It was an order for Ramulas to be taken to Gullytown for two years. This was by order of the king for tax evasion.

Ramulas sank to his knees holding the note.

***

Shigar sat smiling in his chambers. He had not felt this way in a very long time. The magical energies he felt to the west had steadily been growing, and last night it was joined by a magical artefact. He knew both magical properties were linked in some way.

He sighed, knowing that Zachary would need to be told of this new revelation, and Shigar did not want to deal with the king's temper or the paranoia that would consume the king and Princess Aleesha.

So, for now, he was content to keep this his little secret. Shigar was surrounded by people and yet he felt alone. This revelation brought him a semblance of happiness, and he would not give it up for anyone.

The king could be told of the crystal tomorrow.

***

'What's wrong?'

Ramulas looked up to see Jacqueline standing next to him with a concerned expression. He stood and handed her the note. As she read it, Ramulas saw that it was late in the day. He could not believe that he had spent so long searching for the crystal.

Once again, the idea of being a leader entered Ramulas' thoughts. He pushed them away with a bitter taste in his mouth. Nothing could change for him now.

'What are we going to do?' Jacqueline asked in a wavering voice.

Ramulas took a deep breath as he formed the words he needed to say. Then with a sigh, he said, 'I have to leave first thing in the morning. Word will be sent and another sheriff will come to take me away. I cannot go to Gullytown.'

Tears filled Jacqueline's eyes. 'What of me and the girls?'

Ramulas shook his head, thinking of Gullytown and the need to find the crystal. The thoughts were so overwhelming that all Ramulas wanted to do was go to sleep.

'They will come for me. When they come, tell them I have gone to somewhere far away. You and the girls will be safe and I will return in a few days when I think they have gone.'

'Why do you have to leave? Can't we talk to the sheriff and say this is just a mistake?'

Ramulas looked at Jacqueline, thinking that if she had not spent the coins, then this would not be happening. He did not need the pressure of looking for the crystal and dealing with avoiding the sheriff. But he forced a smile. 'This is the only way I can protect my family. I need to pack the cart for tomorrow.'

He walked away from Jacqueline, and she followed. 'But there must be something we can do. I don't want you to go—stay here, and we can talk to the sheriff together.'

Feelings of rage and despair flooded through Ramulas. He wanted to say so many things, but he needed her to be strong for the girls. He remembered the two men in Bremnon who were going to Gullytown.

'If I do not leave, they will take me to Gullytown,' he said before embracing her. 'Do not worry—I'll be home soon.'

He walked to the barn with the weight of the world on his shoulders. Ramulas prayed that things would work out the way he told Jacqueline. If they didn't, Ramulas did not know what he would do.

11

The door of the workshop opened, and Thomas looked up from his tools. His natural welcoming smile quickly faded when he saw who had entered.

It was one of the king's secret agents, accompanied by four soldiers. The early morning sun streamed through the windows, highlighting dust motes in the air.

The soldiers walked through Thomas' workshop as if browsing. The agent walked over to Thomas, wearing a sinister smile. 'Hello, my good man,' the agent said. 'We have word that one of your locals has possession of magical power. I would like information about that person.'

Thomas shrugged. 'I do not know of any person.'

The agent gave a slight nod to one of the soldiers, who knocked tools from a shelf.

'You have no right!' Thomas exclaimed.

'We have every right,' the agent replied in an icy tone before nodding to another soldier.

This time a cart was tipped.

Rage filled Thomas' vision as his Khilli heritage came forth, and he charged the agent, who pulled out a rod and struck Thomas across the head. As Thomas hit the ground, the four soldiers lay their boots into him.

After a moment, the beating stopped and Thomas was pulled to his feet.

The agent walked over to him. 'If you hear of anyone with this power, I will need to be informed. We will be staying in Bremnon until it is found. I will leave a message with you for anyone who hides this person.'

The agent delivered three solid punches to Thomas' face, each of which rocked his whole body.

'It would be in your best interest to help us,' the agent said as Thomas was released and collapsed to the ground.

Thomas watched the agent and soldiers walk out into the street. He felt sorry for whoever this person was.

***

A lump had formed in Ramulas' throat, making it hard to breathe. The cart was packed with a few days' food and supplies, and the weapons lay under the covers.

This would be the first time Ramulas had left his home and family. He had never been away for more than a day. Jacqueline had tried to convince him during the night to bring her and the girls with him. However, Ramulas insisted they would be safer at the farm.

They stood in the barn, which smelled strongly of fresh straw in the morning breeze. His wife and daughters came to say goodbye.

Jacqueline smiled. 'We have something for you. But you will need to close your eyes.' Something was placed around his neck and tied at the back. 'Now open your eyes.'

Ramulas looked down to see a necklace made from woven strips of leather. In the middle of the necklace were three locks of hair. Two long—one blonde and one red—and a short brown lock in the middle.

'This is for you to know that we will always be with you,' Jacqueline said.

'My one is in the middle, Da,' Grace said excitedly.

Ramulas found it hard to talk with a heavy heart. He hugged Grace before Jacqueline and Kate joined them.

'This is very nice, but I must go,' Ramulas said before remembering something. 'While I'm gone, I don't want either of you girls to be using any of your tricks. Is that understood?' Both girls nodded, and he was satisfied.

He waved to Kate and Grace, who returned the gesture happily. They had been told their father was going on an adventure and would return with wonderful gifts for them.

***

Pip crouched in a fighter's stance with her back pressed up against the still-warm stove, which caused sweat to drip down her spine.

Her opponents stood on either side of a large table, trapping her.

The boy held his short staff in both hands, whereas the girl scraped hers along the table, sending cups and plates crashing to the flagstones. Each wore a stern expression.

Two throwing knives appeared in Pip's hands as if by magic.

'What are you waiting for, you cowards?' she taunted.

Her two opponents rushed in, swinging their short staffs. Pip ran at the girl and jumped over the swinging staff. Stepping in, she pushed her opponent's swinging arm, causing her to lose balance. When the girl turned, Pip delivered a kick to her backside, sending her sprawling past the table.

Pip spun and used her throwing knives to parry three strikes to her head from the boy. As he pulled back his staff for a heavy strike, Pip threw both her knives. They hit the mark, embedding in the staff.

He dropped the staff and turned to run. Pip launched herself through the air to land on him and drive him to the floor.

She turned him over and straddled him, and then she drove her fingers into his lower ribs. He began to squeal in delight as Pip felt a staff hit her across the back.

'Pippa, do you have to excite the twins every time you come here?'

Pip flinched. She hated being called Pippa. Her sister was the only one she allowed to do so.

She stood, holding a twin under each arm.

'I need to make sure they'll look after their mother while I'm gone.'

Pip sighed as she put the twins down and retrieved her throwing knives. She looked at her sister and wondered how they could be so different. But Pip was thankful to have the two-year-old twins in her life.

***

On the way to Bremnon, Ramulas thought about what had transpired since the last time he came to town. He had met Oriel, who had opened up some of the mystery of his past. It was still hard to comprehend that he came from another world and that he had magical abilities.

Ramulas' perception of everything in life had changed. Before he met Oriel, the most important things for Ramulas were his family and preparing the crops for harvest.

Now Ramulas had the weight of the world on his shoulders. He had to stop Remus and the first legion from coming into this world. Before he could do that Ramulas needed to find the young woman who saved him and then get the crystal. And he needed to avoid the sheriff or be sent to Gullytown.

And the last thing Ramulas needed was for the sheriff or anyone else to discover his daughter's unusual talents. There would be no telling what trouble that would cause.

But deep down, Ramulas knew that he was doing the right thing by leaving home. The sheriff would focus on him and leave his family alone.

***

Ramulas arrived in Bremnon and slowly made his way to Thomas' workshop. He noticed a change in the people of the town. As Ramulas travelled through the marketplace, he received quizzical and probing looks from people who knew him.

He noticed that everyone in Bremnon seemed subdued. Something had happened in town that had affected the people.

Ramulas pulled his cart to a stop outside Thomas' workshop and walked inside. Thomas looked up from a wheel he was repairing.

At first, he was shocked. Then a smile spread across his face. 'What are you doing here?' Thomas asked as he placed the tools on the ground.

Ramulas smiled. 'I'm passing through, I have business in the Symiak mountains past Keah.'

Thomas stepped back in shock. 'Do not tell anyone you are going there.'

'Why not?' Ramulas asked.

'The king's secret agent is in town. He has been looking for someone who has magical powers. If anyone is acting strange, they will be taken for questioning.' Thomas noticed Ramulas' expression when he mentioned magic. 'In fact, the king's agent has been making people's lives around here very difficult. The only way to make him leave is to give him what he wants, or someone who knows where this person is. Some people have weathered harsh questioning,' Thomas said.

It was then that Ramulas noticed the dark markings around Thomas' eyes. He had been beaten recently. 'Thomas, I didn't know,' Ramulas said, stepping forward.

'Stay where you are,' Thomas said, holding out his hand, 'As soon as you walked in the door, I noticed a change in how you hold yourself. You have lost weight from your face and your shirt is very tight on you. You have always been strong, but you have never had muscles on your arms like that before. Who grows muscles like that in days?'

'Thomas, I am sorry for what you have been through.'

'Tell me, Ramulas,' Thomas said softly, 'are you the one they are looking for? Do you have magical power?'

'Thomas, I did not mean for anyone to get hurt,' Ramulas pleaded. 'I didn't want this—it was thrust upon me.'

'Tell your story to the king's agent,' Thomas said.

'What? I thought we were friends,' Ramulas said.

Thomas nodded his head, looking past Ramulas. When he turned, Ramulas saw four soldiers and the king's agent gathered around his cart. The cover had just been removed.

'My weapons!' Ramulas said as he raced for the door.

Thomas stood in shock at Ramulas' statement. As he followed Ramulas out into the street, he wondered what had happened to his old friend. Ramulas had changed so much in the short time since he last saw him. The way he turned and moved toward the front door reminded Thomas of soldiers he had seen in battle. But how could Ramulas move in such a way?

Once outside, Ramulas placed a hand on his cart. 'Is there a problem here?'

The king's agent was dressed in black leggings and vest and had a dark cloak pulled around his shoulders. He had short dark hair and a beard that was waxed to a point below his chin. He was Ramulas' height, but thin with sickly pale skin.

The agent had his hand on the folded blanket that covered his weapons. He turned to Ramulas while his thin fingers danced across the material.

'Is this your cart?' the agent asked with a sly smile. 'I have not seen you in town. We should talk after I see what you have in here.'

The four soldiers closed in around Ramulas to within arm's reach. Ramulas thought that if he had his weapons he could fight the soldiers, but he did not know how to use them properly.

As soon as the weapons were found, Ramulas would be searched and then taken away for questioning.

Ramulas needed a miracle.

Thomas stepped out of his workshop and said to the agent, 'You asked me to tell you of anyone who has the magical power. I have found him.'

Ramulas almost collapsed hearing this from Thomas. He did not know what to do. He could not see things getting any worse. The four soldiers closed in on Ramulas and held him tightly.

'Oh no,' was all Ramulas could think to say.

***

Remus stood watching the black hole. The blue energy strand had begun to grow once more. However, small purple dots floated around the strand. This signified that the crystal had been moved. The other four warlords and a score of red wizards crowded around the black hole, working on spells.

He turned to Omega. 'Why has the crystal moved? And what of the two soldiers who were sent to watch over it?'

'The link to the soldiers was severed soon after they arrived on Oriel's world, and we have no knowledge of who has possession of the crystal.'

Remus thought for a moment about the best course of action to take. The crystal had been dropped in farmland, the perfect place to stage an army. The last thing he needed was for the crystal to be taken to unfavourable ground.

He waved at the black hole. 'Change your spells. Try to persuade the person carrying the crystal to return it to where it came from.'

The colour of the magical stream flowing into the black hole changed as the warlords and red wizards attempted to influence the person holding the crystal.

***

Pip sat on the floor in the middle of Jenna's small apartment, holding the crystal in her hands. Pip was so absorbed in the artefact that she was oblivious to Makayla and Tao running around. Jenna had tried to calm them to no avail.

In the past few minutes, tiny purple shapes had danced and moved within the crystal. Pip had second thoughts about this being an ordinary gem that would buy her freedom. She knew that it was something magical.

Pip knew nothing about magic, except that a magician had burned her family's house to the ground. She needed to do something. Then it occurred to her: the farmer with the purple aura. She found the crystal on his farm. It came with the soldiers she killed. Maybe he would know what to do with the crystal. Pip's head snapped up.

She saw a shaft of purple light outside. Running to the window, she saw that the purple light was two streets away. Pip thought that this would be her chance as she quickly gathered her things.

Pip saw Jenna and the children; she had a plan in which they would play an integral role. After Jenna understood what she was supposed to do, they all left the house. Pip ran down the street while Jenna led the children the other way.

Pip arrived at her position and waited for Jenna to play her part. Looking down the street, Pip saw the man's horse and cart outside a workshop. A glowing purple light shone from within the workshop. She was content to wait until he came out.

Pip's mood suddenly soured when she saw the king's agent and soldiers walk over and inspect his cart. Then the mysterious man came rushing out into the soldiers' arms. Pip had come so close, only to feel it slipping away.

12

Shigar looked up from the book he was studying. He placed it on the table as he stood. Shigar tilted his head as he looked to the ceiling. It was very faint, however, Shigar knew that he felt it.

The magical artefact had moved. Its magical energies were stronger than the person with magical powers. With the artefact, he could no longer feel the person, which made things very interesting. After a quick internal battle, the magician decided that Zachary would need to be told. After all, if the artefact came to Keah, he would be the one to study it.

It had not moved much, but it was closer to the city of Keah. He needed to inform King Zachary. He left his chambers and walked through the hallways, trying to contain his excitement.

Shigar arrived at Zachary's chambers to find two royal guards at the door. They gave a slight nod before opening the door, allowing him to enter.

He walked into the king's chambers to find Zachary speaking with his councillors. Aleesha sat next to her father and gave the magician a smug smile as he entered. Zachary looked up to see Shigar at the end of his chambers.

Shigar made a slight motion with his hand and Zachary sent the councillors away. The magician waited until they were gone until he approached his king. Aleesha remained by her father's side.

Shigar politely coughed before speaking. 'My king, this is for your ears alone.'

'I am the princess!' Aleesha proclaimed, 'And what you tell my father will be said in front of me.'

Shigar was caught in a dilemma; he had something important to say, however, he did not think it was for Aleesha to hear.

After a moment, Zachary turned to his daughter. 'Aleesha, leave us.'

Aleesha looked at her father in shock. 'But I want—'

'Leave us now!' Zachary demanded.

She stormed past Shigar, throwing him an evil look. Shigar knew that he would need to watch out for reprisals from Aleesha.

Zachary leaned forward in his chair. 'Tell me.'

'A magical artefact has come into the kingdom to join the person with magical power.'

'Where is it now?'

'I cannot tell for certain,' Shigar said with a shrug. 'All I can tell you is that it is in one of four towns. Turtha, Bremnon, Rylek, or Covedon.'

Zachary placed his chin in a cupped hand and thought for a moment. 'I have an agent in each of those towns. We must let them know someone has the artefact, and to look for anyone acting suspiciously.'

'Shall I inform the aviary to ready pigeons?' Shigar asked.

'James!' Zachary called.

The hulking brute stepped out from behind a tapestry and walked to Zachary.

'I need a quill and paper.'

When James had left, Zachary leaned back on his throne. 'I want this message to go to all four towns. And magician—tell me if the artefact moves again.'

James returned with quill and paper. Zachary quickly wrote the messages before handing them to Shigar. 'Send them now.'

Shigar hurried out of the king's chambers and made his way to the aviary. He hoped the agents would receive the messages in time.

***

The agent walked up to Thomas with a sadistic smile. 'You know of this person with magical power?'

'Yes, I do,' Thomas answered.

'Then where shall I find this man?'

'His name is Nathan, and he lives south of Rylek.'

'Rylek is half a day's ride from here. What makes you think this man has the artefact?'

'I see him a few times a year when he comes to trade. The week before you came, he was asking me where he could sell a magical item he had found. I thought he was foolish, then I remembered the change in his body.'

'What change?' The agent asked.

'He had grown bigger across his whole body within a short time, and for a person that thin, it was strange.'

'Are you sure about this?'

Thomas nodded. The agent pondered for a moment before looking at Ramulas. 'Release him. We must make haste for Rylek.'

The soldiers quickly released Ramulas and followed the king's agent down the street. Ramulas leaned against the cart and let out a sigh of relief. The sound of his heart beating sounded like a wild horse running inside his chest.

'My friend, what has happened to you?' Thomas asked.

'There is much to explain and not enough time. But you need to trust me. When this is all over, I will tell you everything over a drink. But I am looking for a young lady who is good with throwing knives—have you seen her around?'

Thomas opened his mouth to talk, but was interrupted.

'Excuse me, sir—could my children pat your horse?'

Ramulas turned to see a plain-looking woman with two young children who eagerly looked at the horse.

Ramulas communicated with the horse and told it to allow the children to pat it. He came to the front and showed the children how to act with a horse. After a few moments of patting, the woman thanked Ramulas and dragged her children away.

'I do not know of a woman who can throw knives. Why would you be searching for someone like her?'

Ramulas looked at Thomas. 'She has something that I need. I hope it will be returned. But thank you for sending the agent away.'

Thomas laughed. 'They won't be finding Nathan in a hurry. This time of year, he hunts the plains between Rylek and Covedon. It would take days or even weeks.'

'What will you do when they find out you lied to them?'

'Oh, I have a feeling that you will do what needs to be done before that time.'

Ramulas sighed. 'Thank you once again, but I must be going.' They shook hands and Thomas' eyes widened in surprise at the strength in Ramulas' grip. Ramulas climbed onto his cart and pulled the covers over before communicating with the horse that they would be leaving.

Ramulas took the east road out of Bremnon to Nasad. A few days prior, he led a normal life. Ever since Oriel came to Ramulas, his whole world had been turned upside down.

***

Jenna took several minutes to calm her children down after her sister had left. She sat them at the table for the morning meal.

Passing the window, Jenna caught her reflection. She wore a full-length brown dress. Her dark hair, which she subconsciously used to hide the scars on the left side of her face, fell past her shoulders. She was the same height as Pip and slightly broader across the shoulders.

Looking at her children brought a smile to Jenna. Makayla looked similar to Pippa and even had the same mischievous smile. Tao looked like a miniature version of her husband, who was killed before the twins were born.

It was bittersweet having a reminder of the man she loved while knowing he was taken from her in a very violent way. Jenna had almost died that day, as well.

Jenna and her husband were beaten as a warning to Pip. Jenna smiled at the thought. That man had underestimated his sister at the cost of his life.

***

Pip watched as the dark-skinned man came out of the workshop and spoke to the agent. The one thing that stood out for Pip was the purple energy surrounding the farmer. The last time Pip had seen him, the energy had risen off him like steam from a boiling pot.

This time, however, he had purple flames dancing on his shoulders. Pip knew his magic had become stronger since the last time she had seen him.

A minute later, the agent and four soldiers walked away from the cart. Pip smiled as Jenna brought her children up to the horse.

She pulled her cloak around her and ran for the rear of the cart.

By the time she had reached the cart, the two men were talking to Jenna.

Pip climbed into the cart and gave a quick wave to Jenna before ducking under the cover. Once she was comfortable lying on her side, Pip partially pulled the cover to remain hidden.

Pip lay still as the men spoke. She held her breath as the cover was pulled over properly. Once the cart began to move, Pip thought about the best way to reveal herself to the mystery man without scaring him into doing something stupid.

***

Two miles out of Bremnon, Pip decided to show herself. Even from under the cover of the cart, she could smell how the grass on the side of the road was sweeter, being made from the natural springs in this part of the kingdom rather than stagnant irrigation water closer to Bremnon.

Pip smirked. Nobody else could have trained themselves to know where in the kingdom they were by smell alone. And she knew exactly where they were on the King's Road.

Pip's stomach had begun to growl with her being so close to the food sacks. She smelled the individual scents of bread, cheese, salted meat, and nuts.

It was becoming impossible to stay hidden. Pip sat up in the cart while pulling back a section of the cover. She looked at the man's back while purple flames danced on his shoulders. He had not noticed her yet; he watched the road ahead.

'Hello,' Pip said softly.

'By the gods!' Ramulas shouted as he jumped in his seat.

One moment he was looking at the road ahead, and the next there was a young woman wearing a cloak in his cart. Ramulas recognised her as the woman who killed the legion soldiers. He was startled and sent those feelings to his horse. The animal kicked up its front legs and began to run.

Ramulas turned from the woman and sent calming thoughts into the horse. A moment later, he pulled the cart to a stop.

'I did not mean to scare you,' Pip said by way of apology.

'How? What are you doing in my cart?' Ramulas asked. 'And where is the crystal that came with the legion soldiers?'

She shrugged as she pulled the crystal from within her cloak. 'I needed to talk to you,' she said, handing it to Ramulas.

'Why would you need to hide in my cart to talk to me?' he asked, becoming a little suspicious. 'And why did you steal the crystal from me?'

A mischievous smile spread across Pip's face as she held her hands out. 'I did not steal the crystal. It was lying on the ground. It had no owner, so I claimed it as my own. I need to talk to you about the magic you possess.'

'What magic?' Ramulas asked.

Pip let out a long sigh and rolled her eyes as she pointed to the crystal. 'You have a purple aura surrounding you. It is the same colour as the shapes dancing with the crystal. I think in some way it is connected to you.'

Pip smiled as Ramulas subconsciously nodded.

'I can see we started on the wrong foot,' she said, holding out her hand. 'I'm called Pip. What's your name?'

Ramulas stared at the outstretched hand as if it were a wasp's nest. He had seen what she had done to the soldiers on his farm. However, Pip smiled and thrust her hand closer. A moment later, he accepted her hand.

'Ramulas,' he answered.

As he took her hand, Pip squeezed and pulled herself into the front seat next to him with the agility of a cat. Ramulas quickly moved a few inches away from her, and he found himself sitting on the edge of the seat. This was the third time this strange woman had thrown him off balance.

Ramulas looked at her smiling up at him. He did not know what to make of her. He wanted as much space between them as he could.

'If you move across any further, you'll fall off the seat,' Pip said.

'What are you doing here?' Ramulas asked, trying to regain control.

'The last time I saw you in Bremnon, you saved your daughter from the hell hound. Then I followed you home, and I have been watching what your girls can do. Do your daughters have magic like you?'

'I have no magic,' Ramulas stated.

Pip smiled. 'Lies.'

'What?'

'I said "lies". I can tell when people lie or are about to lie.'

Pointing at Ramulas, Pip said, 'You are about to tell another lie.'

Ramulas opened then closed his mouth not knowing what to say. A few minutes earlier, he had been thinking about the warrant for his arrest and being sent to Gullytown, worrying about his family not having food for the winter, and concerned about his daughters' new-found abilities and needing to find the crystal. Now, he had this strange young woman sitting next to him claiming to know about his magic.

'I want you off my cart,' Ramulas said.

The smile on Pip's face grew wider as she placed a hand on her chest. 'You wouldn't leave a poor defenceless girl alone on the king's highway.

There are bandits who might take advantage of me,' Pip said with an expression of mock terror.

Having seen how Pip had killed the soldiers, Ramulas knew she was far from defenceless. He found himself between a rock and a hard place. He did not want this stowaway on his cart, but he could not leave her in the middle of nowhere. He scanned the road ahead looking for any suitable farmhouses where he could leave Pip. When he found none, a solution came to mind and he turned to Pip. 'I will take you back to Bremnon.'

'I would rather travel with you. You're heading in the direction I need to go,' Pip said with a shrug, 'But if you want to take me back to Bremnon, then I guess I will have to go back to your farm and talk to your family about your magic. I can see purple flames dancing on your shoulders, and your girls have unusual talents.'

'What would my family know—' Ramulas said before stopping himself.

A sensation of shock swept through Ramulas like someone had thrown a cold bucket of water over him. Not only did Pip claim to know about his magical ability, but she had been spying on him and his family. How much did she know?

'What do you want from me?' Ramulas whispered.

'You have special abilities, and I find that curious. I have been searching for something and I think I can find it through you.'

'What are you searching for?' Ramulas asked.

'I will tell you when I find it,' Pip said. 'Let's make a deal. Take me as far as Nasad, and after that, we part ways.'

Ramulas thought for a moment. He had been looking for this young woman in order to retrieve the crystal. Now that he had it, he did not want her with him. However, she had been watching his daughters, and Ramulas didn't want word to spread about what they could do.

He thrust his hand out towards Pip. 'I will take you to Nasad as long as you do not speak of what you saw with my girls.' They grasped hands, sealing the deal.

Ramulas communicated with the horse, and the cart moved toward Nasad. Pip smiled as Ramulas moved back to his original sitting position. She noticed the reins for the horse lay at Ramulas' feet.

Over the next few minutes, she watched Ramulas out of the corner of her eye. At first, he was rigid and taut, then gradually he relaxed. Pip wanted to know who this person was to draw her to him.

Pip could see great power within Ramulas; she could also see that this was a newly acquired power, and he was still coming to terms with it.

'That's a good trick.'

'What is?' Ramulas asked, coming out of his reverie.

'The way you spoke to your horse to make it walk,' Pip said, pointing to the reins at Ramulas' feet. 'A normal person would flick the reins, and I did not hear you make any noise. Can you do that with other animals as well?'

'But I—' Ramulas began.

'Lies,' Pip said, cutting him off.

Ramulas looked at Pip as thoughts raced through his head. He tried to think of an excuse as to why the horse moved without him using the reins. Pip stared at Ramulas with an expression of determination. She saw him thinking of a solution, and she was ready to catch him in another lie.

Ramulas let out a long sigh and turned to the road ahead. Pip smiled and looked up at the sky. There were a few clouds, but it was mainly clear. It would be a warm day, and she would become hot in her cloak.

'You don't mind if I remove my cloak?' Pip asked as she took it off.

Ramulas' eyes widened as Pip removed her hood and thick purple hair flowed over her shoulders. She shook her head and removed her cloak, and Ramulas' mouth opened.

Pip had throwing knives that covered almost every part of her body. They were strapped to her thighs and forearms and she had several pockets sewn into her vest—these pockets held twelve knives.

He had seen the way she killed the legion soldiers but hadn't realised she carried so many knives. Ramulas looked at Pip in disbelief. 'Why do you need so many knives?'

'Oh, these?' Pip said innocently. 'I need them in my line of work. I am one of the best thieves in Keah's history. These knives help people keep their hands away from me.'

'Thieving is against the law. If you are caught stealing, you will be sent to Gullytown,' Ramulas said in shock.

An expression of anger flashed across Pip's eyes before vanishing. 'I only steal out of necessity. It is not *what* you steal, but *who* you steal *from* that is important.'

Ramulas was at a loss for words. He had never met a thief before, let alone had one sit next to him. From the way Pip held herself, he knew there was more to her than just being a thief.

Pip held a bronze coin in her hand for Ramulas to see. As soon as he looked at it, she tossed it in the air and he caught it in midair.

'What is this?'

'I am hungry and wish to share your food.'

Ramulas held the coin for a moment while he looked at Pip, he was unsure how to respond. Ramulas focused and sent his awareness out around the cart like a fishing net. The first feedback he received was from the horse—it was content. Then Ramulas narrowed his focus solely on Pip.

The feedback from Pip was fragments of anger, sadness, and desperation. Behind those feelings, Ramulas saw that Pip was doing what she thought was right, and he could feel that she was very protective over people close to her.

Ramulas lost the awareness and it was replaced with a pounding headache. He had only tried this on animals and never on a person before, and after this experience, it would be a long time before he tried it again.

***

Pip watched Ramulas catch the coin then focus on her. The purple flames that danced upon his shoulders started to grow, before exploding outwards. It took self-control not to flinch as the flames passed through her. The cart was surrounded by a purple flaming bubble, and then the bubble closed in on her.

Through this, Pip could feel who Ramulas was and the urgency of the journey he was taking. After a moment, the flames returned to his shoulders once more.

***

Ramulas looked at Pip for a moment, wondering whether it was wise to share food with a thief. Then he remembered that Pete and Fran had taught him to show kindness to everyone. 'Help yourself—there is food in the sacks behind you,' Ramulas said.

Pip turned and looked in one of them. She pulled out a loaf of bread and a wedge of cheese. Pip broke the loaf in half and gave some to Ramulas with a piece of cheese. He took it with a grunt of thanks.

They ate in silence as Ramulas watched the different farms pass by. He was astounded at the size of some farms. The cart came to the top of a rise that allowed Ramulas to see for many miles.

For Ramulas, the view was breathtaking, as he saw the different shades of green and yellow throughout the fields. Small black dots moved around in faraway paddocks, which Ramulas knew to be cattle.

'Why do you need the crystal?'

Ramulas was shocked at the question and did not want to talk about the legion. How could he expect anyone to believe him when he had trouble believing it himself?

He shook his head. 'I need to take it somewhere.'

Pip knew there was more to the story, but saw Ramulas was hiding something that was important to him. She shrugged, knowing that she would find out what she needed to know.

They finished eating and Pip turned to Ramulas. 'Have you any water to drink?'

Ramulas slapped his hand against his head. 'Damn,' he swore, 'I had planned to buy water skins in Bremnon. After the scare with the soldiers and the agent, all I wanted to do was leave. We will stop at a farm and ask for water.'

Pip laughed. 'You might not find such a friendly welcome from farmers along the king's highway. Remember, there are bandits and thieves who travel this road,' she said with a wink. 'Strangers are not welcome. But there is a stream down the road. I water my horse there.'

'Where is your horse?' Ramulas asked.

'Back in Bremnon,' Pip replied, as if the answer were obvious.

Pip instructed Ramulas to follow a small track that led away from the highway. He looked at her, searching for a hidden agenda. When he saw none, Ramulas communicated with the horse, and they followed the track.

Ramulas focused and spread his awareness in front of them. There was nothing ahead except for animals. A few minutes later, they came to a small clearing that led to a stream.

Ramulas stopped the cart and unhitched the horse away from the water. He walked the horse to the stream and saw the water was wide and shallow. He bent down, cupping his hands to drink a few mouthfuls of water. Pip walked next to the horse through the water. Her leggings were rolled up to her knees.

She saw Ramulas looking at her. 'This is a wonderful place. I come here every time I visit—every time I come to Bremnon.'

Ramulas noticed the change in Pip as she corrected her sentence. 'You seem to know things about me, but I know nothing about you. Who do you visit in Bremnon?'

The smile on Pip's face disappeared, replaced by a painful expression. Without a word, Pip walked over to the cart and sat on the seat. Ramulas watched her in amazement. She crossed her arms and refused to look at him. Ramulas shook his head in bewilderment at how women did not know how to express their feelings.

He tried a few more times to talk with Pip to no avail. She would not look at Ramulas, let alone talk to him. He was shocked at how quickly her attitude had changed. Ramulas had hoped to stay by the stream for a short while.

However, with Pip giving him the silent treatment, he decided to hitch the horse and continue their journey.

13

Remus, the warlords, and red wizards watched the black hole. The blue energy strand still grew, but the purple dots remained. They knew the crystal continued to move. Remus was furious. He needed the crystal to stop moving.

They had to find a new way to stop the crystal from moving. Then a faint echo of magic came through the black hole. The warlords and red wizards knew it was not from Oriel. It came from the person in possession of the crystal.

Remus smiled. They would use this person's magic to focus on them. Remus knew of an ancient spell that would kill the person holding the crystal. Then their worries would be over. However, it would take some time to prepare the spell.

Soon the person would die a painful death and the crystal would remain where it was.

***

After a few minutes of silence, curiosity got the better of Ramulas, and he glanced at Pip. 'Why would you join the thieves' guild?'

A flash of anger crossed her expression before disappearing. 'Our house was burnt to the ground and our parents taken to Gullytown three years ago. My sister and I had no family in Keah, so that was our only choice.'

The memories of that awful time flooded back like a tidal wave of despair for Pip.

Pip walked through the streets of Keah. Jenna and she had been sent to the markets by their father and returned with food. As they came closer to their home, a thick column of smoke could be seen rising into the sky. The wind blew the smell of burning wood in their direction.

Jenna and Pip looked at each other before quickening their pace. As they turned the corner Pip and Jenna saw a crowd gathered around their burning house.

Pip screamed, dropped the groceries and ran to the house. Her heart beat fast in her chest as she pushed through the crowd of people. Once she was through the crowd, the sight before her shattered her world.

A sheriff stood in front of the house with half a dozen soldiers. Her mother and father were on their knees before the sheriff. Her mother looked at the ground, and her body shook with sobs. Her father's face was swollen and covered in abrasions from a recent beating.

'No!' Pip screamed as she ran forward. Feelings of anger and rage Pip had never felt before exploded within her. Her face heated and she felt light-headed as she ran to her parents. Two soldiers drew their swords and stepped forward.

Pip skidded to a halt when her father's eyes met hers. He smiled and slowly shook his head. Then he said, 'You must look after your sister.'

Pip fought against the rage within her as she turned to see her sister standing at the edge of the crowd. Jenna was distraught and didn't know what to do. Pip looked back at her father, who nodded to Jenna.

Pip walked away as the sheriff shouted to the crowd, 'This man and his wife have been charged with stealing from the kingdom and will be sent to Gullytown. Let this be a lesson to those who break the law.'

The sheriff waved his hand, and Pip held her sister as they watched their parents taken away. The anger in Pip grew as she swore to kill those responsible for taking her parents.

After the soldiers and sheriff had left with the prisoners, a magician stepped from the crowd. Pip gasped as the magician waved his hands through the air while chanting. The fire in the burning house died down and finally vanished with a *pop*. The smell of burning timber seemed stronger and hung in the air.

She realised that the magician had taken part in destroying their home. He would go onto the list of people Pip needed to kill.

The energy had all but left Pip as she sunk to the ground with her sister. The gathered crowd slowly drifted away, leaving the sisters alone in front of their burnt home.

Pip had called out to neighbours who had once been friendly with her family. However, everyone ignored her pleas for help.

Pip felt a cold hard stone form inside her chest. After all these years of her father helping the people around him, they had turned their backs on his daughters.

She promised herself that she would never care about anyone except for Jenna. Pip had seen the true nature of people, and she would never forget how they were in her time of need.

***

Pip came out of her reverie to see Ramulas wearing a worried expression. 'What's wrong?'

A myriad of thoughts raced through Ramulas' mind after hearing Pip's tale of what happened to her family. Would the same happen to his family? Did he make the right decision to leave them at the farm? He didn't know what to do. Maybe Pip would know.

He turned to the young thief, fighting back the rising bile in his throat. 'Does that happen to everyone who goes to Gullytown?'

'Does what happen?'

'Their house being burnt down.'

'Why?'

Ramulas swallowed and quickly told Pip the events of what happened with the five silver coins, up to the point the dog attacked the sheriff, and he found the note. He thought that by leaving home, he would keep his family safe.

Pip saw the mounting worry in Ramulas and knew that he would not be able to handle the truth. If she told him the truth, he would likely race back to his farm. So, she forced a smile and patted his hand.

'You did the right thing; the sheriff will look for you for a few days and your family will be safe.'

Ramulas breathed a sigh of relief and thanked Pip.

***

Grace sat next to the barn, holding her hand a few inches from the ground. She smiled as her powers moved several small stones. The shadows of clouds blocking the midday sun caused her to peer up, and Grace saw the sheriff coming down the path to her home. She knew something was wrong. He rode a horse and was followed by two mounted soldiers. None of them looked happy. She turned and ran inside to her mother.

Jacqueline saw Grace's concern and walked outside. She was shocked to see the sheriff had returned so quickly. *He was only here yesterday.* She breathed a sigh of relief that Ramulas had left that morning. She noticed that the sheriff's right foot was heavily bandaged.

The sheriff and the soldiers stopped their horses ten feet from the house before the soldiers dismounted. The sheriff pulled out a small scroll from his vest and looked at Jacqueline with a stern expression. The sound of the soldier's boots grinding the stones beneath his feet echoed in the silence.

He unrolled the scroll and read, '*I am here for Ramulas of Bremnon. He is guilty of stealing from the kingdom and is sentenced to two years labour in Gullytown.*'

Jacqueline's hands clutched at her heart as she fought for breath. She slowly shook her head hoping the sheriff and soldiers would leave.

The sheriff turned to the soldiers. 'Search the house.'

'No!' Jacqueline said, stepping forward. She was surprised at the authority of her voice, but she would not allow the soldiers in her house with Kate and Grace inside.

The soldiers hesitated for a split second before continuing for the door. Jacqueline's maternal instinct overrode all sense of fear. She stepped forward, halting one of the soldiers with her hand on his chest.

'Stay away from my girls.'

She screamed as the soldier pushed her out of the way and opened the door. Jacqueline's scream was cut short when the soldier was knocked back. His head arced upward with a spray of blood coming from his nose.

Kate followed him out with her staff jabbing him several times in the stomach. He tripped and fell off the porch only to land on his rump in front of the sheriff, who wore a shocked expression.

'Kate,' Jacqueline said, alarmed, 'stop that.'

Before Kate could respond, the other soldier drew his sword and looked at the sheriff, who nodded. Jacqueline's heart skipped a beat as Kate moved to the soldier, spinning her staff. Fear gripped Jacqueline, and all she could do was watch.

The soldier stepped forward with a cruel grin and thrust the sword at Kate's chest. She stepped to the side and struck the knuckles of his sword hand before jabbing him in the groin.

As he doubled over in pain, Kate ran from the house.

'Get her!' the sheriff yelled.

Both soldiers gathered themselves and moved after Kate.

'Kate, stop! Put the staff down!' Jacqueline called before looking at the sheriff. 'Please don't hurt my daughter.'

The sheriff gave her a sinister smile. 'The king's men have been attacked. The punishment is death.'

A cold shock ran through Jacqueline. 'Run, Kate!' she screamed.

Kate ran back to the house and Jacqueline's heart sank. Then Grace appeared beside her. Grace waved her arms and a few small stones rose from the ground and flew at the soldiers.

The soldiers screamed in surprise as they were struck by the stones. As they turned, Kate beat them both around the arms and upper body with her staff. Jacqueline was too stunned to move. Kate sent the staff in dizzying patterns, and after a few seconds, both soldiers dropped their swords.

Kate threw her staff into the air. While the soldiers watched the arc of the staff, Kate dived into a forward roll and came up holding one of the swords.

Both soldiers backed away hesitantly while looking back at the furious sheriff.

'Kate,' Jacqueline managed to call, 'put the sword down.'

Kate shook her head and a few more stones hit the sheriff and soldiers, which brought a giggle from Grace.

'Girls, stop this at once and come to me,' Jacqueline said in a no-nonsense tone.

Grace's hands dropped to her sides and Kate slowly walked to her mother while still holding the sword, her eyes never leaving the soldiers.

'Drop the sword, Kate.'

Kate shook her head. 'After they leave.'

'Do you know what you have done?' the sheriff screamed. 'We are the king's men, and there will be punishment.'

Jacqueline winced, seeing that the sheriff had been struck in the face by Grace's stones. Blood flowed from two small cuts on his cheek. If anything, this enhanced his outrage.

The sheriff motioned to the soldiers, who sheepishly climbed on their horses. If looks could kill, Jacqueline knew that she and the girls were in a world of trouble.

'We will return,' the sheriff said softly, 'Next time we will be ready for your tricks.'

A sense of foreboding came over Jacqueline as she watched the trio ride away. She knew that when the sheriff came again it would be very bad for them.

Jacqueline looked at her girls. Kate stood protectively in front of her, while Grace swayed on her feet, exhausted.

'Why did you girls do that?'

'They hurt you, mother,' Kate answered.

'I feel tired. I need to sleep,' Grace said.

Jacqueline shook her head. 'Girls, grab as much as you can carry. We need to leave now.'

'Where are we going?' Grace asked.

'Away from our farm. We have upset the sheriff.'

As the girls raced inside, Jacqueline wished that Ramulas was here. He would know what to do. Then she remembered that they had come for him, wanting to take him to Gullytown. A wave of guilt washed over her. This was her fault for losing the silver coins in Bremnon.

14

Ramulas looked at Pip. 'How did you become one of the best thieves in Keah?'

Pip shrugged. 'I'm good at what I do.'

'Were you a thief before this?'

'No, but the master of shadows saw something in me and agreed to train me.'

Pip drifted away to the first time she laid eyes on the master of shadows.

Pip and Jenna had begged for help from those they knew. But everyone had turned away, pretending they did not know the girls.

The sisters walked the streets until they found themselves in the markets. They had not eaten all day and were both hungry. Pip watched a baker plying his wares, waiting for the opportunity to steal something.

Two young street rats came up to Pip, and one of them smiled at her. 'You're going to get caught.'

Pip jumped at the statement and looked at the two boys. They were no older than twelve and dressed in rags. Their faces were dirty and their hair unkempt.

'If you want food, come with us to the master. He'll feed you.' Pip wanted to argue that they were not hungry and was not trying to steal. But a look at Jenna changed her mind. She nodded, and the sisters followed the boys.

After walking through a maze of streets, Pip found herself in a section of the city she had never seen before. There were so many people crowded in the narrow streets. Every building seemed run-down and several of the window shutters had fallen away.

They were close to the docks, and she saw dark-skinned sailors, Feyans, and Nihon with their flat faces and almond eyes all mixed in with the people of Keah.

Pip and Jenna were shown into an old warehouse. The windows were shut, and the only light came from a score of candles set on the tables. A large man in a loose silk shirt rose from his seat when they entered. Six men along the walls stepped forward, hemming in the sisters. The space smelled stale, and Pip knew the windows did not open much, if at all.

'What do we have here?' The large man said in a low, gravelly voice.

One of the young boys smiled. 'We found them in the market. They're hungry and looking for food.'

'Is this true?' The large man asked, looking at the sisters.

Jenna nodded, and he continued, 'We are the shadows, thieves of Keah. I am the master of shadows; you may join us, and you will never know hunger again. But nothing comes for free. You will both need to work.'

Pip thought for a moment. She and Jenna had never worked before. 'What work will we do?'

The master of shadows walked over to the sisters, and Pip could feel power emanating from him. He stood before them and smiled.

'We always need new whores; I think you two will bring in good money.'

Jenna gasped and stepped back. A feeling of rage exploded within Pip. She had just lost her parents, watched their home burn down, and now they were expected to be whores.

With a scream of rage, Pip threw herself at the master of shadows. With a speed that belied his size, he knocked her down with a backhand. Pip landed hard, growled, and launched herself at him again and again. The other men in the room stood and watched in amusement.

After the third time, the master held her by the neck and laughed. 'This one has a lot of fire. I like that. I think you will be suited in other areas. You and your sister will be spared from the brothels. But you need to understand one thing. Never attack me again.'

With that, he picked Pip up and slammed her to the ground.

***

'Why did you leave your horse in Bremnon?' Ramulas asked.

'My sister lives in Bremnon,' Pip offered, 'with my niece and nephew. I visit her whenever I can, but I work in Keah.'

'Why don't you live in Bremnon or your sister come to Keah?'

'She cannot live in Keah, and I cannot live in Bremnon.'

'Why?'

'It is a long story.'

Pip thought back to that time.

After a few months, Pip had moved up to the senior ranks of the shadows. She was quick to anger and used her knives on anyone who threatened her or her sister. It was rumoured that Pip could walk into King Zachary's chambers at night and steal his gold tooth while he slept.

Her sister, on the other hand, was only trusted to pass messages throughout Keah. Jenna had fallen in love and married a lower member of the shadows.

A senior member of the shadows was jealous of Pip's rapid rise, and they constantly argued. He was not used to people standing up to him; especially a young girl who thought she was equal to, if not better than, most men. He wanted to hurt Pip, but she had risen to a position where she was protected by the master of shadows.

He knew to touch Pip was to die a slow, agonising death. So he decided to take his frustrations out on Jenna. He organised for Pip to take an item into the town of Nasad.

When she had gone, he killed Jenna's husband and beat Jenna to within an inch of her life. He was protected by the same law that prevented him from killing Pip. He was safe.

Or so he thought.

Pip returned home to find Jenna close to death. She was concerned for the baby her sister carried. With the help of a priest and healer, Jenna was able to walk after two months. Then Jenna was told she would be having twins.

The day after Jenna began to walk, a certain senior member of the shadows was found hanging in the poor section of Keah. Both his hands had been removed; the body was covered in puncture wounds.

That night the master of shadows sent for Pip. She nodded to the messenger and walked to her execution. Pip knew she was unable to run with Jenna still being sick. She would plead her case so that her sister could live.

Pip entered the master's lavish chambers, which were hidden below an old warehouse. She was surprised to see him without his guards. The candles along the walls flickered, throwing shadows along the walls.

'The punishment for your crime is banishment,' he said in a soft gravelly tone.

He glided across the floor and loomed over her like a cobra. A loose black silk shirt hung off his broad shoulders, hiding his body. His bald head shone in the candlelight as he leant down.

'You have impressed me greatly with your skill. That is why you live, and why I banish your sister.'

'But she—' Pip began.

He exploded into a blur of motion, and Pip heard humming through the air. His arms spun patterns in front of Pip. Every now and then, his weapon passed so close Pip could feel the air move her hair.

After a few seconds, he stopped and held two pieces of wood, each a foot long. They were joined by a thong of leather. One blow from these would have killed her.

He calmed himself. 'I understand your anger. But all actions must have consequences, and I still need you to work for me. Take your sister from the city.'

Pip had taken Jenna to Bremnon where she would be safe. She continued working for the shadows and returning when she could to visit Jenna, Makayla, and Tao. These three people meant the world to her. Pip provided Jenna with money to live and save. Pip planned to one day stop working for the shadows and live a normal life.

***

Pip turned to Ramulas. 'Your turn.'

'My turn with what?' Ramulas asked.

'I have told you about me, and why I do what I do. Now I would like to hear why you are on this journey, and why you need the crystal.'

Ramulas was shocked at her statement. Pip had opened up and shared some of her story with him, and it would be rude if he did not return the favour. But how much should he tell this thief from Keah? He had only met her when attacked by the legion soldiers, and she was asking him to tell her things he had not even told Thomas.

Ramulas looked at Pip. She had mentioned that she saw flames on his shoulders. Ramulas knew he would find this journey into unknown places difficult.

Ramulas sighed, not knowing where to begin. 'I do not know if you will believe my story.'

'I know when someone lies to me.' Pip said, raising an eyebrow.

Ramulas began his story from the day Pip had first seen him in Bremnon, which was when he first met Oriel. She had told him that she had come from another world, and an army of soldiers and scores of magicians were coming for her. Apparently, he was the only one with the power to stop this army.

But Ramulas was just a farmer. He had been from his first memory at eighteen. Oriel had told Ramulas that he also came from her world, and he had been a powerful battlemage. Oriel had been coming to him the last few nights.

Now he needed to take the crystal to the Symiak mountains to prevent the army from coming into this world. The crystal would transform into a doorway soon, Oriel had told him. Ramulas finished, knowing that he had left out certain details of his family. However, he was certain Pip knew most of his story.

'I believe you,' Pip said with a nod.

Ramulas was shocked. 'Really?'

'And you could talk to animals before you met Oriel?' Pip said, stating more than asking.

Ramulas nodded. 'How did you know?'

'You seem more comfortable with talking to animals. You're uneasy when you talk about the crystal.'

Ramulas saw several columns of smoke from behind a group of hills ahead.

Pip noticed what he was looking at and smiled. 'That smoke is coming from Nasad; we will be there shortly.'

Ramulas felt apprehensive about entering a new town, a place he had not been to before. However, the excitement of new experiences far outweighed those feelings.

***

As they rounded the hill, Ramulas saw that Nasad lay in a long, narrow valley. The town was almost twice the size of Bremnon. However, Nasad was not as densely populated.

Nasad was spread along the valley, with a few houses on its outskirts. As they came into the valley, Ramulas had a better perspective of the town. More double-storey buildings lined the main street, and there were more people here than Ramulas had seen before in one place.

A few people gave curt nods of greeting as they passed. A few outcast Khilli walked the streets, mingling with Feyans and a few people with colourful material wrapped around their heads.

'Close your mouth before you swallow a fly,' Pip said.

Ramulas looked at Pip and almost jumped out of his seat in shock. Pip was wearing her cloak with the hood pulled down low.

'How did you do that?' Ramulas asked, 'I did not see you move.'

'You were too busy looking around.' Pip said distractedly. 'You were so busy looking at Nasad, I could have jumped off your cart without you noticing.' Ramulas looked at Pip in disbelief.

'This is Nasad,' Pip said with a sweeping motion of her hand. 'As agreed, we part ways here. But first, tell me where you will stay the night.'

'I don't have much money and planned to sleep in my cart,' Ramulas replied.

It was Pip's turn to be shocked. 'Are you serious?'

Ramulas nodded.

Pip shook her head. 'You will be a target for thieves. I will take you to a place where it will be safe for you to stay.'

'I cannot afford much.'

'Let me worry about that,' Pip said.

Pip guided Ramulas through Nasad to one of the smaller two-storey inns at the end of town. The battered sign outside read *The Weary Traveller*. Pip jumped down from the cart and made her way inside while telling Ramulas to wait. A short time later, she returned with a smile.

Pip jumped back into the seat next to Ramulas. 'I have secured lodgings for the night, and a stable for your horse. Bring the cart around the back.'

When they arrived at the stables, Ramulas found a groom waiting. The cart was placed in the stables near the horse, and Pip reassured Ramulas that this inn was safe. They brought his possessions upstairs. Ramulas held his weapons wrapped in a blanket.

His room was on the first floor. It was small and sparsely furnished, with only a bed, table, and chair. There was a window looking out over the stables. It was late in the afternoon by the time Ramulas placed his things on the table.

'Stores will be closing soon,' Pip said. 'Best you get water skins and any other supplies you might need.'

Ramulas nodded, not fully comprehending what Pip had said. He was finding it hard to absorb being in a place so far from home and everything he knew. Pip held his hand gently before bending his little finger.

Ramulas gasped in pain as he pulled his hand away. 'Why did you do that?' he demanded.

Pip shrugged. 'You were daydreaming. We need to get supplies.'

Ramulas opened and closed his hand a few times bringing feeling back to his finger, then he followed Pip outside.

They passed three other inns before Pip led Ramulas into a series of stores to buy Ramulas' supplies. He did not need much besides water skins, but Pip haggled for every item before paying for them. She would not listen to Ramulas when he said he could not repay her.

They returned to the Weary Traveller and walked into the common room. Ramulas was hit with a wall of noise as a bard played his lute and sang. Groups of people were attempting to talk over one another.

The common room was a large square area. Half of the tables were occupied. Pip led Ramulas through the noise to a corner table.

When they were seated, Pip ordered two ales and two bowls of stew from a serving girl. After it arrived, Pip spoke between mouthfuls.

'After I finish this,' Pip said, pointing to the stew with her spoon, 'I will go. The road to Keah will be long, you will need rest tonight.'

'Where are you going?' Ramulas asked.

Pip gave a slight shrug. 'I don't know.'

When her meal was finished, Pip pulled a peach out from under her cloak. 'Do you like peaches?' she asked as she tossed it in the air towards Ramulas.

He followed it through the air and caught it just above his head. When he looked back at Pip, she had gone. Ramulas quickly looked around and under the table, but she was nowhere to be seen.

15

Shigar sat on the floor with his legs crossed, feeling the energies flow around him. His eyes were closed, and he waved slow, lazy patterns through the air around him. The presence of the magical artefact had grown stronger throughout the day.

It was moving closer to Keah. Now, it had stopped. He knew it lay somewhere to the north-east of the city, probably a day's ride away. However, he was unable to pinpoint exactly where.

Shigar opened his eyes, uncrossed his legs, and allowed his arms to fall by his side. A tired smile played across his face. Using magic to track the movement of the artefact was mentally draining. However, it was almost intoxicating thinking about the foreign power of the artefact.

Shigar knew that King Zachary wanted to be informed when the artefact moved closer to Keah, but the magician needed to be fully alert before speaking with his king. His thoughts had become clouded and disjointed. Shigar needed to rest before speaking to anyone.

He walked over to a high-backed red leather chair. Shigar sat down, closed his eyes, and was instantly asleep.

The magician opened his eyes and was fully recovered. He left his chambers and made his way through the hallways to Zachary's chambers. After a few moments, Shigar came across a page, who he grabbed by the shoulders.

'I need you to send an urgent message to the king. Tell him I have news that he alone needs to hear.'

The page nodded once before racing away. Shigar knew that Zachary would want to send men out to find this artefact. But there were two major flaws with this plan: the first was that he did not know exactly where the artefact was. The second was that the artefact could slip through the search parties. Shigar was the only one who could feel its presence, and only through meditation. He arrived at Zachary's chambers to find the doors open.

The royal guards closed the doors as Shigar entered. He was shocked to see Zachary walking over to meet him. This was rare indeed; Zachary usually enjoyed the power of sitting on his throne and looking down on the people that came to see him.

'Tell me what has happened,' Zachary demanded.

'The artefact. It has moved again. It has come closer to Keah from the north-east.'

Zachary's eyes widened as though he had been slapped. 'Where is it now? We must find it.'

'That is the problem,' Shigar said, shrugging. 'I do not know exactly where it is. The artefact is somewhere in-between Nasad and Covedon.'

'Then send every available soldier out to look for it.'

'There are many different roads, and the soldiers will not know what to look for. If they begin to suddenly search everyone coming from the north and east, the person holding this artefact will become suspicious and dispose of it.'

'How did the artefact escape my agents' attention?' Zachary said to himself before turning away from Shigar. 'James!' he called.

The hulking brute came out from behind a tapestry near Shigar, which made him jump. He had always thought James only had one secret entrance into Zachary's chambers. This was another thing Shigar stored in his memory.

The brute was told to fetch quill and paper. After James left, Zachary focused on Shigar. 'I want word sent to my agents for them to return to the city.' Then the king's eyes widened in realisation. 'I could have you travel with the soldiers; you will be able to find the artefact.'

Shigar shook his head. 'There will be too many distractions on the road. I need to meditate within my chambers to feel its location. And there is the chance I could travel on the wrong road and miss the artefact completely.'

James arrived with quill and paper and handed them to his king, Zachary sent him away with a wave of his hand. Zachary quickly wrote something on the paper and handed it to Shigar.

'What am I supposed to do? Just sit on my throne and wait for it to come to me?' Zachary asked.

'Yes,' Shigar said with a smile. 'Since it has begun to move, the artefact has been heading in our direction. I would say that by tomorrow night, the artefact will be within the walls of Keah.'

Zachary smiled as a thought came to him. 'Once it is within my city, there will be no escape. And the person who possesses this magical artefact will be questioned. I want this person and their family and friends to be placed in the dungeon and questioned by James.'

An involuntary shiver ran through Shigar at the thought of what James had done to other people during his questioning.

'What if this person has children?' Shigar asked.

'Then they will not last long under James's questioning. Now leave, and keep me informed of the artefact,' Zachary said.

Shigar held back a comment on how wrong it was to torture a person's family. He knew the devastating effect it had on Zachary when his wife died.

Shigar hoped that the person who held the artefact did not have a family. It would end badly for them.

***

Remus stood with the other warlords and red wizards, watching the blue energy strand. It had begun to swim through the black hole in a fluid motion. The side filaments moved once more, making it appear as a giant centipede. The thin red strand of energy that had broken into segments had slowly begun to join again.

'What does this mean?' Remus asked, pointing to the black hole.

'The crystal has stopped moving,' one of the red wizards replied.

Remus' eyes widened at this news, and the red wizard braced himself for an attack. He had seen how Remus had dispatched his companion.

'Where is it now? And how far has it been moved?' Remus asked.

The red wizard shrugged and looked helplessly at Remus. 'We do not know. This new world is foreign to us. All we know is that the crystal has moved, and now it has stopped.'

Remus was furious as he paced back and forth in front of the terrified red wizard.

After a moment he stopped. 'Anchor the crystal now so that it cannot be moved.'

The red wizard took a tentative breath. 'If we attempt to anchor the crystal too early, it might break. Then it will take far longer to retrieve Oriel.'

Remus bowed his head and pinched the bridge of his nose with his thumb and forefinger. Since the crystal had been moved, Remus had ordered all magic into the opening the doorway to cease, they could not risk anything stopping them from retrieving Oriel. He fought against the rising frustration. Again, they had come so close, only to risk losing it all.

Remus raised his head. 'We will cast the spell that will kill the one holding the crystal. Once the person has died, the crystal will no longer move.'

The red wizards sat in a circle while the four warlords channelled magical energies through them. Remus watched the magical streams flow into the blue energy strand for a few minutes, ensuring the magic did not disrupt the black hole or the strands.

Satisfied, Remus walked back to his chambers. He needed to study in case they could use the crystal to reach Oriel. Remus knew that Oriel was their only hope for remaining powerful. He needed to sacrifice everything to retrieve her.

If Remus could not get to Oriel, life as he knew it would be over.

There were things to prepare before he would be ready to travel to Oriel's world. Remus had always known there was something different about her, but he did not realise how powerful she had become. In the battle before Oriel escaped, she had caught Remus unawares. This time it would be different: the odds would be in his favour.

Walking into his chambers, Remus picked up a small, polished wooden box. Placing it on his desk gently, he opened the lid to find a crystal ball sitting on a red velvet pillow. Remus picked it up and smiled.

This was the secret weapon that would give him the advantage over Oriel. He gave the crystal ball a soft shake and smoke began to form within.

'You are bound to obey my commands. Tell me what I need to defeat Oriel's magic,' Remus said.

Out of the smoke came the face of a foe Remus had killed and imprisoned the soul of within the ball. This soul had no choice but to obey Remus' commands.

Remus smiled as he focused on the face of Oriel's teacher.

Antok looked back helplessly.

***

Jacqueline sat at the small square wooden table with Kate and Grace. They ate in silence as a cauldron hung above the fire by the wall.

She looked around the wooden shack, which was half the size of their home. Their possessions lay against the wall in three sacks. Uncertainty flooded through Jacqueline, but she gave her girls a brave smile.

They had travelled six leagues through the fields to Matthew's farm. The hut was empty, and Matthew was nowhere to be seen; they had known him for years, and Jacqueline hoped he would not mind them staying with him for a while.

Once the girls had finished eating, Grace looked at her mother. 'Where will we sleep?'

Jacqueline looked at Matthew's bed on the other side of the room and sighed. 'While Matthew is away, we will use his bed.'

'When will we go home?' Kate asked.

Jacqueline forced a comforting smile. 'In a few days. Then it will be safe to return home.'

Jacqueline saw the worry in her daughters and knew it would do no good to berate them for what they did to the soldiers. Ramulas was gone, and the sheriff searched for him. They were away from home, and she was not certain when they could return. Jacqueline pushed away feelings of despair. She needed to be strong for her girls.

***

Ramulas had moved from the corner table and now sat in front of the firepit in the middle of the common room. He stared into the fire, hypnotised by the sound of wood popping while it burned and the patterns of smoke as it formed lazy tendrils toward the ceiling.

Ramulas had spoken to the serving girl, offering to pay for the food and drinks, only to find that Pip had already paid. The number of people had doubled in the common room, along with the volume of noise. There were two different bards on opposite sides of the room, fighting to be heard over the noise of the patrons.

Ramulas had adapted quickly to block out most of the noise and focus on the fire.

Even though Ramulas was surrounded by groups of people talking, laughing and enjoying themselves, he felt very much out of place, and more importantly, he felt alone. This was the first night away from his family, and the emptiness inside threatened to consume him.

Ramulas stood and walked away from the fire and up to his room. He opened the door to find an empty bed, table, and chair. His shadow danced across the room as the candle behind him flickered in the slight breeze.

He missed his family and wondered how they were without him. Had the sheriff come to the farm and did Jacqueline send him away on a wild goose chase? And would he be able to return home after dropping the crystal?

Too many questions and no way to answer them—Ramulas could only think of one thing at a time. After he was rid of the crystal, he would worry about home.

Ramulas could not sleep—not then, anyway. He closed the door and walked downstairs.

Ramulas found himself at the stables behind the inn. He communicated with his horse to let it know he was coming. The stable door was open, and his horse was in the fourth stall on the right, its head hung out the door waiting for him.

Ramulas sent calming thoughts to the other horses as he stroked the neck of his own horse. Through communication, Ramulas learned that his horse had been fed, however, it was in a strange place and wanted to return home.

'We will be home in a few days,' Ramulas whispered to the horse.

Ramulas heard the faint sound of metal placed on wood. He knew that someone had entered the stables. Turning, he saw a boy a little older than Kate walking slowly toward him. The young boy held a crossbow, and it was aimed at Ramulas.

'Shouldn't be here,' the boy said in a strained voice.

Ramulas slowly raised both hands to show he held no weapons. 'I was checking my horse. I'm staying at the inn.'

'All the same, it's my job to keep people away from the horses,' the boy said.

'I can see that you are doing a fine job. I will return to the inn.'

Ramulas walked out of the stables and back to the inn. Even though Ramulas had not spent much time with his horse, it still put a smile on his face.

The horse was a real connection to Ramulas' home and family. He entered the room, closed the door, and went to bed. The faint sounds of music and laughter drifted up from downstairs.

Ramulas soon fell asleep, and then the fog rushed into Nasad.

16

Remus smiled as he replaced the crystal ball back into its wooden box. Through Antok, he found Oriel's true weakness. She would look for a family or a father figure. Once she found them and made a connection, Oriel would do anything for them. All Remus needed to do in this new world was find the person she was closest to and attack them.

Oriel would make a mistake and fall into his trap. Remus knew that the best-laid plans needed to be simple. He would find this person and make them suffer enough for Oriel to show herself.

***

Ramulas woke to find himself inside Oriel's cavern. She greeted him with a smile. 'Welcome, Ramulas. You need to train in order to remember who you once were.'

She waved her hands, and his weapons floated before him, and Ramulas stepped back.

Oriel shook her head. 'Take them. You need to be ready if the legion comes. You are the only one who can stop them.'

Hesitantly, Ramulas reached out a held his weapons. He gasped as they transformed to silver. Then he saw fragments of his past flash before his eyes.

Ramulas saw himself spinning the war hammer and battleaxe, shooting streams of energy into hordes of barbarian tribes. Then he blinked, and they were gone.

Standing before him were four legion soldiers. Each looked at Ramulas with open hatred, pulling out their swords.

'Fight them,' Oriel said calmly, 'and it will help your memory return.'

'I can't. I don't know how to use these.'

The leading legion soldier burst forward with blinding speed, slashing at Ramulas' face with its sword. Ramulas stepped back, lifting the battleaxe, catching the sword. He swung his war hammer in a small arc and hit the soldier in the left shoulder.

The soldier's face became a mask of fury as it struck the battleaxe again, before lowering its sword and thrusting at Ramulas' stomach.

Ramulas skipped back while pushing down with his battleaxe, pushing the sword to the side. He then hit the soldier in the head with the war hammer. Ramulas winced as he heard the soldier's neck snap. He smiled in disbelief as the soldier fell to the ground.

Ramulas was surprised at how natural it felt to fight with the weapons. However, self-doubt still clouded his mind.

The second soldier moved a little cautiously as he came at Ramulas, but he was still fast. However, Ramulas was able to see where the strike would come from. He lifted his battleaxe to block the downward swing of the soldier's sword then stepped forward, delivering an overhand strike with his war hammer, hitting the soldier square in the face.

Blood and gore exploded from the soldier's face; his jaw hung by a strip of flesh. Ramulas dropped his weapons and was shocked at what he had done. He saw that Oriel wore a concerned expression.

'Ramulas. You must return, there is danger.'

His world turned white.

***

Grace woke in the middle of the night, disoriented; someone had called her name. She could not understand why she was sleeping with her mother and sister. Then she heard her name called again.

She slowly sat up in bed as memories returned. A soft voice called her name from somewhere outside Matthew's hut. Grace carefully climbed out of bed and walked out into the moonlit night. Two shapes stood by a grove of trees near the hut, and they waved to Grace.

She was curious to know who would be outside in the middle of the night. As Grace walked closer, she saw that the people wore funny clothing, then the two stepped into the moonlight and Grace gasped in surprise.

Standing in front of her was a man and woman. Their skin was dark, rough, and covered in vines and small leaves. The woman's hair consisted of thin branches sweeping up two feet from her head; they were covered in bright green leaves. The branches on the male's head were only about half a foot long.

Small branches protruded from their arms and legs; their eyes shone green as they smiled at her. They were twice her height, and the man broad across the shoulders.

'Hello?' Grace said hesitantly as she stepped toward them.

The woman squatted and tilted her head to the side. 'Hello,' she replied, perfectly imitating Grace's voice.

'Who are you?' Grace asked.

The woman smiled. 'We are dryads. We came because we could feel your magic, and we want you to come with us. My name is Eady.'

'Where?'

'To our home,' the female dryad said in a sing-song voice. 'There are many more like us.'

'Where is your home?'

'It is far away, but we can take you there.'

Grace's eyes widened as the male dryad walked into the trunk of the tree.

Eady smiled at Grace. 'Would you like to come with us?'

Grace smiled, held the dryad's hand, and walked into the tree.

***

The sound of screaming woke Ramulas. He sat up, trying to gather his bearings in the dim room. The scream cut through him once more. It was then Ramulas realised that the screams were coming from his horse. He was hearing it in his mind.

He quickly dressed, grabbed his weapons, and raced downstairs. Ramulas burst out the rear door as he sent calming thoughts to his horse.

Ramulas stepped into the stables to find a figure leaning over a body. It was the stable boy, who Ramulas saw was dead, still clutching the crossbow in his hand.

The figure became aware of Ramulas and stood. Ramulas' mouth instantly went dry and all strength left his body.

Standing in front of him was a druid.

The druid raised its arm to point at Ramulas with a scaly hand.

His heartbeat was almost deafening as it pounded in his chest. The druid took a slow step toward Ramulas. Memories of his last encounter with a druid returned.

Somehow finding the strength in his legs, Ramulas walked back a few steps until he was outside the stables. His weapons hung uselessly in his hands. No matter how much he tried, Ramulas could not move them.

The druid had followed him and was six feet away. Ramulas found himself frozen in place. His muscles refused to obey his commands. The next thing Ramulas realised was that the druid was three feet away from him.

Then Ramulas was hit from the side.

A shoulder charged into his midsection, sending him sprawling to the ground, and both weapons flew from his hands. A small hand covered his eyes and a light body lay on top of him. The person hid the side of their face next to his.

'Do not look at it,' Ramulas heard Pip say. 'They ignore you if you do not look them in the eyes.'

Relief flooded through Ramulas as Pip spoke. She had broken the spell that the druid held over him. However, that relief was short-lived.

Ramulas felt the presence of the druid as it stood over them, then he felt Pip being lifted away from him.

'No, no, no, no,' Pip said rapidly.

She grabbed Ramulas' shirt with her free hand, and he reached out blindly to wrap his arms around her waist. Ramulas pulled Pip close and held her as tightly as possible. He felt her being pulled a few more times. Each time, Ramulas and Pip held each other as tightly as they could.

The druid released Pip and stood over the pair for a moment before it moved away.

Ramulas focused and communicated with his horse in the stables.

The danger had passed, which meant the druid had left.

'It has gone,' he said with a sigh of relief.

He released his grip on Pip and she rolled off. She sat beside him, trying to steady her breathing.

Ramulas sat next to her and asked, 'What are you doing here?'

'I should ask you the same thing,' Pip said as she punched Ramulas in the shoulder.

Ramulas pulled away in shock. 'What was that for?'

'For almost having me taken to the Druids' Labyrinth.'

Ramulas stood and offered Pip his hand, which she refused to take. She rose to her feet in a fluid motion. Pip glared at Ramulas and was as taut as a bowstring.

'I heard my horse screaming, and I came down to investigate.'

'Then next time leave it be,' Pip said, pointing a finger to the stables.

'But my horse is the only connection to my family. I would be devastated if anything were to happen to him.'

Pip shook her head in frustration. 'I don't understand you, putting a horse's life before your own.'

Ramulas' response was cut short when fog came racing toward them.

'Where did that come from?' Pip asked.

Ramulas smiled. 'Oriel is here.'

Before Pip could respond, the fog cleared and Oriel stood before Ramulas.

'I see the danger has passed.'

'Yes.' Ramulas sighed. 'It was a druid. It almost took me away.'

'What is a druid?' Oriel turned to Pip and smiled. 'And who is this?

Ramulas quickly explained the story of the druids and of how the young thief came to be with him. Then he looked at Pip and saw a confused expression.

'What is wrong?' Ramulas asked.

Pip laughed. 'A woman appears out of a fog and you ask what is wrong.'

'This is Oriel. She is the reason I am taking the crystal to the Symiak mountains.'

Pip shook her head. 'Where does that language come from?'

Ramulas looked at Pip in confusion. 'What language?'

Pip shook her head. 'I can't understand what you are saying.'

Oriel smiled and waved a glowing hand in front of Pip. 'I am sorry,' she said in the common tongue, 'Ramulas and I were speaking the Language of Lodec, the world where we both come from.'

Pip's mouth fell open when she detected that Oriel was not lying. However, she quickly recovered. 'When were you going to tell me that?' she asked Ramulas.

'Ramulas is on an important quest,' Oriel said. 'He will need as much help as he can. I will show you what he will be facing.' Oriel waved her hands while chanting. Pip fought the urge to run as the tingling sensation of magic covered her body.

Pip gasped as visions of the legion marching through Bremnon came to her. The columns of soldiers seemed endless, and the way they moved in a synchronised manner shocked her. She had seen the soldiers of Keah and knew the legion soldiers were far superior.

'Ramulas will need to prepare in case the legion comes to this world. And he will need help,' Oriel said before looking at Ramulas, 'My magic is weak, I must go.' As the fog came in to claim Oriel, Ramulas looked at Pip. He needed her help but felt self-conscious asking for it. He took a deep breath and spoke from the heart.

'Pip, I never wanted any of this; I still don't—it scares me to death. But I am doing this for my family. I want to keep them safe. Will you come with me to the Symiak mountains where I will drop the crystal?'

Pip shook her head. 'No.'

Ramulas was astounded and felt foolish for being so vulnerable. 'Why? You saw the legion. If I don't take the crystal to the mountains, the legion will come here.'

'I have a sister, niece, and nephew. That is my world. I will not risk them being hurt. I have travelled with you far enough,' Pip said before disappearing into the night.

Ramulas felt helpless as she walked away. For a moment, he thought that she would help. More than ever, the weight of the world rested on his shoulders.

***

Grace's sight vanished and she felt as if she were being pulled down a very narrow hallway. She stepped out of a tree to find herself in a great forest. She looked around in awe at the large trees that surrounded her.

'Can you see?' Eady asked.

Grace nodded. Even though it was night, she was able to see quite far into the forest.

The female squatted in front of Grace. The dry leaves and twigs on the forest floor crunched under her weight. She waved her hand in an arc to the surrounding trees.

'This is our home, and there are hundreds more like us. We have all felt your magic and want you to become part of our family.'

Grace was astounded and was unsure what to think. A short while earlier, she had been sleeping in Matthew's hut with her mother and Kate. Now she stood in a forest with two magical creatures, and they wanted her to be part of their family.

'I have a family,' Grace said, thinking of her da and wondering when he would return.

'If you join our family, we will show you so many wonderful things.'

Grace was curious. 'How do I be a part of your family?'

Eady smiled. 'We will show you soon. But when you are with our family, you will become as we are. And you can never leave.'

Grace shook her head, not liking what she heard, and the female dryad still smiled. 'We will wait for you to make a decision. We have been in this forest for hundreds of years and we have learned how to wait for what we need.'

Grace felt a bit uncomfortable and looked to the tree she had come out of. 'I want to go back to my mother and Kate.'

The female dryad nodded. 'We will bring you to your home, and we will call on you again.'

***

Something brushed Ramulas' nose lightly, which brought him out of his sleep. He shook his head and grunted under his breath. The tickling sensation returned to his nose. This time it was softer and more irritating. Ramulas brushed at his nose and heard a giggle.

Ramulas opened his eyes to find himself in a room he did not recognise. He sat up in his bed and rubbed the sleep from his eyes. Ramulas saw Pip sitting on the edge of his bed with a long white feather in her hand.

'Time to wake up,' she said with a smile.

He looked outside to see that the sun was just rising. The events of the day and night before came back to him. He felt stiff sleeping in a strange bed.

'What are you doing in my room?' Ramulas asked. 'How did you get in?'

Pip shrugged. 'I'm able to walk through walls—or so some people say. I still find you special, and I think you might help me find what I am looking for.'

'Why are you here? Last night you were worried about your family and did not want to be with me.'

'Don't worry about that,' Pip said pointing to the window. 'If we don't leave now, we will be held for questioning.' Ramulas looked down at himself and saw that he had slept in his clothes. He hopped off the bed and walked to the window. The owner of the inn stood with a sheriff and a handful of people outside the stables.

'What do we do?' Ramulas whispered.

'I'm able to vanish like this,' Pip said as she snapped her fingers, 'but I think I will travel with you to Keah. You need to gather your things and follow me downstairs. I have a plan.'

Ramulas followed Pip out the rear of the inn and walked towards the stables. Pip had her cloak pulled tight around her and the hood covered her purple hair. Ramulas' weapons were wrapped in a blanket and tucked under his arm. Pip had come up with a plan—all Ramulas had to do was play along.

The sheriff saw the pair and stepped away from the small group. 'State your business.'

'We are on our way to Keah,' Pip said, 'We stayed at the inn last night, and we are getting our horse and cart.

The sheriff shook his head. 'There was an incident last night. No-one is to leave until they have been searched and questioned.'

Pip gasped in mock terror placing both hands on her cheeks. 'Oh my, what could have happened last night?'

'The stable boy has been murdered, and there have been reports of a druid in town.'

Pip shrieked and ran up to the sheriff, grabbing his vest with both hands. 'A druid! Please, sir sheriff, do not leave my side,' Pip wailed as she collapsed and wrapped her hands around his legs. 'The druid is coming for me, you must save me.'

The sheriff looked down at Pip then at Ramulas in shock. He attempted to loosen her grip a few times, but each time Pip just screamed louder. Windows from the inn and surrounding buildings began to open in the early morning light.

'How do you stop this?' the sheriff asked Ramulas.

Ramulas gave a helpless shrug. 'She would feel safe if we were on the road to Keah. But we will need to be searched and questioned.'

The sheriff made some quick calculations. He did need to question and search everyone, but this young woman would cause a riot. He would be better off letting them go, then he could return to his investigation.

'Take your horse and cart and leave for Keah,' the sheriff said before turning to Ramulas. 'And keep her quiet.' Ramulas nodded, walked over to Pip, and whispered in her ear, which seemed to calm her. Within two minutes, they were sitting on the cart and ready to leave.

'Goodbye, brave sheriff,' Pip called out between sobs.

Ramulas flicked the reins and they moved into the main street. Pip continued her act of a distraught female until they had left Nasad.

'That was fun,' she said, winking at Ramulas.

'How did you know that would work?' Ramulas asked in astonishment.

'Oh, that's easy; men are very uncomfortable around a crying woman. They will do almost anything to help them,' Pip said waving a hand. 'The sheriff was left with no choice but to allow us to leave.'

'That was dishonest,' Ramulas replied.

'You have a lot to learn,' Pip laughed. 'A lot of rich people use dishonesty to get where they are. They would not think twice about taking all that you own.'

Ramulas was shocked at the resentment in Pip's voice. They travelled the next half an hour in silence.

Pip looked across and saw Ramulas wearing a sombre expression. 'What are you thinking about?'

'I wish we could have helped the stable boy.'

Pip shrugged. 'Better he dies than us.'

Ramulas' eyes widened in shock. 'Are you always this cold?'

Pip nodded. 'I only help the people I love.'

Ramulas smiled. 'You saved me from the druid—does that mean you love me?'

He laughed as Pip punched him in the arm.

17

Remus watched the black hole with calm resolve. He needed the crystal to stop moving. The warlords had found an ancient spell that would make the holder of the crystal extremely unwell and eventually die.

It had taken a short while and cost him five red wizards, but it did not matter to Remus—all he wanted was the crystal to stop moving.

Remus nodded to the warlords, who channelled the spell through the red wizards and into the black hole.

Remus wished he could witness the effect of the spell.

***

'That's a nice trick you have with your weapons,' Pip said.

'What trick is that?'

'When you hold them, they're silver, and out of your hands, they turn to wood. I noticed that when I knocked you to the ground.'

'They are a part of me. They will only change in my hands.' Ramulas said, 'How did you know about closing your eyes around the druids?'

'Oh, I learn things here and there,' Pip said casually.

'Look,' Ramulas said, 'If we are going to travel together, we need to trust one another. I would have liked to have known that before meeting the druid.'

Pip sighed. 'I know a thief from Turtha who went missing for two weeks. When he returned, he was a broken man. He had lost a lot of weight and said that he had escaped from the Druids' Labyrinth.'

'The Druids' Labyrinth? I thought that was just a myth,' Ramulas said.

'Not according to him. He said that he was very lucky to be placed on the top level of the labyrinth. Others were placed in the lower levels and had to fight their way up. It wasn't easy for him to escape, but he did,' Pip said with a faraway look. 'Have you heard the story of the druids?'

Ramulas nodded. 'I think everyone has.'

'Well, all of those monsters and creatures the druids were said to have caught are running around within the labyrinth. For months after my friend's escape, he refused to sleep indoors. He said that he needs to feel free. He told me that he knew the secrets to finding the way out of the labyrinth. The most important thing was to go to the tavern for help.'

'What's in the tavern?' Ramulas asked.

'That's what I asked him, and he said that I never want to find out.'

The crystal began to softly hum and vibrate. Pip's eyes locked on to the bulge in Ramulas' vest.

Ramulas began to feel nauseous as the farms on either side of the road seemed to tilt from left to right. Every small bump on the road was magnified. He felt as if the cart were a boat travelling down a wild river. Ramulas hugged his stomach tightly as his face contorted in agony.

Then he fell off the cart onto the road.

***

Pip watched Ramulas as the colour drained from his face. He began to sway in his seat slightly, before clutching his stomach in pain and falling from the cart. Her hand shot out to grab him but just missed. Pip picked up the reins and pulled the cart to a stop before jumping to the ground.

Ramulas lay on the ground at the rear of the cart. He clutched his stomach and rolled from side to side. His complexion had paled, and he was sweating.

A cold sensation exploded inside of Pip. She had allowed herself to get close to another person and he was gravely ill.

She could not let another person she cared for suffer. She needed to do something.

Pip put her hand against Ramulas' cheek and quickly pulled it away. Ramulas' skin felt as if was on fire. The crystal had intensified its humming and vibrations.

Ramulas had become sick when the vibrations first started.

Pip knew that if she removed the crystal, it would help him. Pip took the crystal out and threw it away from the cart. Ramulas continued to burn inside as Pip knelt next to him, feeling helpless. Ramulas was dying and there was nothing she could do.

***

Shigar felt the energies of the artefact change as it moved closer to Keah. He smiled to himself; not only could he feel where it was, but Shigar could tell which road it was moving along. It was coming straight for Keah as he had predicted.

Excitement built up inside of him at the prospect of this foreign magic coming towards Keah. It had been a long time since Shigar had known happiness, and he would not allow this opportunity to pass.

Shigar knew that as soon as he told Zachary where the artefact was, the king would send soldiers charging up the highway to Nasad. Without knowing what properties the artefact possessed, that could be very dangerous.

The last thing Shigar wanted was to lose the artefact. He decided to wait until the artefact was in Keah before he told Zachary.

The energies in the artefact had changed once more, telling Shigar it had stopped. This was good. It would give him time to prepare for the artefact's arrival. When it did arrive, Shigar wanted the artefact contained so he could study it.

There was a faint humming within the energy of the artefact. He was very curious about what this meant.

***

An idea came to Pip and she smiled while cutting away at Ramulas' vest. She needed to find a way to cool him down. After a few seconds, Ramulas felt cooler.

The front of Ramulas' vest and the crystal lay on the ground. His breathing and complexion were returning to normal. The crystal continued to hum and vibrate but did not seem to have any more effect on Ramulas. He came to and found Pip standing over him smiling.

'If you keep lying down, it will take a while for us to reach Keah,' Pip said.

Ramulas sat up and instantly regretted the movement as his head swam. He leant against the side of the cart. 'What happened?' Ramulas asked.

'That crystal in the front of your vest,' Pip said, pointing to it on the ground, 'started to hum and vibrate, which made you very sick. I threw it away and I cut away your vest.'

Ramulas looked over and saw that the crystal was still vibrating. He pulled himself up and slowly walked to his vest. Ramulas bent down and picked up the crystal. As he held it close to him, the sickness returned. He dropped the crystal and stepped back. 'Oh, that feels strange.'

'What is it?'

'Wait,' Ramulas said as he stepped toward the crystal. He waited a moment before stepping back.

He looked at Pip. 'The crystal makes me feel sick when I come close to it, and when I walk away, I do not feel its effects.'

Pip smiled at Ramulas. 'I will put it in the rear of the cart.' The young thief wrapped the crystal in a blanket and placed it in the back. She watched as Ramulas hesitantly walked to the front of the cart and was not affected.

As the cart continued on to Keah, Pip was lost in her thoughts. She had never gone out of her way to help anyone the way she had helped Ramulas, except for Jenna and her children. Pip prided herself on not having to rely on anyone, or have people rely on her.

Yet here she was helping Ramulas through situations she would normally walk away from. Pip's instincts screamed for her to stay with this man. There was something special about him she could not put her finger on.

***

Ramulas glanced at Pip out of the corner of his eye. She was a very strange person. She had saved him several times from certain doom in a short period of time. He felt indebted to her. At the same time, he could not understand how he came to enjoy the company of the young thief.

'Thank you,' Ramulas said.

Pip looked at him with genuine surprise. 'For what?'

'For helping me. Without you, I don't know what would have happened to me.'

Pip nodded, not knowing how to respond to such a compliment. Besides her sister, no-one had ever thanked her before. The closest Pip had come was a small nod of acknowledgement.

She looked up at Ramulas sitting next to her, searching for any sign of deceit. When Pip saw none, she noticed something under Ramulas' shirt.

'What have you got there?' Pip asked pointing to the top of his shirt.

Ramulas looked down and smiled as he pulled out the leather necklace. 'My wife and two daughters made this for me. They each tied a lock of their hair into the leather so I would remember them on my journey.'

Pip watched Ramulas closely. She had learnt long ago to mainly ignore what people said and to read their body language. That was how to tell what a person's real intentions were.

Ramulas held the necklace what great reverence. She could see that he held much pride, love, and sadness within the handmade necklace. Pip could tell the necklace represented his family, and Ramulas loved them very much.

'You will be happy when you return to them,' Pip said.

Ramulas replied, 'The sooner I complete my task, the sooner I will be able to go home.'

Pip smiled to herself as Ramulas wiped tears from his eyes and complained about dust on the road. It was typical of a man not to show his emotions. For some reason, men were taught that showing sadness meant weakness. To Pip, that was stupid.

Ramulas and Pip noticed that the crystal had stopped humming. They looked at each other before Ramulas communicated with the horse, and the cart pulled to a stop.

They climbed down from the cart and walked to where the crystal lay. Ramulas made his way with trepidation. He was fearful of becoming sick once more. They reached the rear of the cart without Ramulas suffering any ill effects. He reached out and touched the blanket that held the crystal, and nothing happened.

'It seems safe now,' Pip said, 'I think you should take a look inside. But if you start to feel sick, walk away.'

Ramulas hesitated. What Pip said made sense, but he was anxious about what would happen when he opened the blanket.

He took a deep breath and picked up the blanket and placed it on the ground. He let out a sigh of relief when nothing happened. Ramulas knelt next to the blanket and slowly unwrapped it. He was amazed to see Pip's foot tapping impatiently on the ground nearby.

After a moment, Ramulas had opened the blanket, and he saw the front of the vest Pip had cut away. Still, he had no feelings of nausea.

Ramulas picked up the vest and allowed the crystal to fall into the palm of his hand. Pip was kneeling by his side in the blink of an eye. He heard the sharp intake of her breath as Pip saw the moving images coming from within the emerald crystal. She was transfixed with the crystal and did not want to look away.

'In all my life I have never seen anything like this,' she whispered in awe, 'The shapes in the crystal were moving before you came into Bremnon.'

'This crystal will turn into a doorway that the army chasing Oriel will come through. It will anchor soon; then it can no longer be moved. That is why I need to take it to the Symiak mountains.'

'It is beautiful,' Pip said.

'And it is also dangerous.'

Ramulas dropped the crystal into the blanket, rolled it up, and placed it back on the back of the cart.

***

Remus nodded in satisfaction after the red wizards and warlords completed their task. They had successfully sent the ancient spell into the energy strand.

The red wizards assured Remus that both strands would return to normal within six hours. There was no indication of what had become of the person who held the crystal. If the spell had worked, the person would have been cooked from the inside.

Remus left instructions for the warlords and red wizards to continue their work on the black hole. As Remus walked down the hallways, he thought of the crystal anchoring in Oriel's world. Once it anchored, he would have a clearer picture of where the first legion would be facing.

He arrived at the training ground. The three captains—Redemption, Reckoning, and Retribution—were overseeing training drills of the legion.

They turned to Remus and spoke as one. 'We have increased the legion's training in preparation of retrieving Oriel.'

They turned to the legion and clapped once. The sound was amplified in the large courtyard. The soldiers of the legion scattered like leaves in the wind, running through arched entrances that lined the courtyard.

A few minutes later they returned, each with a pack strapped to their back. They stood in columns awaiting further instructions. 'The first legion and all their supplies can be moved through the portal in under an hour,' the three captains said.

Remus allowed a smile to play on his face. 'You have done well. Continue training the legion. The time to leave will come soon. We must be ready.'

The three captains bowed as Remus walked away. He had been so close to losing everything after Oriel left. Now Remus could almost taste the power when he consumed Oriel. Remus knew that he should thank Oriel for, without her escaping, the legion would not have found this new world to conquer.

***

Jacqueline sighed as she looked across the fields in the direction of their farm. It was mid-morning and she had already deflected questions from her girls about their father and when they would be going home to their farm.

What meagre food supplies they had brought from their home were added to Matthew's. She calculated they would have enough food for a week. After that, she was not sure what to do.

Would Ramulas have returned by then? Would it be safe to return home? And how long would the sheriff continue to hunt for them?

What would she say to Matthew when he finally came home?

One thing that took Jacqueline's worries away was watching Grace talking to a group of trees near Matthew's hut. What would possess Grace to talk to trees? It did not matter, as long as it kept her happy.

***

Ramulas and Pip made small talk as they ate and came closer to Keah. Trees and bushes lined the sides of the road, and birds could be heard singing in the warm sunny morning. Both were lost in their own thoughts until Ramulas saw an overturned cart.

He was instantly alert and communicated for the horse to increase its pace. Pip pulled her cloak tight around her body and covered her face with the hood. As they came closer to the cart, they heard a woman calling for help.

She was kneeling next to the cart, next to a man whose lower half was trapped beneath the wooden frame. Her cries for help increased when she saw Ramulas and Pip.

'Whatever happens,' Pip whispered. 'Do not stop. Keep moving.'

'We cannot leave them there!' Ramulas said in shock.

'Keep moving.'

They were twenty yards from the overturned cart. Ramulas could see that both the woman and man were hurt and bleeding.

'Thank the gods.' The woman wept as she held her arms out to Ramulas. 'My husband is hurt, and we need your help.'

Despite Pip's warning, Ramulas communicated with the horse and their cart came to a stop. He heard Pip curse under her breath. He ignored Pip, only thinking of the people in trouble. He had been brought up by Pete and Fran to help those in need.

'How can we help you?' Ramulas asked.

The injured man and woman pulled out hidden crossbows from under the cart just as two men with swords came out of the trees on either side of the pair. Ramulas' heart skipped a beat, and confusion froze his movements.

'We will take all of your possessions,' the woman said with a smile.

Pip jumped up in her seat and opened her cloak in one fluid movement. Her hands blurred through the air as four throwing knives were embedded into the overturned cart. The four bandits all dropped their weapons in surprise.

'Pip,' the woman said as she took a step forward, 'I did not know it was you.'

'This trap is only to be used on caravans,' Pip said as she jumped from the cart.

Ramulas was still in a state of shock as Pip retrieved her throwing knives. He remained in the cart as Pip angrily spoke to the bandits before they walked into the trees. After a minute, she climbed back in the seat next to Ramulas.

'We can leave now.'

Ramulas communicated with his horse, and they began to move.

'How did you know that was going to happen?'

'Because I was the one who thought of the trap. But they should only use it to rob rich merchants, and I hid my identity so I could catch them in the act. If they had seen me, they would not have tried to rob you.'

Ramulas' mouth hung open in shock.

'They were wrong in attacking your cart. I am happy that I was with you. There have been reports of bandits attacking lone travellers along the king's highway They have always denied it was them. Now I will report this to the master of shadows.'

'Why?'

'Even though we are thieves, we still live by a code.' Ramulas was about to ask for an explanation when he saw a mountain range as they rounded the bend.

'What mountains are they?' he asked, pointing ahead.

Pip followed his finger. 'They are the Symiak mountains. We will be in Keah within the hour.'

Ramulas eyes widened as they came around the hill. The mountain range stretched as far as the eye could see. How was he going to find the proper place to drop the crystal? Then Ramulas saw the city of Keah.

Keah was enormous, surrounded by a wall. From this distance, all the people milling outside Keah's wall reminded Ramulas of an ant mound.

'There must be at least a thousand people in the city of Keah,' Ramulas said.

'There are tens of thousands,' Pip replied.

'Ten thousand? How do they all live together?' he asked.

'I said *tens of thousands.* You will see how they live when we enter the city.'

Ramulas saw a large body of water dotted with small sailing boats next to Keah. 'What do you call that large lake—the one with the small boats?' Ramulas asked.

'We call that the ocean, and those small boats are ships.'

18

Shigar rose from his seated position and stretched his body like a cat. He could feel that the artefact was close. It was within ten miles of the city.

The magician was in two minds whether to tell King Zachary of the artefact or wait until it was within the walls of the city. If the king was informed of the artefact outside the walls, they could apprehend the person as they came through the gates.

However, if he waited for the artefact to come into the city before he told the king, it could be lost. This was his reason for being truly happy in many years, and the magician did not want to let that slip away.

In an instant, Shigar's mind was made up. He left his chambers and walked down the hallways; within moments, he came across a page.

'You there,' Shigar said with authority, 'I need you to run to the king and say only these words to him: "It is almost here." Do you understand?'

The page nodded once before running to the king's chambers.

'Ah, the vigour of youth.' Shigar mused as he followed the page.

A short while later, he arrived at the king's chambers to find Zachary and a score of soldiers waiting for him. Shigar quickly explained the energies of the artefact grew stronger, which meant it was coming to the city.

'Then we will ride out with the army and take the artefact from whoever is holding it,' Zachary stated with hunger in his eyes.

Shigar inwardly smiled. He had prepared for this response from Zachary. 'They will see us coming from miles away. Without knowing the properties of the artefact, I do not know what will happen. It may even vanish back to where it came from.'

Shigar had thrown out the bait and waited for the king to take it. He knew that the last thing Zachary wanted was to lose this magical artefact. Shigar did not have to wait long. 'What do you suggest I do then, magician?' Zachary asked sarcastically.

'We wait for him to enter the gates before closing the trap. Inside a city of this size, a lot of soldiers in one place would not stand out. I will wait above the west gate and signal when he comes through.'

Zachary nodded. 'I will stand with you; I wish to see who holds this artefact. We must prepare.'

Zachary and Shigar walked towards the west gate, and the king gave orders to the soldiers following them. One by one, they ran off to fulfil their tasks.

By the time Zachary and Shigar stood above the west gate, hundreds of soldiers lined every street near the western wall.

Half were in plain sight, and the other half were hidden from view.

Once the person with the artefact entered the gate, Shigar would point them out, and the soldiers would rush in. The person would be caught before they knew what was happening.

Shigar smiled to himself at the turn of events. It had seemed like a lifetime ago that Zachary held onto his every word and did not look upon him with disdain.

Inwardly, Shigar wished they could return to the way they were, but those thoughts were quickly dismissed. He knew that once he had solved the mystery of the crystal, Zachary would have no further need of him.

Shigar was once told that being alone was the most painful experience. He had discovered that being surrounded by people who made you feel alone was worse.

All Shigar wanted was to find a place where he belonged. Maybe one day he would find a place to call home.

***

Ramulas shook his head in amazement. The people in this part of the kingdom had gone mad. They were a mile from the massive walls of Keah. People, horses, carts, and wagons flowed into the city from the west.

It was midday and there was not a cloud in the sky. Ramulas coughed from the dust kicked up by so many hooves in a confined space. The sense of being hemmed in almost caused Ramulas to turn back. However, they were about to enter the city. From there, he would go into the mountains and be rid of the crystal.

Several roads merged into the main highway. They moved at a slow pace. Ramulas watched as the cart driver next to him cut off several people. It looked like a confused mess at the gates. To Ramulas, it looked as if there was no order at all.

'How will we get into the city?' he asked Pip.

She waved at the gate. 'This is normal. The soldiers make sure the people keep moving.'

It took a few minutes to get within one hundred yards from the gate. Ramulas was astounded at the sheer number of people flowing in and out of the city. The sounds and sights surrounding his cart were almost overwhelming.

There were people of all different colours, and people wearing clothes Ramulas had never seen before. He was stunned to see several men wearing flowing white robes, which reminded him of dresses worn by women. These were dark-skinned men but different from the Khilli.

He saw Nihon people from across the seas. Ramulas could not help but stare. They were a head shorter than Ramulas and had flat faces and almond eyes. They spoke rapidly in a language that he could not understand.

The road to the gate began to narrow, carts and wagons were entering the city in single file. The cart driver next to Ramulas flicked his reins and his cart cut in front of him.

'Out of my way, you fool!' he shouted at Ramulas while shaking his fist.

Ramulas was in shock. Never before had someone been so openly rude to him. His body tensed as he was about to communicate with man's horse and send the man on his way.

Pip lay her hand gently on Ramulas' arm. 'Let him go in front of us. If you cause a scene, soldiers will be on us like flies to a corpse.'

Ramulas allowed the man to push in front as he looked up at the soldiers walking along the wall. The wall towered over the people. Ramulas judged it to be at least fifty feet high.

The gate was half as high as the wall. It was made of two solid iron doors, only one of which was open, thus causing the bottleneck of people.

Finally, they came to the gate and were waved through by the soldiers. As they passed through the gate, Pip felt the hairs on the back of her neck stand on end. She looked at Ramulas to see if he had released a spell. The purple flames on his shoulders had not changed, so Pip knew it was not him.

Pip ignored the feeling as she instructed Ramulas to follow the rude cart driver as he turned right. Something was out of place, but Pip could not put a finger on it. A small voice inside told her to run, but she could not see any danger.

The first thing Pip noticed was a large number of soldiers inside the wall. Something must have happened while she was gone.

It did not matter; the soldiers were none of her concern.

***

Shigar and Zachary stood above the gate dressed in brown hooded cloaks. They watched as the flood of people poured into the city.

The energy of the artefact was extremely strong. Shigar knew it was very close.

Suddenly, the energies of the artefact had changed. Shigar cast a quick spell over the people below to see who had the artefact.

Then Shigar felt it pass beneath them. He grabbed the king's arm and pulled him to the other side of the wall. He pointed to the cart.

'That cart there,' Shigar said with excitement. 'He is the one who holds the artefact.'

Zachary made a signal to a sergeant in the street below.

A moment later, the street exploded into action as soldiers from both sides of the street converged on the cart. People screamed and ran as the soldiers pounced on their prey.

Zachary smiled; from his vantage point, the manoeuvre had worked perfectly. The artefact would soon be in his possession, and he wanted James to question this man. He did not want the man to die before telling him where the artefact came from.

***

As they moved slowly down the road, Ramulas' senses were overloaded with the sights, sounds, and smells coming from the stalls and stores on either side of the road.

An old man with a brown weathered face came up to the cart holding two live ducks by their necks. He yelled in a language that Ramulas could not understand, but the intention to sell the birds was clear. He wore a white robe and a piece of cloth tied tightly around his head.

A spice vendor called out the quality of his wares while standing next to large mounds of powders and containers of seeds. Ramulas could not believe the vast array of colours—from shades of orange, red, and yellow to green, brown, and black.

The next stall housed a Nihon vendor that sold quality tea. Outside his store sat four Nihon playing a board game with multicoloured tiles. Ramulas was mesmerised at how quickly their hands and tiles moved across the board.

'Something is about to happen,' Pip said.

Ramulas turned to look at Pip and saw that she had become extremely tense. Her focus was on the road ahead. He followed her line of sight just in time to see soldiers from both sides of the road rush forward with their swords drawn.

Pip grabbed Ramulas' thigh and said, 'No.'

'Don't move. If you move, you'll die!' A sergeant called out as he walked forward.

Ramulas felt helpless as he watched the soldiers surround his horse and cart. Pip looked around frantically. Then Ramulas noticed the cart in front was surrounded as well. The rude cart driver stood up in his seat, yelling abuse at the soldiers.

The sergeant ran up to his cart. 'Sit down and shut your mouth!'

'Do you know who my father is?' The rude man screamed.

The sergeant jumped up onto the cart and hit the man in the jaw with a mailed fist. The man's head snapped back, and he collapsed into the rear of his cart.

As the sergeant jumped down to the ground, all of the soldiers stood to attention. Ramulas turned to see a man in black robes with dark hair and a short beard. Behind him walked a regal man who wore a red vest that had a black eagle over his heart.

Pip sucked in her breath as the man in the robe led the regal man to stand in front of Ramulas' cart.

'The king and his magician,' Pip whispered, 'What are they doing here?'

The magician placed the forefinger and middle finger of both hands on his temples. He faced Ramulas, and Pip murmured for a few seconds before turning away. He knew that neither of them possessed the artefact. It was ten feet away from them.

Shigar could feel that the person who possessed the magic was close, but the artefact's power was stronger than the person's. The still figure of the rude cart driver lay in the rear of his cart, roughly ten feet from Ramulas and Pip.

'This is the man,' Shigar said as he pointed to the other cart. 'He possesses the magical artefact.'

The jaws of Ramulas and Pip dropped simultaneously at the magician's words. They quickly glanced at each other, knowing they needed to get away from this situation.

'Search the cart,' the sergeant called.

'Do not!' Shigar ordered. 'This has to be done carefully. Take him and the cart to the palace.'

The soldiers moved away from Ramulas' cart and began to clear the road ahead. The king and Shigar climbed into the front cart and led the procession of soldiers to the castle as the soldiers began to move away. Pip squeezed Ramulas' hand. 'Wait,' she whispered. When the soldiers had moved twenty yards, Pip nodded to a small alley to her right. 'Go in there slowly.'

He followed Pip's directions down a few narrow streets, and soon they were in the front yard of an abandoned house. The high fence sheltered them from the street.

Pip jumped down from the cart. 'We have to leave your horse and cart here. As soon as they discover they have the wrong person, they will come looking for us. The last time we were seen was in this cart.'

'I cannot leave my horse and cart here,' Ramulas protested.

'What do you suggest then?' Pip asked.

Ramulas gestured to the high fence. 'We can hide here as well.'

Pip grunted in frustration. 'I may as well dance on the roof while calling out for the king. The king's magician knows when the crystal is close. We need to move; it is our only choice.'

She removed her cloak to reveal her throwing knives and opened a door at the side of the house. Inside, Ramulas saw two troughs full of water.

'What is this?' he asked.

'Sometimes we steal a horse or two. This is a good place to hide them. Now take what you need. We have to leave.' Deep down Ramulas knew she was right. He did not want to leave the horse, but to be seen with his horse and cart meant capture. The animal was the only link to his family, and he felt sick having to leave it. He communicated with the horse, saying that he would return shortly.

He unhitched the horse, donned a new vest, and removed the blanket from the cart. Ramulas was cautious when unrolling the blanket in case the crystal caused him to become sick once more. Once the crystal was unwrapped, Ramulas felt no ill effects and placed it inside his vest.

'I need to take my weapons.'

'You cannot walk around with a silver war hammer and battleaxe. Keep them covered. We need to go now.'

Ramulas ensured that his weapons were covered in a blanket, and then he looked at Pip. 'You cannot go out into the streets like that!'

Pip smiled. She remembered her own father saying the same thing when Jenna wore a dress that showed her legs. However, Pip knew Ramulas was referring to her throwing knives.

'I am known to dress like this in Keah.'

Pip walked to the gate, motioning for Ramulas to follow. They walked out, and Pip closed the gate, placing a flower on the latch. 'This tells the other shadows that the house is being used. No-one will enter.'

Pip led Ramulas through a few narrow streets filled with double-storey stores and houses until they came to a main street near a large market square. Ramulas held his weapons close. He felt lost in the sea of people that moved around him.

Ramulas saw vendors' tables set up along the aisles and pens with horses, cattle, and pigs and cages full of birds stacked on one another. The smell of the animals reminded him of his farm.

Pip took his hand and led him through the market to a small table next to a food vendor's cart. After sitting Ramulas down, Pip spoke to the vendor and returned with two plates of spiced meat.

Ramulas saw that there were several other food vendors selling all manner of foods. He had to look twice at the Nihon vendor who sold what looked like fried insects on sticks. The vendor smiled at Ramulas while eating one of the insects with an audible crunch.

'Eat your food and stop looking around,' Pip said as she popped a piece of meat into her mouth.

'Why?' Ramulas asked.

'Because it will help you blend in with the crowd. Once the king's magician finds out he has the wrong man, he will come looking for you.'

'What do we do?'

'What we are doing now: hiding in plain sight. But you need to relax. I have things that I need to do. Stay here and I will return soon.'

'But they will find me here,' Ramulas said.

'No, they won't. They are looking for two people in a cart, not one man eating in a busy marketplace. You will be safe here. Wait for me to return.'

Ramulas watched Pip disappear into the crowd, and then looked down at the strange food in front of him. From the food to the diversity of the people around him, everything felt alien to Ramulas. All he wanted was to drop the crystal off and return home.

**

Pip stood outside a warehouse and tapped her hand on the wall in a sequenced pattern. She heard the answer and sliding of the lock. She glanced around before disappearing in through the door.

Pip stood in total darkness and attempted to gauge how many shadows were in the room with her. She could hear breathing and faint movements. But there was something else in the darkness with her.

'Hello, Pip,' a soft voice said near her.

Pip threw herself into a forward roll as the shutters were taken from the lanterns, bathing her in light.

Pip saw that she was in a large room with stacks of barrels lining the walls. Six burly men stood near the barrels. They were dwarfed by the master of shadows, who glided toward her.

'I expected you back in the city days ago. Where have you been?'

Pip rose to her feet. 'The king's agent was in Bremnon. I needed to keep Jenna safe.'

The master chuckled, sending a shiver through Pip. 'But you have been a busy girl. Just before your arrival, there was a lot of activity inside the western wall. Too many soldiers in one place is never a good thing. Do you know why the soldiers were there, young Pip?'

Pip's mind raced. She recognised that the master of shadows knew about the ambush and her escape. He knew almost everything within the city walls. But how much did he know about Ramulas? Pip decided it would not be wise to withhold too much information.

'I met a man in Bremnon. He has something that the king is looking for.'

'Hmmmmm,' the master said as he held his chin in a cupped hand and paced. 'What is this thing?'

'Something magical,' Pip replied, not wanting to reveal too much.

The master raised an eyebrow. 'Something? What sort of thing?'

'A crystal,' Pip said.

The master smiled, and Pip knew what was coming. 'Did you see this crystal?'

She nodded. 'I had it before returning it to him.'

The master stepped closer to Pip with a growing smile. 'Why would you do such a thing? A fine thief such as yourself should have brought it straight to me.'

Pip sighed and quickly told the story of Ramulas' mission, the legion, and Oriel. By the time she finished, the master of shadows had stopped smiling.

'Pip, I would like to speak with this Ramulas. I have heard of the agents looking for some powerful magic. Bring him to me, please. And I want no more trouble with this man.' Pip nodded and left the warehouse with a myriad of thoughts. The master of shadows would want to question Ramulas, look at the crystal, and find a way to profit from this situation.

That was the way of all the shadows, but Pip knew Ramulas needed to take the crystal out of the city. However, she could not betray the master of shadows. Jenna's safety depended on what she did. And Pip would not allow any more harm to come to those she loved.

***

They had ridden for several minutes in the cart when Shigar became confused. The power of the artefact was gradually waning.

The rude cart driver moaned as he regained consciousness.

It was then that Shigar realised his error. 'Stop!' he shouted.

Zachary looked at him in shock, and the soldiers turned in surprise.

'Tell me what has happened,' Zachary demanded.

'We have the wrong man,' Shigar said in shock.

'How is that possible?'

'When the artefact first came into this world, I felt that it was attached to a man, and it suppressed the feeling of his magic. Then when it entered the city, there were two carts: one with this man, and another with a man and woman.

'When we reached the carts, this man,' Shigar said pointing to the limp body behind them, 'was unconscious, which led me to believe he was in possession of the artefact. Then the energies were slowly fading, I thought it was because he was unconscious, but now?'

'Where is the artefact?' Zachary demanded.

'It is with the man and woman on other cart.'

Zachary looked as if he had just been slapped. Then the driver behind them came to his senses. 'What are you two doing on my cart?'

'Gullytown!' Zachary screamed pointing at the man.

Once the man was pulled off the cart and dragged away, Zachary ordered everyone back to the place where the two carts were first seen.

Shigar's heartbeat quickened. Days prior, his life had been given new meaning when he felt the foreign magical energies. His hopes had risen as the artefact came closer to the city. Now he let it slip through their fingers. The magician could not let this new lease on life slip away.

He needed it; the artefact gave him a purpose for the first time in his life.

They rushed through the streets with soldiers clearing the way ahead. They arrived at the spot only to find the other cart was nowhere to be seen.

'Where have they gone?' Zachary asked.

Shigar closed his eyes and held his hands out in front of him and waved his fingers slowly. Taking slow, deep breaths, he moved his hands through the air, feeling for the energies of the artefact. After a moment, his eyes snapped open. He pointed to the narrow street Ramulas and Pip had taken.

'Down this way,' the magician said.

Three scores of soldiers followed the cart down through the streets until they arrived at the abandoned house where Ramulas had left his horse. Again, he closed his eyes and felt the faint energies of the artefact.

'They stopped in here before moving,' Shigar said before leading Zachary and the soldiers to the market square.

19

Ramulas had eaten half the meat on his plate when he felt the first sensation. It was a whimper that brushed the edges of his consciousness. Then it built into a scream of terror, before being cut off abruptly.

Ramulas felt the animal's fear just before it was killed. Then he felt the fear of other animals who were awaiting the same fate. Another presence found its way into his consciousness. This animal was filled with rage and fury.

Suddenly Ramulas understood what was about to happen. 'This is barbaric,' he said as he stood.

Ramulas quickly walked to where he knew the animals were.

***

Pip returned to the market square in time to see Ramulas disappear into the crowd. She had to bring him to see the master of shadows.

'I told him to wait there for me,' Pip said as she made her way through the throng of people.

Luckily, Pip was able to track Ramulas by following the purple flames that danced on his shoulders, sending a shaft of purple light into the sky. It took her a minute to catch up with Ramulas in front of a warehouse.

Pip grabbed Ramulas by the arm and spun him around. What she saw caused her to release his arm and step back. Ramulas' face was a mask of fury. Tears filled his eyes and he held his weapons so tightly that the muscles on his arms bulged. 'Stay out of this,' Ramulas whispered before walking into the warehouse.

Pip quickly glanced back at the market before following Ramulas into the warehouse. She needed to bring him to the master of shadows.

When Ramulas entered, he saw a large group of men gathered in a circle in the middle of the empty building. They were shouting and cheering over the sound of a dogfight. A small dog yelped in pain and terror as a larger dog attacked it.

Ramulas waded through the crowd. Each step brought a tightening to his chest, pushing men aside until he came to the centre. He was appalled at the sight before him. Ramulas stood at the edge of a pit dug into the earth. It was roughly ten feet wide and three feet deep.

A hell hound stood in the middle of the pit with a smaller dog in its jaws. The pit itself was littered with body parts of other dogs. The scene broke Ramulas' heart, and a raging heat spread through his body.

Ramulas communicated with both animals. The smaller dog was close to death, and even though it pained him, Ramulas put it out of its misery. He waved his hand, sending purple mist over the small dog, and it became still. Then with another wave, Ramulas covered the hell hound and it fell asleep in the middle of the pit.

As both dogs collapsed, a large man with a bushy beard turned to Ramulas. 'What have you done? We were having some fun.'

Ramulas looked at the man as a warm sensation exploded in the pit of his stomach. He jabbed the man in the chest with a finger. 'You dare kill animals for sport?'

The man looked behind Ramulas and nodded. Several pairs of hands grabbed Ramulas from behind. The front of Ramulas' shirt tore as the hands tightened their grip. The warm sensation grew inside of Ramulas.

'What do we have here?' The bearded man said as he came up to Ramulas.

He leaned forward and reached for Ramulas. Cold ice rushed through Ramulas' veins as the man took hold of the necklace given to him by Jacqueline and his girls.

'No, you don't understand,' Ramulas said.

The man smiled, showing black-stained teeth. Then with a jerk, he pulled the necklace away from Ramulas.

'Aaaaaargh!' Ramulas screamed.

The cold sensation in the pit of his stomach exploded and rushed throughout Ramulas' body. Then everything slowed around him. Ramulas could feel the individual fingers of each hand that held him.

Ramulas sent magical energy outwards in a massive surge. Men around him were lifted and thrown back in slow motion. The bearded man's eyes widened as he turned to run.

Everything around Ramulas returned to normal speed. He was momentarily surprised by what he did, but the rage flooding through him cancelled any rational thoughts.

'No,' he growled.

Ramulas focused on his anger. He saw men running toward him armed with clubs and swords. They were covering the bearded man's escape.

Ramulas flicked his cloth bundle into the air and caught his weapons as they came free. He smiled at the men's reactions when they saw the transformation. Memories of his past life flashed before him.

Deep inside, a part of Ramulas knew what needed to be done.

There were six men in all. Ramulas took a step toward them.

He could hear the moaning of the men who flew through the air, and he saw them rolling around in pain. Orders were called out for others to attack Ramulas. He also heard Pip calling for him. Ramulas ignored her and ran at the men.

Ramulas began to spin as he reached the first man. He knocked aside a thrust from a sword and delivered a bone-shattering blow to the man's knees with his war hammer.

The next man had a club that he swung at Ramulas, who cleaved it in two with his battleaxe. The top half of the club spun through the air, followed by the hand that had held it.

Two men with swords rushed at Ramulas only to be thrown back after blows from his war hammer. The two remaining men stood in shock. Both had dropped their swords and held their stomachs. Each was hit with one of Pip's throwing knives.

Ramulas turned to see Pip running toward him. 'The soldiers are coming! You have to leave now!' she cried.

***

Pip looked back at the market square in time to see soldiers converge on it. She ducked into the warehouse and shut the door behind her. Pip saw Ramulas disappear within a group of men who were watching a dogfight. Two seconds later, the dogfight stopped, and Pip could hear Ramulas arguing with someone.

'This is not good,' Pip said as she moved closer.

There was a scuffle in the crowd before Ramulas screamed.

Pip dashed forward, pulling out two of her throwing knives. Without warning, bodies flew through the air. She was surprised as an invisible force pushed her away along with the others. Pip saw the flame around Ramulas expand before returning to normal.

Pip saw a young boy come in from the street. He tapped his shoulder when he saw Pip. This was a signal that soldiers were coming.

Pip needed to get Ramulas out of there.

***

Shigar and Zachary arrived at the market square with three score soldiers. A small spark of hope reignited within his chest as he felt the recent echoes of the artefact.

'The artefact was here very recently,' Shigar said, 'but there are too many people. I cannot feel where it is.'

'Clear the square!' Zachary called.

The soldiers rushed in and cleared half the square in a few moments. Then Shigar felt a surge of energy on the other side of the square.

'Oh my—he is over there,' Shigar said as he pointed in the general direction of the warehouse. Zachary ordered the soldiers across the square.

The spark of hope grew as Shigar realised he would have the artefact soon. With a wave of his hand, Shigar led the soldiers to the warehouse.

Shigar held up his hand outside the building, stopping the soldiers. 'He is inside.'

***

Pip grabbed Ramulas' arm and pulled him toward the rear door of the warehouse. 'Quickly! We need to move. I will meet you outside.'

As the young thief led Ramulas outside, he was overwhelmed at how he had used his weapons. He had never fought before, or so he believed. But the weapons felt very much a part of him, and his body seemed to know how to move.

Pip gave Ramulas a push in the direction of the rear door before running to retrieve her knives. Ramulas came out of the warehouse into a narrow alley. He saw the bearded man duck around the corner. Ramulas saw that he still held the necklace. He ran after him.

Ramulas turned the corner into a narrow street and ran directly into the path of Zachary and Shigar. He stopped fifteen feet in front of them. Scores of soldiers surrounded the cart the king and his magician sat in.

Ramulas' eyes met with Shigar's as he searched for a way out.

However, Ramulas realised he would be able to communicate with the animals. He smiled at Shigar as he spoke to the horse.

'That's the man!' Shigar shouted, 'I need him alive.'

The horse ran to the left, bringing the cart with it, blocking half of the soldiers and knocking a few over. Ramulas turned to run as Shigar cast a spell.

After three steps, a strong wind blew towards Ramulas, kicking up a cloud of dust from the ground. Tiny particles of grit flew into his face as Ramulas inhaled a mouthful of dust.

Ramulas stumbled as he choked and coughed. Then he heard soldiers running up behind him. He spun with his weapons and struck a soldier. Ramulas spun three more times, knocking several soldiers down. Then a bout of coughing shook his body.

Ramulas looked up to see blurry shapes rush at him from all sides.

A soldier launched himself through the air to tackle Ramulas around the waist. He staggered under the weight but remained standing. Then the weight of other soldiers brought him to the ground. Mailed fists, boots, and sword hilts rained down upon Ramulas until he fell into unconsciousness.

***

After Pip retrieved her throwing knives, she followed Ramulas out the door. She saw at least ten soldiers beating Ramulas as he fell to the ground.

Pip was torn between rushing to help Ramulas, which she knew would be suicide, and holding back and waiting for an opportunity to help him later.

Pip cursed as she hid between two crates and waited to see where the soldiers took Ramulas. Never before had she felt concern for anyone except for Jenna and her children. However, there was something special about Ramulas.

The master of shadows would be angry. He had told her that he wanted Ramulas brought to him with no more trouble. How would she explain this?

She inwardly flinched when Ramulas' flame disappeared during the beating.

***

'That is enough!' Zachary shouted.

The soldiers stopped their assault and stepped away. Cuts and abrasions covered Ramulas as he lay still on the ground.

Shigar climbed down from the cart, followed by Zachary. The magician cautiously approached Ramulas and opened his hands above the prone figure. He could feel the strong energies of the artefact flowing up towards him. Shigar murmured a simple spell and the crystal began to glow within Ramulas' vest.

'This is indeed the one,' Shigar said to Zachary. 'I will need to study the artefact in my chambers.'

Zachary motioned with his hand and several soldiers picked up Ramulas' limp form and placed him in the cart. Zachary scanned the laneway and saw the few people who were there before had vanished.

Shigar picked up Ramulas' weapons for Zachary to see. 'They are made from wood, yet when he held them, they were silver.'

Zachary's eyes widened at the realisation, then he looked to where Ramulas lay.

'Come, I'll show you,' Shigar said with excitement in his voice.

Soldiers moved away from the cart as the king and magician came to inspect Ramulas. Shigar muttered a few words before turning to Zachary.

'I have cast a spell to ensure he sleeps for a few hours; he will not harm us.'

Shigar moved the war hammer into Ramulas' open hand. Everyone around the cart gasped and took a step back as the weapon transformed. Once the war hammer was removed from Ramulas' hand, it returned to a wooden weapon.

'I will need to study his weapons and the artefact,' Shigar said. 'The only safe place for this one is in the tombs. I do not know the extent of his magical power, and magic does not work within the tombs.'

Zachary nodded. 'We need to return him to the palace.' Zachary motioned for the sergeant to come to him. Once he was close, the king spoke softly for a moment. When he had finished, the sergeant stepped back and bowed slightly.

Then the sergeant stepped away from the cart and began screaming orders to the soldiers. Ten raced to the palace and the rest formed a cordon around the cart.

'We are ready, my lord,' the sergeant said softly to the king.

Zachary nodded, and the entourage moved forward.

***

Minutes before Ramulas fought the men in the warehouse, Grace stood by the tree where the dryads had gone into. She had attempted several times to call them to no avail.

The moment Ramulas sent a surge of energy through the men in the warehouse, Grace had a spontaneous reaction. A warm sensation exploded inside her stomach and flowed through her body.

The air around her burst into flame as her hands were covered in purple energy. Then the energy exploded in Grace's face, sending her flying backward into one of the trees. Grace landed face down in the dirt and lay very still.

A figure stepped out from the trunk of a nearby tree. The dryad walked over to Grace and gently picked her up. She held Grace in her arms and walked away from the tree.

20

The cart arrived in the courtyard of the castle. Shigar jumped to the ground when it came to a stop. He walked to Ramulas and opened the vest pocket and removed the crystal. He held it out for the king to see.

Zachary and Shigar were transfixed by the dancing shapes within the emerald crystal. The sergeant and a few of the soldiers leaned in to look as well.

'I will need to study this artefact and the weapons in my chambers. Send this one to the tombs, and I will see what magic he has brought to us,' Shigar said.

After Ramulas had been taken to the tombs, Zachary followed Shigar to his chambers. When they were alone, he pointed to the crystal. 'I want to know everything about this crystal and the man's weapons. I don't care what you have to do.'

Zachary turned and walked from the chambers without another word.

Once Shigar was certain that he was alone, he began a little dance around the table. He never hoped in his wildest dreams to have such a powerful artefact sitting in his chambers. He could feel that the artefact was the key for him to finally find happiness.

After a minute of dancing, Shigar sat at his table and examined the crystal.

***

The afternoon sun shone down on Matthew's farm as the dryad walked with Grace in her arms. If she walked with Grace into the trees and transformed Grace into a dryad, she would be able to heal this human child. But Grace had been adamant: she did not wish to enter the trees.

The dryad walked to the door of the hut and stopped when she heard two females talking inside. Besides Grace, the dryads had not come in contact with people for hundreds of years. She wanted this meeting with Grace's family to be one of acceptance.

Kate saw the dryad enter the house and let out an ear-piercing scream, and pointed to the creature holding Grace. Jacqueline looked at the dryad and screamed as well.

Kate's demeanour changed as she danced sideways, and picked up her staff leaning against the wall. Kate spun the staff as she moved in front of her mother, before crouching into a fighter's stance. She held one end of the staff toward the dryad like a spear.

'Kate, what are you doing?' Jacqueline scolded. 'Put that down and come back here.'

The sound of her mother's voice brought Kate out of her trance. She dropped the staff and held onto her mother. The two backed into the corner of the small hut wearily looked at the dryad.

Then Jacqueline's maternal instinct took over. The need to protect her daughters flooded through her. She pushed Kate behind her and stepped forward.

'What have you done to my daughter?' she demanded, pointing an accusing finger at the dryad.

'I assisted Grace after the incident,' the dryad said in a sing-song voice. 'She needs to lie on her side and have poultice placed on her head.'

'What incident?' Jacqueline asked. 'And how do you know her name?'

'A part of her magical ability came to fruition, and she was unable to control it. We must lay her down,' the dryad urged.

Jacqueline led the way to Matthew's bed, where the dryad lay Grace on her side. She had lost colour, and her breathing was shallow. Jacqueline moved to her youngest daughter, and the dryad raised her hand.

'Please allow me to heal her first,' the dryad said with a calming smile.

Jacqueline wanted to push the creature out of the way and comfort Grace. But there was something about the way the creature treated her daughter, placed her on the bed, and spoke of her. It was as if it saw Grace as part of her family.

The creature laid its hand over the left side of Grace's face.

After a few moments, the hand came away, and the whole side of her face was covered in moss.

'She must rest until the morning,' the dryad said as it stood.

'What are you?' Jacqueline asked.

'I am a dryad; I came because my people can feel her magic. She has been to our home and is welcome to return.' The dryad walked out of the hut. Jacqueline and Kate knelt by the bed, shocked at what they had witnessed.

A weariness came over Jacqueline as she sat next to Grace. Ramulas had left and the sheriff searched for him. He would also be looking for her girls after they attacked the soldiers. Now they were away from home and Grace had been hurt.

Jacqueline did not know what to do or who to turn to. What of the creature calling itself *dryad*? What would she do if it returned? After the initial shock, Jacqueline was scared of the uncertainty and did not know what she was going to do.

Maybe when Matthew returned, he would be able to help.

It was too much to comprehend along with thinking about both girls having special abilities. Jacqueline wished Ramulas was home. She wondered what he was doing.

***

Ramulas woke in a dark place face down on a bed of rotting straw. The coppery taste of blood lingered inside his mouth. He wondered where he was and how he came to be here.

Ramulas pushed himself up onto his hands and knees with a grunt. Every part of his body seemed to be on fire and stiff. He looked up to see a faint light coming through a doorway.

Then memories of the day with Pip and entering Keah came back to him. He had run into the king's magician, and the soldiers had beat him senseless.

His eyes became accustomed to the dim light. He saw a wall to the left of him. Ramulas crawled to the wall, then used the cold bricks to pull himself up into a standing position.

Ramulas leaned against the wall for a few seconds as a bout of dizziness threatened to send him back to the floor. He used this time to look around the room. It was roughly ten feet square with no visible windows. The floor seemed to be bare except for the pile of straw, and the only source of light came from the door.

Ramulas used the wall as a guide and support as he made his way to the door. Reaching it, he realised that he was not in a room.

Ramulas was in a cell. A wave of anxiety threatened to overwhelm Ramulas. How would he get out? How long had he been here? Thoughts of his family came to him. He needed to return home.

The door was barred. It was made from thick iron bars that prevented him from leaving. Ramulas held onto two of the bars and looked down the hall to see a torch in the wall.

Ramulas pressed his body up against the bars and realised that the crystal was no longer in his vest. Panic flooded through Ramulas as he ran back to where he woke in the straw.

He dropped to his hands and knees and frantically searched through the straw. Ramulas soon found that both his weapons and the crystal were nowhere in the cell.

'Damn you,' Ramulas whispered in the darkness.

A wave of despair swept over him as he collapsed to the floor. He had left his family for the first time to place the crystal in the Symiak mountains. Now he found himself locked in a cell without his weapons or the crystal.

Ramulas was away from his family and had no idea when he would see them again. He hoped that now he was gone from the farm the sheriff would leave his family alone.

He sat with his back against the bars for what seemed an eternity. He worried about his family and the crystal. Then he heard footsteps coming down the hall. Ramulas quickly stood near the bars. The footsteps grew louder, then a large shadow passed the torch.

A hulking brute stopped on the other side of the bars. He was almost as wide as the door and slightly higher than it. He wore dark leggings and a dark woollen shirt. He had short-cropped blond hair and eyes void of emotion.

The brute held a ring of keys in his hand. He used one to unlock the door, then he leaned forward and walked into the cell.

'I need the crystal back,' Ramulas pleaded, 'You don't understand what will happen.'

Ramulas was silenced by a backhand from the giant, which sent him crashing into the far wall. The brute stood over Ramulas before he had time to recover.

'Now, James,' a voice called from the hallway. 'You know that you are not supposed to be in there yet.'

James stepped away from him and walked out of the cell.

Ramulas looked up to see the magician standing in the doorway.

'You are a special person with some very interesting items. One way or another, we will find everything we need to know about you and them,' the magician said.

Shigar played with a ring on his finger before waving his hand through the air. A ball of bright light appeared in the middle of the cell. Ramulas threw a forearm across his face to shield his eyes from the sudden brightness.

Shigar walked over to Ramulas and looked down at him. 'You fare quite well after your capture. A lot of your wounds have healed extremely fast. That is good—you will live longer through questioning.'

Shigar turned to walk out of the cell.

'The crystal,' Ramulas said softly. 'I need it. Something very bad will happen if I do not have the crystal.'

Shigar raised an eyebrow. 'And what bad thing is this?'

Ramulas was in a dilemma. If he told the truth about the crystal opening into a doorway for the legion to come through, he would then have to explain Oriel and his own magical abilities.

His inner voice screamed for him not to say anything. They would find out about his girls; he did not want the king's men to know what his daughters could do.

If they found out about his magical powers, they would go to his farm and find out about Grace and Kate. Ramulas shook his head. 'Nothing.'

'Oh, I think there is. And one way or another, I will find out what I want to know.'

The ball of light flickered a few times before disappearing. Shigar shrugged and walked out. As James locked the cell, a thought came to Ramulas.

'How long have I been here?'

Shigar turned to him. 'You cannot expect me to answer your questions when you do not answer mine.'

Shigar walked away as James took one last look inside the cell before following the magician.

Ramulas heard the jingling of keys as they were placed on the wall. He waited for the footsteps to recede before making his way to the cell door. Ramulas saw that the keys had been placed on the opposite wall. He wondered how he could reach them.

***

Shigar walked up the stairs that led away from the tombs and thought of the ball of light he made appear in the cell.

The ring he wore on his finger allowed him to use magic within the tombs. However, the magic he could use was limited. The tombs had a powerful spell that acted as a dampener for magic. He wished he could see the prisoner's reaction if he attempted to use magic within the cell.

***

Oriel stood within her cavern facing east with great concern.

Since coming to this world and meeting Ramulas, she had formed a connection with him. Oriel could feel where Ramulas was.

A short time prior, she had felt a great surge of magical energies created by Ramulas. After that, the connection with Ramulas was severed. Oriel could feel his life energies one moment, and the next it had vanished. It was as if Ramulas had dropped off the face of the earth or had died. Ramulas could not be dead, Oriel told herself.

If Ramulas was dead or something had happened to him, what had happened to the crystal? If it had been left in an open place and given a chance to anchor, Remus would have no problem bringing the legion to this world. Where was the young thief who helped him with the druid? Did she have the crystal?

Oriel needed to rest. She needed to send her astral image to the city of Keah to find what had happened to Ramulas.

***

The red wizard entered Remus' chambers and waited for the warlord to look up from the pile of scrolls. After a few moments, Remus motioned for the red wizard to speak.

'There has been another development with the crystal.'

'Has it moved again?' Remus asked as he stood from his chair.

'The energy strand has changed again. You will need to see for yourself.'

Remus gave a slight nod before following the red wizard out of his chambers. He knew by the red wizard's demeanour that something was wrong. They were close to the crystal anchoring; Remus did not want things to fall apart now.

When they arrived at the black hole, Remus noticed the blue energy strand had grown again. The side filaments were moving and helping the strand to swim through the air. The thin red strand had not changed.

Then Remus saw the purple dots floating through the black hole. 'What are the those?'

'The crystal has stopped moving. It has been separated from the one who carried it. The purple dots represent another who possesses the crystal. He is using magic.'

'How is this possible? And now we have another magic user with the crystal,' Remus said in shock. 'How many magicians are on Oriel's new world?'

The red wizard shrugged. 'The only thing we know is that he uses magic to examine the crystal.'

'How can you say for certain?'

'Echoes of his spells have been coming through the black hole.'

'How will this affect the crystal and the portal?' Remus asked.

'As with the Oriel, this assists in strengthening the passageway. And soon the crystal will anchor. Once that happens, nothing will affect the crystal.'

Remus held his chin in a cupped hand as he thought. How did the original person lose possession of the crystal? And the person who now had the crystal, did they know what it was? Is that why they were using magic?

This brought another train of thought to Remus. The person who had the crystal must be a powerful magic-user.

But the question was how powerful?

Dropping the hand from his chin, Remus turned to the red wizard. 'Continue feeding magic into the black hole until the crystal anchors. Then we will evaluate the situation.'

Remus turned and walked away without waiting for a response.

21

Ramulas heard footsteps coming down the hall. He quickly stood and walked to the centre of the cell. Shadows in the hall began to dance as torches were carried to the door. Ramulas saw the king with James and a Khilli warrior.

James had the ring of keys in one hand and used a key to unlock the door before stepping away. As he stepped away, Ramulas saw the Khilli carrying a tray with a jug and a loaf of bread.

The king opened the cell door and stepped inside.

'The crystal and weapons you had in your possession—where did you acquire them? And what powers do they hold?' Zachary asked while glaring at Ramulas.

Ramulas held his tongue, not wanting to talk. The king held a presence of power about him, of someone who was accustomed to people obeying his every order. Ramulas did not want to reveal anything about his family. If they found out that Grace and Kate had special abilities, he did not know what would happen to them.

When Ramulas did not respond, Zachary spoke again. 'I know you have travelled from the north-east with the artefact for the last two days. I also know that you entered my city with a woman. Was that, perhaps, your wife? I have my men searching the city for her as we speak.'

Zachary smiled at the prisoner's reaction when he mentioned him travelling from the north-east and the man's wife. He saw the prisoner's eyes widen in surprise. Zachary would find what he needed to know from this prisoner before allowing James to play with him.

'One way or another, I will find out everything I need to know. If you tell me now, I will allow you to walk out of here a free man,' Zachary said.

A glimmer of hope flashed in Ramulas' eyes before vanishing. Even if he told the king everything about the crystal, he did not think the king would believe him. And Ramulas' inner voice warned him not to say anything.

Ramulas stood where he was and remained silent while an internal struggle ensued. If he spoke, the king might let him return home. But he needed to take the crystal to the Symiak mountains, or the people he loved would suffer.

Zachary smiled as he stepped forward with his hands clasped behind his back. 'The sooner you talk to me, the less pain you will experience.'

The king stood before Ramulas, studying him for a moment. Then he turned and walked out of the cell. As James locked the door, the Khilli placed the tray just outside the door. 'Please help yourself if you become hungry or thirsty,' Zachary said, waving at the tray before walking away followed by James.

The Khilli stood just outside the door holding a torch and locked eyes with Ramulas. He made a slight gesture toward the tray with his hand. He shook his head before walking away.

As the shadows gathered once more within the cell, Ramulas wondered where he had seen that Khilli before. The image of the fight with the hell hound in Bremnon flashed before Ramulas' eyes.

He was the Khilli that helped Grace in the fight with the hell hound and the men. It was the day he first met Oriel. Ramulas was happy to see a familiar face. That happiness quickly faded and was replaced by anxiety.

The Khilli had seen him in Bremnon. The sheriff who was with the Khilli had come to his farm with the collector of tax. As soon as the Khilli told the king, the sheriff would lead him to Ramulas' family. He did not want anyone to know about his daughter's abilities.

Ramulas paced the cell, worrying about the welfare of Jacqueline and his daughters. What could he do to help them or divert the king away from his farm? After pacing for what seemed an eternity, he had run out of solutions. With his mind beginning to wander, Ramulas knew he needed to rest.

Then he saw the tray with the bread and drink. Ramulas' stomach growled as he made his way to the door. He knelt down and reached through the bars.

A boot came out of the darkness and pinned his wrist to the floor. Ramulas gasped in pain as James moved into view. He had been hiding in the darkness, waiting for Ramulas to take the tray.

James smiled as he brought a club down on the back of Ramulas' hand. Ramulas screamed as he felt something break. This was followed by an explosion of pain that ran up his arm. James lifted his foot, allowing Ramulas to pull his hand back through the bars.

Then James unlocked and opened the door.

Ramulas held the injured hand against his body and scuttled away from the door. James bent down and picked up the tray and placed it inside the cell. He picked up the bread and tore a chunk off before dropping it. James chewed the piece as he locked the door and walked away.

Ramulas sat on the floor cradling his injured hand. He realised that was what the Khilli was trying to warn him about. Ramulas didn't understand why they would want to lure his hand out to injure it. Then after James had hurt him, he left Ramulas the tray.

Ramulas sat wondering if this was another trick. His hand began to throb as the pain increased. He looked down at his hand and attempted to form a fist. Pain shot up his arm, almost causing Ramulas to faint.

Ramulas knew there was something wrong, and that he needed a healer. A bitter laugh escaped his lips. Ramulas knew he would not be seeing a healer any time soon. He removed his vest and wrapped it around the injured hand.

How long were they going to keep him here? Why didn't they let him take the crystal into the mountains? Ramulas knew that he could not explain the crystal without bringing harm to his family. He would just have to find some way out of this mess.

Ramulas stood and made his way to the tray with both eyes on the door, expecting it to open at any moment. When he reached the tray and the door did not open, Ramulas quickly took the loaf and moved to the rear of the cell. He would wait until the pain subsided before he ate.

***

Pip hid in the shadows of a laneway opposite the servant's entrance of the castle. She had followed the soldiers and Ramulas from a distance. Once she saw him taken into the castle, Pip ran off to see the aftermath of the dogfight in the warehouse.

Pip recognised a few lower-level people from the thieves guild in the group. She needed to ensure the dogfight was not organised by the shadows. If it was, then Pip would have to choose between Ramulas and the thieves guild.

After a few enquiries, Pip discovered the shadows only played a minor role in the fight. Pip heard many differing stories about what had transpired with Ramulas.

No-one seemed to know who this stranger was and where he had come from. Pip spread her own rumours to add to the confusion.

One story that made Pip laugh was that a man swore he witnessed the whole thing, and he saw Ramulas transform into a green dragon.

From the shadows of the laneway, Pip watched people pass. She waited for a certain person. After a few moments, a young girl in a black dress and dirty apron stepped out of the gate carrying a bucket. Her hair was pulled under a black woollen cap.

The young girl tipped the contents of the bucket into the gutter and turned to see Pip standing behind her. 'Hello, Sara,' Pip said as the young girl jumped in shock.

'Don't be sneakin' behind me, Pip,' Sara whispered.

'I need some information. A man was brought into the castle with the king and his magician. Do you know of him?'

Sara nodded. 'They have him in the tombs.'

'Try to find out what you can about him,' Pip said. 'I will return soon.'

'I will, and the master of shadows wants to speak with you,' Sara replied as she returned to the castle.

Pip nodded, knowing the master would not be pleased.

***

The sheriff looked down the path to Ramulas' farmhouse. He slowly turned his head, searching for any sign of life. The only sounds were of birds calling out in the sunny morning.

Other farmers were ploughing their fields for the next season, and farms this time of year were hives of activity. However, this was quiet. It was too quiet. He smiled and raised a hand. The ten soldiers behind him led their horses into the farm.

The sheriff followed while a silent rage seethed inside of him. He had been embarrassed twice here; his throbbing foot was a constant reminder. He would ensure Ramulas spent the rest of his days in Gullytown and his family suffered a great deal.

He approached the farmhouse as soldiers called out while searching the buildings. The sheriff knew by the confused expressions that the mother and daughters were not home, and the feelings of frustration and rage boiled within him.

Soldiers came out of the stables and barn only to look out into the fields for the family. The sheriff climbed off his horse and limped over to the door. Anger overrode any feelings of pain or discomfort in his foot.

Walking into the small house, he could see no-one was home. He stood near the stove and lay his hand on it. The metal was cold. It had not been used since the day before. The sheriff assumed they had left after the girls attacked him and the soldiers.

He walked to the kitchen table and swept the plates onto the floor. They broke as they hit the tiled floor. Two soldiers burst into the room.

The sheriff looked up. 'Burn everything. The house, barn, and stables. I want them to have nothing.'

The soldiers nodded.

By the time the sheriff had climbed back onto his horse, all three buildings were alight. The sheriff led the soldiers to the front gate to watch the buildings burn. The barn and stable caught first, followed by the house.

Columns of black smoke spiralled into the clear blue sky. The sheriff watched the surrounding fields to see if the family would show themselves.

When the stables collapsed, he gave the signal to return to Bremnon. He hoped that he would find them soon. He would not stop looking.

***

Grace groaned as she turned her head.

Jacqueline was by her side in the blink of an eye. 'Oh, my darling—how do you feel?'

Grace sat up and removed the poultice from her face, dropping it to the floor in disdain. 'What happened?'

Jacqueline watched as her youngest swayed in bed and looked around the hut. 'There was an accident.'

'What?' Grace asked as Kate sat next to her.

'A dryad brought you inside after you had an accident.'

All signs of weariness left Grace as she focused on her mother. 'You saw a dryad?'

Jacqueline nodded. 'Yes, she carried you in here. The dryad said that you have been to their home.'

Grace smiled, swinging her feet from the bed, and stood. She held her mother until a wave of dizziness passed. Then she smiled. 'I will show you where they come from.'

Grace led the way, holding her mother's hand for support. By the time they reached the tree, Jacqueline saw Kate's worried expression.

'What's wrong?'

Kate pointed across the fields toward their farm. Jacqueline's heart sank as soon as she saw the rising black smoke. Jacqueline knew that it was their farm on fire. She knew the sheriff had returned, and now their home was gone.

More than anything, she wanted Ramulas to be with them. Even if he was running from the sheriff, they would still be a family.

She wondered what Ramulas would say when he found out.

'Mother?' Kate said.

Jacqueline looked down at her daughters and almost burst into tears. Where were they going to live? What were they going to do? And how would Ramulas find them when he returned?

But she needed to be brave for her girls. 'There's nothing to worry about. When your father returns, we will sit down and plan our adventure.'

She was glad that her daughters smiled; she would have broken down otherwise. Jacqueline could not see things getting any worse for them.

***

'I asked for no trouble,' the master of shadows said in a soft tone. 'Your friend was involved in a dogfight, and then attacked soldiers guarding the king; we are known as the shadows, because as thieves we like to remain unseen.'

She looked around the same warehouse, and there were only two other shadows present. If the master planned to kill Pip, there would have been many more.

Pip bit down on her tongue. To talk out of turn could mean death for her and Jenna. The shadows prided themselves on stealth and cunning, and in one day Pip had brought attention twice to herself. She knew that the master was not pleased.

'Your friend is locked in the tombs. Forget him. There is much for you to do,' the master said with a dismissive wave as he walked to within two feet from her.

Pip took a deep breath. 'The crystal is dangerous. He needs to take it out of the city and into the mountains.'

The master leaned forward. 'I need my best thief to forget about this man and work for me.'

Pip nodded, withholding her arguments about how important the crystal was. The master smiled and told her what needed to be done.

'Pip, I have an important job that requires your unique skills.'

She looked at the master of shadows across the dim-lit room. Two of the shadow's enforcers stood behind the master. Pip only half-heard what was being said. She thought about how to help Ramulas.

'Pip, are you listening to me?' The master of shadows asked in a low voice.

She nodded.

As the master explained what he needed, Pip thought of the ramifications of what would happen if she helped Ramulas. She would be tracked down and killed. Pip could disappear, but Jenna and her children would be easy to find.

***

A small crowd had gathered at the docks, surrounding a source of excitement.

As Pip made her way to the crowd, she thought of what the master of shadows had said. People had come from across the sea. They were using parlour tricks to relieve people of their money. That would not be a problem if they had asked for permission from the shadows.

However, they were here without permission.

And that meant their problem came in the form of Pip.

Pip pushed her way through the crowd, and even though it was the middle of a sunny day, she wore her cloak and had the hood pulled down low.

Pip suppressed a laugh when she saw the scam. The leader stood behind a small table with his back to the bay. He had three cards facing up on the table, two black and one red.

'Now keep your eyes on the red card,' the man said as he flipped the cards, and moved them around swiftly, 'If you find the red card you win. Step up, this is an easy game to play.'

Pip saw through the man's false smile as his blue eyes darted behind the blond hair that fell over his face. She also noticed the man's two minders—one on either side of the table. Both were over six feet tall, covered in muscle, and wore sailor's clothing.

The man at the table gave a slight nod, and a sailor stepped out of the crowd. He pulled a bronze coin out and announced loudly that he would like to play.

Pip saw the man at the table gesture slightly with his hand. The sailor pointed to the middle card, which was quickly flipped to show the red card.

'We have a winner!' the man at the table cried out. 'Step forward and try your luck.'

Pip watched as two people came forward and quickly lost coins. However, more people were eager to play the game.

Pip stepped forward and waved away a large man who wanted to play the game. He went to protest, but paled and stepped back when Pip removed her hood.

'I wish to play your game,' Pip said, placing ten silver coins on the table.

The crowd murmured in excitement; this was more than most people earned in several months.

Pip focused on the man running the scam. His eyes widened for a fraction of a second when he saw the coins, then a calculating expression crossed his features.

'Young lady, follow the red card,' he said with a hungry smile.

Three cards were flipped to show two black and a red. They were turned face down and swiftly moved around the table. Then in a swift move, the red card was removed from the table and replaced with another card. It happened in the blink of an eye. Most people would have missed it, but Pip was better than most.

'I choose the middle card,' Pip said after the cards had stopped moving.

The man hid his smile as he turned the middle card to reveal a black card.

'I am truly sorry,' the man said with a shrug, 'you chose wrongly and have lost.'

He reached out for the coins and Pip slapped his hand away.

His two minders stepped forward and scowled at Pip.

'What are you doing?' The man asked. 'You lost and now you must pay. This is a fair game.'

'Show me the red card,' Pip said softly.

The man's eyes darted from Pip to the crowd as other people called to see the red card.

Tension began to build around the small table.

Pip's hands shot forward and held up the other two cards, before returning them. The crowd's shock quickly turned to anger when they saw the scam for what it was. Three black cards were on the table, and the red card was nowhere to be seen.

The man's minders closed in on Pip as he reached for the coins. In one fluid movement, Pip opened her cloak and pulled out one of her throwing knives. The man screamed as the knife went through the back of his hand, pinning it to the table.

Pip grabbed the coins as she vaulted the table. Lashing out with her foot, Pip kicked one of the minders in the throat. He gasped, holding his neck as he fell into the water.

With a roar, the other minder rushed at Pip, only to find she had slipped between his legs. Then he felt an explosion of pain from his buttocks as Pip stabbed him repeatedly.

He ran two steps before joining his companion in the water.

Pip turned to see the crowd had not moved; and the man knelt on the ground whimpering, his hand still stuck to the table.

'The shadows control the city of Keah,' Pip proclaimed loudly, 'We do not take kindly to those who come here and steal from our people.'

A few people cheered while others muttered in agreement. Pip grabbed the man's wrist and pulled her knife out. He gasped in pain as blood poured from the wound, and he collapsed to the ground.

Pip leaned in to whisper in the man's ear. 'I am but one of many shadows in this city. If you return, we will not be so nice,' Pip scanned the nearby ships. All faces looked down in amusement, except for the deck of one ship. She saw a few concerned faces.

Pip winked at them as she kicked the man into the water.

'I would get your friends out of the water before the sharks come.'

Pip had been sent to deliver a message, but her mind was on Ramulas. Her instinct told her that she needed to free him soon, or the kingdom would be in a great deal of trouble.

22

Shigar sat at his table, mesmerised by the crystal. Piles of books and scrolls littered the table where he sat. Time was lost to the magician as he cast spells into the artefact.

What he had before him exceeded his wildest dreams. So far, he discovered that the crystal did not come from this world, and neither did the weapons. *What a find*, Shigar thought to himself.

This would be something other magicians would dream of their whole life and never attain.

The more Shigar studied the crystal, the more questions he had for the prisoner. He sat back and sighed, not knowing what to do. There were purple shapes dancing within the crystal every time has cast spells, but he did not know what that meant. Maybe the prisoner would be able to shed some light on this.

Once Shigar was finished studying the weapons and crystal, he knew Zachary would return to treating him with disdain. So, how much of the crystal's magic should he reveal to someone who barely knew he existed?

He decided to pay a visit to the prisoner once he had studied the crystal in more depth.

***

Pip made her way back to the dark laneway opposite the castle. Ramulas' capture weighed heavily upon her shoulders. He was in the tombs, fives levels below the dungeons. There was no possible way to get him out of there.

The master of shadows was upset and wanted Pip to forget about him and return to work. But a small voice inside said that she needed to help him. Caught between her inner voice and the master, Pip knew that there would be ramifications if she made the wrong choice. She would just have to make sure no-one found out what she was doing.

People were sent to the tombs and never seen again. Why didn't Ramulas stay in the market where she had left him? Then she wouldn't have this dilemma. Pip knew she was unable to change the past. All she needed now was an opportunity.

The air behind Pip dropped in temperature, and she was instantly alert while seeming calm. Her father referred to this as the swimming duck. When you see a duck moving calmly along the surface of the water, you do not notice the rapid movement of its feet.

'Hello,' a voice behind Pip said.

Pip spun and thrust two of her knives into Oriel's stomach.

Pip's eyes widened as the knives passed through Oriel and into the crates behind her. Looking down, she saw that her hands had disappeared into Oriel's green robes.

She gasped and pulled her knives out of Oriel's image. 'Don't be sneakin' up on people like that.'

Oriel smiled. 'I am sorry, but I have come to find out what has happened to Ramulas. I have lost contact with him.'

Pip's body seemed to sag at the mention of Ramulas, and she quickly told Oriel of yesterday's events. By the time she had finished, Oriel was extremely concerned.

'If the crystal is not taken to the mountains, the legion will come through into your city. I have shown you visions of them, and I have seen the soldiers of this city. They will be no match for the legion.'

Oriel's statement and demeanour made Pip very uncomfortable. She was not sure what she could do.

'How long until the legion comes to Keah?' Pip asked.

Oriel shook her head. 'They will come any day. Once they arrive, the warlords and legion will kill and enslave as they move north to find me. Nothing will be able to stop them.'

The urgency in Oriel's voice shocked Pip. She knew that Oriel feared the warlords, but what could she do? Ramulas was in the tombs, and it would take a miracle to break him out.

Then an idea came to the young thief, bringing a smile to her face. 'Could you use your magic to help me get Ramulas out of the tombs?'

Oriel shook her head and smiled sadly at Pip. 'I am very weak. Just coming to you is draining my magic. You must find a way to free Ramulas soon.'

Pip nodded. 'Don't worry, I will.'

The young thief put on a brave face while wondering how she would get him out of the tombs. She knew this was urgent and she would need help, but Pip would find no help from the shadows.

'Ramulas is strong,' Oriel said. 'Once you free him, he will know what to do.'

Oriel looked at Pip, knowing that Ramulas had not had enough training to remember who he was and what he was capable of. If he stayed locked up for too long away from his family, she knew that it would destroy him.

Oriel hoped that Pip would be able to free Ramulas before he lost faith. If that happened, everyone in the kingdom would suffer. 'I must return. I am weak. Do what you can to free him. He is our only hope.'

Pip silently cursed as Oriel faded in front of her. She needed to free Ramulas as soon as she could, but had no idea where to start. The feeling of letting down another person she cared for resurfaced, followed by a sense of failure.

Pip's world seemed to close in on her, and she found it hard to breathe. So much to do in so little time. Where would she start?

***

Remus, the warlords, and the red wizards stood in silence watching the blue energy strand. It had grown to almost four feet long and was close to forming a doorway. However, something had happened. The strand moved through the air in jerky movements.

Spells into the black hole told the warlords that the magician on Oriel's world was the cause of this. His magical prying had stalled the process of the energy strand.

Remus had had enough of the delays and setbacks. He would handle this personally. He instructed the warlords and red wizards to cast spells that would allow him to go to the crystal.

There was no word of the two soldiers who had been sent through the crystal. And any more sent through would give warning to the magic-user.

He knew he could only be on Oriel's new world for a short while, but while he was there Remus would destroy the magic-user, cause as much havoc as he could, and anchor the crystal. He would give the people on Oriel's world a taste of what to expect when the legion came.

***

Ramulas had eaten the loaf and drunk the water from the jug. He had his fill when half the loaf was eaten, however, his anxiety of the predicament he was in could only be held at bay through eating. His hand continued to throb, but the act of eating distracted him.

He worried about Jacqueline and his girls and hoped they were coping without him. But he needed a way to get to the crystal.

The king and his magician did not understand how much danger they were in. But Ramulas could not talk in fear of them finding out about his daughters.

The concept of time was lost to Ramulas as he paced back and forth in his small cell. He replayed in his mind the circumstances that landed him in this cell. He thought about how he would have acted differently if he could go back in time.

Light footsteps coming down the hallway broke his train of thought, and Ramulas stopped pacing. Shadows played upon the wall as the person carrying a torch approached. Ramulas felt his heartbeat quicken as anxiety threatened to overwhelm him.

Then the Khilli stopped outside the door. 'Do not worry, I have come alone,' he said softly.

Ramulas watched the door fearfully, waiting for James to jump out. The Khilli saw his apprehension and wanted to calm Ramulas.

'I remember you from Bremnon,' the Khilli said with a broad smile. 'You showed great courage fighting the hell hound. After telling the tale to my people, they see you as a warrior.'

Ramulas felt a sense of pride at the Khilli's praise, and a small smile played upon his lips. It was the first smile since his capture.

'You have been locked away from your family without knowing when you will see them. I understand what you are going through,' the Khilli said as he lowered his eyes.

'How could you understand?' Ramulas retorted, feeling anger rise within him. 'The Khilli are guards for the sheriffs and the royal family. What could you know about being apart from your family?'

'Not by choice,' the Khilli said as he raised his head to lock eyes with Ramulas. 'My people are as much prisoner as you are now.'

'What do you mean?'

The Khilli looked past Ramulas with a faraway expression. 'Thirty years ago, my people hunted the plains between Turtha and Covedon. The king had sent messages to us several times asking for our warriors to work for the kingdom. The messengers were told that we were a free people and would not fight for another man's cause.

'The king first asked the chief and a few warriors to Keah as guests. After that visit, the king sent for the whole of my people. Both times we refused.

'Then one day, the king himself arrived in our homeland. He came personally to offer his apologies for asking for warriors. The king came with gifts for the women and children of my people, but not enough for all. He said that if my people came to Keah, each would receive a gift and each warrior a weapon of the finest steel.

'My father was the leader of our people. He thought it would be dishonourable to refuse the king after he came with gifts.

'I remember that day well. I was almost of age to be a warrior of my people. It would be the first time in many generations since the whole of the Khilli people had left the open plains.

'The journey took three days to reach the city of Keah. The king and his men showed my people much kindness along the way. Once inside the castle, the king brought my people to a large room—I now know it was one of the training chambers. Along one wall was lined with the finest weapons. Across from the weapons, there was an opening to another chamber. In this second chamber, tables were filled with bolts of colourful silk and food. The women and children were told to enter this chamber.

'Once we had all crossed over, a large metal gate dropped down and separated us from the warriors. Soldiers rushed in and pushed the warriors away from the gate.

'The men grabbed the weapons from the walls and screamed for their wives and children. The king walked out into our side and told the warriors that if they did not drop their weapons, we all would die. The weapons fell to the floor.

'The king announced that he would have his Khilli warriors after all. If the warriors did not do as they were told, their families would suffer. For the sake of their people, the warriors agreed to the king's terms. The king allowed the men to spend a few nights a week with their families, but not all warriors could see their families at one time.

'At that time, our people numbered six hundred warriors. They were divided into five separate groups. Each would spend a day and a night with their families, then others would take their turn.

'Some younger warriors would talk to my father about killing the king and his soldiers, then fighting our way out of the castle. These warriors were very brave and fearless, as they are today. My father said this could be done, but at what cost—how many women and children would be lost? Our people would lose at least half our number.

'We must wait for a time to come when the threat to our families has passed. Then the warriors will seek their revenge. Six months after our people's capture, I became of age and performed the warrior's ritual. The king fell ill soon after and died. His son Zachary was crowned the new king. My father went to Zachary begging for our freedom, but the new king did not listen.

'Since that time, my father has gone to ride his horse through the stars. This is what you would call the afterlife. Now I lead my people. Zachary is not as strict as his father. Half of the women and children walk through the castle freely, while the others are locked away.

'We pass our memories and culture from parent to child. This is in the hope that one day we will be a free people once again. So, you see, I know what it is like to be a prisoner,' the Khilli finished.

'I am sorry for what has happened to your people,' Ramulas said.

'Do not be sorry,' the Khilli said, 'this was not of your doing. My name is K'ayden. I will send my daughter down with food for you. Only accept food from her.'

'Thank you for your kindness. My name is Ramulas,' he said holding up his injured hand. 'I did not know what you were trying to tell me about the tray.'

A stern expression crossed K'ayden's face. 'You must be strong at all times. They will try to break your spirit.'

'What do you mean?'

'You need to be strong. My daughter will come soon. Her name is Ch'oak.'

K'ayden saw Ramulas' confusion at the name. 'In our language, *ch'oak* means "little one".'

K'ayden quickly waved before walking away. 'Little one' was the same name Ramulas called Grace. The story of the Khilli saddened Ramulas. The only thing he ever knew about them was that they worked for the royal family. Not once did ever hear the slightest rumour about them being held captive.

He needed Oriel to help him out of this predicament. She knew magic and would be able to get him out.

A few minutes after K'ayden left, Ramulas felt extremely tired. He looked at the pile of straw that would be his bed. In his sleep, Oriel had always come for him. That thought comforted him as he fell asleep.

***

Ramulas woke to absolute agony. His hand felt as if it were going to explode. He opened his eyes and was shocked to find James kneeling over him. James held Ramulas' injured hand and was squeezing it. Ramulas screamed in pain.

James reached back with a hand and punched Ramulas in the face so hard that his head bounced off the stone floor under the straw.

'Oriel!' Ramulas screamed.

James hit Ramulas two more times in the chest, spreading the pain throughout his body. Ramulas had never felt this helpless before. Where was the magic inside of him that Oriel spoke about? Why couldn't he do anything?

James smiled without emotion and raised his hand once more. Ramulas winced as it came down.

'That is enough!' Shigar said.

He spoke with such authority that James held his hand in check. 'How am I to ask him about the crystal when you continue to beat him? Leave now, and let me work.'

As James walked out, Shigar looked at the battered form of Ramulas. He knew Zachary would have instructed James to question the prisoner. At this rate, the man would die before Shigar found out anything about the crystal and the weapons.

He looked down and saw the man's vest wrapped around his right hand. Shigar bent down to unwrap the vest. The prisoner made a feeble attempt to push him away.

'Let me look at your hand,' Shigar said softly.

He unwrapped the vest and clucked his tongue as he saw the swollen it was. Even in the dim light of the cell, he could tell that the hand was broken.

Shigar left the cell and returned a few moments later with K'ayden. With the Khilli's help, they brought Ramulas out of the tombs to a cell where Shigar could examine the hand better.

It was plain to see that bones and ligaments were broken in the back of the man's hand. Shigar waved his hands over Ramulas while chanting a spell of healing. Ramulas moaned softly as the spell took effect. Once that was done, the magician cast another one and Ramulas was asleep.

'I feel for him,' Shigar said to K'ayden. 'If he does not tell the king about the crystal, he will die very soon.'

They brought Ramulas back to the tombs. K'ayden took one last look at him before following Shigar. His heart was heavy seeing Ramulas the way he was. He had proven to have the heart of a warrior.

K'ayden was powerless to stop the beatings. If he tried to help, his family would suffer.

**

No matter how many times Shigar studied the crystal, each brought a sense of wonderment. The crystal seemed to animate every time he cast spells into it. He wondered what that meant.

The shapes within the crystal had begun to dance, and the crystal itself had changed. Six appendages had appeared on it: three on either side. Through a looking glass, they resembled the legs of an insect.

The weapons were another matter. They appeared and felt like wood. Even when struck, they sounded as wood should. However, they would not burn or even be marked when cut. James had no effect when he struck them with a mace. After a few swings with the mace, the bench collapsed and the weapons were unscathed.

Shigar looked up from his work and realised it was time that he spoke to the prisoner about the crystal. He made his way through the hallways to the dungeon before descending down to the tombs.

He came to the door with his torch to find the prisoner sitting on the bed of straw. 'Ah, you are awake. How is your hand?'

Ramulas looked down at his hand; it was stiff and sore, but it had healed. 'What happened?' he mumbled.

The left side of Ramulas' face had swollen and his eye had closed over from James's beating.

'I healed you,' Shigar replied, knowing that this man was somehow special. Why else would he be in possession of the crystal, which held foreign magic? It was strange and yet so captivating. And it was the first time he had heard of weapons like the prisoner carried, let alone be able to examine them.

'Thank you,' Ramulas said. 'How long have I been here?'

'You arrived yesterday.'

'The crystal. It brings danger,' Ramulas said with urgency. 'It must be taken far from here.'

'Tell me what danger it brings,' Shigar said with growing curiosity.

Ramulas shook his head and instantly regretted it as waves of pain shot through him. 'I am the only one who knows where to take the crystal. It needs to be moved very soon.'

'Tell me what the crystal is and why you need to move it.'

After a few seconds of deliberating, Ramulas slowly shook his head. 'I cannot tell you.'

'If you do not talk, James will come to you again. He is the one who broke your hand. He likes to hurt people, and you will soon die at his hands.'

'But my family ...' Ramulas said.

Shigar's eyes widened at this news. A significant piece of the puzzle had fallen into place. 'You have a family.'

He could see the prisoner trying to think of something to say. Maybe if he approached this in a different way, he would find the answers he was looking for.

'I know you are scared; you have every right to be,' Shigar said. 'I want to help you. The items you brought into the city are unique. I wish to find out everything I can about them.' Ramulas gave Shigar a wary glance. 'I know you do not want to talk, so I will tell you what I know. The crystal and weapons came from another world.' Shigar noticed the prisoner gave a slight nod. 'You have a connection to the crystal, and you travelled two days to bring it here. Your wife knows about the crystal and your journey here.' Shigar had hit a nerve, the prisoner's eyes were full of fear at the mention of his wife. 'The king thinks you will use the crystal to harm him and his daughter. That is why James will eventually kill you,' Shigar said sadly.

'I need to move the crystal to protect the kingdom,' Ramulas blurted out.

Shigar raised his hands as he shrugged. 'All I want to do is study the crystal and your weapons. I will leave you time to think. I am not your enemy. If you help me, I, in return, may help you.'

23

Pip stood outside the burnt building, reliving the bitter memories. This had been the home of her family, the place where so much laughter made everyone feel welcome. She remembered it as if it was yesterday. A magician had been hired to burn down the house. A part of Pip wanted to push away the memories of her parents being taken away—their neighbours standing by and doing nothing. But she could not forget.

At that moment, Pip knew that she would one day kill the magician.

A year later, the same magician was found burnt alive in an abandoned house. Pip loathed magic users, and would not allow them to hurt her family again. However, Ramulas was a different type of magic user. He was different in so many ways.

A wave of guilt washed over Pip. She blamed herself. Not only for what happened to her parents, but Jenna's assault and Ramulas being in the tombs. Why did everyone close to her have to suffer?

The master of shadows had said for Pip to forget about Ramulas and return to work. Pip quickly shook her head. She will continue working, but would also try to find a way to help Ramulas.

***

Pip waited in the laneway opposite the castle until Sara came out of the gate. She waited to see if anyone followed the young girl before walking after her.

In a few seconds, Pip was by Sara's side. 'What have you heard?'

'They have your friend in the tombs. They found some magical items with him. They want to know what it is,' Sara whispered. 'James has seen him twice.'

Pip was instantly concerned. No-one lasted long when James came to see them. 'I need to get into the castle, Sara. Can you find me a job in the kitchen?'

Sara nodded. 'Of course. When do you want to come?'

'Tomorrow.'

'Meet me an hour after dawn, and dress as I do.'

Pip thanked Sara before walking away. She was deep in thought about what she could do to help Ramulas. Once in the castle, Pip had no doubt that she could enter any room, even the dungeon, without being seen. But the tombs were another matter.

To help Ramulas escape would take a lot of planning, time, and people. Those three luxuries were out of Pip's reach. She needed to do what she could without the help of the shadows or the master's knowledge. Pip worked well under pressure and hoped that opportunities came her way.

***

Ramulas sat in the corner of his cell deep in thought. The magician had healed his hand and spoke about wanting to help him. Ramulas was not sure what to think.

The magician had known things about him and the crystal that Ramulas had not told anyone. He seemed genuinely curious about it and Ramulas' weapons. When he said that James would soon kill him, Ramulas did not doubt that for a moment.

The magician had also offered to help him in exchange for information. Ramulas was unsure whether he should talk, and if he did how much would he say.

A soft noise at the door brought Ramulas out of his reverie.

Looking over at the door, Ramulas saw a small dark-skinned figure standing in the torchlight. He stood and slowly made his way to the door.

'Hello, did your father send you?'

The small girl nodded. She was as tall as Grace but lithe. She wore a plain brown dress and had long black hair that was woven into beads. Her hand reached through the bars and handed Ramulas an apple before shooting a fearful glance up the hall.

'Thank you,' Ramulas said as she raced away.

He smiled, looking down at the apple. It was strange that something so small and insignificant could mean so much to him. But Ramulas knew that after everything he held so dear had been taken from him, something as simple as the gift of an apple meant the world.

Ramulas closed his eyes as he slowly ate the apple, savouring every bite. He even ate the core, not wanting to leave any evidence. Even in this dark place, Ramulas had found a reason to smile.

After a few minutes of pacing, Ramulas heard footsteps coming down the hallway. His smile faded as he placed himself against the rear wall. His heart began to race in anticipation of who might be coming to the cell. The magician soon stood at the door with a smile.

Relief flooded through Ramulas as he saw it was not James.

'Hello. I have come in the hope of sharing magical knowledge with you,' the magician said.

Ramulas stepped away from the wall and wondered what the magician wanted. And how much could he say without any harm coming to his family?

'King Zachary was very worried when I told him that I felt your magic and the presence of the crystal come into this world,' the magician said with a wave of his hand. 'He thinks you might use its powers against him or the kingdom. That is why James will keep coming to see you.'

Ramulas held out his hands in a pleading gesture. 'But the crystal will bring something very bad to this land. That is why I must move it soon.'

'You need to tell me what this bad thing is, so that we can prepare for its arrival.'

A bitter laugh escaped Ramulas' mouth. He had seen the soldiers in the city of Keah. They would stand no chance against the first legion.

It would be like letting a pack of wolves amongst a flock of sheep. 'You would never understand,' Ramulas said with a shake of his head.

Shigar wanted to scream in frustration at the prisoner's pigheaded behaviour. He was doing his best to help this man. The only way for that to happen was for him to find out about the crystal.

Shigar decided to try a different tactic. 'I have been rude in not introducing myself. My name is Shigar, the king's magician. What should I call you?'

Ramulas was silent for a moment before saying, 'Thomas.'

Shigar knew the name Thomas was false, but he shrugged. At least he had a name for the prisoner.

'Well, Thomas,' Shigar said, 'I will talk, and if you do not want to answer, I will understand. However, a simple nod or shake of your head will suffice. I cannot tell the king what you have not said.'

Ramulas nodded.

'The crystal and your strange weapons—I take it they are connected in some way.'

Ramulas thought for a moment. They had both come from the world where Oriel said he was born. He looked at Shigar and nodded.

'Come closer so I can see you properly,' Shigar said.

Ramulas stepped closer to the bars. Shigar looked at him from top to bottom. He motioned for Ramulas to show him his hands, which Ramulas did.

'You have worked on a farm or workshop most of your life. You have the hands and body of someone used to hard work.'

Again, Ramulas nodded.

'The crystal and the weapons came into your possession around the same time. And they are not from this world.'

Ramulas nodded.

'The use of magic is quite new to you. Your family knows about your magical ability and your journey to move the crystal.'

Ramulas stiffened, which to Shigar was as good as a nod. 'I have been studying the crystal. It is quite fascinating. I have seen shapes dancing within it, but it has started to change. It is growing legs.'

'It has begun to anchor,' Ramulas said with panic in his voice.

'What will happen when the crystal anchors?'

'Then it will be too late. Everyone will be enslaved or killed,' Ramulas said in a defeated tone.

'Everyone in the castle?' Shigar asked with concern.

Ramulas slowly shook his head as his shoulders sagged. 'Everyone in the kingdom.'

Shigar was stunned. The prisoner said the statement so calmly that he knew it was true. He needed to study the crystal more in order to find a way of moving it himself. He focused on the prisoner once more. They had caught more than they bargained for with this one.

'If I were to move the crystal, where would I take it?' Shigar asked.

Ramulas looked at him in disbelief. 'Only I am able to know where to move it. The people who made the crystal have very strong magical powers—that's why you need to let me go.'

This was another shock for Shigar. The prisoner mentioned powerful magic users making the crystal. And he knew it came from another world. This was very interesting, and yet daunting at the same time.

'I am sorry, but the king sees you as a threat. I cannot grant you freedom. But I will talk to him for you.'

Ramulas held his hands out in a helpless gesture. 'I did not choose the burden of the crystal. I am only doing this to keep my family safe,' he said as another bitter laugh escaped his lips. 'When the crystal anchors, it will be too late.'

'I will see what can be done,' Shigar said with a sad smile.

As Shigar walked away, he viewed the prisoner in a different light. He knew the name Thomas was a lie. However, everything else the prisoner had said was true. He knew that this man was doing what was right, and doing it for the safety of his family.

Shigar could see that the prisoner had a code of honour in that he lived by. He would talk to Zachary and try to explain that the prisoner needed to be freed and move the crystal before something bad happens.

Then he pushed that thought away. Zachary would not listen to reason; he had not been reasonable for many years. His daughter and paranoia ruled his thoughts. The prisoner in the tombs had more passion and character than most men he had seen.

For a fleeting moment, Shigar thought that the prisoner would make a great leader, better than Zachary. As soon as the thought entered his head, the magician was shocked. Where did this come from?

He knew that he was not happy within the castle, but why would he think that his salvation might come from the prisoner?

Thomas' eyes told another story. It was as if he had already seen what would happen if the crystal was not moved.

***

Pip sat in the darkest corner of the bar. She wore an old shawl and slowly drank ale from a pewter mug. Upon casual inspection, Pip looked like an old sea witch from the docks. Her hands and face were covered in glue. As the glue dried, it caused her skin to wrinkle.

Her shawl was left each night on one of the fishing boats. Anyone that walked past would smell the strong aroma of the ocean. Pip would cough and wheeze each time she spoke to the serving girl.

She had been monitoring the movements of a rich merchant who had come to Keah from across the far sea. He was accompanied by two large dark-skinned guards who wore long silken blue pants and lethal-looking curved swords. They were bare-chested and covered in tattoos.

With them was a small, rat-faced man whose eyes would dart from person to person. The merchant himself was a rotund fellow of middle age, which was very unusual for a Nihon; they were usually thin. He wore white silk robes. He had gold rings on each finger and he had a weakness for pastries.

The pastries were Pip's key to relieving the merchant of his wares. The top floor of the inn had been reserved for the merchant and his party. Two more large guards stayed in the room to guard his wealth. Pip needed to leave no trace of who committed the crime.

Pip could smell the pastries coming out of the oven in the kitchen. She slowly stood, knowing that timing was everything.

Pip heard the tray of pastries being placed on the bench in the kitchen above the noise. She slowly hobbled toward the bar near the merchant. As Pip reached her position, the tray of pastries came out of the kitchen carried by the serving girl.

She opened a small pouch and emptied the contents into her hand.

Pip grabbed the serving girl by the shoulder as she walked by.

''Ere now, young un,' Pip croaked, 'How bout one o these for old Gertie?'

'You there, stay away from that tray!' the rat-faced man called out.

'Oh, there's sure to be enough for all of us. Maybe I could have a bit o this one or that one. Oh, there's a nice one,' Pip croaked hopefully.

The rat-faced man had reached them, and Pip released the serving girl while giving him a sour look. As she walked back to her table, Pip hid her smile. Every time she had pointed to a pastry, Pip sprinkled a fine white powder over them. It blended in perfectly with the icing sugar.

This powder was a powerful laxative which would have them losing control of their bowels. And they all loved pastries. After they finished eating, Pip silently watched them go upstairs.

**

The top floor was in turmoil. Pip sat next to the first-storey window overlooking the street. It was dark and the only lights showing came from lanterns and candles within buildings.

She heard the stampede of desperate men running to the lavatory. Pip forced the window after hearing the stampede from the room. By the smell in the room, someone had been too late.

Looking around the room, Pip saw a number of fancy chests and trunks. However, she was only here for one. After a quick search, Pip found what she was looking for. Pip stopped at the window and looked back at the treasures, but the commotion outside the room had brought unwanted attention from other guests at the inn.

After dumping her shawl, Pip ran across the rooftops until she came to a marked chimney. She knelt by it and removed a few bricks for the chest to fit inside then covered the hole. It was time for a bath and to prepare for her first day of work in the castle.

Pip could not get thoughts of Ramulas out of her head. The sense of guilt weighed heavily upon her shoulders. She would do everything she could to help him. Pip did not want to fail another person she cared for.

***

Grace woke to the sound of someone calling her name. She sat up with a smile, knowing the dryads had returned. With slow, deliberate movements, Grace climbed out of bed without waking her mother or sister.

Coming out of Matthew's hut, she smiled as two dryads stepped out of the shadows. Grace quickly ran to them. The sound of leaves crunching beneath her feet broke the night's silence. 'Mother and Kate told me that you came before,' she said with excitement.

Eady nodded. 'We felt your magic grow, and I helped you.'

It was exciting for Grace to have these dryads come again. They seemed to be half-tree and half-person. They took away the worries Grace was feeling with her da gone, having to leave home, and knowing that it burnt down.

'Would you like to come to our home?' Eady said. 'Our children would like to play with you.'

Grace nodded, and the dryad took her hand, leading her into the tree. She was surprised to find they came out into a different part of the forest.

Even though it was night, Grace saw that they were in a clearing surrounded by thick forest. She could see a pond with various smooth rocks as its border. Small fish swam in the water, glowing with faint light.

Grace was in awe. 'What is this place?'

Eady smiled. 'This clearing is very special to us.' Then she swept her hand to the water. 'This is the mystical pool where we made our transformation from people to dryads. To become one of us, all you need to do is step into the pool willingly.'

Grace shook her head. Her da had gone, and she needed to go back to her sister and mother.

Eady saw her hesitation. 'Very well. We will await your decision. But for now, would you like to see the rest of our family?'

Grace nodded then gasped as hundreds of male, female, and child dryads emerged from the surrounding trees. The adults walked towards Grace with welcoming smiles, with the children close behind.

'If you join our family, you will be able to play with our children.'

A thought occurred to Grace. 'How long have you been in the forest?'

'Over two hundred years.'

Grace was shocked. 'You don't look that old.'

She placed a hand on Grace's arm. 'Once you become a dryad, you don't grow old.'

'How can you not grow old? Everyone grows old.'

The dryad smiled. 'This forest has magic, just like you do. That is why we want you to join our family.'

Grace thought of the predicament her own family were in and it caused her to sigh.

'What is wrong?' The dryad asked.

'Our home is gone. We are living in Matthew's hut, and mother said we have not much food.'

Eady smiled and waved her hand behind Grace. A few dryads melted into the trees, only to return a moment later with armfuls of fruits and berries.

'Take this to your family, and we will call on you again.'

Grace nodded dumbly, not knowing how they pulled food out of the trees.

24

Pip made her way down several laneways before coming to the abandoned house where Ramulas' horse and cart were kept. She stopped her hand just before reaching the latch. The flower had been moved.

Someone had entered the yard.

Pip stepped away from the gate and entered the house next door. She found this house also vacant. Pip climbed up the side and onto the roof. She peeked over into the yard next door.

The horse and cart were gone. In their place were four soldiers. Two hid behind the fence and two were inside the house; all four were alert. Pip's heart skipped a beat. How had they found the horse and cart?

The shadows had never lost anything in that yard before. Pip quickly climbed down from the roof and made her way into the lane. She walked away toward the market. Pip needed to find out how the soldiers had found the horse and cart.

After speaking to several of her contacts, Pip learned what had happened. The king, his magician, and the soldiers returned to where they stopped the carts. The magician had used spells to track their movements to the abandoned house. The horse and cart were removed, and soldiers were now watching the house.

Pip decided to keep a low profile and try to find out as much as she could without causing trouble.

***

Ramulas had had the urge to relieve himself for a while, and it was getting progressively worse. However, there was no chamber pot or bucket for him to use. Ramulas needed to go soon, and he had called for someone up the hall a few times.

No-one had answered, and the pressure was almost unbearable in his lower stomach.

A minute later, Ramulas ran to the rear corner of his cell that was clear of straw. He pulled down his pants, then squatted down to empty his bladder and bowels. Ramulas covered his waste with some of the straw.

After a few minutes, the smell of his waste filled the small cell. It did not seem to matter how much straw he used, it still smelled. A sense of shame washed over Ramulas that he was forced into such an act.

A short time later, he heard footsteps coming down the hallway, accompanied by the flickering light of a torch. Shadows danced along the walls as the people came closer. The king and James appeared in the doorway.

'What is that foul smell?' Zachary asked while wrinkling his nose in disdain. 'This prisoner has relieved himself in his own cell. Why, he is no better than a pig.'

'I tried to call someone,' Ramulas said.

'You dare speak to your king!' Zachary screamed.

James took this as his cue. He lay the torch on the floor, unlocked the door and walked into the cell.

Ramulas' heart began to beat rapidly as James walked towards him. James wore the same cold smile as when he last beat Ramulas.

Ramulas' body was still stiff from the previous beatings, but this time he would fight back.

Ramulas was terrified of conflict, but he would not lie down and be treated like some animal.

He waited until James was three feet from him, then Ramulas feinted to the right and spun to the left. He hit James in the body with his left hand before delivering a right cross to the brute's jaw.

Ramulas was rewarded with a soft grunt from James. A boot to Ramulas' chest sent him bouncing off the rear wall of the cell. James pounced onto Ramulas as quick as a cat, raining blow after blow upon him. Ramulas did the best he could to protect himself.

However, James's strength rocked his body, sending pain through every fibre of his being.

'Take the pig to his new home,' Zachary said.

Ramulas was grabbed by the hair and pulled kicking into the hallway. As he was dragged from his cell, Ramulas saw the king following with an evil smile. They passed a few doors before Ramulas was thrown into another cell.

He landed in two inches of mud that covered the floor. James followed Ramulas in and kicked him around the cell. Several times, Ramulas tried to move out of the way but only succeeded in slipping in the mud. James only stopped when every part of Ramulas was completely covered in the wet, clammy filth.

'When you wish to talk about the crystal's magic, I will release you,' Zachary said.

James walked out and locked the door behind him, and the two walked away.

Ramulas lay in the mud, staring at the ceiling. His body ached from the beating, and each breath hurt. Just when the simple act of receiving an apple had made him smile, the beating he had received, and being covered in mud, brought his morale to a new low.

Ramulas had always taken pride in his appearance. He might not have been able to afford the best clothing, but he had always ensured to dress well. Now that was taken from him.

He did not know how he would react when K'ayden or Ch'oak came to see him. What would they do if they saw him in this state? A stronger sense of shame washed over Ramulas. What would he say if Jacqueline and his girls saw him like this?

He stood and did the best he could to remove as much mud as possible. However, that sent Ramulas into a deep depression. It did not matter how much mud Ramulas removed, he was surrounded by it, and the damp, musty smell seemed to cling to his bones.

Once again, time had no meaning for Ramulas. He was left in a mud-covered cell with only his thoughts for company. After a while, his eyes became heavy, and Ramulas decided to close his eyes.

***

Remus stood with the warlords and red wizards watching the energy strand. It still moved while jerking sporadically. All magic had been focused to stabilise the strand to allow Remus to enter Oriel's world.

The magic-user on Oriel's world was still using spells to study the crystal. This delayed its anchoring. Whether he knew what he was doing was irrelevant to Remus; the magician on Oriel's world would suffer.

It was as if the warlords took two steps forward, only to be pushed back one. Even though things were not going to plan, Remus did not show his anger and frustration. That would wait until he crossed over.

Once the magician had been dealt with, the crystal would be anchored. Then Remus would see what fun he could have before he needed to return. He wanted to take his rage out on as many people as possible in the shortest amount of time.

***

Pip waited outside the servants' entrance to the castle. After a moment, Sara joined her. Sara checked Pip's clothing; they were almost identical.

'Follow me to the kitchen and keep your eyes down,' Sara said 'If someone talks, just ignore them and keep walking.'

Pip nodded and followed Sara into the courtyard of the castle.

In the early morning light, Pip stole quick glances and saw several servants rushing from one place to another. The eight soldiers in the courtyard appeared bored and were not paying anyone close attention. Pip suppressed a smile as they entered the castle.

The two guards at the door gave the two a casual glance as they entered. Sara led Pip through a series of hallways that were filled with servants. Again, no-one gave Pip and Sara a second glance. Pip heard the kitchen before she saw it.

The clamour of noise did not prepare Pip for the turmoil in the kitchen. The seemed to be a chorus of voices mixed in with the banging of pots and pans.

It was a large open space with two long wooden tables dividing the room. Against the rear wall were two fire pits and several ovens. There were at least thirty servants cooking, preparing, or cleaning.

Sara took Pip through the people to a fat balding man who wore a dirty white apron. He was yelling out orders and looked quite stressed. 'Roger, this is my sister. She cannot talk, but she will work for food.'

Roger's annoyed expression brightened at the news. He looked Pip up and down. 'Take her to help wash the pots and stoke the fires.'

Sara nodded, and Roger turned to Pip and spoke loudly while using arm gestures, 'You help clean and keep fires burning.'

Pip nodded while biting back a retort. Roger turned away from them and continued to yell instructions.

Sara led Pip first to the ovens and then the washing area. She said that Pip was there to help. Sara said goodbye before going to work. She told Pip she would try to find out more about Ramulas.

After a few hours, the front of Pip's dress was soaked, and her hands had several splinters from the wood. But Pip did not complain; she performed each job that was given to her and adapted well. She had memorised the hallways coming into the kitchen and listened to the gossip in the kitchen. Not one person had mentioned Ramulas in the tombs.

***

Ramulas stood in the doorway of the barn, squinting in the midday sun. He watched as Grace chased the horse around the fields. He communicated with the horse every time Grace fell behind. It would slow, allowing her to catch up before taking off once again.

Ramulas smiled to himself. He was content with his life and family. Then a jolt of pain shot through Ramulas' body. He heard someone banging metal on metal far away in the distance.

'Eat your food, pig.'

Ramulas almost cried when realising he was in the muddy cell. He wanted so much to return to the dream with his family, but he was in hell so far away from home. And he had no idea when, or if, they would release him.

He looked around the dim cell and saw through the faint light that a jug and loaf of bread had been dropped near the door.

Ramulas' whole body was stiff and sore as he moved. But he needed food and water. His throat was parched and his tongue swollen. If Ramulas did not eat or drink, he knew that he would be too weak to fight back or do anything.

He reached the bread and picked it up out of the mud. Half of the loaf was covered and could not be eaten. The jug had tipped and Ramulas saw there was only enough for a mouthful.

'I need more food,' he croaked through the bars, 'More water.'

He heard men laughing nearby. 'Pigs eat what they are given. If you talk again, James will see you.'

Holding the bread, Ramulas attempted to brush away some of the mud. But he seemed to spread it over the loaf. Despair threatened to overwhelm Ramulas as he ate what little of the loaf he could.

Ramulas laughed bitterly as he thought of the crystal. When would it anchor and when would the legion come through? He had done all of this for his family, and now he had failed them.

Ramulas' eyes filled with tears as a sense of helplessness became his new world. He wondered what had become of Pip. Did she escape? Or was she locked away as well?

***

Lunch was served to the workers in the kitchen. Pip joined the line and found Sara with a small Khilli girl.

230

'Follow us after you get your food,' Sara whispered.

Pip nodded and followed the line until she was handed a bowl of thick broth and a chunk of bread. She found Sara and the Khilli girl near the ovens. When they were all seated, Sara looked over her shoulder before speaking.

'This is Ch'oak. She has seen your friend in the tombs.'

Pip's jaw dropped being close to someone who had seen Ramulas. 'How did you see him?'

'My father first met this man in Bremnon, and in this man, my father saw the heart of a warrior. My father has spoken to him in the tombs. He has told me to bring him food.'

'How does he fare?' Pip asked.

'He has been beaten, and his eyes are full of sadness.' This statement broke Pip's heart. She remembered Ramulas being happy when speaking of his family, and she saw he had a strong spirit. That spirit would soon be broken if Pip did not get him out of the tombs.

'I need to see him. How do I get into the tombs?' Pip asked.

Ch'oak shook her head. 'No-one is to go down there. Through the dungeons is the only way, but the guards will see you.'

'How do you go down there to see my friend?' Pip asked.

'I have always gone into the tombs. My father teaches me the ways of our people. There are secret ways only known to the Khilli.'

'Is there another way into the tombs?'

Ch'oak shook her head and Pip's mind began to race. There was a way to free Ramulas. She just had not found it yet.

'I will come to work here for the next few days,' she said to Ch'oak, 'If something happens to my friend, I want you to tell me.'

The Khilli nodded.

Pip spent the rest of the break trying to formulate a plan to free Ramulas. There needed to be some way to get him out of the castle without angering the master of shadows. Her chances were slim, but she would find a way.

***

Jacqueline stood in stunned silence staring at the abundance of food on the table. Grace waved at the fruit with a smile as if she had performed a magic trick.

'Where did all of this come from?' Jacqueline asked.

'I told you. The dryads gave this to us. They know we have not got much food, so they helped us.'

Jacqueline shook her head, not wanting to believe what she saw with her own eyes. There was enough food for her and the girls for a couple of weeks. One of her prayers had been answered by the gods. She had spent most of the time praying to the goddess of harvest and the god of luck.

But what would this mean? Grace had said she had gone to the dryad's home once again. Jacqueline did not like this situation. Ramulas was gone, the sheriff searched for their whole family. She did not want to lose Grace as well.

The aroma of the fresh food filled the small hut, but she needed to say her piece. 'Grace, I do not want you going with the dryads again.'

Her daughter's smile disappeared. 'But they are my friends,' Grace said, waving her hand once more at the food. 'And look, they are helping us.'

Frustration and worry for her husband came to the surface. 'Grace, your father has gone! The sheriff has burnt our farm, and we have nowhere to go. I do not want you leaving my side.'

Grace could not understand why her mother was so angry. The dryads had given them food and were her friends. It was boring on Matthew's farm and she wanted to go home.

'This isn't fair!' she yelled at Jacqueline, 'You never let me do anything.'

Before Jacqueline could respond, Grace ran out of the hut.

25

Ramulas awoke to the rattle of keys as the door was unlocked. His muscles protested as he sat up in the mud and saw four soldiers by the door. He stood and backed against the rear wall. The mud seemed to have seeped into his soul.

'Your wife is here,' one of the soldiers said. 'She wants to see you.'

Ramulas' heart skipped a beat. How did they find Jacqueline? Was she hurt? Where were his daughters?

Did his ears deceive him? Was this some strange dream? The soldier who spoke looked at Ramulas expecting a response, when none was forthcoming, he looked at the muddy floor. He did not want to enter and get his boots dirty.

'You need to bathe and have clean clothes before you see your wife,' the soldier said.

These words prompted Ramulas to take a few hesitant steps toward the door. The soldiers stepped back, allowing him room. A few feet from the door, Ramulas stopped. He was unsure if this was a prelude to another beating.

'Hurry,' the soldier said, 'Or we will send her away.'

Ramulas quickly walked out of the cell and was escorted to the end of the hall. He saw a cell open opposite the stairway. A partition with a small bench blocked the view of the rear of the cell.

On the bench were some neatly folded clean clothes. Ramulas was led around into the rear and found a tub half-filled with steaming water.

'Wash yourself and call out when you are finished,' one of the soldiers said before walking away.

Ramulas stood by the bath, mesmerised by the steam coming out of the water. He heard the fading footsteps of the soldiers as they walked away. He walked around the partition and saw that the clean clothes were still on the bench.

Ramulas walked to the tub and slowly peeled off his muddy pants and shirt before dropping them on the floor. Once he was naked, Ramulas could feel mud clinging to every part of his body.

Ramulas stepped into the bath and let out a sigh. He was surprised to find a scrubbing stick in the tub. Using the stick, Ramulas cleaned every inch of his body.

Once he was clean, Ramulas lay in the tub and allowed the warm water to soothe his aching muscles. After a few moments, Ramulas thought he heard a noise out in the hallway.

'Hello, is anyone there?' he called out while sitting up in the tub.

When no response came, Ramulas lay down in the tub once more. Then his inner voice told him something was wrong. He stepped out of the tub and walked around the partition to look into the hallway. Something was amiss.

Ramulas' knees weakened when he saw the bench was empty. Someone had taken the clean clothes.

Ramulas' heart began to race in his chest as he fought for breath. Then one of the soldiers appeared in the doorway, and Ramulas jumped back.

'You must get dressed. Then we will take you to your wife.'

'The clean clothes, where have they gone?' Ramulas asked, pointing to the empty bench.

The soldier shrugged. 'That is not my concern. You need to get dressed.'

'But the clothes are gone,' Ramulas pleaded.

'If you are not dressed soon, your wife will be sent away.'

Ramulas walked back into the cell. He looked at the pile of muddy clothes he had removed. He was torn between wearing the dirty clothes or refusing to wear them and not seeing her.

His mind was made up and Ramulas quickly dressed in the muddy clothes. Ramulas picked up his shirt and held it away from his body in disgust. He wanted nothing to do with the dirty clothes, but this meant seeing Jacqueline.

He fought back the bile that rose in his throat. After being clean the feeling of the wet, muddy clothes clinging to him brought waves of nausea.

Once dressed, Ramulas held his hands away from his body and opened his legs slightly. The muddy clothes felt cold and clammy as they clung to his skin. He worried about what Jacqueline would say when she saw him in this state.

The realisation of his wife coming to see him sunk in. How did they find her? Had K'ayden betrayed him and told the king of their meeting in Bremnon?

The soldier walked into the cell and stopped Ramulas' speculation. 'We must leave. Your wife is waiting.' Ramulas followed the soldier out into the hallway to find the king and three other soldiers waiting for him. He grimaced with each step, feeling the mud stick to his clean body. Two soldiers walked up the stairs motioning for Ramulas to follow. As Ramulas took his first step into the stairway, the king stepped forward. 'Where do you think you are going?' Zachary screamed.

Ramulas flinched. 'I am going to see my wife.'

Zachary wrinkled his nose in disdain. 'Look at you, pig—even after a bath, you are an animal. Take him back to his cell.'

The four soldiers unsheathed their swords and pointed them at Ramulas, who stood in a state of shock. 'No, wait. My wife is here,' Ramulas pleaded.

Zachary motioned with his hand, and Ramulas was prodded down the hall with the swords. He begged the whole way to see his wife, but his requests fell on deaf ears. With each step away from the stairs, his hope for freedom faded.

He was led passed the muddy cell back to his original cell.

Ramulas turned to Zachary. 'Please, I beg of you. Let me see my wife,' he said as tears streamed down his eyes.

'James!' Zachary called.

The door of the cell behind the king opened and James stepped into the hallway. His eyes locked onto Ramulas and he took a step forward. Ramulas' shoulders collapsed in defeat as he walked into the cell.

The door slammed shut behind him, and he heard the key turn in the lock.

'When you are ready to talk about the crystal and where it came from, I will allow you to walk free of this place,' Zachary said.

Ramulas spun to face the king. 'Talk to your magician. He knows what the crystal does.'

'Shigar is studying the crystal. But he said you have not given him any information about it and why it is in your possession.'

Ramulas was speechless.

The king and soldiers walked away, leaving Ramulas to think about his last meeting with the magician. He did not answer most of the questions asked by Shigar, but the magician received his answers by Ramulas nodding and shaking his head.

The king did not seem to know anything about what the magician did about the crystal. This could only mean that Shigar had withheld the information from the king. This was another revelation for Ramulas to digest.

Ramulas looked around the cell and saw that it had been cleaned, with a fresh pile of straw in the corner.

Ramulas was confused. Why would they take him from here, throw him into a muddy cell, bathe him, then return him? He moved toward the straw and a small piece of mud fell from his clothes. An idea came to him.

Ramulas went to the opposite side of the cell, stripping as he walked. When Ramulas was naked, he vigorously shook his clothes, sending mud flying into the wall. When he was finished, Ramulas grabbed handfuls of straw and began to scrub his clothes.

By the time he was finished, Ramulas had broken out into a light sweat and was breathing heavily. The majority of the mud had been removed from his clothes.

Because of the beatings, lack of food, and stress Ramulas felt tired after cleaning his clothes. He dressed and walked over to the pile of straw. Ramulas sat with his back against the wall.

He fought to keep his eyes open. The last time he fell asleep in this cell, he woke to find James hurting him. He didn't want that to happen again. He would try his hardest to stay awake. Ramulas thought to close his eyes for just a moment and was instantly asleep.

***

Pip sat in her small apartment thinking about Ramulas and ways she could help him. She berated herself for becoming close with him. Why did she have to do this?

Her life before him was much simpler. All Pip had to worry about was Jenna, Makayla, and Tao. She knew that soon enough she would find a way to have enough money to leave the shadows. Then Pip saw something in Ramulas she had not seen in a long time.

It was a sense of purpose and doing what he knew was right. She had not seen that in anyone except her father, and that was so long ago. Maybe that's why Pip felt the urge to help him and go against her motto of not caring about those who were not family.

Pip became instantly alert and looked around her small room. Light from the setting sun came in through the shutters to form strips of light along the floor. She sat up on her single bed, which was the only piece of furniture in the small room.

The buzz of people talking and background noise had suddenly stopped. This was strange for a three-storey building in the poor section. It was noisy both day and night.

Floorboards creaked outside in the hall as someone crept towards her room. Pip jumped up into the rafters above the door, with a knife in each hand and waited. No-one ever came to her room; people knew her reputation for violence.

When the intruder entered, Pip would drop on them, and they would be dead before she hit the ground. For a few moments, there was silence.

Then a low deep laugh could be heard outside her door. 'Pip, I need a word with you.'

A cold hand gripped Pip's heart as she recognised the master's voice. She dropped as silently as a cat and opened the door. She was greeted by the master and four enforcers.

'I heard a rumour,' the master said with a knowing smile. 'That you were in the castle. Is that true?'

Pip had surmised that the master already knew the answer and wanted a way out of this. She nodded and decided not to talk.

The master and the enforcers blocked the doorway. She knew that at any moment they could rush in and kill her. Things like this usually happened within the shadows to keep people in line.

'You weren't there for your friend with the crystal?'

'I was in the kitchen. I am planning to steal something from the castle.'

The master raised an eyebrow. 'It would not fare well for you and Jenna if this involves your friend. Remember, Pip, I want no trouble for the shadows.'

Pip inwardly breathed a sigh of relief when they walked away. The master had come with a warning. He had trained Pip and knew what she was like when an idea come to her.

Pip could not spend too much time in the castle or Jenna would suffer. She needed to think of something quick, or Ramulas would soon be dead. And when he died, what would happen with the crystal?

***

Ramulas woke to the sound of metal banging on the bars of his cell door. His eyes snapped open, and he attempted to sit up. Every muscle in his body protested. He groaned before falling back on the straw.

The cell door opened and four soldiers walked in. One held a length of chain and another held a torch. Ramulas shielded his eyes from the light, and two pairs of hands roughly pulled him to his feet.

'On yer feet, scum,' one of the soldiers said.

Ramulas stood unsteadily as shackles were clamped on both wrists. He blinked a few times to adjust his eyes to the brighter light. Ramulas saw more soldiers outside.

'Move,' a soldier said as Ramulas was pushed in the back.

Ramulas stumbled to the door and was happy that he did not fall.

Once in the hall, the soldiers formed a tight ring around Ramulas. He was marched to the stairway, where he was forced up five flights of stairs.

Ramulas' legs were on fire by the time they reached the dungeon. He had broken out in a sweat, and his body began to shake. He needed to stop and rest, but the soldiers continued to push him forward.

In a few moments, Ramulas found himself in a small open courtyard. His shackles were attached to a bolt in the ground. This allowed him to stand and move in a three-foot radius. Ramulas looked around and saw a score of soldiers on the balconies above. Each had a crossbow trained on him.

Anticipation of what was to come bought on a bout of anxiety for Ramulas. He searched the courtyard for something to use. Ramulas was confused when he saw a similar bolt in the ground fifteen feet from him. He wondered what that was for.

The king and James entered the courtyard one hundred feet from Ramulas. As they came toward him, Ramulas wondered if he was going to receive another beating.

The king and James stopped twenty feet away from Ramulas. Judging by the shadows on the ground, Ramulas knew it to be sometime in the afternoon, but he could not say what day it was.

The king smiled smugly. 'Hello, pig. Are you ready to tell me of the crystal and how you plan to use its magic against me?'

'You do not understand,' Ramulas said, feeling frustrated. 'I need to take the crystal far from here.'

'We have captured your wife,' Zachary lied. 'We caught her returning to the abandoned house where you kept the horse and cart.'

This statement confused Ramulas. Jacqueline had never been to Keah, let alone knew how to find the house. Could he be talking about Pip?

Zachary saw the confused expression. 'Do not play me for a fool,' he screamed, stepping forward. 'We saw you come into the city with your wife in the cart. We have questioned her. She has told us everything she knows about the crystal. Now we want to hear it from you.'

This did not make sense to Ramulas. He knew the king was talking about Pip. If they had spoken to her about the crystal, the king would be asking about the first legion. What was it that Pip used to say when she knew someone was making up stories?

'Lies,' Ramulas said with a tired smile. He held onto the hope that she had not been caught. He had seen what Pip was capable of and refused to believe they had her.

Zachary took a step back as his face turned crimson. 'You dare speak to your king this way?' Zachary motioned to James, who walked over to a large wooden door to the side of the courtyard.

'You have brought this upon yourself,' Zachary said, 'I want you to know that your wife died during questioning.'

Another lie, Ramulas thought. Then a familiar presence brushed the edges of his consciousness before James led his horse into the courtyard with a chain around its neck.

Ramulas was elated. The horse was his only connection to his family. He communicated with the horse to check on its wellbeing. The horse turned to Ramulas and walked toward him.

The communication was cut short when James jerked the chain, which was then attached to the bolt fifteen feet in front of Ramulas. This confused him until James walked to the side of the courtyard and returned with a blacksmith's hammer. He tossed it in the air a few times as he neared the horse.

'No, what are you doing?' Ramulas whispered as a cold chill ran through him.

When James neared the horse Ramulas communicated for it to move away. When it moved as far as the chain would allow, James looked at Ramulas and smiled without emotion.

Then he ran at the horse and swung with his hammer. There was an audible snap, followed by the horse's scream. James had broken its front leg, and bone protruded from the skin.

'Noooo!' Ramulas screamed as he fell to his knees.

Not only could he hear the horse screaming, but Ramulas could also feel its pain through their connection. The horse fell to its side and pleaded for Ramulas to help it.

Then James took a step and swung again with the hammer. Another snap, and the pitch of the horse's scream raised an octave. Now both its front legs were broken.

Ramulas screamed again as he jumped up from his knees and ran to his horse. After two steps, the chain attached to the shackles pulled him crashing to the ground. The horse called for Ramulas to help and take away the pain.

'Stop it!' he screamed. 'I will tell you what you want to know.'

Zachary smiled. 'It's too late for that.'

Ramulas turned in time to see James swing the hammer and break one of the horse's rear legs.

'Aaaaaargh!' Ramulas screamed as he pulled on his chains.

Ramulas pulled on his shackles until they cut deep into his wrists. Then James broke the last leg of the horse. The horse was delirious from the pain and suffering. It called for Ramulas to help while looking him in the eyes. It could not understand why he could not help.

Then James began to attack the horse's body. Each swing broke a part of the ribcage. Flecks of blood came out of the horse's nostrils with every breath. Ramulas pulled on his chain with all his might to no avail. James walked to the horse's head and smiled at Ramulas.

'Nooooo!' Ramulas shouted.

He saw and felt the horse's last thought. It was of Grace waving her arms and telling the horse what to do. A warm sensation exploded in the pit of Ramulas' stomach and slowly spread through his body. Ramulas became quiet.

Deathly quiet.

He felt something powerful grow within, something that was faintly familiar. It was part of his old magical ability. He had stopped pulling on his shackles. Ramulas looked at James with primal rage. He breathed slowly and focused on the brute. In the tombs, Ramulas had been unable to access his magical ability, but being outside for this short period of time gave him access to them once more.

James's eyes opened in shock as his throat began to constrict as if someone was choking him. His hands went to his neck as he fell to his knees.

A growing pain formed behind Ramulas' eyes—his reserve of magic was almost empty. Ramulas knew he had to stop or suffer.

He saw his horse and pushed with everything he could to kill James. Then Ramulas blacked out from the effort and collapsed to the ground.

26

Zachary walked over to inspect Ramulas' still form. He nudged the body with the toe of his boot. When Ramulas moaned, Zachary knew he still lived. Then he looked across at James in confusion. Just before the prisoner collapsed, James had some sort of coughing fit and grabbed his throat.

Zachary motioned for the soldiers to take Ramulas back to the tombs. When he recovered, Zachary would speak to him again. He needed to know what threat the crystal was.

One of the city's butchers stepped into the courtyard with his apprentice. They quickly began cutting up the horse.

After the prisoner was taken away, Zachary noticed the stone the prisoner was shackled to had been pulled two inches from the ground. But that was impossible. The stone weighed over three hundred pounds and was set into the ground.

***

Grace walked through the trees, still upset at her mother. Why could she not play with the dryads? They were her friends. Then Grace stopped in shock; she could not believe what she saw.

Through the trees, she could see her da and the horse. A large evil man was hurting the horse, and her da was screaming. A warm sensation exploded within Grace and spread throughout her body. She wanted to help the horse.

Grace felt her da's anger toward the man and knew she needed to do something. Screwing her face in concentration, Grace reached out toward the large man and focused her anger on him.

She smiled when he grabbed his throat and dropped to the ground.

Then the vision vanished, and Grace was hit by a wave of dizziness. She swayed on her feet and a comforting hand held her shoulder.

'It's time for you to come home, Grace,' a familiar voice said.

She turned and smiled at Eady, who led her into a nearby tree.

They came out into the sacred grove where she was met by hundreds of dryads. Her dizziness soon gave way to excited energy as children came up to her.

'Remember that when you want to join us, all you need to do is willingly step into the mystical pool. Now, go and play.'

Grace's brown eyes widened with excitement as she ran off with the children.

All of the children sat around the mystical pool. The rules of the game were explained to Grace. One of the children would walk behind the others, tapping each child on the head saying 'Duck.'

When the child tapped someone on the head and said 'Goose', that child had to jump up and tag the other before they made it once around the mystical pool.

This sounded so exciting to Grace, and she sat down eager for the game to begin. In the first two rounds, Grace was tapped on the head and called 'Duck'. She laughed as the child who was called 'Goose' chased the other around the mystical pool.

Then Grace felt a hand touch her head and heard 'Goose'. With a squeal of delight, she jumped up and chased the dryad child.

Halfway around the mystical pool, Grace was almost within reach, when she tripped and fell into the mystical pool.

***

Pip was finishing the last of the pots for the day. She had quickly gained a reputation as a valued worker, helping other people when she had time to spare. Ch'oak walked up to Pip and tapped her arm.

Pip smiled down at her. 'Hello.'

'Your friend is very sad,' Ch'oak said.

Pip gave her a questioning look.

'He was taken to the eastern courtyard, and they killed his horse in front of him. Some of my people saw it happen. Your friend was screaming and crying. Now he has been returned to the tombs.'

Pip covered her mouth to hide the fact she was talking. 'Meet me in the store.'

A moment later, Pip walked into the storeroom to find Ch'oak waiting for her. 'I need to get to my friend. Tell me how to get into the tombs.'

The Khilli's eyes widened in shock. 'You cannot go there. The only way for you is through the dungeon. They have guards there.'

Pip sighed. 'Just tell me how to get to the dungeon. No-one will see me.'

Ch'oak thought for a moment before nodding. 'Follow me.' She handed Pip a tray and placed a few bread rolls on it. She led Pip out of the kitchen and through several hallways. Then they stopped at a downward spiralling stairway.

'The dungeon is below. Give this tray to the guards and walk away.'

Pip nodded and descended toward the dungeon. When Pip reached the lower level, she noticed the hall to the dungeon was curved. There were four empty rooms along the hall before she reached the dungeon. Only the last room could be seen by the guards.

They saw Pip and called for her to come to them. Pip gave an awkward smile as she handed over the tray. One of the guards took it and walked away.

Pip counted ten cells—five on either side of the dungeon. There was another descending stairway beyond them. As Pip walked back to the stairs, she smiled to herself. She had seen young Tom in the cells. He was one of the shadows. Tom gave her a quick wink when he saw her.

He would be able to help Pip with the plan she was formulating.

***

Oriel sat in her cavern, working on spells to return to the city of Keah when she felt Ramulas' presence.

Then her eyes widened in shock. She could feel that he was suffering an enormous amount of pain and torment. By the time Oriel readied herself for astral travel, Ramulas' presence was gone.

Oriel was worried. Since Ramulas had vanished, she had been slightly concerned. She had spoken to Pip, who said that she would try to help. After this brief connection, Oriel could only think the worst and knew that Ramulas needed her help.

If Oriel went to Keah soon, she might find a way for Pip to help Ramulas escape.

***

Shigar was mesmerised as he sat looking into the crystal. The table where he sat was littered with mounds of books and scrolls. The more he studied the crystal, the more he was certain that someone from another world was trying to contact him.

Then he felt a burst of familiar magical energy. It was so raw and powerful, and it lasted a few seconds before vanishing. He stood from his chair and walked into the hallway. He headed toward the energy.

Shigar walked out onto the balcony of the eastern courtyard. What Shigar saw shocked him.

The butcher and apprentice were busy dissecting the dead horse. Shigar noticed that it was chained to a bolt anchored to the floor. It was the horse that had pulled the prisoner's cart into Keah. He knew something very wrong had happened—every major bone in the horse was broken and blood-soaked the marble floor.

He motioned for a nearby soldier over to him. Shigar asked what had happened. The soldier told the magician what he had witnessed, and by the end of the story, Shigar's face had turned ashen. Zachary had gone too far.

Shigar turned from the soldier and made his way to the tombs. Zachary's fear of things he did not understand had led to this behaviour. With each day that passed, the magician felt the rift between Zachary and himself growing wider. The prisoner showed more traits of being a leader than the king.

Shigar needed to talk to the prisoner to see how he fared after such an ordeal.

Shigar arrived at the prisoner's cell and held up his torch. He could see the prisoner curled up on the bed of straw. He took the keys from the wall, unlocked the door, and walked in. The state of the prisoner took Shigar's breath away.

The prisoner hugged himself while softly humming. His eyes were open, yet he focused on something only he could see. Shigar leaned over and snapped his fingers in front of the man's face a few times. When the prisoner did not react, Shigar knew he had witnessed a trauma so great that he had retreated to a place deep inside his mind.

Shigar had seen cases like this before, and most people never recovered. Only on a few rare occasions did they return from the safe place within. However, this usually took the voice of a loved one or a dramatic event. Shigar did not know where this man's family was and did not think he would be able to survive another dramatic event.

He gave the prisoner one last look and stood before walking from the cell. The prisoner did not deserve to be treated this way. He was only doing what he thought was right for his family. Shigar had lost the last of his respect for Zachary.

Up until six years previous, Zachary would have been seen as a fair king by the people. Then his wife died.

Zachary was devastated and was left to raise his nine-year-old daughter on his own. Over the years, he grew bitter toward the people of the kingdom and refused to listen to reason from his advisors. Over the years, Shigar felt disillusioned as the friendship with Zachary slowly crumbled.

The Zachary he once knew was now just a memory.

***

James walked into the cell holding something wrapped in a cloth. He smiled when he saw Ramulas curled on the floor. He knew that somehow this man had used magic to try to strangle him. James had come to return the favour.

Walking up to Ramulas, the brute unwrapped the cloth, revealing one of the horse's leg bones. He had seen how upset the prisoner was when he beat the horse to death. Now he wanted to beat the prisoner with a bone of his own horse.

Ramulas had given no reaction by the time James stood over him. He just stared into space. James was used to, and fed off, fear from people. He kicked Ramulas, which sent him crashing into the wall. Still, there was no reaction. James exploded into motion.

He savagely beat Ramulas with the bone for a few seconds, then he stood back and waited for a reaction. Ramulas had not screamed or attempted to defend himself. He lay on the straw with blood seeping from fresh injuries. James dropped the bone and walked out of the cell. He would come back at a later time and find a way to make the prisoner scream for mercy.

27

Witnessing the brutal death of his horse and hearing that they had killed Pip sent Ramulas deep within himself. The burden of the horse being killed weighed heavily on his consciousness more than he was able to cope with. It was the one link to his family.

Added to that was Pip's death. She was doing her best to help Ramulas in his quest. Now she had died because of him.

He had abandoned all hope of regaining the crystal and returning home to his family. Now the legion would come to his world and destroy everything. The place Ramulas had retreated to was warm and safe. He saw no reason to leave.

***

Grace sat in the mystical pool, not knowing what to do. The dryads in the clearing had gathered around, and every one of them was smiling down at her.

'Welcome to our family,' one of the children said.

'But I fell in,' Grace said. 'I didn't mean to.'

'To join us, one must enter the mystical pool willingly,' Eady said. 'You fell in. If you wish to join us, stay in the pool a while longer.'

'Mother said no,' Grace replied.

'But by falling into the pool you have been affected by its magic,' Eady said.

'What magic?' Grace asked.

'You will find out soon.'

Grace looked at the dryads around her as she stepped out of the mystical pool. She expected them to be disappointed that she did not join them, but they still smiled at her. One by one they stepped forward and hugged her. Then the dryads walked into the trees.

Grace was astonished that even though the dryads went into the tree she could see them. 'I can see them in the trees.'

'I know,' Eady said, 'You are now a part of our family. You will share our magic.'

Grace was excited at the prospect of this and wanted to tell her da. Then the reality of her situation dawned on her, and she wanted to go back to her mother and Kate.

'My family will be worried; I should go back now.'

Eady smiled and led Grace to a nearby tree. She stepped out and saw her mother and sister standing near Matthew's hut. Both of them saw Grace and ran to her. Jacqueline stopped within arm's reach of Grace and she gasped in shock. Grace had green eyes.

From the day grace was born until earlier that day, her eyes had always been brown. Now they were a bright emerald green.

She grabbed Grace by the shoulders. 'What happened to your eyes?'

Grace smiled. 'I fell into the mystical pool.'

***

Pip came to work in the kitchen, anxious to hear news of Ramulas. She washed pots until Ch'oak came into the kitchen. The Khilli girl came over to Pip holding a few biscuits.

'I will give these to your friend and see how he fares.'

'Let me come with you,' Pip whispered.

Ch'oak shook her head. 'You cannot come. I will return soon.' Ch'oak walked from the kitchen and made her way to a hidden passageway that brought her to the tombs. At the bottom of the stairs, she went to Ramulas' cell.

Looking through the door, she saw Ramulas curled on a bed of straw. She put her hand through the bars holding the biscuits.

'I have brought you food,' she called.

He did not seem to hear her. Ch'oak called out a few more times, each time speaking louder. She was about to walk away when a large shadow fell over her. She looked up in time to see James's giant hand reach down for her.

Ch'oak squealed and tried to jump back, but James grabbed a handful of her hair. She screamed in terror when he lifted her off the floor.

***

Ch 'oak's scream reached Ramulas in his safe, own little world. A part of him heard the scream of a young girl, and his first thought was that Grace was in danger.

Ramulas eyes snapped open, and he found himself in a world of pure physical pain. The girl screamed again, which brought Ramulas to the present moment. He fought through the pain and sat up. He saw James lift Ch'oak by her neck and begin to strangle her.

Ramulas felt anger explode within.

As Ramulas pushed himself up he felt something under his hand. Looking down, he saw the horse's shinbone. At first, he was repulsed, then he saw the jagged end of the bone.

Ramulas picked it up and ran screaming at the door. His first strike through the bars glanced off James's upper arm, drawing a small line of blood. James looked at Ramulas and took hold of the shinbone with one hand.

In his other hand was Ch'oak, who was held aloft by the throat. As Ramulas screamed and fought with James for control of the bone, Ch'oak feebly kicked out and slapped James's tree trunk-like arms. Her kicks were becoming weaker with each second.

James pulled the bone from Ramulas and threw it behind him down the hallway. Ramulas hit James, but his blows had no effect. His strength was rapidly leaving him. Ramulas threw one last punch with the last of his strength and missed James completely.

Ramulas let out a cry of despair as he collapsed to the ground.

He was helpless to help Ch'oak.

***

Pip looked at the door where Ch'oak had left a short while before. *She should have been back by now,* Pip thought. A small voice inside said that something was wrong and Pip needed to go into the tombs. The only thing stopping Pip was that she could not just race through the dungeon. She decided to give Ch'oak a bit more time to return.

28

K'ayden walked down the spiral stairway into the tombs when he first heard Ramulas scream. He came out into the hallway to see James's wide back. Ramulas and James wrestled with a bone while Ramulas screamed in rage. K'ayden could not interfere because his family would suffer.

Then James tore the bone from Ramulas and threw it behind him. As he threw the bone, K'ayden saw that James was strangling his daughter.

The bone landed at the feet of a very angry warrior father.

K'ayden picked up the bone and raced silently towards James. He thrust the sharp end of the bone into James's lower back. James gasped in pain and shock. He dropped Ch'oak. Before she hit the ground, K'ayden ripped the bone out of James's back, and he repeatedly stabbed the side of the brute's neck.

A fountain of blood-covered Ramulas as he sat against the cell door. K'ayden pushed James aside and embraced his daughter.

Tears of joy ran down his face, and his heart sang with happiness that he had arrived in time.

After a moment, K'ayden checked to see if Ch'oak had been hurt, then he looked at James's body. This would bring trouble for his people, and Ramulas would certainly be killed. Then he asked his daughter what she was doing in the tombs.

She told K'ayden about Pip, who wanted to help Ramulas escape. K'ayden thought of a plan in which Pip could help. He sent Ch'oak to bring her from the kitchen.

Ramulas would leave the tombs, and James's body would be found. The blame for the brute's death would fall on the escaped prisoner, and the Khilli would not suffer.

***

The moment Ch'oak walked into the kitchen, Pip knew something had happened. Before she could say anything Ch'oak held up a hand for silence. 'Come with me; your friend is in danger.'

'Show me your secret ways,' Pip said.

'I cannot. My people will be punished.'

On the way to the dungeon, Ch'oak told Pip of the events as they unfolded. Pip knew that if she did not help Ramulas escape from the tombs he would die. She would not allow that.

Pip walked alone down into the dungeon. As she neared the last room before the dungeon, Pip gave three short soft whistles. A second later, she could hear young Tom yelling and banging on the bars of his cell. When the guards began to yell, Pip ran into the room.

Within the dim room, Pip saw that Tom was causing a riot in his cell. The guards had their backs to her, focusing on him. Pip found some straw and old cloth on one side of the room. She removed her flint, and after a few strikes, the straw caught fire. Pip blew on it a few times and built a fire before leaving the room.

Tom screamed out 'fire!' and Pip saw the guards rush into the room. Pip ran behind them and shut the heavy wooden door before pulling the latch across and locking them inside. Pip ignored the faint pounding on the door as she ran through the dungeon and into the tombs.

Pip came out into the tombs to find a Khilli warrior waiting for her. Ramulas and James both lay in the hallway covered in blood. The cell door was open and the key hung in the lock. 'Help me take your friend from here,' K'ayden said.

As Pip walked to Ramulas, K'ayden spoke in Khilli. She turned to see Ch'oak standing behind her, holding a sheet. Pip was surprised at how quiet the young Khilli was. She had not heard a sound.

254

K'ayden bent over Ramulas and removed his shirt. Then he took the sheet from his daughter and proceeded to wipe the blood from Ramulas' body. He spoke once more in Khilli, and Ch'oak ran for the stairs.

'Come, help me lift him,' he said to Pip.

They bent down to pull Ramulas to his feet, stood on either side, and draped his arms over their shoulders.

'My friend, you must walk, and we will take you from this dark place,' K'ayden said.

Ramulas looked at K'ayden as if seeing him for the first time. 'Your daughter. I could not save her.'

'She is safe, my friend. Now, we must hurry.'

The three of them made their way down the hallway to the stairs. Ramulas was able to walk in short bursts with the help of Pip and K'ayden. By the time they reached the stairs, the sensation of pins and needles in Ramulas' legs was almost unbearable. After three flights of stairs, his body began to shake.

'I need to rest,' Ramulas said.

'We must keep moving. Rest will come soon,' K'ayden replied.

Ramulas nodded and concentrated on placing one foot in front of the other while blocking out the pain.

The group arrived at the dungeon, and Pip and K'ayden placed Ramulas against a wall.

'Whatcha doin' there, Pip?' Young Tom asked with a smile.

'We need to get this one out of here,' she said, pointing to Ramulas.

'Take me with you, I can help.'

Pip looked at the lanky young man with his mop of messy dark hair and plain clothes. Pip did not want to draw any unwanted attention to herself.

'Can you leave here without being seen?' she asked.

Tom gave a wry smile. 'Of course.'

Pip removed the keys from a peg on the wall and unlocked Tom's cell. She turned to see Ramulas staring at her in wonder.

'They told me you were dead,' he slurred.

'Lies,' Pip said as she reached down for him.

K'ayden, Pip, and young Tom struggled to help Ramulas to the stairs that led out of the dungeon. At the top of the stairs, Ch'oak waited with a cart used for laundry. A small pile of sheets lay near the cart. Ramulas was bundled into the cart and the sheets were thrown over him.

'We can help you no more,' K'ayden said. 'If we are caught, my people will suffer greatly.'

Pip nodded her thanks and the two Khilli disappeared. Pip found that the cart was not hard to move.

'I'll be fine. Leave without attracting too much attention,' she told young Tom.

Pip moved the cart towards the kitchen wearing a bored expression. People who saw her would think she was a servant on another errand.

A short while later, Pip reached the kitchen and leaned into the cart. 'Stay quiet. I will return soon.'

Walking into the kitchen, Pip made her way to the barrels that held rotting food. Using two buckets, Pip filled them with rotting fruit and took them out to the cart. She covered the sheets until it looked like a refuse cart.

Pip moved the cart through the castle to the courtyard. The smell of the rotten food forced Pip to think of pleasant things or she would have vomited.

Pip slowed her breathing and walked toward the open gate. In her mind, she could hear alarms beings called and see soldiers racing for her. However, no-one gave her a second glance until she was almost at the gate.

'Where do you think you are taking that cart?' A voice called behind her.

Pip turned to see two soldiers twenty feet away and walking to her. Pip's first thought was to leave the cart and run into the city streets. But she could not leave Ramulas. 'I was taking food to my sick mother,' Pip said in a voice that made her sound simple.

'Who said you could take food from the castle?' one of the soldiers asked.

'The kitchen said this was bad and I could take it,' Pip said as she reached into the cart and pulled out a rotten apple. She thrust it toward the two. 'You can have some too.'

Both soldiers wrinkled their noses and stepped away from her.

'This is a good one,' Pip said as she took a bite from the apple.

'Ew. Get away from here,' one of the soldiers said before they waved her through the gate.

The apple was rotten to the core, but Pip did not spit it out until she had passed the gate. Words from the master of shadows echoed in Pip's mind. She had done exactly what he warned her not to. But deep inside, she knew that Ramulas was important.

Pip just hoped she had done the right thing.

She made her way to the poor section near the docks. Pip stopped outside an abandoned house near the southern wall. She scanned the street and found that no-one was paying her any attention.

It was a small two-room house that had been neglected for months and was in need of repairs. *An unpainted house about to fall down would be the last place for people to look for Ramulas*, she thought.

Pip pulled the cart into a rear room of the house and tipped Ramulas onto the floor.

She took one look at Ramulas and knew that she needed help. Pip piled as much of the rotten food into the cart, and lay Ramulas on the sheets.

'Stay here. I will return soon,' she whispered.

'Wait.' Ramulas croaked, trying to reach out for her. 'Where am I?'

'You are in a house by the docks.'

'I need to go back into the castle and get the crystal,'

'What?!' Pip said in disbelief, 'You need to rest here for a while. Then we can think of a way to get the crystal.'

Ramulas nodded once before passing out.

Pip left, knowing she would need a lot of help and that the master of shadows would not be pleased with her. She needed to find a way for Jenna and herself not to be killed by the shadows.

***

Shigar looked up from his work. He could feel the familiar magic of the prisoner once more. However, this time it was different.

It was so faint that Shigar had almost missed it, and it was moving through the castle. He decided to investigate. Shigar left his chambers and made his way to the tombs.

Shigar was in the hallway leading to the dungeon when he heard a faint pounding on the last door. He pulled the latch and two of the dungeon guards collapsed in front of him, gasping for air. A thick plume of smoke drifted from the room, and Shigar instantly knew that something was wrong.

'Tell me what happened,' he demanded.

'There was a fire in the room,' One of them said, 'We went in to look and the door closed behind us.'

Shigar walked into the dungeon to find all of the cells empty. He came back to the guards. 'How many people were locked in the dungeon?'

'Just one,' the same guard replied between coughs. 'He began to yell before the fire.'

'Well, now you have none,' Shigar said. 'Send for help.' Shigar walked down into the tombs with a feeling of trepidation. He knew that the empty dungeon and the guards being locked away had something to do with the prisoner in the tombs.

Shigar reached the bottom of the stairs and saw James lying in a pool of blood. He walked over to inspect the scene. The cell door was open, and Shigar was not surprised to find it empty.

He took a closer look at James. The brute had been stabbed in the lower back once and suffered multiple stab wounds in his neck. Shigar laughed when he found the horse bone that was used as a weapon. How ironic that James was killed by the bone of a horse he slaughtered.

It was obvious that James had come to torment the prisoner, and the prisoner had killed him. King Zachary would have to be told what had transpired.

Shigar made his way to see Zachary. He knew the king would be furious with the missing prisoner. The dungeon was empty and the guards were nowhere to be seen.

29

Pip had tracked down Old John; he was looking for potential targets in the market square.

'John, I need your help,' she said, coming up behind him.

He turned and smiled. 'What job has the master of shadows got you doing?'

'No-one knows about this. I need help to keep what I'm doing quiet, which is why I need you.'

John took one last look around the market square. 'Today would be good for lifting a few coins.'

'This is important,' Pip said before walking away.

Old John followed her through the streets until they were near the docks. Pip led him into the abandoned house. The pungent aroma of rotting food assaulted them as they entered. Pip took Old John to the rear room where Ramulas lay unconscious on the floor.

'We need to help him.'

'He must be someone important, but I have not seen him before.'

'He is very special. I just helped him escape from the tombs. Soldiers will be looking for him soon.'

Old John nodded slowly as the gravity of the situation sank in. 'Do you know what you have done? You have broken a direct order of the shadows. The master will not be happy.'

Pip glared at Old John. No-one spoke to her in this way without punishment. She decided to let this pass. There were bigger things to worry about. Pip needed to explain to the master of shadows why the city will be placed under martial law.

'Our future—and the future of everyone in the kingdom—rests with this man,' Pip said, pointing to Ramulas.

Even though Pip knew she needed to keep people in the dark about Ramulas, she needed help in getting him back into the castle.

'Stay here and watch over him. I will return soon.'

Pip quickly made her way to the master of shadows, formulating a plan as she walked.

***

Shigar found himself outside the king's chambers. The royal guards opened the door allowing him entry. Zachary was talking with a few merchants. Aleesha sat by her father's side and gave the magician a smug smile when she saw him.

Shigar walked towards the throne, and when Zachary looked up, Shigar shook his head and waved at the merchants. Zachary smiled politely and asked for them to leave.

'I think it would be best if Aleesha left with the merchants,' Shigar said.

'You dare speak about a princess in such a manner?' she demanded.

Shigar ignored her and spoke to Zachary. 'This is most important.'

Zachary nodded. 'It is fine for my daughter to be here. Tell me what is important.'

Shigar sighed. 'The prisoner has escaped the tombs.' Zachary looked at Shigar in shock and was silent for a second. 'James!' he shouted.

Shigar slowly shook his head. 'James is dead. I found his body by the tombs.'

The colour drained from Zachary's face. 'Guards!' he called.

Eight royal guards rushed into the cambers. 'I want all of you to stand guard and watch over my daughter. A dangerous prisoner has escaped from the tombs. Do not let any harm come to the princess.'

The royal guards nodded and formed a tight circle around Aleesha. About to protest, a glare from her father silenced her.

Zachary turned to Shigar. 'Take me there.'

As they walked from the chambers, Zachary addressed the two guards at the door, 'There has been an escape from the tombs. No-one is to leave the castle, and I want every inch of this place searched.'

The two royal guards raced down the hallway.

By the time Zachary and Shigar reached the stairway into the dungeon, six soldiers accompanied them. The party made their way into the dungeon to find two extremely worried guards.

'We do not know what happened, lord,' one of the dungeon guards said. 'We saw a fire, then we were locked in the room.'

'What is he babbling about?' Zachary asked.

Shigar retold the story of how the guards ended up locked in the room, and how the lone prisoner in the dungeon went missing.

By the end of the tale, Zachary was furious. 'Throw them both in the cells.'

The soldiers pounced on the guards and threw them into a nearby cell. Zachary glared at them once before heading down the stairs to the tombs.

Zachary stood over James's body while a royal guard held a torch. The blood around the body had begun to thicken, but Zachary knew this had been recent. In the king's own opinion, he was surprised that the prisoner was able to best James in combat, but the evidence was lying at his feet.

'He has left something behind,' Zachary said, pointing to the bloody shirt that lay near the wall. 'Fetch the dogs. We will use them to track the prisoner.'

As two of the royal guard left, Zachary turned to Shigar. 'James was not supposed to be in the tombs. I wonder what brought him down here, and I wonder how the prisoner got hold of the bone?'

Shigar shrugged while thinking, *Because James was a sadistic animal, and he brought the bone to abuse the prisoner.*

They waited by James's body until four tracking dogs came into the tombs. The animal's handler picked up the bloody shirt and allowed the dogs to sniff it. At once, they began to bark and pull at their chains toward the stairs.

The small group followed the dogs through the castle, taking the same route Pip had when pushing the cart. Within a few minutes, the dogs had led them into the courtyard. The dogs barked and pulled at their chains toward the locked gate.

Zachary's heart skipped a beat. The prisoner's scent led out into the city. 'Captain!' he shouted as he walked into the courtyard.

The captain quickly walked out of the guardhouse and met Zachary halfway across the courtyard. 'My lord, the gates were locked as soon as we received word.'

'A dangerous prisoner has escaped the tombs. He was injured. Did such a man come through here?'

The captain shook his head, 'No, my lord. Only servants have passed through this gate.'

Zachary looked at the dog's handler, a small scruffy man who had the appearance of his dogs. 'Could the dogs have made a mistake?'

'No, my lord, they could follow—'

'Enough,' Zachary said, holding up his hand and turning to the captain. 'He came through this courtyard. He would have been in disguise or had another person help him. I want to know anything out of place that happened today.'

The captain called the eight soldiers in the courtyard to him. He repeated to them what the king had said. By the end of his speech, two of the soldiers stepped forward and spoke of the serving girl pushing the cart full of rotting fruit.

'And you did not think to check the cart?' the captain screamed before cuffing one of them behind the ear.

Zachary walked up to the captain, and the two soldiers cringed. 'I want every gate in the city locked. No boat or ship is to leave the docks. The city of Keah will be locked down until this prisoner is found.'

The captain walked away screaming orders to his men. The gate opened and Zachary spoke to the royal guards. 'Follow the dogs; I want this prisoner brought back to the castle alive.'

Zachary wore a grim smile. It would take time for all of the gates to be closed. The prisoner could have left by then. And it would be dark in a few hours. His men needed to search as many places as they could by then.

'I shall return to my chambers to see if I am able to feel his presence within the city,' Shigar said before walking away.

Zachary gave the magician an absent wave. He was busy watching the dogs head toward the docks.

***

Pip stood outside a small, rundown building in the poor section. All of the windows had been boarded up, but those on the street knew to stay away from here.

Pip knocked a pattern on the door and waited. She heard bolts being pulled and turned to see a crossbow trained on her from a nearby window. Pip knew that the real danger lay in the poison dart within the door aimed at her stomach.

'What do you want?' A muffled voice called out.

'I wish to buy fruit,' Pip replied.

'Do you know what is in season?'

Pip smiled. 'Apples are good today, but oranges are better on the morrow.'

The door opened, and Pip stepped into a small room with three barrels against the far wall. Other than the barrels, the room was empty. An old lady stood by the door with a crossbow and nodded to the barrels.

Pip went to the one on the right, opened the lid and climbed in. Once the bottom was removed, Pip found a ladder descending into darkness. The lid was replaced as she made her way down.

After a few moments, Pip stood in pitch blackness and felt along the wall. She found a symbol etched in the darkness on the wall.

Pip followed these until she came to the ladder she needed.

This was the shadow's underground highway. It consisted of tunnels running under half of the poor section. Travelling needed to be in darkness. Anyone seen with a torch was to be killed.

At the top of the ladder, Pip knocked twice, three times, and then once. Something heavy was dragged away and the trapdoor opened. Before Pip could recover from the intense light, she was pulled up through the trapdoor.

Two pairs of hands held her in place while her vision adjusted. Then the two large enforcers stepped away.

Pip looked around the large room filled with expensive furniture. The master of shadows sat behind a heavy wooden table near an open window. The smell of the ocean was thick, and the sounds of gulls and sailors could be heard.

'What has brought you here, Pip?' the master asked. 'It must be something important to disturb me.'

Pip took a deep breath, knowing the master would not be happy. 'I have helped my friend escape from the tombs. He is close to death and needs help.'

The master became quiet, and Pip could see him controlling himself. He slowly looked past Pip and waved his hand. The door opened and the enforcers left the room.

He stood and slowly made his way over to Pip who dared not move. The master could kill her in an instant. Then who would look after Jenna?

He stopped two feet from her. 'Tell me why I should not send people to kill your sister and her children.'

Pip's heart skipped a beat as her insides turned to ice; this was her biggest fear. She needed to word this in a way that the master would see a benefit in Ramulas.

'I had to do it,' Pip whispered with her eyes downcast. 'He is special, and there is something coming to the kingdom. Only he can stop it.'

The master's hand shot out, grabbing Pip by the neck. She did not attempt to struggle as he lifted her off the floor.

He held her weight with ease. Pip knew her life could be lost at any moment. 'Pip, I want you to bring your friend here. It would not be good if the soldiers found him first.'

Pip gasped for air as she was dropped to the ground. The door opened, and the master instructed the two enforcers to go with Pip and return with the friend. She took a few deep breaths before leading them out into the street.

***

Remus smiled at the energy strand. It had grown to six feet and was growing rapidly. With all of their magic, it would not be long until the portal opened.

The strand turned on itself as it swam through the black hole. Every now and then, the strand would rub against the edges of the black hole, causing flashes of white light.

Then the strand stopped swimming and throbbed. The warlords and red wizards were awestruck as they saw the strand grow.

A blinding light exploded within the black hole, dazing everyone, and magical energies filled the chamber. Remus blinked a few times before his sight returned. Elation surged through him when he saw the black hole had been replaced with a golden arch.

The arch was eight feet tall and wide enough for three men to walk abreast. The sound of rushing wind came from within the darkness of the arch. The anticipation of going to Oriel's world was almost intoxicating.

The warlords and red wizards quickly recovered and cast more spells into the arch.

'How long until I am able to enter?' Remus asked.

One of the warlords smiled. 'It will be very soon.'

***

The trio stopped opposite the abandoned house, and Pip turned to the two enforcers. 'Wait here and keep a lookout for soldiers. I will be back to get you.'

They both nodded, and she entered the house, where the smell of rotten food was still strong.

Old John saw Pip and gave a sigh of relief. 'This one has been callin' your name in his sleep.'

Pip knelt by Ramulas and saw that he had started to shake. He lay on the wooden floor wearing only pants, and his injuries had swollen.

'The master is not happy and wants to see Ramulas now,' Pip said, 'Two enforcers wait outside.'

Sharp whistles could be heard from outside. Pip and Old John looked at each other. It was the shadow's code for danger approaching.

'Quickly go outside and see what it is,' Pip said.

Once Old John left, Pip turned to Ramulas, who had opened his eyes. 'The crystal, where is it?' he whispered.

'It is still in the castle.'

Ramulas attempted to sit up; he moaned once before falling back to the cold floor.

'Stay on the floor. We need to get you well before you can return to the castle. The master will know what to do.'

Ramulas knew that by the time he had recovered it would be too late. 'The crystal has already begun to anchor. Once it does, everyone in the kingdom is doomed. Remus will bring the legion.'

Pip heard the urgent tone of his voice. 'I am getting help. We just have to avoid the soldiers who are looking for you. Where would the crystal be?'

'It is in the magician's chambers with my weapons.'

'Oh, joy. That will be fun,' Pip said sarcastically. 'Let's hope the magician is out when we come for the crystal, or we might be turned into toads.'

Pip looked to Ramulas for a response, but he had fallen back into unconsciousness.

Old John burst into the room with the enforcers. 'Dogs are coming this way.'

'Quick, help me move him,' Pip said.

Old John shook his head. 'They are too close.'

'Show me,' Pip said, running out into the street.

30

Pip, the enforcers, and Old John walked out of the house to see the dogs and soldiers fifty yards away. People quickly moved out of the way as soldiers shouted orders over the barking of the excited dogs. The shadows crossed the road and mingled with the crowd.

Her heart dropped; she had come so close, and for the second time, she had lost Ramulas to the soldiers. Pip felt sick to the stomach knowing that she had left him in the house. He was unconscious and helpless as a babe.

Since meeting Ramulas, she had come to see him as a father figure. Pip hoped with all of her heart that the dogs would lead the soldiers past the house.

All she could think about was how upset the master of shadows would be. He would not take this lightly. Pip knew that Jenna and her children's lives hung in the balance. She needed to do something. But what could she do?

Pip prayed to the god of thieves for the dogs to pass the house, holding on to one small shred of hope.

That hope shattered as the dogs led the soldiers up to the front door. As they entered the house, a thick fog rolled in from the docks. The fog was so dense Pip could not see three feet in front of her.

***

Shigar sat on the floor with his legs crossed and eyes closed. He could feel the prisoner's presence near the docks. The magical energy was very weak, and Shigar needed to concentrate in order to keep the connection.

He could feel that the prisoner was close to death. Shigar had his doubts about the prisoner leaving the castle unassisted, and doubts about who really killed James.

Shigar's eyes snapped open.

An extremely powerful magical energy had come into the city of Keah. He could feel that this magic was connected to the crystal, and also connected to the prisoner. He quickly stood and left his chambers.

Then both the prisoner and powerful energy disappeared. Shigar stopped just outside his door. He could not understand how both magical energies could just vanish.

For the first time in years, Shigar ran. He made his way to the southern balcony to where he could look out into the city. He instantly understood what had brought him there. Shigar was confronted by the thickest fog he had ever seen. And it was summer; fog was only seen in winter.

Echoes of foreign magic lingered in the air.

As Shigar stood wheezing and fighting for breath, he felt the hairs on his arms rise with the static energy in the air. This was something truly special.

'Oh my,' was all he could say.

Each time Shigar thought he had the prisoner figured out, another layer would reveal itself. He would not inform Zachary of what he discovered. Shigar would keep this to himself.

***

Pip stood perfectly still in the fog, listening to the people panic around her. A smile played across her face as she heard Old John taking short, sharp breaths.

'Walk back two steps until you are against the wall,' she said calmly.

After Old John and the enforcers stepped back, Pip counted silently in her mind. It was too late in the year for fog, and she had never seen one like this before. Pip knew this was something strange.

After two minutes, the fog began to lift until Pip could see for thirty yards. People around her had ceased to panic as their vision returned, and Pip laughed. Take something from people that they take for granted, and they will always panic.

Pip focused on the house across the street where she had left Ramulas. The dogs had led the soldiers inside before the fog rolled in. Now she waited for them to emerge from the house.

When they finally did, Pip saw that Ramulas was not with them. The dog's behaviour had changed. When she last saw them, the dogs were pulling on their chains toward the house. Now the dogs sniffed the ground as if searching for a trail.

The soldiers and the dog handler began to argue with each other, pointing in different directions. Some wanted to return the way they had come from, and others wanted to go to the docks.

Eventually, they came to an agreement and walked toward the docks.

Pip waited for them to disappear into the fog before rushing across the street. The three shadows followed her to the house. They entered and made their way to the rear room where they had left Ramulas.

Pip found the blankets on the floor, but Ramulas was nowhere in sight. She knelt down to touch the blankets. They were still warm, which meant Ramulas had to be close by. She had left him only a few minutes ago, and he had trouble moving without assistance. Ramulas could not have gone far.

The four shadows searched the house, yard, and nearby yards for Ramulas. They searched every possible hiding place, but they could not find him. For the first time in many years, Pip felt lost. She was unsure what to do. She sat on the floor by the blankets.

'What do we do now?' Old John asked.

Pip looked up with weary eyes and shook her head. 'The master will not be happy. Tell him that I will wait here and hopefully Ramulas will return.'

'Are you sure he will return?' one of the enforcers asked.

Pip shrugged. 'I can only hope. He is new to this city; I will wait here until tomorrow. Then I will see the master.' After Old John left, Pip wondered where Ramulas had gone.

***

Oriel felt Ramulas' energies once more. This time they were very weak. It took her some time to prepare spells strong enough to return to the city. Once Oriel arrived in Keah, she found Ramulas lying in an empty house close to death. She left with Ramulas just as the soldiers entered the house. Oriel took him back to her cavern.

Ramulas lay on the floor of the cavern covered in abrasions, bruising, and lacerations. His breathing was shallow.

Oriel felt terrible and responsible for his current situation. But she needed him to be well enough to move the crystal. She could feel Remus' magic and knew that he would be coming to this world soon.

She knelt over Ramulas and slowly waved her hands over his body while chanting softly. Small flecks of red energy floated down to Ramulas' body. As the flecks touched him, they were absorbed, and his wounds slowly began to heal in front of her eyes. When all the wounds had almost healed, Ramulas began to moan and move. 'Stay still,' she whispered, 'I am almost finished.' Within a minute, all Ramulas' wounds had closed over. He looked up and gave Oriel a tired smile. 'Have I died?'

'No,' she replied. 'You were very close, but you are alive.'

Ramulas began to laugh, then held his stomach in pain. 'Oh, that hurts.'

'What happened to you?'

Ramulas told Oriel of the arrival into Keah where they met the king and his magician, who were looking for the crystal, being captured, put in the tombs, and tortured.

Ramulas said that the king was threatened by the crystal and its unknown magic. That is why he was abused by James. However, Ramulas focused more on the relationships he formed while locked away, the time he spent with Shigar and K'ayden.

Shigar was the king's magician, but was very interested in Ramulas as a person, and how he came upon his magical abilities. He had proved through his actions that he would not betray Ramulas' trust. K'ayden provided food and comfort for Ramulas when he could. He also was the one who helped Pip in Ramulas' escape.

'You were seriously injured,' Oriel said. 'Every bone in your arms had been fractured, along with half of your ribs. Your internal organs have been damaged, and you are bleeding on the inside. I need to help you heal. If I do not help you, you will die in ten minutes. The crystal will anchor very soon. I need you healed so that you can take the crystal to the mountains.'

Ramulas nodded. 'Then heal me.'

'I am sorry,' Oriel said with a sad smile. 'This is going to hurt.'

Oriel's hands glowed red then she pressed them against Ramulas' chest. Ramulas screamed as steam rose from his body.

***

He lay on the floor recovering from Oriel's treatment. The pain was excruciating, and Ramulas felt every fibre of his body as the injuries healed. Once Oriel had finished, Ramulas' body had succumbed to shock and his strength had left him.

He felt totally exhausted and could hardly move. However, he could feel his strength slowly returning as he sat up. Ramulas saw Oriel watching with worry in her eyes. 'Oh, I have not felt this tired before,' he said as a bout of dizziness swept over him.

'It was the only way to heal you quickly,' Oriel said as she walked over to him, 'But you are not fully recovered, I did not have enough power for that. I just hope you will recover in time to stop the legion from coming to this world.'

Ramulas opened his eyes in surprise. With every passing second, he could feel his body becoming stronger. He slowly stood and smiled at Oriel. Then he felt soreness deep in his bones and knew he had not fully healed.

'I need to tell you why it needs to be you who moves the crystal, and face Remus if he comes here.' Oriel took a breath before continuing. 'In the world where we both come from, a warlord ruled the lands sixty years ago.

'During this time, the army was made up of farmers pressed into service, fighting off the barbaric tribes. Then the tribes joined forces and invaded the capital. The army was overwhelmed, and the tribes stayed in the city for six months before they were bribed to leave. The warlord did not know what to do to stop this from happening again.

'He was served by two wizards who were very loyal to him. The two wizards were in fact twins and very competitive with one another. Time after time, they would attempt to outdo each other to become the warlord's favourite. They attempted to solve the tribe problem.

'But throughout all of this, their love for each other far outweighed their want for recognition from the warlord. Being competitive was always a sport to them with no malice.

'One day they were both working on a spell in their chambers when a wraith appeared before them. It told the twins they could become more powerful in magic if they would allow the wraith to possess a part of their souls.

'When the twins asked what would happen to them when they were possessed, the wraith said they would have to kill and destroy everything to become powerful. Both twins said they would not do such a thing. The wraith said it would wait in the chambers until the next day, to see if they would change their minds.

'The twins walked away from the chambers and stopped studying for the day. During the night; the youngest of the twins rose from his bed silently, so as not to wake his brother who slept nearby. He came to the chambers and found the wraith waiting for him. The wraith knew the youngest would come to him. It asked the wizard to step forward and embrace true power.

'But he asked what would happen to his older twin. The creature became dark and said that he must destroy his older brother, for he was the only one with the power to stop him when he became stronger.

'However, the younger twin could not think of killing his brother and did not want the power. The wraith was cunning and offered a proposal. He said there was one thing he would do for the younger twin: when the wizard took the wraith's hand, his brother would be banished to another world where he would be no threat to him, and therefore he would live.

'Reaching out, the younger twin only thought of power as he took the wraith's skeletal hand. What the wraith did not say was that woven into the banishment spell was a forgetfulness spell. So, both twins would not remember each other.

'The youngest twin is Remus, and you, Ramulas are the elder twin. You were a natural leader of people in your old life.'

An image of Remus appeared before him.

Ramulas was in shock. 'So that explains the dreams I have had.'

'Remus and you both studied magic, but you have an advantage over him. You studied to be a battlemage. They have more of an advantage over warlords and wizards.'

'In what way?'

'You will find out soon when your power returns. I need to get you back to the city. I will tell you more tomorrow night.' Ramulas started to reply but was engulfed by the fog.

Once Ramulas had left the cavern, Oriel felt fatigued. It had taken most of her magical ability to help him. She needed to rest in order to recover. She knew that if Ramulas faced Remus, he would not be ready. It would take months of training for him to be ready. They did not have that luxury.

Ramulas was the only thing with the power to stop Remus and the first legion. Oriel put all of her hopes in Ramulas dropping the crystal in the Symiak mountains. That would be their only way to stop the legion. If Remus came now, Ramulas would not stand a chance.

***

Pip sat against a wall in the rear room of the house. She was ten feet away from the pile of sheets where Ramulas had been. Her eyes were closed as she thought of what to do next.

Part of her wanted to look through the city for him, but she knew that to be an impossible task. If he had not come back by morning, she would return to the master of shadows. She knew he would be extremely upset. Without Ramulas, her and Jenna's life hung in the balance. Then the temperature in the room dropped dramatically, and she became instantly alert.

'Hello, Pip,' she heard Ramulas say.

Her eyes snapped open, and she jumped to her feet when she saw Ramulas standing before her. Her mouth hung open as she saw that he stood with any injuries and his eyes full of power.

He stood bare-chested, and Pip saw that he had a tattoo of a green dragon on his chest.

'What happened to you?' she whispered.

Ramulas smiled. 'I was sick, and now I am better.'

'I helped you escape from the tombs. You could hardly walk without assistance. Now you have returned with a tattoo—where did that come from?'

Ramulas looked at Pip in confusion, before glancing down at his chest to where she was pointing. He gasped in shock when he saw it.

'I was not aware of this,' he said in awe. 'This must have been put there by Oriel when she healed me.'

Pip's face grew stern as she walked up to Ramulas and punched him in the arm.

Ramulas laughed as he rubbed his arm. 'What was that for?'

'Don't disappear like that again,' Pip said shaking a finger at him.

A wave of dizziness swept over Ramulas, and he swayed on his feet. Pip grabbed one of his arms and helped him to sit down. 'I guess I am still recovering,' he said. 'I think I will rest for a while.'

'Rest as much as you can until dawn. Then I will take you to the master of shadows. He will know what to do.'

'What can I do to repay you?' Ramulas asked.

'For now, stay here until I return,' Pip said before racing out of the room.

Pip ran through the streets, her mind full of thoughts. She was so happy that Ramulas had returned and was better. But she could tell he was still sick and would be in no condition to break into the castle any time soon.

If there was a way to fix things, Pip would find it.

31

Shigar's eyes opened in surprise.

The prisoner had returned to the city. One moment there was no trace of him, and the next he was here again. A smile spread across the magician's face. He was worried that he might have lost the prisoner.

Shigar walked from the cluttered table in his chambers out into the hall. He was tired from studying. Now, however, energy in the form of hope flowed through him. He needed to talk to the prisoner, who he felt was near the docks and still recovering.

The magician's thoughts were broken when he encountered Zachary and a score of royal guards.

'Magician,' Zachary said, with wild eyes. 'Have you any news of the escaped prisoner?'

'No,' Shigar said. 'I have been searching, but could find no trace of him in the city.'

The king came to within inches of Shigar. 'I want him found. He could be out there somewhere planning to kill Aleesha and me. I do not even feel safe in my own castle.'

Shigar held out his hands. 'I do not know where he is. And I am still in possession of the crystal and his weapons. He cannot harm you without them.'

'Are you sure?'

Shigar nodded.

'What are you doing out of your chambers, then, magician? Go back and protect the crystal! And inform me when he returns.'

Shigar bit down on his tongue to suppress his smile. Walking back to his chambers, Shigar could not believe how easy it was lying to Zachary. After all these years, he thought there might be a way out of this empty life.

***

Pip stood in an abandoned warehouse with the master of shadows and eight enforcers. She had just told of Ramulas' return, and how he was too sick to come.

Anger simmered behind the master's eyes as he looked around at the cobweb-covered crates. Then he focused on Pip. 'Do you know what is happening in the city?'

Pip stayed silent, not wanting to anger the master more.

'The city has been locked down, and teams of soldiers search for your friend. I have been told that they will not stop until he is found. This will be very bad for the shadows.'

He focused on Pip. 'Bring him here now, and I will judge for myself if this man is worth the trouble you have caused.'

The master waved his hands, and four enforcers walked over to Pip. She knew each one of them personally, and they were to help her bring Ramulas to the master. As the group left the warehouse, Pip played the master's words over in her head. He had put the blame squarely on her shoulders.

For the sake of Jenna and herself, Pip needed the master to see Ramulas was worth the trouble.

***

They entered the abandoned house, and Pip found Ramulas sleeping on the floor in the rear room. She bent down to shake him, and he woke with a start.

She smiled down at him while he looked at the enforcers. 'They are with me. Come on, we need to take you to see the master.'

Ramulas nodded and was helped to his feet and brought outside to a wagon with two horses. Pip seemed calm in the sea of madness on the street. People were filled with panic and frantically searched for hidden enemies as they rushed by. News of the city shutdown and soldiers roaming the streets caused them to abandon all logic.

She helped Ramulas into the wagon before she and an enforcer jumped into the front seat. Ramulas heard a whip crack and the wagon began its rocky movements. He closed his eyes and listened as they made their way through the city.

The rocking motion was somewhat comforting and relieved some of the worries about the crystal. As soon as Ramulas dropped it in the mountains, he would be able to return to his home and family.

Then he heard Pip curse and the shots of alarm from soldiers. A cold chill ran through Ramulas as he heard calls for the wagon to be stopped and searched.

'Stay quiet,' Pip said.

Then the voices of the soldiers grew louder, and Ramulas could not believe how many there were. Then the canvas was removed from the barrels in the wagon, and Ramulas froze holding his breath.

'What are you doing?' Pip shouted.

'By the orders of Kind Zachary, we are to search everywhere for the escaped prisoner.'

'I have only barrels of wine, there is no-one else on my wagon.'

'Open every barrel,' the soldier called, 'starting with this one.'

Ramulas almost jumped when he heard the thump so close to his head. How were they going to get out of this situation?

***

'I can see them in the trees!' Grace said excitedly.

Jacqueline and Kate looked at the trees where Grace pointed.

After a second, two dryads stepped out from the trunks. Jacqueline was still recovering from Grace returning with bright emerald eyes and had made her promise not to go with the dryads until her da returned.

Eady and a male dryad walked towards them with welcoming smiles. Then the female spoke to Grace. 'Why have you not answered our calls? The children wish to play with you.'

Jacqueline stepped in front of her daughters. 'My husband is missing, and my girls will stay with me until he returns.'

Eady's smile grew as she looked at Jacqueline. 'We wish your family no harm, and we have sent food to help you in this time of need.'

Jacqueline's maternal instincts told her not to let her daughters out of her sight until Ramulas returned. 'Thank you for the food, but my girls will stay with me. Grace will not go into the trees again any time soon.'

Eady nodded and looked around. 'Very well. When it is safe, some of the children will come here to spend time with your daughters. Would this be to your liking?'

Jacqueline saw both Kate and Grace nod their heads vigorously.

As a mother, she had her reservations about the dryads. However, Jacqueline thought that if she controlled how they interacted with Grace it would be safer.

Grace had run off once already, and she did not want that to happen again. If the dryads came to Matthew's farm, Jacqueline would be able to keep an eye on both girls, and that put her at ease.

Jacqueline nodded. 'You may come here, and know that my daughters are not to leave this farm until their father returns.' The female dryad smiled while Kate and Grace danced, kicking up clouds of dust. Several dryad children came out of the trees to join the girls.

***

Pip and the enforcer stood by while twelve soldiers carried the four barrels from the wagon. She crossed her arms and scowled at the sergeant. Hammers were brought forth and the soldiers started to smash the barrels.

'Hey!' Pip shouted, moving forward. 'Who's going to pay for this?'

The sergeant smiled while pushing Pip back. People in the street had stopped to watch the spectacle. The first barrel cracked. A small trickle of red wine could be seen before another blow sent the barrel's contents flowing along the cobblestones.

One by one, the other barrels were broken and the smell of wine filled Pip's nostrils. Her anger increased with every damaged barrel. Once the soldiers had finished, Pip and the enforcer were told to move on.

'This is not fair,' Pip shouted, 'Who is going to pay for this? My family is waiting for me to bring money home.'

The sergeant shrugged. 'Take it up with the king. We search for an escaped prisoner, and do not care for your petty problems.'

As they disappeared, Pip tapped the side of the wagon. 'You did well. We will be with the master soon.'

Ramulas felt the wagon move once more and was surprised that he was not discovered. He focused on the rocking motion and the sound of the people to take his mind off his family. He would be home again with them soon, and all of this would be behind them.

The wagon stopped and Ramulas heard the creak of a wooden door. Hushed voices surrounded the wagon as it moved into a building. Hidden latches were pulled and Ramulas fell from the false bottom of the wagon onto the floor.

He crawled out and dusted himself off. Ramulas looked around the large warehouse and saw ten large men lining the walls along crates and barrels. Pip stood next to an even larger man dressed in a black silk shirt. His bald head seemed to shine in the light as he glided to Ramulas.

'So, Pip,' the master said, 'this is your friend. The one who has brought trouble to my city.'

Pip nodded. 'He is important. He needs to get into the castle to retrieve the crystal.'

Ramulas flinched at the mention of the crystal. The more people that knew, the greater the chance of people finding out about his daughters, and he wanted to ensure that his family stayed safe.

The master smiled at Ramulas, which caused an involuntary shiver to run through him. His heart beat faster as the large man came closer.

'Pray tell,' the master said in a soft voice, 'why this crystal is so important that Pip would risk death to rescue you.'

The statement shocked Ramulas. He could not understand how Pip could be in danger. He looked at this man, knowing he must be the master Pip spoke about. He was the one who would be able to help.

'If I do not take the crystal into the Symiak mountains, something bad will happen.'

'And what is this bad thing?' the master asked.

Ramulas saw Pip nod behind the large man and he took and deep breath. He told of Oriel, Remus, and the legion that would come to the kingdom once the crystal anchored, and the importance of him taking it into the mountains.

Once he had finished, Ramulas waited for the master or the others in the warehouse to scoff or call him a liar. However, the master's expression grew stern and he walked a few feet away. He crossed his arms and looked at Ramulas. 'I believe you.'

Ramulas was so stunned he almost fell over. His mouth opened to speak, but he was silenced by the master's upraised hand.

'Pip says you are still weak; I can see that it will be a few days before you can return to the castle. You will stay with us until this time.'

Ramulas stepped forward. 'I need to get the crystal before it's too late.'

The master's expression changed, and Ramulas lost his breath. 'If you attempt to enter the castle now you will fail, and blame will fall on the shadows. This is my family, and I will not have anyone bring trouble to my home.'

The master walked into the shadows along the far wall, and Pip came up to Ramulas. 'Come with me, I will take you to a safe place.'

***

The men screamed as they were dragged away from the gate.

Pip watched the scene from the shadows. A patrol of soldiers pulled a merchant and his guard away from the west gate. He had been waiting in line for the gates to open with the other merchants. A fight broke out, and he used the opportunity to move his wagon forward. Soldiers saw this and he was accused of causing a riot and sent to the dungeons.

As he was dragged away, other merchants raided his wagon. Pip shook her head seeing the first signs of anarchy.

In the two days since Ramulas' escape, the tensions within the city had grown. Everyone now knew that the soldiers looked for the man who escaped from the tombs.

When Ramulas first escaped, there had been no reward, now it was ten gold pieces and a promise that the city could return to normal. The gates and harbour being shut down had upset a lot of important people. Many merchants were losing money each day the city was locked down.

Word had spread that if the prisoner was not found in two days, people would not be able to leave their houses. *There would be a lot of killings*, Pip thought.

The master had also felt the pressure, and this was the last day shadows were allowed in the streets. The soldiers were throwing people into the dungeons for the smallest of reasons. It did not seem to matter that the cells were already full.

Pip made her way back to the hideout, thinking about Ramulas. A healer had been giving him herbal medicine to make him strong, but it was too slow for the master. Pip had been planning a way for them to get into the castle. The master was slowly losing his patience, and she needed a way in soon.

Pip saw people passing her with arms, sacks, and carts loaded with food and supplies. They were readying for being locked in their homes. No-one outside of the shadows could be trusted. If Ramulas was found with the shadows, every one of them could look forward to Gullytown.

She backtracked and circled around the building before entering. Pip flashed hand signals as she ran for the hidden panel in the wall. As soon as she entered, the two burly men pushed a large heavy table in front of the section.

32

Shigar hid his emotions as Zachary paced in front of him in his chambers. Four royal guards stood at the door.

'Tell me what I am supposed to do, magician,' the king said as he stopped to face him. 'There is a mad man out in the city somewhere planning to kill Aleesha and me.'

Shigar waved his hand at the piles of books and scrolls littering the table and floor. 'I have been studying and have not felt any trace of the escaped prisoner.'

'Do you care about your king, magician?'

Shigar nodded as he watched the madness in Zachary's eyes. He reminded Shigar of a young page caught in the king's chambers without permission. There was a mixture of fear and panic brewing just beneath the surface.

'Then do better!' Zachary shouted sweeping his hand across the table, sending scrolls flying into the wall. 'I am your king, and if you do not find this man, I will have you sent to Gullytown.' Shigar kept his composure as Zachary stormed out of the room. He looked down at his scrolls and felt sad. The mess on the floor represented his life. He needed a way out of this life.

He walked over to the window and looked out towards the poor section. Since returning, Shigar had felt the prisoner move around that area of the city. Shigar was happy to keep this information to himself.

There was something about the prisoner that connected with Shigar. He wanted to talk to this man to find out what it was.

The only problem was that he was unable to leave the castle.

***

Pip entered a large room filled with lavish furnishings, tapestries, and paintings. The master of shadows sat in a highbacked red chair opposite Ramulas. Eight enforcers sat on silk cushions, drinking and talking amongst each other.

Everything appeared fine, but Pip's inner voice screamed for her to run. The master stopped mid-conversation and turned. He motioned for her to come closer, his face devoid of any emotion. Pip stopped six feet from him and readied herself.

'My favourite thief, how does business go in the streets?'

She knew that all business had stopped from last night, and the shadows were losing money. Pip did not answer, and the master stood and took a quick step to her. In the blink of an eye, his hand shot out and grabbed a handful of her hair.

Pip screamed in surprise as she was lifted in the air. 'Now, Pip, I have been told that the price for your friend will be fifty gold coins on the morrow, and a pardon for any who brings him into the king. I think the shadows would like a pardon.' Ramulas stood and backed away in shock, knowing where this was leading. The enforcers moved in to close any escape routes.

'I think the king's soldiers will be able to deal with the crystal. Jenna and you must be punished for what has happened here.'

Pip held onto her hair and screamed, 'No, leave my family alone!'

The master laughed. 'And tell me, Pip, who is going to protect them? It won't be you, because I am going to teach you a lesson, and there is no-one to help you.'

The master of shadows threw Pip to the wall, and she fell to the floor with a moan. The enforcers turned away, knowing what was about to happen. The master reached down for Pip.

'Stop!'

The master froze and slowly turned around. Pip's eye's widened in shock at what she saw, and the enforcers were stunned.

Ramulas stood straight and tall with a determined look on his face. He walked over to put himself between the master and Pip.

He looked the master in the eyes. 'You will not touch her like that again. Pip is under my protection, and I will do what I can to protect her.'

The silence in the room was deafening. For a few heartbeats, no-one moved. The enforcers and Pip looked from Ramulas to the master, waiting to see what would happen.

No-one had ever stood up to the master before and lived to tell the tale. The master himself looked like he was about to explode.

'Are you willing to die to protect Pip?' the master asked in a low voice.

Ramulas coughed and winced before nodding. Everyone in the room knew that he was still recovering and had no chance against the master, but he still stood his ground.

Suddenly, the master laughed and slapped Ramulas on the shoulder, sending him crashing to the floor. Tears rolled down the master's cheeks as he laughed harder.

He pointed to a dazed Ramulas. 'You would stand up to me for her?' Then he turned to Pip. 'By this time tomorrow, I want the both of you in the castle.'

The laughter stopped and he looked down to Ramulas. 'You are either very brave or a fool. Never do that again, or you will die very slowly.'

The master motioned with his hand to Pip. She ran to Ramulas and took him from the room.

Once in the street, she turned to him. 'What were you thinking? He could have killed you.'

'I wanted to do what was right.'

At that moment, Pip saw her father in Ramulas and silently began to cry.

***

Pip smiled as she stood next to Ramulas. Two enforcers waited by a few crates and sacks filled with items she ordered from the market. The master of shadows sat behind his table in his luxurious quarters. He looked at the young thief and knew she had come up with a plan.

'Tell me, Pip—how are you going into the castle?'

Pip gave a mock bow to the master. 'This is my wounded duck. And it will help us enter the castle.'

The master raised an eyebrow. 'How will a wounded bird get you past all the soldiers?'

'When Jenna and I were young, our father would take us to the lake in the spring and summer. Sometimes we would see a duck that appeared to be hurt and could not fly. Jenna and I would follow it until it flew away.'

'But how will this help you enter the castle? One injured bird would not attract the attention we need.'

Pip's smile grew. 'This wounded duck will get the whole city's attention.'

The master listened intently as Pip explained her plan. By the time she had finished, he wore a smile almost as large as Pip's.

If things worked out the way she said, then the shadows would be rich beyond their wildest dreams.

'I have received word that by mid-afternoon the soldiers will be placing a curfew on the people of Keah. They will be locked away in their homes until your friend is found. I want you in the castle by midday. There is much to do and so little time.' The master called out instructions and the room exploded into a hive of activity. Pip grabbed Ramulas by the hand and dragged him out into the street. They only had a few hours to get ready.

***

The master of shadows sat silently as the sergeant stood before him. After a minute, the sergeant began to fidget and readjust parts of his uniform. The master of shadows smiled; the balance of power had just tipped into his favour.

He had six of the largest enforcers standing silently along the walls of the room. They were as silent as the crates and barrels lining the walls. He wanted the sergeant to know who was in control of this situation.

'Two months ago, you were found in one of my brothels with a dead girl beside you,' he said to the sergeant. 'A very uncomfortable position for you to be in. I offered you a way out of the mess you caused. In exchange, you were to grant me one small favour. Now is the time to ask for that favour.'

'What do you want from me?' the sergeant asked.

'Your uniform. I will return it to you tomorrow.'

'I cannot—' he began.

'I still have the girl's body,' the master of shadows lied. 'And witnesses who saw you in the room with her.'

The sergeant's body slumped. He found himself between a rock and a hard place. He slowly began to undress. Two of the enforcers walked over and took his clothes. When the sergeant had finished, he was given a brown robe.

'Please remain here as our guest until your uniform is returned,' the master of shadows said with a smile.

The sergeant stood defeated and full of shame. He wished he could go back to that night two months ago. Things would be a lot different for him.

***

Pip pointed to the sergeant's clothes on the table. 'You will need to change clothes in order to enter the castle.'

Ramulas walked to the table and began to undress while the master of shadows focused on Pip. 'There has been a development. The gates will be open in the morning to allow merchants in the city. We could work that in with your wounded duck plan.'

Pip nodded. 'We need to prepare now.'

She motioned for one of the large men to take the canvas sack.

As they left the room, the master of shadows glided over to Ramulas with the fluid steps of a seasoned fighter. He handed Ramulas a rolled sheet of paper.

'This is a map of the castle. It shows the way to the magician's quarters. Study it well until Pip returns. She will read the map once her work is done. After you have both memorised it, the map will be returned to me.'

Ramulas nodded and began to look at the map. After what only seemed a few moments, Pip appeared by his side.

'The wounded duck is ready, and our people move into position.'

The master of shadows nodded. 'Show me.'

Pip led the small group outside to where Old John held the reins of a horse. Ramulas saw a cloaked figure sitting on the horse. He could sense that the horse was about to bolt down the street. Ramulas concentrated and sent calming thoughts to the horse.

'Stop that,' Pip whispered, punching him in the arm.

'But the horse is about to run; the rider will be thrown,' Ramulas replied.

'We want the horse to run—need it to run,' Pip said, pointing to the saddle, 'and that rider will not fall.'

Ramulas looked at the saddle and saw several ropes holding the rider in place. He looked at the cloaked figure but was unable to see the face under the hood.

'Why is the rider tied to the saddle?' he asked Pip.

'The rider is my wounded duck; I have explained this before. He will help us get into the castle. We will wait here until Old John sets the wounded duck free.'

As Old John led the horse away, Ramulas looked at Pip. 'Who is the wounded duck?'

'You ask the wrong question. You should ask, "*What* is the wounded duck?"'

Pip quickly explained what the wounded duck was, and how it would help them get into the castle. By the time she was finished, Ramulas was smiling.

'Are you sure this will work?' he asked her.

'Nothing in life is certain,' Pip said, 'but that does not mean that we do not try.'

Pip looked at the map with Ramulas, and they studied the route they would need to take.

***

Old John led the horse to the west gate. Word of the curfew had spread and the streets were full of people buying last-minute items. By the time he arrived at the gate, he was struggling to keep the horse under control.

It was spooked, foaming at the mouth. Its eyes were wide, and it was pulling on the reins. Old John could sympathise with the horse—the dummy tied to it was a living thing; actually, living things.

The dummy's legs were filled with live crabs that were constantly moving, and the body held a surprise for whoever stopped the horse. Old John found himself one hundred yards from the gate, and he saw a line of people, horses, and carts along the wall waiting to leave the city.

As John got closer to the gate, he saw a merchant come through the gate into the city. This brought howls of protest from those waiting to leave. The tide of people was pushed back by a score of soldiers.

One of the gates was open, and six soldiers stood guard, only allowing people into Keah. Old John was twenty yards away.

He could see that it was more chaotic outside the gates than in the city. There was no orderly line, just a mass of screaming people, horses, and carts trying to push their way in. Old John came to within ten yards of the gate.

A team of four horses pulling a wagon came into the city, and one of the soldiers saw him.

'Halt! Come no closer.'

Old John saw that the gate was now clear. 'We have come with a message from the king!' he said loudly as he came closer to the gate.

The soldiers looked at each other in confusion then back at John, who was attempting to control the horse.

'What is the message?' one of them asked.

Old John saw that the gap in the gate was closing and he was six feet away. '*Yaaaaah!*' he screamed as he slapped the horse on its rump.

The horse reared back before bolting through the opening. Two soldiers were knocked to the ground as the animal raced past.

Old John removed a small pouch of ground pepper from his vest. He opened the pouch and spun it above his head. Soldiers rushing in to grab him were stopped by fits of coughing and sneezing. Old John held a cloth to his face as he ran into the city waving a hand above his head.

A boy sitting on a nearby rooftop saw the signal. He quickly stood and waved both hands in the air. The signal was repeated and passed through the city.

Finally, Pip saw the signal.

33

Pip looked at Ramulas. 'We leave now. Remember to act like the sergeant who stopped our cart when we came into Keah, and walk with confidence.'

'Pip.' Both Ramulas and Pip turned to the master of shadows, who stood looking out the window. 'Pip, you are my best thief. If you were anyone else, I would have killed you and your sister by now many times over. I do not need to tell you how important it is for you to come back to work once he has the crystal. Your friend will go into the mountains by himself.'

She nodded.

Ramulas looked at Pip in her black robe. She was dressed as a priestess of the sea goddess. To see a priestess and a sergeant walking through the city would not turn any heads—this is what Pip had told him.

'How far to the castle?' he asked her.

'A few minutes' walk, but we will ride part of the way.'

Pip led Ramulas to a side street to a waiting carriage.

Once they climbed in, the driver cracked his whip, and they began to move. The carriage rocked and swayed as they moved down the street. Ramulas looked through the black lace curtains as he heard shouts of alarm, followed by soldiers running to the west gate.

'The wounded duck has left the city. For a short while, all eyes will be looking to the west, and the castle will be open.'

After a few minutes, the carriage stopped. When they hopped out, Ramulas saw they were a block away from the castle. His mouth became dry and the palms of his hands were sweating. A score of soldiers raced out of the castle towards them. Ramulas was frozen. He could not move.

'We move now, sergeant,' Pip whispered as she pushed him from behind.

Ramulas took strong, confident steps toward the castle with Pip by his side. In his mind, he could see the soldiers surrounding him and Pip before dragging them to the castle. He let out a sigh of relief as they ran by.

As they walked into the courtyard, Ramulas heard a commotion from within the castle and saw four soldiers rush inside. Four more soldiers waited in the courtyard. When they saw Ramulas and Pip at the entrance of the castle, they ran up to them.

'What are you doing here, sergeant?' one of them asked.

Ramulas turned and struck the soldier across the face. The soldier spun as he fell, an arc of blood coming from his mouth. Ramulas' heartbeat sounded like a drum, and he felt as if he was going to throw up, but he pushed the anxiety away.

'You dare question me?' Ramulas shouted down at the soldier.

'Forgive him,' another soldier said. 'We thought you would be at the west gate, or at the rear of the castle.'

Ramulas looked at him. 'What's happening at the rear of the castle?'

'After we were told someone rode out of the west gate, almost every soldier rushed to the gate. And now we have groups of thieves coming through the rear of the castle.'

'Who told you those lies?' Ramulas screamed. 'I want every man to the west wall.'

The soldiers saluted, picked up their comrade, and rushed into the streets. Pip and Ramulas walked unchallenged into the castle.

***

The horse carrying the wounded duck charged through the west gate, into the sea of people waiting to come into the city. It pushed through the small gaps in-between people, horses, and carts.

People called out in protest to the rider, but they made way for the crazed horse. In a short time, the horse had broken through the mass of people and raced to the southwest. The jolting had agitated the crabs, and they increased their movements within the leggings. This was pure terror for the horse and encouraged it to run faster.

The people outside the gate saw an opening amidst the chaos. They moved as one, trying to enter the city. As the soldiers continued to choke on pepper, two carts became lodged in the gateway. The two owners hurled abuse at each other.

After a few seconds, the soldiers had begun to recover and raced to the gate.

'Rider out of the gate!' one of the soldiers screamed from the wall.

A sergeant at the gate pointed to the two carts. 'Clear the way.'

Six soldiers moved forward as the sergeant ran into the street, where he could be seen from the wall. 'Sound the alarm!' he called through cupped hands. 'Escape!'

He ran back to the gate as it was being cleared. A bell could be heard, and the sergeant knew that a brazier would be lit, sending green smoke into the sky signalling an escape.

Once the gate was cleared, the sergeant stepped through to see the congested mess of people, horses, and carts. 'I want a path opened for me now!' he screamed.

As the soldiers rushed forward, the sergeant saw two men on horseback. He walked to them with a grim smile. 'In the name of King Zachary, off your horses. I have need of them.'

The riders looked at each other, unsure what to do.

'Your horses or Gullytown,' the sergeant said.

Both climbed down from their horses and handed their reins over. The sergeant and a soldier climbed onto the horses. He screamed at the people as they pushed through the mass.

By the time both horses were out in the open, the escaped horse seemed like a speck on the horizon. The sergeant kicked his heels into his horse and gave chase.

Two factors worked against the sergeant and the soldier. The horse they were chasing carried a much lighter weight, and it was fuelled by sheer terror.

A few minutes after they left the gate, scores of cavalry left the gate and joined the pursuit. Within ten minutes, they had caught up with the runaway horse, forming a giant V around the horse.

Despite repeated calls to halt, the rider in the hooded cloak ignored them. The riders closed in; the king had given orders that the rider was to be taken back alive. When a soldier was close enough, he grabbed a handful of cloak and pulled.

As he pulled on the cloak, it opened and six ducks flew into the sky.

It was at that moment they knew they had been duped. They were several miles from the city.

'Back to the city. We have been tricked!' the captain shouted.

As one, they turned and raced back to the city.

**

Remus smiled as he stood in front of the golden arch. The warlords and red wizards had just completed their final spells. Blue and red mist swirled within the arch.

Remus tossed in a small silver ball and the mists combined, turned purple, and slowly thinned.

'As soon as the mist clears, I will go to Oriel's new world and deal with the magic-user who has possession of the crystal. Then I will show the people of this world a taste of what to expect when the legion comes,' Remus said.

After what seemed like an eternity, they had finally opened the way to Oriel and restored hope for regaining their power. Remus' magical symbols glowed in anticipation of what he was going to do.

Oriel's escape was a blessing in disguise. If she had stayed and been consumed, the warlords would not have known about this new world. Their world was slowly dying from constant wars. There seemed no hope until Oriel escaped. Remus would have to thank her just before consuming her soul.

The was so much to do in so little time.

***

Shigar had been studying the crystal for the past few days while secretly monitoring the escaped prisoner. He could feel the prisoner's health improving as he moved around the poor section of the city.

He must have someone helping him move around to avoid the king's soldiers.

However, the crystal had slowly changed. The shadows were more prominent and moved at a faster pace. Then he heard a cracking sound and purple mist flowed from the crystal. This alarmed Shigar, and he wondered if this had anything to do with the crystal anchoring.

The energies of the prisoner changed and became stronger, diverting the magician's attention from the crystal. He had left the poor section of the city and was now in the courtyard of the castle.

This filled him with excitement. For so long, Shigar had yearned for somewhere he belonged, and he felt that somehow this prisoner could offer that to him.

Shigar looked at the crystal in front of him. He knew the prisoner would somehow return for it. Then he felt the prisoner enter the castle. The magician needed to prepare for this important meeting. He began to gather spells and potions that he might need.

***

Ramulas and Pip walked into the castle as if they belonged. They walked by a few servants as they made their way through the maze of hallways, but no-one gave them a second glance.

Ramulas made a couple of wrong turns, which were corrected by Pip. After a few minutes, they stood outside the magician's chambers. It was the only room on this floor with its door open.

'I have a bad feeling,' Pip whispered as she looked around. 'This was too easy; this might be a trap.'

Ramulas saw the crystal on the table and walked inside the magician's chambers.

'Does the word "trap" mean anything to you?' Pip asked as she followed him in. Ramulas ignored her as he reached out to pick up the crystal.

As he held it in his hands, Ramulas noticed mist rising from it. The shapes within were more prominent as they danced beneath the surface. Ramulas knew deep down that the crystal would anchor soon, and they needed to get to the mountain quickly. He went to place it in his vest and realised that he wore the sergeant's uniform.

He dropped the crystal into a small pouch attached to his belt then scanned the room for his weapons. Ramulas found them in a corner near the bookshelf. A sense of relief washed over him as he walked over to them.

As he picked up the weapons, Ramulas heard the creak of a door opening and he froze. Ramulas slowly turned with his weapons ready. To his shock, he saw Pip looking through the magician's desk. Her head was hidden in one of the doors.

'What are you doing?' he whispered. 'You almost scared me to death.'

Pip pulled her head out. 'I'm just looking for a little something to take with me.'

'Well don't,' Ramulas scolded. 'This is the magician's chamber, and I want no trouble with him.'

Pip saw a small crystal bottle filled with amber fluid. She quickly dropped it into one of her pockets.

Ramulas saw this and walked over to her. 'Put that back. It will only bring us trouble,' he whispered.

'I would listen to him if I were you,' Shigar said as he came out of a doorway on the side of the room.

He smiled as the duo moved away from each other. Pip's hands disappeared inside her robe and came out throwing two knives at Shigar. Both knives were deflected by an invisible wall in front of the magician. They flew wide, embedding in books on opposite sides of the chamber.

'I am not here to fight with you,' Shigar said, holding his hands up.

Ramulas stopped circling to the left but still held his weapons ready. 'I have come to claim the crystal and my weapons. It will anchor any moment; I need to take it far from the city.'

Shigar nodded as he saw Pip holding two more knives. 'You two make a good fighting team. Very wise for you to separate. I can only target one of you, and I am sure that when I do, the other will strike me down. So, you see, I have no wish to fight.'

'We will be leaving then,' Ramulas said as he motioned for Pip to come over to his side.

'And how, pray tell, will you leave the city?' Shigar asked. 'That was a fine trick sending most of the cavalry from the city. But they are on their way back. When they return, no-one will be able to leave.'

'We will find a way,' Pip replied defiantly.

'I know of a way for you both to leave the city safely,' the magician offered.

'Why would you help us?' Ramulas asked.

'I am helping you because I have served King Zachary for many years, and I have made too many excuses for his behaviour since the death of his wife. Things changed for me when you were placed in the tombs.

'Zachary allowed his fear of the unknown to rule his decisions, and you showed true character when you suffered through your ordeal. You continued to put the welfare of others ahead of your own, even after suffering so much loss. We do not have much time. Follow me, and I will show you the way.'

Shigar walked back to the door he appeared from. Ramulas looked at Pip, who just shrugged as she retrieved her knives.

Ramulas nodded to Pip, and they followed Shigar through the doorway. They found themselves in a smaller room filled with bookshelves. One of the bookshelves swung away from the wall, showing a stairway descending into darkness.

Shigar stood smiling by the entrance. 'At the bottom of the stairway is a tunnel, which travels north for two miles. You come out behind a small hill; you will not be seen by those on the wall. You will find a hut near the tunnel and also something to help you on your journey.'

Shigar paused before asking, 'What are your plans once you are rid of the crystal?'

Ramulas smiled. 'Home to my family.'

'The city may still be locked down. Find your way back to the hut when you return. I will see if I can help you.'

'What can I do to repay you?' Ramulas asked.

'Do what you know to be right,' Shigar replied, 'And once the young lady gives me my potion, you can both leave.'

Pip gave Shigar a defiant look before handing him the crystal bottle. Shigar held it and shook it vigorously, and a pale blue light began to shine from within. In moments, all three were bathed in its light.

He handed the bottle to Ramulas. 'Your name isn't Thomas, is it?' he asked with a smile.

'It's Ramulas.'

'And I am Shigar, magician to King Zachary. Now, you must go quickly.'

Ramulas and Pip descended down into the darkness a few feet, and then they heard the door close behind them. Pip reached over and took the crystal bottle from Ramulas. He would need both hands if something happened in the tunnel. She could cope with one hand.

The stairway was wide enough for them to walk side by side. The light from the crystal bottle illuminated them and the stairs below. The walls were rough, and yet the stairs were smooth and uniform. Ramulas saw lichen built up on the walls, and the air was damp with moisture. The temperature dropped as they descended.

After a short while, they found themselves at the bottom of the stairs, which continued as a passage. Pip stopped and tilted her head to one side.

'What's wrong?' Ramulas asked.

'There is something down here with us,' she whispered, with plumes of fog coming from her mouth.

Ramulas glanced up the stairs then down the passageway ahead of them. But he was unable to see past the circle of amber light. 'I can't see anything.'

'I can feel it,' Pip said. 'I want to try something.' Pip hid the crystal bottle under her robe. Their world became dark, and all Ramulas could see was Pip's face illuminated by the bottle in her robe.

Soft moans and sighs came at them from every direction, and the air around them became extremely cold. Pip quickly pulled out the potion and flooded the area in light. Pip and Ramulas gasped in shock.

Several spectral figures floated in front of them, their skeletal hands reaching out for them. When Pip pulled out the potion, the spectral figures covered their eyes and swam into the darkness.

'By the gods,' Ramulas said, gripping his weapons, 'what are those things?'

Pip glanced around, looking at the edges of the light. 'I don't know what they are, but I think the light hurts them somehow. I can see them trying to find a way in.'

Ramulas walked closer to the edge of the light and saw faces that were rotting with decay smiling back at him. 'I don't know how long the light will last. I want to be out of this tunnel as soon as we can.'

Pip nodded in agreement, and they quickly walked down the passageway.

***

Ramulas could feel a slight breeze in the passageway, and he could see a faint light ahead. He turned to tell Pip, but he could tell that she had also seen it.

'We are almost there,' she said, taking the words out of his mouth.

Their pace quickened and, a few minutes later, they pushed through a wall of vines and were outside. Ramulas closed his eyes and breathed in a lungful of fresh air. Then he felt the strong presence of an animal close by.

His eyes snapped open.

To Ramulas' left was a small hut. Next to the hut was a large horse. It was almost twice the size of a normal horse.

Its face was covered with a guard, and its body was covered in studded leather.

'It's a warhorse,' Pip said in awe.

Ramulas had heard rumours of warhorses. They were bred for fighting, and with the right rider, they could plough through enemy ranks. However, they were said to be rare. There were only one hundred in the kingdom.

Ramulas focused and communicated with the warhorse as he walked towards it. He sent it calming thoughts and told it that Pip and he were friends. He found that it was a majestic creature that had been treated well. It accepted them both.

Then Ramulas laughed.

'What's funny?' Pip asked.

'Rufus. The warhorse's name is Rufus.'

'How do you know that?' she asked.

'He just told me.'

Ramulas walked over and patted the warhorse on the neck. It felt strange being a foot above his head.

'There are blankets and provisions tied the back of the warhorse,' Pip said pointing to Rufus.

Ramulas looked to the right and saw the Symiak mountains reaching up for the sky. He touched the pouch containing the crystal. He smiled, thinking of his family. Ramulas could picture each individual face in his mind. Soon he would drop the crystal and return to a normal life back on the farm.

Ramulas looked at Pip. 'Thank you for helping me. Without you, I would never have gotten this far. But we will part ways now.'

'Why?'

'The master told you to return as soon as I had the crystal. I don't want anything to happen to your family.'

Pip waved a dismissive hand. 'Don't worry about him. I'll talk to him when I return. You heard him: I am his best thief. Nothing will happen to me. I only want to go a little way into the mountains.'

Pip watched Ramulas as he thought it over and finally nodded. She knew that Jenna's life and her own hung in the balance. But there was something special about Ramulas. The urge to stay with this man was almost overwhelming.

For the first time in many years, Pip threw caution to the wind and did not think of the consequences. She was certain that Ramulas held the key to her family's freedom. She didn't know what it was, but Pip needed to stay with this man.

'Let's go into the mountains. I will be happy when this crystal is out of my life.'

Ramulas climbed up onto Rufus and found two leather pouches on either side of the saddle. Pip told him they were used for lances. Ramulas smiled as he placed the handles of his weapons into the pouches. Once his hands were free, he reached down and helped Pip to sit behind him.

He communicated with Rufus, and they made their way into the mountains.

34

Oriel sat in her cavern worrying about Ramulas. She had sent him back to the city before he was fully recovered. She could feel Remus and the warlords working on their spells, and they were very close to opening the portal.

If Oriel had more time training Ramulas, he would have remembered who he was and the power he possessed. Then he would have a chance against one or even two of the warlords.

However, Ramulas had only just experienced some of his past, nowhere near enough to awaken his true potential. She hoped that something would happen to prevent the warlords from coming through into this world. Ramulas would have no hope of surviving.

Oriel was almost strong enough to return to Ramulas. She hoped to be able to help him move the crystal, or guide him to the place where it should be dropped.

***

As they rode toward the mountains, Ramulas saw large moss-covered rocks scattered amongst the tree and grass. Coming closer to the mountains, he noticed the trees thinning and the rocks covered in less moss.

Within an hour, Rufus had brought them to the base of the mountains.

'Now we're here, where do you drop the crystal?' Pip asked.

Ramulas searched the mountains. 'I don't know. I'm supposed to see a sign of where to take it.'

Pip sighed. 'And if you don't find this sign?' Ramulas ignored her as he continued to scan the mountains. Then he saw a pale shaft of red light shooting into the sky in the northeast. His heartbeat quickened.

'There,' he said pointing to a faraway mountain peak, 'That red light.'

Pip followed his finger searching for the light. 'I can't see any light,' Pip replied.

'Trust me,' Ramulas said, 'I can see the red light, and that is where we drop the crystal.'

Pip shook her head. 'Never trust anyone that says "trust me".'

'Trust me, we will be there soon,' Ramulas laughed. He laughed louder when Pip punched him in the back.

They rode toward the shaft of light, following the tracks in between the mountains and slowly climbing higher. The sense of excitement was almost intoxicating to Ramulas. Communicating with Rufus, he found that the warhorse was not tired. By midday, they had covered about half the distance to the light.

Ramulas spoke to Pip about what he wanted to do when he returned home. By the time he had finished, she laughed. 'Everything you want to do includes your family. Why don't you want to do things by yourself?'

'My family is everything to me. Why would I want to do anything without them?' he said before turning to Pip. 'If you had enough money, how much time would you spend away from your sister?'

Pip did not answer, and that spoke volumes to Ramulas.

A few minutes later, they spotted a caravan moving along the road four hundred yards below them.

'That is the caravan to Salvation,' Pip said.

Ramulas saw ten wagons and several riders for each wagon. 'There must be something special in those wagons for that many guards.

Do they have bandits along this road?'

'Not bandits—they have Symiaks,' Pip replied.

'Symiaks!' Ramulas said in shock, 'I thought all the monsters in the kingdom were taken by the druids?'

Pip sighed. 'Well, the druids must have missed some. Because Symiaks are in the Symiak mountains. I thought you knew that.'

'I thought it was rumours told by travellers.'

'Well, those rumours are very real, and I don't want to meet any up here.'

***

The terrain became increasingly difficult as they climbed into the mountains. Some sections of cliffs had collapsed and blocked paths. Ramulas debated whether he and Pip should climb off Rufus and walk.

A short time later, they came upon a canyon that opened up for the next mile. As they entered the canyon, Ramulas heard Pip gasp and become rigid behind him.

'What's wrong?' he asked.

'Look at the shadows on the ground.'

Ramulas looked down at the ground. The jagged shape of the cliff edge and several rocks could be seen. Then one of the rocks moved. It ran for a few yards in a crouching position, then huddled back down.

Pip turned to look behind them and thumped Ramulas on the back. 'Ambush! They're behind us—go!'

He communicated with Rufus, and they raced along the canyon.

The shadows of what Ramulas thought were rocks transformed into Symiaks. Hooting and grunting echoed throughout the mountains, adding to the fear building in Ramulas and Pip. Spears and small rocks were thrown from above, narrowly missing the pair.

He quickly glanced behind to see six creatures chasing them. There were about a dozen above them, and two jumped out of hidden cubbies just ahead of the warhorse.

Ramulas' heart skipped a beat when he saw these creatures close up. They were a foot taller than him, broad across the shoulders, with arms hanging to their knees holding crude spears and clubs, and they had tusks protruding from their lower jaw.

In Ramulas' wildest nightmares, he never thought to encounter such creatures. The pair in front quickly closed in to intercept them. 'What do we do?' he shouted to Pip.

'Go, go. Don't stop,' came the panicked reply.

Ramulas communicated with Rufus, and the warhorse ploughed through the two Symiaks, sending them flying to the side like leaves in a storm.

Pip gave a yell of triumph before saying, 'Oh no.'

'What's wrong?' Ramulas asked as they came to the end of the canyon.

'Look up there.'

Ramulas looked at the end of the canyon and saw several Symiaks pushing large rocks on top of the cliff. Smaller ones bounced down the cliff face, and he knew that the larger rocks would block their exit.

He willed the warhorse to go faster, and they made it through just as the rocks fell behind. The crashing and clouds of dust almost caused Ramulas to fall from shock. But he gripped the reins as they came out into a junction.

Ramulas had a choice of right or left. His mind and heart were racing as Pip held onto him tightly. The hooting and grunting seemed to come from everywhere. He was frozen with indecision, not knowing which way to go.

Then two Symiaks charged at them from the right with spears.

Ramulas turned the warhorse to the left, racing down a path that was wide enough for three to walk abreast. He had to ensure that Rufus did not trip over some of the larger rocks scattered on the ground.

Ramulas saw a shadow from above and looked up in time to see a Symiak drop down. Pip cursed as the creature landed on top of both of them. Ramulas was pushed forward and did all that he could to not fall off.

He could feel Pip and the Symiak fighting behind him as he willed the warhorse to go faster. Every time the Symiak was pushed against him, Ramulas threw back an elbow, causing it to grunt.

Ramulas saw a narrow gap ahead that would just be wide enough for the warhorse to pass through. He called back to Pip warning her about it.

Then the weight shifted behind Ramulas as they passed through the gap. Pip cursed and the Symiak grunted. Ramulas turned in time to see her push the creature to the side. Its head hit the protruding rock, and the Symiak fell to the ground. The hooting and grunting followed them down the narrow path.

Ramulas realised his mistake as soon as they entered a cul-de-sac. It was roughly two hundred yards wide with two cliffs and an opening, which was a precipice looking over the mountains. He knew they had been led into a trap.

Ramulas looked over the side and saw a sheer drop that would kill anyone who fell. As they turned toward the entrance, Ramulas felt Pip's body tense, and he knew why.

Four Symiaks stood at the exit.

'We need to get out of here,' Pip said, 'If they catch us in here, we're dead.'

Ramulas communicated with Rufus, and they charged the creatures, who all brought up crude spears at the last moment. Rufus reared back and kicked out at one, sending a broken body to the ground. Pip sent two knives into a second Symiak, and it dropped its spear and staggered back.

A spear grazed the warhorse's leg, causing Rufus to turn away from the Symiaks. Ramulas saw something that shattered hopes of a quick escape. Ten Symiaks raced toward them.

Over a dozen Symiaks came into the cul-de-sac, and Ramulas did not know how Pip and himself were to fight them. He knew that she was good with knives, but against this many, he thought she would have trouble.

'What do we do now?' he asked.

'We fight or die trying.'

'I don't remember how to fight with these weapons,' Ramulas said pointing to the war hammer and battleaxe.

'Just swing them around, you might hit one,' Pip said sarcastically as she climbed off the warhorse, 'We will have a better chance on our feet.'

'Oh no. We're in trouble,' Ramulas said as he joined Pip on the ground.

'You didn't think I could count how many there were?'

'Not them,' Ramulas replied before pointing to the left at a much larger Symiak. 'Him.'

Pip was frozen to the spot as the group of Symiaks came in through the entrance. They fanned out and approached slowly. A sense of calmness came over Ramulas as he took hold of his weapons. Then a kaleidoscope of fragmented memories flooded through him.

'I think I know how to use these,' Ramulas said, raising his weapons. 'I will finish this quickly.'

'You *think*?' Pip said incredulously, 'You're not going to fight them all are you?' Pip asked.

'No, just the big one,' he said. 'I hope that when I defeat him, the others will run off. Stay with Rufus until I fight this one.'

Pip shook her head at how Ramulas had changed from a naïve farmer to the person she saw now. But knew that even if Ramulas did somehow defeat the larger one, the other Symiaks would be too much for the both of them.

Ramulas stepped a few feet away from Rufus and waited for the large creature to come to him. He held both weapons ready.

It stopped ten feet from him, holding a club as big as Ramulas with ease. It was almost twice his size, had a barrel-like chest, and its arms were corded with thick muscles. Two yellow tusks protruded from its mouth. Its hands hung to its knees. It wore a necklace full of curved teeth.

Ramulas could feel the savagery and power lying dormant beneath the Symiak's calm demeanour. 'We want no trouble,' he offered the creature.

The Symiak grunted as it picked up the club and readied it for a swing.

'Fight!' Ramulas yelled to both Pip and Rufus.

Ramulas breathed in and glanced behind. Pip had run to the left, and two Symiaks were down with throwing knives in their bodies. But there were too many for her to handle.

Protect her, he communicated to the warhorse.

Ramulas spun towards the large Symiak without really knowing what to do. He just hoped more of his memories would return.

As the fragmented thoughts swirled through his head, Ramulas held onto one. It was of him fighting barbarian tribes in his home world. Ramulas ran at the Symiak.

The battleaxe cut into the Symiak's shin, followed by the war hammer hitting the creature's kneecap. It took a step back and raised its club. Ramulas ran forward, giving no quarter as he struck at the Symiak's body with blows from both weapons.

The Symiak kicked out with its foot, catching Ramulas off guard. He was sent sprawling along the ground and was thankful he still held his weapons. The creature stood with blood flowing from its wounds, yet it seemed unaffected. And this caused Ramulas to doubt himself.

The ground shook as the large Symiak raced toward him with its club held high. Ramulas pushed the doubt away, got to his feet, and rolled through the creature's legs, striking its groin with his war hammer. It grunted and doubled over holding its neither region.

Ramulas dropped the war hammer and ran at the Symiak with his battleaxe held in two hands. The weapon hit it in the head with a resounding crack, which echoed across the cul-de-sac.

All fighting stopped as the creature toppled forward. Ramulas looked at Pip thirty yards away and the Symiaks that were nearby. The duo shared a look of hope as Ramulas removed the battleaxe and picked up his hammer.

As soon as the weapon was removed, the Symiaks came to their senses and attacked with renewed fury.

'Pip, run!' Ramulas called as he ran to her aid.

Pip threw two knives and slashed at the Symiaks closest to her. Rufus waded through the creatures, kicking out at the ones on her left. Several were either dead or suffered broken limbs that took them from the fight.

Ramulas saw that there were only six creatures left, and they might have a chance of actually winning. He reached Pip and struck out at the closest Symiak with his battleaxe. It roared in pain as it fell with a gash to its face. Blood sprayed over Ramulas as he smiled at Pip.

The hooting and grunting started again, causing Ramulas and Pip to look at the entrance in time to see at least a score of Symiaks rush in to join the fight. More could be seen from the cliffs above—there were at least two score.

Pip's body sagged as she looked at Ramulas. 'Can this get any worse?'

Ramulas saw the Symiaks come in and wondered how they were going to get out of this. Then his whole body felt as if it was covered with hundreds and hundreds of ants. The urge to drop his weapons and scratch was almost overwhelming.

Rufus kicked out at a Symiak who came too close to Ramulas. Then he saw the expression of shock on Pip's face as a magical doorway opened in front of Ramulas.

An arc of red energy threw Ramulas back, and Pip could not believe her eyes as she saw someone very similar to Ramulas come out of the doorway. He wore a red robe and a breastplate with glowing symbols. Then Remus looked at her and smiled without emotion.

Remus snapped his fingers. Glowing white balls hit Pip and the Symiaks, slamming them to the ground. Pip looked at Ramulas in sadness. The spell had taken away her ability to control her muscles. She was unable to help him.

35

Remus stood at the arch as the mists cleared. The time had come to go to Oriel's world and kill the meddling magician who had the crystal, and then he would find what he could about this new world.

He and the warlords had prepared spells for when he crossed over. Remus looked forward to causing as much damage as possible and finding any information about Oriel's location.

The passageway was ready, and Remus stepped into it. Dazzling multi-coloured lights almost blinded him as he walked through to Oriel's new world.

As Remus stepped through, he saw Ramulas and knew instantly that this was the person who was helping Oriel. Anger flooded through Remus as he sent Ramulas flying through the air.

Then he saw a young woman in the midst of fighting several creatures and a large horse. He did not know who would be friend or foe, so he attacked them all.

He walked forward with a smile, thinking that this world would soon belong to him.

***

Ramulas' eyes widened in shock as he saw Remus come through the magical doorway. He hit the ground and fought back the fear building within. He wasn't ready to face the warlord yet. He needed to remember how to use his weapons.

Then he quickly stood while silently berating himself. His weapons lay on the ground several feet from him.

'That should have killed you,' Remus said, walking forward. 'Tell me where Oriel is or I will kill everyone that you care for.'

A warm sensation exploded within Ramulas and slowly spread throughout his body. He fought to hide the surprise. The fragmented images were somehow more tangible, and he could remember some of his past.

Remus waved his hands through the air and the magical symbols glowed on his red breastplate. Ramulas realised too late that his brother was casting a spell.

A solid beam of red light struck Ramulas in the hip, spending rolling waves of agony down his leg. He stepped back and placed a hand where he was hit. A wave of panic washed over him as he felt that the crystal was no longer in the pouch.

The pouch had torn open. Ramulas turned to see the crystal lying near the edge of the cliff, purple mist rising from it. Ramulas knew that he had to retrieve the crystal and drop it in the designated place to stop the legion from coming through.

As he ran to the crystal, another beam of energy knocked it over the edge.

'No!' Ramulas shouted as he turned back to Remus.

Pip and the Symiaks were starting to recover, and Remus chanted before clapping his hands. A wave of red energy sent them flying through the air and knocked Rufus over.

Anger built within Ramulas as he walked toward Remus. He had come so close to finishing his quest and being able to return to his family. Now that the crystal was lost, he did not know what to do.

Remus waved his hands, sending three fireballs at Ramulas. Ramulas shrugged each one off as he walked forward. They stung, but his anger blocked the pain.

'Why won't you die?' Remus asked.

With every spell used on Ramulas, a small doorway of his memory was revealed. Spells and their components danced before him in blue flame.

Ramulas focused on the first as he looked at his brother.

With each breath, the air surrounding Ramulas dropped in temperature. The sensation of pins and needles covered his whole body, and Ramulas held out his right hand toward his brother.

A look of disgust came over Remus as a six-foot translucent white wall surrounded him. 'Battlemage,' he spat.

Ramulas' hand was covered in a white nimbus, which he knew was connected to the wall surrounding his brother. Remus attacked the wall with spells, only causing showers of multi-coloured sparks. Each failed spell brought more rage from the warlord.

Ramulas concentrated and closed his hand. As his hand closed, so did the wall around Remus. The warlord glared at Ramulas. 'I will return and feast upon your soul. I know your tricks now.'

Then the white wall touched Remus and a vortex of white shot into the sky before exploding. A wind storm tore through the cul-de-sac for a second before vanishing. Ramulas saw that Remus was nowhere to be seen.

A sense of relief washed over him that he had survived the warlord's attack. However, that was short-lived as he remembered the crystal. What was going to happen now?

Howling brought him back to the present moment, and Ramulas thought of the scores of Symiaks. He saw that they now looked at him with fear and slowly moved away from him. Pip sat on the ground with an expression of wonderment.

Ramulas slowly looked around and saw that even the Symiaks on the cliffs above were moving away. He wanted to take advantage of the situation and ran toward them screaming and waving his arms. Like frightened cattle, the creatures tripped over one another to get away from him.

After a few moments, Ramulas, Pip, and Rufus were alone. He walked over to the young thief.

'The crystal is gone,' Ramulas said, 'It went over the cliff. I don't know what to do.'

This was one of the few moments where Pip did not feel confident and in control. She had risked the wrath of the master of shadows to Ramulas, and it was all for nothing. What would she do now?

Then a thick fog swept over the mountain.

***

Once the sea of white cleared, Oriel stood before them on the mountain wearing a sad smile. 'I could not come any earlier to help with the crystal. I felt Remus' magical energies, and if I had come, he would have killed me.'

'The crystal,' Ramulas said, pointing to the cliff. 'I lost it when I fought Remus.'

Oriel's eyes widened in shock. 'You fought Remus? How are you still alive?'

He shrugged. 'I just know that when we fought, I remembered some of my past. Now those memories have vanished. But now the crystal has gone, what will happen?'

Oriel nodded to Pip and walked to Ramulas placing a comforting hand on his shoulder. 'You cannot be too hard on yourself. Now we need to prepare for the coming of the first legion.'

'But after dropping the crystal, I thought it would be safe to return to my family?'

Oriel shook her head. 'I am sorry, but because the crystal was not positioned in the right area, Remus will be coming to this world.'

'Damn,' Ramulas said feeling the frustration build within him.

He stepped away from Oriel and began to pace in front of Pip.

Oriel wanted to offer him words of comfort, but she knew that Ramulas needed this time to himself.

After a moment, he stopped to face her. 'How do we prepare?'

'You both will need to come to me and train your army.'

'Where are you? And I don't know one thing about training people.'

'You will have people drawn to you who will help you in your journey. You have already met a few of them.'

Images of Pip, Shigar, and K'ayden flashed before Ramulas' eyes. He understood why Pip and K'ayden would help him, but he was unsure of Shigar's motives. He explained to Oriel how Pip and he had entered the castle to retrieve the crystal and his weapons, and then of their meeting with Shigar and how he helped them escape and provided them with a warhorse. Ramulas finished by expressing his uncertainty of whether he could trust the magician or not.

Oriel smiled. 'This magician has risked much by helping you. At any time, he could have betrayed you to the king. I think he is one of the people you will need on your journey. You should accept his help.'

'Is there a way I could move or destroy the crystal?' Ramulas asked.

Oriel shook her head. 'Nothing can be done with the crystal now; it has started to anchor. You need to focus on what will happen, and come to me.' Oriel took the hands of Ramulas and Pip. 'I will show you where I am.'

The rocky ground and mountains fell away as they floated one hundred feet into the air. Ramulas fought against waves of dizziness that swept over him. Pip gave a squeal of surprise.

Oriel gave their hands a gentle squeeze. 'Do not worry. You are safe.'

Then they moved away from the mountains and over open fields. They started slowly before increasing speed; the landscape below was a blur.

To the left, he saw the city of Keah and the ocean. Then Ramulas realised he could not feel any wind. At the speed they were moving, wind should have been pulling at their clothes and hair.

Looking across at Oriel and Pip, he saw that no wind affected them.

They flew above the town of Rylek and over the thick forest of the Darkwood. Ramulas saw the Devil's Ridge Mountains growing in the distance. The fields beneath them continued to pass at an almost blinding speed.

A few moments later, a large forest came into view at the base of the Devil's Ridge Mountains. As they flew over it, Ramulas could see that it was larger than the Darkwood. He saw a castle surrounded by a small town at the base of the mountains.

A curved wall separated the town from a small clearing at the edge of the forest. They came to a stop and floated above the town.

Oriel pointed to a cliff north of the town. 'I am trapped within this mountain. This town is where you will need to come and train your army.'

'What is this place?' Ramulas asked in awe.

'This town is called Sanctuary.'

'Sanctuary?' Ramulas said, 'That is a place of myth and legend; a story to tell children.'

'This place is very real. It has been lying dormant waiting for someone like you to come.'

'What do you mean "lying dormant?" You make it sound as if Sanctuary is a living thing.'

Oriel nodded. 'It is a place of ancient magic.' Oriel released Ramulas and Pip's hands and they were back on the mountain once more.

'How did we return so quickly?' Pip asked.

'We never left,' Oriel said, 'What you experienced was an illusion. If you do not come to Sanctuary, Remus will lead the legion across the kingdom. Everyone will suffer. You are their only hope.'

Pip looked at Ramulas as he let out a sigh and nodded.

'I thought this would be all I needed to do. I want to return home to my family.'

'When the legion come, they will hunt your family. Remus knows you now and will come for the ones you hold dear. You need to prepare.'

Just when Ramulas was so close to returning home, it was once again taken from him. However, this time he knew that he needed to do this to protect them.

'I will come with you,' Pip said with a smile.

Ramulas shook his head. 'No, you are in enough trouble with the master of shadows. You need to go back to Keah.'

Pip folded her arms and shot him a defiant look. 'No-one tells me what to do. I am coming whether you like it or not.'

Oriel nodded. 'You will need her skills along the way.'

Ramulas thought for a moment before reluctantly agreeing.

Pip vividly remembered every detail of Sanctuary in her mind. She knew that Ramulas would lead her to some utopia, a place where Jenna and herself could call home. She silently congratulated herself for listening to her instincts about staying with this man.

'When do we come to Sanctuary?' Ramulas asked.

'You will need to leave in the morning. Find the fastest route here.'

'I will go through Bremnon. Pip and I can bring our families with us.'

Oriel shook her head slowly. 'You must take the fastest route to Sanctuary. Stopping at your farm and Bremnon to see your families will distract you from your quest, delay you, and allow the legion to begin their slaughter. When you have reached Sanctuary, you may send for your family.'

Ramulas winced upon hearing this. Jacqueline and his girls would be expecting him home soon. Now things had taken a dramatic turn for the worse. Ramulas could feel the weight of the responsibility for what he had to do on his shoulders. But knowing he had a duty to fulfil was causing Ramulas' internal conflict.

Oriel saw the turmoil of mixed emotions within Ramulas and decided to ease his mind. 'Until I came into your life, you were living as if in a dream, going from day to day performing the same menial chores without purpose, and your true powers lay dormant. Now that these powers have been awakened, you cannot return to your old life. You have found a purpose. The only way for you to go is forward.'

Ramulas looked at Oriel with pain in his eyes as he gestured with his hands. 'I was so close to going home, and because of one mistake, I will be away from my family for longer. How do I explain what has happened?'

'You will find a way,' Oriel said with a smile. 'Someone you trust could send a message to your families for you. You must accept help from those who come to you.' Oriel saw confusion in Ramulas' expression. 'Do not worry about that for now. I want to ask you a question that will help you see things differently.'

Oriel waited for Ramulas to nod before continuing. 'When I first came to you, why did you choose to help me? You could have refused and gone back to your farming life, so why did you make that choice?'

The question caught Ramulas off guard, then he began to ponder with his chin resting in a cupped hand. After a moment, his eyes widened as the answer came to him.

'There has always been something missing inside of me, and I wasn't sure what it was until you came into my life. I had dreams of being a leader, and now I find that was part of my past.'

Oriel smiled. 'Self-discovery is a wondrous thing. Now you have walked on a different path, it will be difficult to turn back. There has always been something powerful inside of you waiting to be released. Only a part of it has shown itself so far. You will become stronger as your journey continues. I will speak to you when you are closer to Sanctuary.'

'In such a large forest, how will I know how to reach Sanctuary?'

'I will leave a beacon for you to follow, and remember time is against you. You need to take the fastest route to Sanctuary.' Fog filled the cavern, and a moment later Ramulas found himself standing near Pip and the warhorse.

Then he heard the whisper of Oriel's voice. 'There are leaders and followers. Ramulas, you must choose what you want to be. Pip is the first of many who will help you build your army.'

Oriel disappeared in a sea of fog, leaving Ramulas and Pip alone with Rufus.

Pip smiled at Ramulas. 'We had better rest. We have a big day tomorrow.'

About the Author

I was born in Melbourne in 1970, and from my earliest memories I was always captivated by reading. I fell in love with fantasy in my early teens and discovered a way to escape into a new world.

I attempted to write novels from the age of twenty-two and couldn't find the way to piece it together properly. Then in 2015 one of the main characters of *The Ramulas Chronicles* came to me, followed by other characters and the rest of the fantasy series.

I have found something that I love doing and my characters are constantly running through my mind. I live with my son and his dog, and I am extremely happy to be able to share my world with lovers of fantasy.